PINK SUNRISE

SIERRA CHANDLER

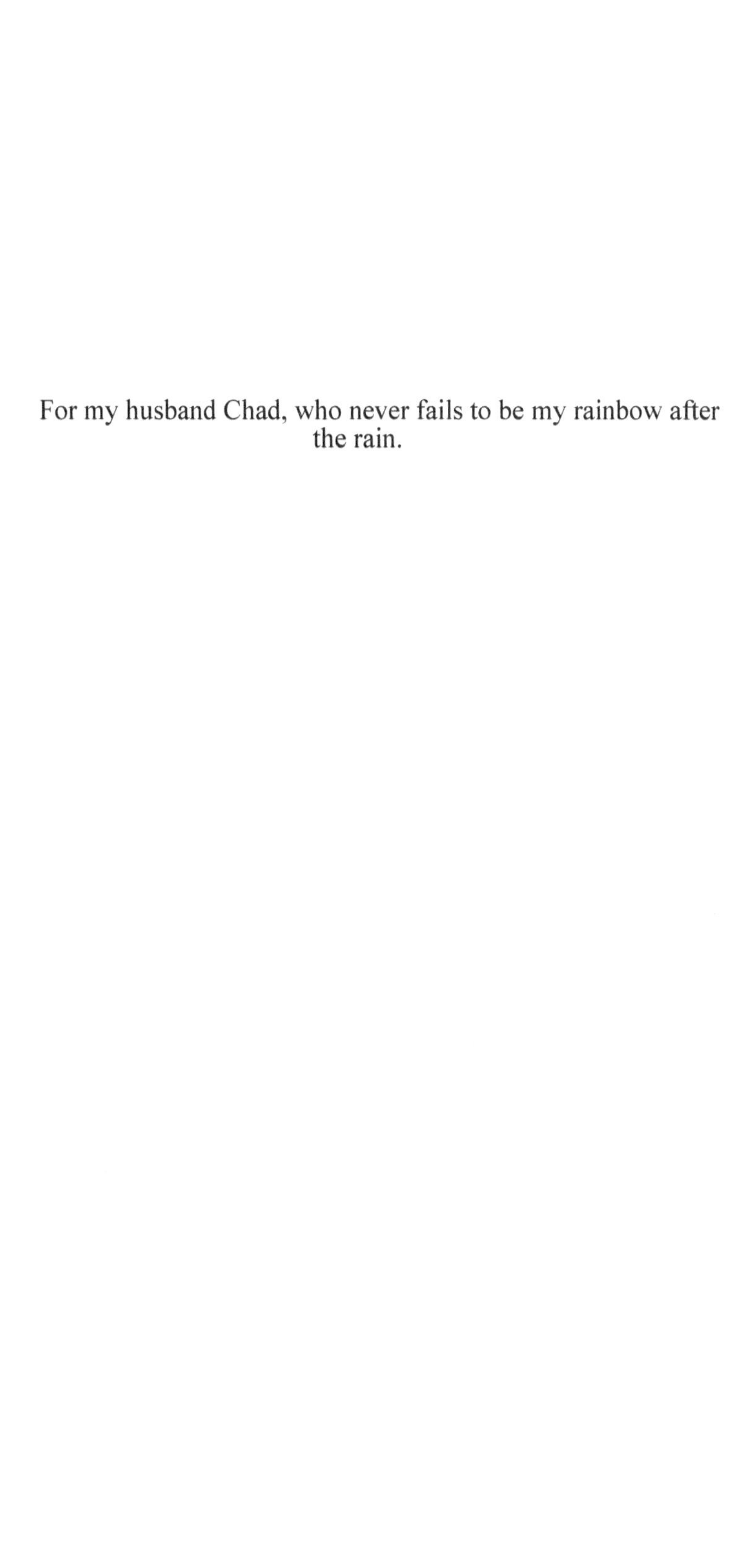

For my husband Chad, who never fails to be my rainbow after the rain.

Chapter One

When Hanna found out that her fiancé had been caught steaming up the windows of his car with an exotic dancer, she was lost. If it hadn't been for the photo, she would have refused to believe it. Even after she saw the smutty image online, she still tried to think of a plausible explanation. Naturally, she fell short.

The day before the shocking discovery, Hanna and her team had been working on a trade show booth they were hired to design and complete for their client, BabyDreams. The luxury nursery bedding and decor company was partaking in the upcoming, Toddler and Baby Expo in Halifax. The BabyDreams owners, Janice and Stacey Lee were a mother-and-daughter team who found Hanna's event planning company, Richards and Co. on social media. They knew Hanna and her team were the ones to create the unique and special look they wanted. After three days of installation, the booth had come together exactly as Hanna and the team had planned. It was designed to look like a beautiful posh baby nursery, complete with a decorative crib, rocking chair, chandelier, and even a faux window to showcase the company's curtain line. An elaborate overhead balloon creation stretched across the width of the booth in a wide arch and two additional balloon bouquets flanked both sides of the front, creating a dreamy entryway for visitors. A pink fur rug covered the floor, while a rotating lamp cast moving images of baby animals, dancing across the walls. The focal point was the tulle fabric canopy that appeared to float up from the ends of the crib. The material came together in a large ornate bow, then disappeared upward into the pearly overhead balloon display. As the end of the day neared Hanna stood back to assess the booth. If the result wasn't what she envisioned, she would stay until it was. It was a standard she had set for herself since working with her first client over five years ago.

The Richards and Co. designs were created by Hanna, with input from Ethan, her brilliant and extravagant designer. Ethan's appearance was just as coordinated as his impeccable designs. One would be hard-pressed to find a hair or thread out of place on either his short-styled haircut or ever-stylish wardrobe. The carpentry was executed by Shauni, a hardworking and talented handy-woman who Hanna had met during a renovation at her dad's. Hanna was so impressed by Shauni's carpentry skills, that she offered her a job on the spot. Before hiring Shauni, Hanna's first, full-time employee, she had relied on various contractors. Some were reliable and great to work with but others were not, leaving her in desperate situations.

Knowing how valuable Shauni was, Hanna was happy to have found her. Despite Shauni's petite size, she possessed surprising physical strength, as well as a feisty and fearless attitude. Her Hawaiian ancestry awarded her beautiful, glossy dark hair and large, showy brown eyes. It was Shauni's task to oversee the building of custom pieces needed for the booth setups and special events. Large items were constructed and built to spec offsite at the Richards and Co. studio, then brought to the event location later and installed by the team. For larger projects, additional tradesmen like electricians and labourers were outsourced if needed but usually, the three-person team was able to complete the final projects on their own. They all played an important role in the completion of the final product. Thanks to Hanna's dedicated and hardworking group, she hadn't disappointed a client or herself yet. Hanna felt pretty good about the BabyDreams booth and smiled as she admired the end result. She gave Ethan and Shauni a customary high five when they came over to stand beside her.

"Awesome job guys! I think we nailed it! Hanna pulled her phone from her back pocket to snap some photos, then sent a quick email to Stacey and Janice Lee to let them know the booth was ready for the expo's opening day. She thanked them for trusting Richards and Co. with their event. "Shauni, my love," Hanna lifted her chin toward the faux-framed window. "That window looks completely legit!"

"Thanks!" Shauni chimed proudly. She gave a quick bow and then continued to pack up the tools. Ethan then cleared his throat loudly, as if he was hinting at something.

"Oh, soooorry!" Shauni drawled sarcastically, rolling her eyes. "The frosting on the window was Ethan's idea. I'm just the putz that designed and built the thing." As Shauni spoke animatedly, her little ponytail swung side to side like the tail of a peppy Pomeranian.

Ignoring Shauni, Ethan puckered his lips and tapped his cheek to suggest that he deserved a kiss for his brilliant contribution. Hanna laughed, grabbing his jaw between her thumb and fingers and delivered an exaggerated kiss on his handsome, boyish face. "Moo Wah!"

After Shauni made a loud gagging sound, they all laughed and continued tidying up the booth. The Richards and Co. team was a tight-knit group who, for the most part, worked together harmoniously. All in their late twenties, they were more like good friends or by some standards, family. Hanna was exactly where she wanted to be in life. She operated a successful special event business and in a few months would be marrying the man of her dreams, Jacob Barber. Jacob too was a successful entrepreneur and the founder of Nextech Cashless Payment Solutions. Hanna adored Jacob and she loved working with her talented team. Most days, she couldn't help but feel blessed and even guilty for being so lucky. When the tools were all packed away in their cases and the booth was swept and wiped, it was time to call it a day. Hanna grabbed a stack of empty cardboard boxes and loaded them onto Shauni's tool cart.

"Ok you two, I'm calling it. Let's get outta here."

The team left the exhibition center and shared an Uber back to the hotel. Hanna looked forward to a long relaxing shower and early night to bed but first, the three friends shared a quick meal in the hotel's restaurant and a bottle of wine to celebrate. The BabyDreams booth was typical in size but required more planning and man-hours than most of their projects. They had travelled to complete the booth, requiring the bigger items to be built on-site. It had been a long three days for the crew and it felt great to have completed it. Hanna missed Jacob and was ready to be home again. She was excited to tell him about the booth and how well it turned out. He texted earlier and said he had a late dinner scheduled with some clients and would call her just before leaving for the restaurant to meet them. The one-hour time difference between them made it nearly bedtime for Hanna and Jacob would be calling any second to say goodnight. As she was stepping out of the shower, her phone rang.

"Perfect timing," she said, as she threw on a bathrobe and answered her phone.

"Hi!"

"Hey, gorgeous."

Hanna smiled warmly at Jacob's greeting. Something about the man's voice did it for her. It always had. It was enough to cause her to lose focus. She realized it was her turn to speak after he asked her how the booth turned out. Hanna told Jacob about her hectic day preparing the booth for her client, BabyDreams. She described the posh nursery with the pretty rocking chair and the ornate crib with the big bow made of tulle.

"It made me think about babies," she said sheepishly. Hanna loved teasing him, knowing on the other end he was silent and stunned. Jacob wanted kids but he was also firm on when he wanted to have them. She then pictured him breaking into an instant sweat, needing to loosen his tie for air. When he said nothing, Hanna continued. "You can breathe now Honey. I'm not talking about having a baby today. I was thinking….," grinning, she paused, then to further poke him, asked sweetly, "Maybe…..next month?"
Her comment generated a loud and exaggerated chuckle from Jacob. "Hahaha! Should we maybe focus on getting married first sweetie?" he joked uncomfortably.

She loved the sound of his deep laugh, even the dramatic and phoney ones, clearly expressing his lack of desire to have a child.

"I know, I know," she quietly apologized. "I just miss you."

"I miss you too sweetheart. Only one more night."

Hanna was eager after not seeing Jacob for three days. "Should I stop by your office on my drive home from the airport or are you working from home?"

Jacob let out a quick, quiet snort. "You're adorable. I'm gonna try." He then quieted his voice. "Wanna send me some pictures before I get going to the restaurant?"

Knowing what he meant, Hanna removed her bathrobe and went to stand in front of the full-length mirror. Turning to the side, leaning seductively on the door frame, she captured a reflection of her curvy naked profile from head to toe. Hanging just past her shoulder blades, her wet, deep honey hair looked darker than usual. She rested her head and one hand on the door frame and gave the camera one of her classic wide smiles that touched her eyes, shaping them into sultry crescents. Hanna's large green eyes were striking and unique, like two bright emeralds.

"Sending it now....did you get it?"

"Mmmmmm, my god you're sexy," came his answer.

"Is that enough incentive to meet me at home?" Hanna asked innocently.

"Damn right, it is." They ended their call shortly afterward. She blow-dried her hair for a few minutes, read a chapter of her novel and then turned out the lights.

CHAPTER TWO

When Hanna's cell phone rang early the next morning, she thought it was Jacob. She answered in her soft, sleepy morning voice. "Good morning my sunshine." Her eyes closed again but a faint smile touched her lips anticipating Jacob's voice.

"Um, Hanna?" Ethan sounded out of breath, his pitch slightly higher than normal.

Disappointed it wasn't Jacob, Hanna grumbled and yawned, stretching her back. She laid still, blinking away the morning sleep from her eyes, patiently waiting for Ethan to address his early morning concern. Hanna had less to worry about since hiring Ethan because he made every effort to do the worrying for her. When the moment of silence became awkward, Hanna became concerned. Ethan finally explained that someone he followed on Instagram had posted something she needed to see. She feared it was a negative review of her company, an incident that had yet to occur.

"Did we finally get our first negative review?" Hanna prodded.

Ethan wished it were something that trivial. "No," he said glumly, "not exactly."

Hanna hadn't heard him sound this ruffled since his favourite barber Tommy had moved out of province.

"Ok," she said, throwing back the covers. "Let's see it. Send it over, I'll have a look."

Now out of bed and heading for the washroom, Hanna clicked on the text to see what Ethan wanted to share. After a few minutes, she finally processed what the dark image was. It was a picture taken through the steamy windshield of a car, a Tesla to be specific. The front seats had been tilted forward giving the occupants in the backseat, extra room while unintentionally, providing the camera a full view of the act.

Hanna peered at the faint image of a man sitting beneath a naked woman. Facing the man, her dark wavy hair hung in long waves over her back and her knees were bent high on either side of her generous hips. The man's hand came around grasping her bottom while his other arm was bent upward, holding her body against him. The woman's profile concealed his face but his large bare legs made it obvious what they were doing.

Why Ethan thought Hanna needed to see it, finally hit her when she spotted the car's license plate. The three-letter plate in the photo was intentionally blurred but one letter could still be made out. The legible letter was an *X*. Hanna knew Jacob's plate was *NEX*.

An abbreviation for his company's name. Nextech. After a few laboured breaths, her response came in sections. "Is that…….Jacob's……car?"

Chapter Three

Adrenaline could do incredible things to a person's body. When injected during severe allergic reactions, it could save someone's life. For Hanna, it felt like dying. Her hand, now shaking uncontrollably, struggled to hold the phone. The ringing in her ears made Ethan's voice sound like a mosquito buzzing defiantly around her head. If she didn't get some oxygen soon, she would easily faint. She took several deep breaths, remembering Ethan was still on the line. She could hear him more clearly now.

"Hanna, honey, we're coming over. Just open your door when we get there ok?"

Moments later, Hanna opened the door, allowing Shauni and Ethan to enter. Looking from Ethan to Hanna, Shauni tried to figure out what was so dire. Ethan had frantically knocked on Shauni's door just moments before and when she opened it all he said was "It's Hanna," and then gestured for her to follow. Shauni grabbed her phone, following Ethan across and down the hall to Hanna's room. Now inside, the two of them stood there watching her. Sitting on the bed, Hanna's hands came together in a praying position, held gently against her mouth. Shauni wore a look of utter confusion while Ethan anxiously anticipated the detonation of an emotional land mine. When Hanna started to sob quietly, Ethan went forward, sat beside her on the bed and put his arm around her. Fearful to ask what had happened, Shauni waited for clues as to what had transpired between bedtime last night and this morning.

In the three years working alongside Hanna, this was the first time Shauni had seen her cry. As sharp-tongued as Shauni liked to be, the fiery little character still possessed a sensitive nature. Whenever she had been in the presence of someone crying, it almost always prompted her to tear up with them. Besides, this was Hanna, and it was startling to see her in such pain. Shauni ducked into the washroom grabbing Hanna some water and tissues to wipe everyone's tears. Hanna's crying had now somewhat subsided. Ethan slowly pulled back from their embrace and Shauni handed out the Kleenex's.

"Ok you two," Shauni sobbed, "it's time to tell me why we're all crying."

Hanna reached for her phone and handed it over for her to see.

Shauni scanned the photo and stopped crying after reading the informative caption below the image. It read, *Mandy givin' her besta in a Tesla!*

She lifted her eyebrows and pursed her lips. "Wow." Sounding surprised and annoyed she added, "Good for Mandy."

Ethan assumed Shauni hadn't grasped the situation. After he gave her a quick double take, he leaned in and whispered loudly. "It's Jacob!"

Shauni rolled her eyes. Hanna's reaction to the online image made it obvious to Shauni, who the man in the photo was.

"Yes, thank you, Sherlock," she said dryly. "Maybe they're just talking." Shauni handed the phone back to Hanna, while Ethan gave her a look of disdain. It was Shauni's way of dealing with terrible situations and Shauni being Shauni, didn't hold back after Ethan's look.

"Ok ok, Mr. Self Righteous. Let's not get our knickers in a knot!"

Ethan self-consciously glanced down at his short, trendy Capri pants and responded defensively. "Look who's talking. If you can't say something sensitive maybe don't say anything at all."

"Sensitive? Seriously?" She raised her eyebrows. "Are you the sensitive one who kindly brought this to light?"

The quip stung but the incriminating post wasn't something Ethan could sit on or ignore. He had battled with himself that morning, debating the call but his loyalty to Hanna had triumphed so he built up the courage to call her.

"Wouldn't yoouuuu want to know if your partner was cheating on you?" Ethan threw back haughtily.

Hanna usually found the banter between them entertaining but the traumatizing circumstances didn't allow it today.

"Guys please," Hanna said solemnly. "I'm already fighting a headache, and for the record," Hanna stared at the photo with a sour expression. "They seem to be doing a lot more than just talking." She sounded stuffed up from crying.

Ethan and Shauni turned to Hanna in sync. Her puffy, red eyes drew guilty expressions from each of them.

"Let's apologize to each other so we can figure out what I'm supposed to do. My wedding is in three months!"

Shauni looked at Ethan, forcing a grimace to her face.

"I'm sorry that I was defensive and yes of course I would want to know." Sounding more sincere she added, "You did the right thing."

She then turned to Hanna with fresh tears in her eyes "I'm sorry Hanna."

Ethan crumbled with emotion. He grabbed both Hanna and Shauni, hugging them over tightly. "We'll figure this out guys, we always do."

The trio had coffee and breakfast delivered to the room and ate while they talked, trying to help Hanna come to terms with the new information. They each held their device and sat together on the bed, examining the picture of Jacob, the woman and the steamed-up

Tesla. The image of *Mandy givin' her besta in a Tesla* had been posted by the user Nightqueen346 and had already garnered over a thousand views. Ethan explained that the image was posted by a low-key influencer he followed because he liked her skin care tips. The influencer also liked to mention in her videos that she moonlighted as an exotic dancer. Hanna was baffled that Ethan's facial care routine had been what led him to the photo of Jacob. The quick internet access that cell phones provided, made the world a smaller place. For influencers, it was all about getting clicks and views. The more shocking the video, the more internet traffic they would receive. And the more traffic they received, the more money they could make. For some, the internet was a weapon or a means of getting what they wanted. If something personal was posted to the right sites, it could spread like wildfire, burning reputations and relationships as it spread. Shauni sipped her coffee, then glared intently at the image on her phone. "Are we only assuming the woman on top of Jacob is a stripper?" Shauni inquired, "And do we know for sure that this guy in the photo is *actually* Jacob? What if it's not even him? Should you call him to ask?"

Hanna appreciated Shauni's logical voice of reason and shook her head. "I texted him and asked him to call me but he hasn't responded. Technically we don't know that she's a stripper. Not that it matters. And in Jacob's defence," Hanna continued, "he has lent his car out to friends before but..."

She paused momentarily, zooming in tightly on the photo to let them have a closer look. Tapping at her tablet screen, Hanna pointed out the wolf head tattoo on the man's forearm.

"I think it's safe to say that this implicates him. The chances of it not being Jacob are pretty slim. If it isn't Jacob, then it's a man with the same tattoo, same car and the same license plate."

Staring at the wolf tattoo, Shauni had the urge to let out one of her trademark gagging sounds but held back.

Ethan let out a long deflated "ugggghhhh. I got my hopes up it wasn't him for a second." He then flung himself backwards onto the bed like a child who'd just been sent to his room. Hanna and Shauni smiled weakly at his theatrics. After the initial shock of the photo had worn off and they had talked for almost an hour, Ethan and Shauni finally asked Hanna the important questions. *What are you going to do? Will you stay with him? Will you call off the wedding?* Despite being logical asks, Hanna didn't have the answers. It would depend, of course, on how things played out after getting home and speaking with Jacob in person.

Chapter Four

The flight back to Toronto seemed to go on forever. The plane was two hours late taking off and a few rows up from Hanna sat a woman with a toddler who screamed on and off for the duration of the flight. Thankfully, she had taken a couple of her migraine pills before leaving the hotel and they had kicked in nicely. Shauni and Ethan both wore earpods and worked or played games on their tablets. Hanna had exhausted herself, imagining the different scenarios that might play out once she finally saw Jacob. She told herself that once they were face-to-face, she would know everything she needed to. She had called him several times that morning without getting an answer and once again before arranging a ride to the airport. After failing to reach him multiple times, Hanna's dignity finally prompted her to stop calling. The one-hour time difference made it about eleven a.m. for Jacob in Toronto. He would be awake. It wasn't like him to not pick up her calls or respond to her texts. The fact that he seemed to be dodging her wasn't boding well for Hanna's situation.

About halfway into the flight, Hanna dozed off. She began to dream about the wedding that was scheduled to happen in three months. From the white wisteria vines to the twinkling lights, everything was just as planned. Jacob stood at the front of the hall, smiling, watching and waiting for Hanna to reach him so they could be married. Holding her bouquet of white roses, she gracefully made her way up the aisle, taking her place beside him. Just as the minister opened his mouth to speak, a large woodpecker flew at Hanna's long veil. She tried to wave it away but this angered it further and it dove sharply at her head. Her long white gloves were now fused at the fingers and she was helpless to his aerial attack. With his tiny claws now grasping her hair for balance, the bird was perched arrogantly, pecking at her head.

Hanna's eyes opened, making her aware she was still on the plane. The inspiration for the head-pecking bird had come from the passenger behind her who was tapping angrily on the screen, built into the back of Hanna's seat. The incessant finger-stabbing was just as aggravating as the woodpecker from the dream. When Hanna thought it would never end, Shauni tilted her chin toward Hanna and announced loudly,

"Did you know that the airlines are now charging you for damaged property? The screens are twelve hundred each!"

When the finger stabbing instantly stopped, Hanna mouthed the words "Thank you."

Chapter Five

The plane landed in Toronto shortly after three o'clock. Hanna, Ethan and Shauni picked up the tool crates from the oversized luggage area, then wheeled them out to the parking garage and into the company van. The company van only sat two, so Hanna arranged an Uber to get her home. Her vehicle had been involved in a minor collision the day before they left for Halifax and was still at the auto body repair shop. Her accident occurred when the woman driving behind her was texting on her phone and drove into the back of Hanna's SUV. The SUV only required a new bumper and some touch-ups, while the woman's compact car was a complete insurance write-off. Thankfully, no one was hurt, but the woman had been charged with careless driving. Hanna's vehicle would be ready in a couple more days. Ethan and Shauni hugged Hanna goodbye and adamantly requested that she reach out if things went badly after confronting Jacob.

As soon as she sat in the back of the Uber, her palms became cold and damp from the building anxiety. When the driver finally pulled away from the passenger pickup area, Hanna took a deep breath and began her journey home. Thinking about the last few days was unsettling. She'd been involved in an accident, been away from home for three days and just found out that her fiancé had cheated on her with a stripper. After thinking about it for hours on the plane, Hanna thought she knew how she would best approach Jacob once she finally saw him. But now she wasn't so sure. Turning onto their street, her nerves felt as frayed as the bottoms of cut-off jeans and her heart hammered in her chest. Jacob was home, or at least his car was home sitting in the garage which, for some reason, had been left open. As the Uber pulled into the driveway, Hanna promised herself, that no matter what Jacob said, she would keep her composure. Even if emotionally, she was losing her mind. After removing her suitcase from the trunk, she thanked the driver again, then took a minute to look at the house she'd shared with Jacob for the past three years. To Hanna it was perfect. It was a large Tudor on a wide lot with a giant oak front door. The door had been what sold Jacob on the house, but the room to grow both inside and out was why Hanna had convinced him that this was the right house for them. With all the original finishes from the seventies, it was horrendously outdated inside. But that made for a happy excuse to beautifully update it with all of the modern finishes. The numerous, renovations took almost a year to complete but the result was even more beautiful than Hanna could have imagined. She entered the code on the keypad for the garage door, then watched as the door slowly came down concealing the vehicle inside. She would never be able to look at the car without feeling disgusted and vowed she would never set foot in it again. Hanna braced herself for the inevitable conversation she would have with Jacob in the moments to come. When she first opened the front door, everything looked as it usually did. The house was clean and bright and in the air, a hint of vanilla, coming from the aroma300 they received as a housewarming gift from her friend Ava. Hanna didn't see or hear anyone, giving her a few extra moments of mental reprieve. As she walked closer to the bedroom she could smell a subtle mixture of Jacob's body wash and cologne floating in the air. On most days she loved the way the bedroom smelled after Jacob had just showered. The duvet had been pulled up neatly over the bed's surface and both sets of pillows were set in place at the head of the bed. Sounds of drawers opening and closing were coming from the en-suite and walk-in closet area. Hanna stood just outside the open bedroom door allowing herself another second to steady her nerves. Then in a moment of weakness, she told herself she could just leave right now, sparing herself the dreaded conversation. After all, what did she need to say to Jacob? The photo and all its vivid details made it irrefutable. He cheated. Still, Hanna needed to see him because she loved him. She needed to hear him tell her in person, that he'd thrown away the life they'd planned together. Hanna rounded the doorway, walked to the large armchair in the corner of the bedroom and sat, waiting for Jacob to finish dressing. When he came out seconds later and saw her sitting there, he was startled.

"Whoa! Shit Honey, what are you doing there? Whew!" Shaking off the surprise, he asked, "You just get home?"

All she could manage was a half-whispered "Yeah."

It wasn't like Hanna not to fawn over Jacob with her affectionate hugs and kisses upon greeting him, especially after being away from him for three days. He approached her cautiously, surveying her unhappy expression. He laid his hands on her shoulders and slowly began rubbing the lengths of her upper arms.

"What is it?" he asked, "A migraine? You want me to get out the body oil and give you a naked rub down?"

Tilting her head up to face him, she asked him as calmly as possible.

"Who's Mandy?"

Jacob's hands went still, falling from Hanna's shoulders and down to his sides. She knew that his sudden look of confusion came more from *her* knowledge of Mandy and not from a lack of his *own* knowledge. He stepped back and now rested his hands casually on his hips. Before today, Hanna had never watched someone she loved, decide whether or not they were going to lie to her. It was surreal in the worst, most painful way.

"What are you talking about?" he asked as if confused and offended.

Hanna was still gazing up into his handsome face praying for some semblance of a confession. It would be easier for her to forgive someone who showed genuine remorse rather than flounder under the shame of their guilt. Her father had told her as a child, the way someone apologizes makes all the difference to what happens next. For Hanna, that statement had never rang more true or held such importance as it did in those few seconds.

"You were with someone in your car," she quietly reminded him. Her statement caused his confused expression to quickly transform into a s*hit she knows,* expression. Jacob wasn't following the same online influencers as Ethan. If Jacob had known about the post, he would have coerced the influencer Nightqueen346 to take it down before someone had the chance to see it. Looking at him, her eyes pleaded with him to tell her what happened. Hanna waited for him to speak but he said nothing. He wore the distant expression she'd seen him wearing when challenging employees on business decisions. Jacob could be stone-cold with an adversary and until now, she'd been lucky to have never been on the receiving end. When Hanna had been mentally playing out the different scenarios on the plane, she hadn't considered Jacob might deny everything. His denial caught her off guard and she didn't know where to go from here. She opened her phone and began tapping and flipping various pages and posts. He would have to admit it if the proof was right there in front of him. The link Ethan sent read *Page Not Found.* She then opened and closed the Instagram app several times and scrolled up and down again. Hanna couldn't find it. It had been removed and she hadn't thought to screenshot the post.

"Shit." She squeezed her phone wanting to pitch it into the wall. She couldn't force him to tell her the truth and he would never be able to convince her that he hadn't cheated. She had seen the damning proof with her own eyes. Hanna heaved a sigh, remembering the promise she made to herself about composure. She needed to go. If Jacob wasn't going to talk, it was pointless to stay. As she stood up from the chair she wiped the tear that began to slide down her cheek, then lightly rested her hands on Jacob's chest. Making sure he understood the severity of the situation, she spoke softly and sincerely. Jacob watched her with a nervous expression.

"I love you, Honey," her throat constricted, "but I need to leave now. I'm so sorry that this happened."

With her hands nearly at eye level, she couldn't help but notice her soft pink cushion-cut engagement ring.

She slid the ring off her finger and sat it on the small glass table beside the chair, clinking as it came to rest. It was the first time she'd ever taken it off. She glanced at Jacob once more as if to say goodbye. He looked as though he was angrily deliberating something. As she turned to leave the bedroom, he caught her arm and pulled her back to him, holding her tightly against his body.

Hanna didn't try to reject him. Instead, she laid both hands across his shoulder blades the way she always did when he held her in his arms. Cradling her head against his chest, he spoke with a shaky voice. "Please don't go."

Hanna slowly tilted her head to find his eyes radiating the same unmistakable sorrow she heard in his hushed voice.

The sheer anguish in his eyes was enough to compel her to stay. *For now.* He held her hands within his own and brought them to his lips, gently kissing them. Looking into her eyes, he was asking her to stay. Jacob had finally shown her a familiar glimpse of the person she had fallen so in love with.

"Are you going to talk to me now?" Hanna asked quietly.

After a slow blink, he nodded in a motion of surrender.

CHAPTER SIX

Jacob and Hanna made their way out to the living room in preparation to talk. The stylish living room was Hanna's most loved room in the house. It was decorated in a luxurious combination of both their tastes. Hanna's decor preference was French and traditional, while Jacob's rugged and stately. The twelve-foot ceiling allowed for a large, modern but whimsical chandelier to hang high in the center of the room. It looked like large floating branches of white and gold ginkgo leaves magically lit from within. A large modular sectional sat paired with a large brass coffee table, crafted to look like a soft-edged, river stone. Opposite the couch were two sets of black flaring wing chairs with tufted leather and tacking around the arms. Hanna thought they were too imposing at first but Jacob pleaded,

"If we have to have a tree hanging from the ceiling, then I'm going to take a chance and say that asking for these cool chairs doesn't make me too much of a bad guy does it?"

His sexy smile swayed Hanna instantly. She surprised him with four chairs instead of the two he was expecting. Jacob settled into the couch and Hanna into one of the leather chairs, where she could face him. Starting at the beginning, Jacob explained how he and his computer engineer Luke had taken their clients out to dinner at Armando's restaurant as planned. Armando's was an upscale restaurant in the downtown financial district of Toronto, located high up on the forty-first floor of the banking tower. It's a favourite amongst the Bay Street traders, bankers, politicians and others who can afford the lavish prices. It's a nice place if you aren't afraid of heights and want a view of the CN tower while dining. A business owner herself, Hanna was no stranger to the wine and dine component of business relationships. Opposite Jacob's clients, Hanna's clients usually preferred a quick lunch meeting or sometimes a late morning breakfast get-together. Jacob's associates had a wolfish appetite for power, fine liquor, expensive meals and anything else that made them feel that they had *arrived*. The contrast between Hanna's clients and Jacob's was like comparing bulls to ballerinas.

Jacob slowly rubbed his hands together, clasped them in front of his chest and began to explain the evening.

"Everyone was drinking during dinner and talks of new deals were going smoothly. We even got them to commit for two more…" He trailed off, realizing he had veered off topic.

"Sorry," Jacob said, giving her an apologetic look. He was uneasy.

"Can I make us a drink?" he asked, perturbed with himself and the situation.

At the current pace, Hanna wouldn't know the full story until sometime tomorrow. The last thing she wanted was to stall the conversation but it was obvious they could both benefit from some liquid courage.

"Sure, I'll take whiskey, on the rocks. Lots." She tried to sound collected.

Jacob gave her a questioning glance as he got up from his seat. Usually, Hanna preferred a white wine but this called for something that, her dad would say, *had a bit of a bite to it*. Jacob walked around the couch to the large, modern, wood sidebar against the wall. Several crystal decanters and glasses on trays sat on the surface. The sidebar was a gift for Jacob that Hanna had custom-made by a local carpenter. It included an ice maker in the center drawer and a mini fridge cleverly concealed on each side. He saw one like it at a resort they once stayed at and thought it was *so swanky*. Hanna wanted to surprise him by getting him one of his own. Jacob reached for the highball glasses and paused, changing his mind. He turned over the two tallest glasses, filled them with ice and began pouring ample amounts of whiskey into both. Hanna watched him in the reflection of the tall mirror that hung above the bar. Jacob was a tall, well-built, achingly attractive man. Hanna felt she would always be mesmerized by him. His light brown hair was cut short in a crew cut that he kept slightly longer on the top. When slicked back, it made him look devilishly handsome. Jacob's eyes were the truest sapphire blue known to exist. Every time he flashed his smile, he made Hanna want to pull him close and kiss him. Everybody seemed to adore Jacob. Women and men were always making fools of themselves around him. People loved his wit, confident charm and of course, his looks. They didn't care whether Hanna had been present or not. It had never bothered her because she knew it was just innocent friendliness on Jacob's part. Sitting there, she stared at his broad form, wondering if she would ever be able to sleep with him again, knowing he had sex with a stranger. She shivered at the thought and looked away.

"Go easy," he said, handing her the glass. "That's a lot for you."

Hanna assessed the tall glass. She hadn't drunk straight whiskey since University.

"I'll be fine. Thanks."

Jacob returned to his spot on the couch after serving Hanna her oversized drink. Normally when they served drinks to each other they would always *cheers* by clinking their glasses together and taking a sip. She sarcastically wondered how this toast should go.

Cheers, Honey, I fucked a stripper while you were gone. Good times!

Hanna took a sip and then immediately another, purposely ignoring Jacob's warning to pace herself. The whiskey seared like liquid fire as it coated her mouth and throat, causing her to question her drink choice. They stared at each other for a minute, and it almost looked like they were a normal couple enjoying a Friday night cocktail together in the comfort of their living room. Jacob hesitated briefly, then continued explaining the evening.

"We had just finished our last bottle of wine when the waitress said the restaurant was closing in another twenty minutes. John and Joel…," he paused, "you know from Encore?"

Hanna nodded. "You mean the two idiots that nearly got you killed on the golf course last year?"

Jacob gave her a look of surprise. Hanna only knew about the incident because Luke had texted Jacob one morning while Jacob was in the shower. Hanna took a peek at the screen when his phone lit up on the washroom vanity. Luke was letting Jacob know that he had contacted the golf course to apologize once again and that he let the manager know he could expect a cheque from Nextech for the value of the two mangled golf carts. The last line of Luke's text was, *Always a party with J and J, isn't it!*

Jacob never mentioned the incident to Hanna.

"Yeah. That's them," he answered. "They were hanging out with the waitresses and trying to get them to keep the bar open another hour for us."

Hanna didn't know that ever happened in the restaurant industry but wasn't surprised that the two gluttons would make every effort to try. She had never been the jealous type but the story of the drunk businessmen *hanging out* with the waitresses had painted a sleazy picture in Hanna's mind.

"When they said they couldn't stay open," Jacob continued, "Joel and John started talking about The Pink Pearl."

Looking somewhat embarrassed, Jacob took a heavy sip from his glass. Everyone from the province and likely the country knew of The Pink Pearl. It was a multi-level strip club that labelled itself the most upscale gentlemen's club in the country. Hanna had always thought the claim was ironic since the men she knew who frequented the club weren't really gentlemen at all. The club was notorious for encouraging the girls to perform *extras* and the waitresses were given bonuses for overcharging patron's credit cards. Hanna glanced at her drink, not realizing the healthy dent she'd made. The whiskey was starting to cushion her nerves but also inhibit the restraint on her overwhelming curiosity. Hanna gave Jacob a look of mild impatience, and he carried on.

"Luke and I didn't want to risk them backing out of the deal we'd just made, so we took them. I drove the four of us because I'd only had a glass or two and I didn't think we'd be there that long.

We all ended up drinking again after we got to the club. Time was flying and I guess I was drinking more than I realized."

He glanced at Hanna, intently gauging her expression. *There was no way he was getting off that easy. If she had to bear the pain of seeing him in the photo, then he would have to explain how the photo came to exist.* Even if it didn't guarantee his eventual exoneration.

"Ok. And?" she encouraged.

Jacob sighed, accepting he would have to surrender more details. "It was getting late and I knew I couldn't drive. The waitresses had already called cabs for the other guys…"

Hanna interjected. "Because they couldn't call for themselves or because the club figured they had already defrauded you out of enough money?"

Jacob smirked at her accurate dig. "Probably both," he admitted.

Hanna couldn't help but feel like parts of the story were missing. Jacob still hadn't filled in all of the blanks.

"What were you doing while Luke, Joel and John were all leaving?"

"I was trying to figure out what I was doing with my car."

The whiskey, now mostly drained, had diminished any restraint that Hanna might have had.

"Is that when you decided to invite the stripper into your backseat?"

Jacob blinked slowly, mentally preparing himself. "She offered to drive my car home, if I paid for her cab ride back to her place, sooo…,"

He inhaled deeply and held his breath. "I said yes," he finished, exhaling loudly as he answered.

Hanna thought she must have misunderstood. "Home? Here?" she asked pointing to the floor, "This house?" Hanna faced the front window, trying to imagine the scene.

As far as Hanna knew, chauffeuring a client home was way above and beyond the usual job description of a stripper, even the ones at The Pink Pearl. This was either a very personal favour or a fully paid service. Either way, it was too many steps over the line for Hanna's already fragile state. She felt like she was eight years old again being spun around on the tire swing at school, her friends spinning her around and around until she threw up her lunch. She leaned forward with her hands on her thighs trying to get some much-needed air into her lungs. This was the second time today she'd nearly hyperventilated. First, after getting Ethan's photo text and now after learning Jacob had hitched a ride home with the stripper he had sex with. She sat staring at Jacob in disbelief, her eyes brimming with tears. If she hadn't gulped so much whiskey and had her vehicle, she would have immediately raced out of there. Pissed off at herself for drinking so much and livid with Jacob, Hanna unleashed on him.

"You are unfucking believable," she seethed. Tears were now streaming down her face. "Do you know just how fucked up that is?"

Jacob hadn't heard Hanna swear twice in one day, let alone twice in the same minute. Now doused in shame, he went to her, sat on the floor in front of her and looked up into her tear-stained face.

"Hanna please," he spoke gently and put his hand on her thigh trying to diffuse her anger. "It meant absolutely nothing to me. It was just sex. Christ, I barely even remember it."

She was offended he thought that would somehow soothe her and pushed his hand away.

"So if I had sex with someone and said it meant nothing, that would make it more forgivable?" she asked skeptically.

After a short pause, he said flatly, "I would forgive you."

Hardly comforted by his hollow remark, she asked herself if they could ever recover from this. She wished she had taken the late flight home instead of flying the next morning. *Would Jacob have skipped The Pink Pearl with his clients and come home alone? Or would Hanna have pulled into the driveway just as Mandy was getting into her Uber? Would the outcome have been any different?* Hanna either had to believe that Jacob had become so intoxicated that he wasn't aware of what his body was doing or that he decided to take pleasure in the other woman's body, thinking he could get away with it. Both scenarios infuriating, with the last, by far more hurtful. Feeling hopeless, Hanna shook her head.

"I don't know if I can forgive you for this," she said somberly, trying to get a hold of her emotions. "This wasn't supposed to be part of our story. We're not in an open relationship Jacob, and you're asking me to downplay what you did."

The more Hanna spoke the more unravelled she felt. "I have so many questions, some of them I'm too afraid to even ask."

Jacob was wearing a wide-eyed expression that Hanna had never seen before. "Ask me Hanna, please!" he pleaded, "I'll tell you!"

Until now she had remained, for the most part, controlled. But the new information about Mandy gave her the nerve to accept his challenge.

"Yeah? Ok! Grrrrreat!" She sounded like the cartoon cereal icon, Tony the Tiger. "Here's one! Why did Mandy the stripper, offer to drive you home?"

Before he could answer, she tossed out another. "How many lap dances did you pay her for before she thought you'd earned a drive home?"

Jacob frowned and stood, so Hanna did the same, abandoning the leather chair. The whiskey had made her wobbly on her feet, but she was determined to continue. Hanna's questions now came like rapid fire, her anger heightening as she listened to herself give the drunken interrogation.

"Whooo's idea was it to fuck in your car? Did you wear a condom? If yes, then where did you even get it?"

Hanna and Jacob hadn't used condoms since the early days of their relationship. If he'd supplied it then he'd bought condoms solely for this occasion. Jacob rolled his eyes and waited for Hanna to be finished so he could begin to answer her torrent of questions.

"Have you done this to me before? Should I be getting tested for STDs?"

This garnered an appalled look from Jacob, which Hanna inwardly enjoyed. She paused to regroup and catch her breath. The combination of alcohol, stress and the excessive energy she expelled during her rant was beginning to subdue her.

She shouldn't be this drunk. She shouldn't have to be asking these humiliating questions, begging for answers. Why was this happening?

Hanna slowly looked around the beautiful room, taking note of all the specially chosen furniture and belongings. She felt tricked by being led to believe the perfect life she had was real. She shook her head slowly at the absurdity then asked Jacob softly,

"Did you kiss her goodbye Honey?" She sounded so sad that Jacob physically winced, but remained silent. Hanna thought back to their last conversation on the phone the night before. "Maybe I shouldn't have teased you about having babies."

Jacob left the room as if he was unable to take it anymore. Hanna watched him storm away toward the bedroom. She couldn't stay here anymore. She told Jacob she had questions that needed answering and to appease her he told her to go ahead and ask. Then when the time came he'd turned and left. Hanna pulled out her phone and began clumsily looking through her contacts, her finger moving in slow dramatic arcs with every scroll. She knew Ava would come to get her. It didn't matter what time it was. Hanna met Ava at University where they quickly became loyal friends. They studied together on weekdays and partied together on weekends. Ava brought Hanna out of her shell and showed her what real fun was. After University they both ended up working in the same city and shared a house until Hanna and Jacob moved in together. Ava wasn't fond of Jacob when Hanna first introduced them four years ago. She told Hanna she wasn't going to be fooled by his looks or cocky charm. There was something about him she didn't trust. Ava agreed to tolerate him as long as he made Hanna happy. She would do anything for Hanna.

Now painfully aware that she was too drunk to operate even a cell phone, Hanna gave up on the contact list and beckoned for Siri to dial Ava's number. She whirled around, dropping her phone as she heard Jacob's heavy footsteps coming purposefully toward her. She had barely registered the cell phone thudding on the rug as it landed. Jacob stood a few inches away from Hanna, grabbed her left hand and swiftly slid her engagement ring back onto her finger. Looking intent he blurted, "I can't give an honest answer as to why it happened. I'm sorry. I know the alcohol played an important role and as I said before, I barely remember anything. Maybe I was a challenge for her because I kept declining her lap dance offers. And 'no' I've never cheated before this. She probably offered to drive me home because she knew it was my name on the credit card that was being illegally swiped all night. Yes, there was a condom, that definitely, did not come from me."

Jacob bent his head and gave Hanna a gentle kiss high on her cheek and her head bobbed like a top-heavy toddler. He brought his hands up, grasping her shoulders to balance her. Still holding her steady, Jacob ducked his head so he could speak to her directly while looking into her eyes. Then softly he said,

"The only person I will ever kiss goodbye is you. And you can tease me about babies aaaall you want." Slowly shaking his head he said, "Nothing like that will ever happen again. It was *one* mistake. I love you, Hanna."

Hanna broke into a quiet sob. Jacob's arms came around her, holding her closely against his strong chest. She was a collage of emotions, a mixture of every sentiment she had felt throughout the day's ordeal. It seemed that each time her crying would begin to subside, seconds later it would begin again. A while later when Hanna was finally finished sobbing, Jacob walked her down the hall and into the bedroom. He turned on a lamp and helped her to take off her clothes. Hanna was thoroughly exhausted and in no condition to ready herself for bed or protest Jacob's helpful assistance. After all, it was soothing to have Jacob care for her the way he was. He slowly pulled the elastic from her ponytail and tussled her long hair, letting it fall in long waves. He then dressed her in her favourite pyjamas, a large white T-shirt that rightfully, belonged to him. He tossed the decorative cushions onto the chair in the corner then pulled down the duvet so Hanna could lie down.

"Ok, let's get you into bed." He spoke in a gentle whisper.

Jacob pulled the duvet up over Hanna's chest, then sat beside her on the edge of the bed. He reached behind her head, adjusting the pillow, pulling it down so it rested against the tops of her shoulders the way she liked. With her head resting against the pillow she sleepily gazed up into Jacob's blue eyes. She raised her hand to his head and ran her fingers through the short hair above his ear. She hadn't touched him affectionately in over three days. Hanna traced her finger over the top curve of his ear then down the side of his face and edge of his clean-shaven jaw. When her finger came to his chin and mouth, she stared longingly at his lips. These were the lips that had kissed her every day for four years. The lips of the man who had promised to kiss her and only her. Overcome by a sudden wave of possessiveness, Hanna pulled Jacob's head toward her and kissed him harder and deeper than she ever had. She broke the kiss only to pull off her T-shirt and toss it aside. Laying naked on her back with her breasts enticingly displayed, she was daring him to refuse her. Jacob removed and tossed his own shirt aside and stood still, waiting for permission to go further. He was sexy, standing there without his shirt, his toned chest muscles and strong arms resting at his sides. Uncertain if they should continue, he asked quietly, "You've had a lot to drink. Are you ok with this?"

In answer, Hanna swiftly undid his belt, then the button and zipper of his pants. Jacob slowly removed the rest of his clothing, giving Hanna a full view of his well-defined, naked body. Without warning, she had a brief, irritating vision of the photo of Jacob she'd seen earlier that morning. Ignoring it, Hanna sat on her knees and used her chin to gesture to the spot where she had laid a second before."Lay down," she said, softly commanding him to comply.

As Jacob laid on his back, she straddled his hips and leaned down to kiss him again, her breasts resting seductively on his chest. She kissed him softly at first and then her kisses became more insistent. She sucked on his lip so hard that he let out a small masculine whimper. His mild protest only encouraged her and she bit gently but briefly at his lower lip. She could feel how hard he was, throbbing beneath her. He ran his hands up the length of her thighs and rested them so he was holding her hips in place on top of him. She swiped his hands away and then lifted slightly so she could guide his length inside of her as she came back down on him. She began grinding against him slowly, then by building speed, intensified the pressure between their bodies. The soft light from the lamp allowed them to see just enough to make out each other's body contours and facial features. Wearing an expression that was almost predatory, Hanna focused intently on Jacob's eyes. Usually, their lovemaking was a harmonious exchange of intimate and pleasurable favours between two compatible lovers. Hanna wasn't making love to Jacob tonight. This was a physical reclamation, an endeavour to regain something that was unjustly taken from her. If she could stay in control of Jacob's powerful body long enough she would undo some of the emotional damage he had caused. The more Hanna spread her legs the deeper Jacob penetrated her and the more he moaned. Her hips fell into a groove that soon had him panting loudly. She leaned down twirling her tongue around his nipple then pulled it into her mouth, sucking firmly and teasing the tip. Maintaining her rhythmic hip rocking, she then did the same for the other nipple.

Hanna's deep thrusts and vigorous licking brought Jacob to the brink of climax. She knew he was ready when he pushed his head backward deep into the pillow, bracing himself for the release. When Hanna halted and raised herself above him, Jacob's eyes flew open in alarm. She took a few steps forward on her knees and hovered her parted legs over Jacob's face. Lowering herself onto his mouth, she compelled him to oblige. Hanna held the headboard with one hand while the other firmly grasped a handful of Jacob's hair. She watched his jaw begin to work hungrily as she rotated her hips in small slow circles, feeding her naked body into his mouth. Jacob loved pleasuring Hanna this way. He found it so erotic that he would be rock hard and ready to erupt the entire time she knelt above him. Following Hanna's orgasm, it would usually only take a few deep plunges inside of her, before he would orgasm himself. Jacob's hands came up to hold her bottom and again she pushed them away.

She clasped and raised his two wrists, holding the backs of his hands against the padded headboard. Confined, she expected him to protest, instead, he continued to relish her most intimate places. She released one of his hands and brought two of his fingers into her mouth to wet them, then guided them to the warm wet opening of her body beneath his lips. His fingers moved steadily inside of her, while his lips and tongue pleasured her on the surface. Now holding the top of the headboard with both hands Hanna allowed the erotic pleasure to flood her body. She swayed her hips front to back, each small thrust edging her body closer to the brim of release. When she could no longer hold back, her upper body jolted as if every nerve ending had been hit with a short surge of lightning. She gave several more slow meaningful thrusts riding out the rippling waves of intensity. When the last wave of pleasure faded, she returned to her original position, sliding down on Jacob's length, taking him deep inside of her. He would be ready to erupt by now. Her pelvis began a rhythm of rise and fall, her hands using his powerful chest to balance. When she knew he was on the brink of exploding, she slowed her rhythm, tormentingly stalling his orgasm. She repeated the taunting once again. She would have to let him come eventually but the physical dominance she held over him had possessed her. If Jacob was going to find release, it would be at her will. Each time she started and stopped, she enjoyed a small dose of empowering energy. The slang term about prolonged erections causing painful *blue balls,* danced merrily through Hanna's mind. After she repeated this ritual several times, Jacob let out a low and throaty laugh. "Oh no you don't, it's my turn now."

His strong hands came to grasp the backs of her thighs in a quick lifting motion. It threw off her balance and she tumbled onto her back, bouncing onto the soft mattress. In one swift motion, he had turned and positioned himself above her. Jacob, now up on his knees, grasped her thighs again and pulled her toward him, her ankles dangling in the air. Dominantly poised above her, he released one of Hanna's legs to align himself, then drove inside, gritting his teeth and panting like an angered animal. After a few quick, deliberate plunges, he came, releasing himself deep within. When Jacob finished his orgasm, he held Hanna impaled with his lasting erection. Realizing that he might have been a little rough, he brought her one foot to his mouth and kissed it softly. Afterward, he rested it lightly on the bed and went to the washroom. When Jacob returned, Hanna was sleeping. She had rolled onto her side and faced the far wall. She often found their lovemaking so gratifying that she would doze off shortly after. Jacob was relieved they were able to reconcile so quickly after such a tumultuous ordeal. He couldn't see that Hanna's eyes were still open, so he turned off the lamp and went to bed. Hanna was lying there, steeping in irritation when she should have been lulled to sleep by her powerful orgasm. Her vivid imagination, an absolute gift where her career was concerned, plagued her mind with images of Jacob's body entangled with the other woman, doing things he should have only been doing with her. After lying there for hours, going back and forth on whether she thought she could bring herself to forgive Jacob, she told herself that it would take time to get over what happened. Jacob had promised her that nothing like that would ever happen again. She wasn't ready to throw away what they shared. Remembering the sincerity in his eyes when he told her he loved her, she finally found herself dozing off to sleep.

25

CHAPTER SEVEN

The next morning when Hanna woke, it felt later than usual. She took a second to assess whether or not she was suffering any side effects from the alcohol and her low-quality sleep. Surprisingly enough, nothing cried out. Thankfully it was Saturday so she would have the day to recover if she eventually ended up with a headache. Jacob was already up out of bed and in the air, Hanna could smell fresh coffee coming from the kitchen. When she went to check the time on her phone, she found it missing from the bedside table. She remembered trying to call Ava right before Jacob came out from the bedroom with her engagement ring. She must have left her phone somewhere in the living room. She threw on a pair of slinky sleep shorts to accompany her large T-shirt and began making her way out to the kitchen. Jacob would be sitting at the island reading from his iPad as he usually did in the morning. When Hanna turned the corner, she saw Jacob leaning back against the counter drinking from his coffee cup. Sitting at the island was Jacob's prized employee, Luke Ramos. Jacob and Luke were dressed in golf shirts, long belted shorts and ankle socks. Jacob turned and smiled widely when he noticed Hanna standing there. Glancing at her outfit, he greeted her. "Good morning sexy."

She hadn't yet put on a bra and her nipples poked sharply at her T-shirt. Hanna wasn't dressed for company and glanced at Luke's back, hoping he would uncharacteristically ignore her. He was one of Jacob's accomplices the night at the strip joint and she wasn't sure she was ready to fake nice just yet. Luke then turned on his bar stool and acknowledged Hanna in his friendly manner as always. Luke was in his mid-thirties, of average height and had a stocky build. He had big brown eyes and short buzzed hair. He had a baby face and a friendly smile that made him look about twenty-five. He was the technical brains at Jacob's company Nextech. Without him, the company might not have achieved the same level of success that it had. Jacob met him at a trade show when Luke was manning a booth. Jacob started a conversation about cashless currency and when Luke offered his insight, Jacob recognized his talent. Hanna and Jacob had invited Luke over for dinner several times since coming on board with Nextech, a couple of years ago.

Luke raised his coffee mug in a cheers-like gesture. "Hey, Hanna."

He smiled cautiously at Hanna, then swiftly turned away after taking note of her skimpy outfit. He must have felt awkward seeing her in sleep attire or maybe he felt guilty being in their kitchen the morning after such an ordeal had occurred. *Was he aware of what happened last night?* Trying not to sound flustered, Hanna replied, "Morning Luke. How are ya?" She was already heading toward the living room to look for her phone. When she saw it lying on the rug, she snatched it up and began slinking back to the bedroom. She waved her hand high in the air, holding her phone as she hurriedly walked by and out of sight. "Bye, guys! Have a good golf game!"

When she returned to the bedroom she contemplated whether the day before had only been a nightmare. She glanced in the corner of the room, catching a glimpse of the suitcase she had yet to empty and put away. She wouldn't have normally left it sitting in the open like that. Sadly it confirmed that the night before wasn't just a bad dream. It had most certainly happened. As far as Jacob knew, they had made up. He seemed genuinely sorry and had even joked about babies with her. He assured Hanna the only person he would ever kiss goodbye was her. In Jacob's eyes, Hanna had even made love to him before bed. The golf game was probably arranged long before last night and she'd forgotten. If Hanna looked in her calendar she would see that she had made note of it as always. It should have been fine that he was going to be out playing a game of golf for the day but it felt like Jacob was gaslighting her. She glanced at her phone noting the dozens of notifications. Ava had called and texted. Her text read,

Hey! Did you pocket-dial me? Sounded like you were crying.
And lastly,
Call me back or text so I know you're ok.

Sounded? Oh my god! Siri must have completed the call and Ava answered. That was when Jacob came out with her ring. She wondered how much of the conversation Ava would have been able to make out. Even if she only heard part of what Jacob had said, it would be pretty obvious what had happened. She needed to text Ava back so she could stop worrying. She could already hear Ava now. *I told you!* or *I knew he couldn't be trusted!*

Hanna needed to gather some energy and mentally prepare before getting back to her. Ava would most certainly spew every inappropriate word she could think of. Hanna could hear distant, loud chuckles coming from the direction of the kitchen. Luke and Jacob were probably heading out to the golf course now. Jacob then called out loudly. "Hanna! You there babe?"

She was tempted to hide, avoiding the uncomfortable goodbye but stalled at the bedroom door instead. Maybe he would just head out if he thought she was in the washroom. It felt strange and wrong to Hanna that Jacob had even considered leaving the house. The whole situation was way too new. Even if they had a golf game scheduled beforehand, Jacob could have easily cancelled it, Luke would have been understanding. She heard the brief rattling of car keys, confirming they were leaving. Then came the low distant rumbling of the garage door opening. They'd left. Hanna stood leaning on the door frame feeling lost. She knew she was partly to blame. Sleeping with Jacob the night before had given him the impression he'd been magically absolved of any wrongdoing.

She was startled by the sound of Jacob's deep voice. "Hey, I was calling you." He wrapped his arms around her waist. "I just came to say goodbye. I should be back sometime after lunch. You wanna go out to dinner tonight? Then maybe we can come home and do that thing we did in here last night."

He slipped his hands up beneath the loose satin of her shorts and cupped her bare butt cheeks, pulling her tightly against him. Jacob kissed her and then looked into her eyes, waiting for an answer. If she turned down his offer she would be taking a step back from reconciliation and delaying the day when she was completely over what he'd done. Since day one, Jacob's sexy smile had seemed to possess an invisible power. Hanna knew that no one else would ever have a smile that held that much influence over her. She jokingly glared at Jacob with her finger resting on her lip, considering his offer. "Uuuuum Sure!" she finally answered and gave him a small smile.

"Ok, Honey! I'll call you on my way home from the golf course." He kissed her on the cheek and then he was gone. She unpacked the suitcase that had been sitting there since last night and threw the clothes into a laundry basket to wash. To make it a full load, she went into the closet hamper to grab a few more items of clothing. On top of the pile was a pair of Jacob's jeans and boxer shorts. She wondered if that was what he'd been wearing two nights before. She shoved her hands into the front pockets searching frantically for...... she didn't even know. When her rummaging failed to yield any findings, she threw the jeans out of the closet and stared at them as if they'd done something to offend her. The only involvement they'd had, was simply being worn on the night in question. *If* they had been the jeans Jacob had worn that night. Hanna rolled her eyes at how ridiculous she was being and went over to pick up the small pile of clothing. Peeking out from one of the back pockets of the jeans was the corner of what looked like a receipt. She pulled on the paper and dropped the jeans to the floor, using both hands to look at it closely. It was a credit receipt for a bottle of Jagermeister from a store called City Convenience. It was dated for over a week ago. If her memory served her correctly, it was the night she'd stayed extra late at the studio with Ethan and Shauni. Summer was their busiest time of year. They had a booth or an event to set up almost every day that week. They were completing as much of the work in the studio beforehand to help the onsite installs and setups go as smoothly and efficiently as possible. They had two events to set up the next day. One was an evening retirement party for a group of senior accountants, and the other was an exhibition booth for a nutritional supplement company. Hanna knew she couldn't be at two places at once, so she and Ethan brought in several temporary team members to help out. The team went over every detail they could think of with the temporary crew. When they were confident the team had the gist of the plan, they let everyone go home. Shauni would prepare the booth with the crew the next day, allowing Ethan and Hanna to oversee the retirement party setup. After the temp crew was gone, they took an hour to load up the van and Hanna's SUV with everything they needed for the two events. When Hanna got home late that night, Jacob had just finished showering and was changing into his sleepwear. Hanna remembered thinking how adorable it was that he had stayed up late waiting for her. He hadn't mentioned purchasing any alcohol only a couple of hours earlier. Jagermeister wasn't something that either of them normally purchased. She had never doubted or not wholeheartedly trusted Jacob before. She was now looking back at dates and checking the time of sale on a receipt she'd found in one of his pockets. *What the hell was she doing?* As she reflected on what she'd been reduced to, the doorbell rang, and at the same time, a notification came through on her phone. Hanna quickly shoved the receipt into one of the drawers on her side of the closet and headed toward the door. Checking the doorbell camera on her phone, the screen featured Ava's voluptuous profile. Hanna glanced down at her outfit, debating a bra, then figured if Luke Ramos had seen her wearing such an outfit, so could her closest friend. Ava Williams was an attractive woman. She was an inch taller than Hanna, with light brown hair cut in a blunt chin-length bob. Long black lashes highlighted her hazel eyes, and her full, sensual lips ignited the imaginations of all men. Ava had a curvy figure with the tiniest waist Hanna had seen on an adult female. Hanna thought Ava was a total show-stopper. As Hanna made her way to the front entryway, Ava rang the bell again and called her cell phone. Hanna didn't want Ava to leave, thinking she wasn't home. She answered, sounding slightly out of breath from her sprint down the long hallway.

'Hi!' she managed.

'Hey, you in there? I'm out front.'

Instead of replying, Hanna opened the front door and stood still in place. Her eyes brimmed with tears, and she was still needlessly holding her phone to her ear. Ava stepped inside and slowly reached for Hanna's phone. She sat it on the long mirrored table against the wall and then brought her attention back to Hanna. "You wanna talk?" Ava's soft, smooth voice put Hanna over the edge. Hanna grabbed Ava and hugged her tightly. They embraced for several minutes before Ava leaned back and used her finger to sweep aside some of Hanna's messy hair away from her face. "Sssshhhh sssshhhh, I'm here now Sweetie. Tell me what happened."

Hanna pulled herself together. She didn't want another headache and knew another bawling session would surely bring one on. She had cried more in the last two days than a teething baby.

She breathed deeply and wiped at her cheeks. "Let's go sit at the kitchen island."

Ava kicked off her sandals and followed behind, glancing around suspiciously for Jacob. Not needing to see her face, Hanna sensed Ava's battle-ready instincts. "You can relax. He's not here," she volunteered, "He's golfing."

Ava shook her head but didn't look surprised. She kept silent, reaching into the cupboard for two mugs, then poured them each a coffee. When Hanna finished blowing her nose and rinsing her hands, she sat on the stool. Ava sat one of the coffees down in front of Hanna then took a seat beside her. Hanna told Ava the entire story, starting with the lurid photo of Jacob in his car. She told her how she couldn't get ahold of him the next day and how he'd confessed only after she asked him who Mandy was. When she told Ava that Jacob had received a ride home from the stripper, she was so disgusted she sat down her mug. Hanna felt like she'd said too much and tried to downplay the facts for Jacob's benefit. "He said it would never happen again and that he barely remembered it. He's hoping I'm putting it all behind me."

"Is that what you want to do?" Ava asked calmly, trying to hide her outrage.

Hanna shrugged looking around. "I want to, but I think it's going to be almost impossible."

Ava tried to appear composed but Hanna knew what she was thinking by the look in her dramatic hazel eyes. Ava's eyes had a voice of their own. She'd learned this about Ava when she met her nine years ago in university. During their first year, the instructor for Ava's women and gender studies course gave her fifty-five percent on her final assignment. Her average was well over eighty, so the low mark was a surprise. It was enough to knock her off the Dean's list for the year. When Ava went to the instructor to speak privately about the low grade, she said that she didn't think Ava took the course seriously and felt that Ava hadn't fully grasped the material. Hanna had been waiting outside the door to offer moral support and had covertly glanced into the room every few minutes. Ava's temper was often quick to ignite but her razor-sharp tongue, along with her iconic arched eyebrows were usually the only weapons she needed. She accused the instructor of judging a book by its cover. Ava was always done up, whether attending an early morning class or working out at the gym. It was a woman's prerogative to want to look beautiful when she felt like it. It didn't mean she should be judged unfairly and it didn't mean she hadn't grasped the material given in the course. When Ava asked the instructor to re-mark the assignment, she curtly said '*no*'. *So much for women supporting women!* Weeks later when she received her final report for the semester, she had surprisingly made Dean's list. Knowing Ava had been justified in her request, the instructor had adjusted the mark. When Ava told Hanna about the changed grade, Hanna thought back to the way Ava's dramatic eyes had pierced the instructor like a laser. She wasn't at all surprised the grade had been adjusted in Ava's favour. That evening they celebrated at the campus bar till early morning.

Sitting at the island, Ava rubbed Hanna's back in slow gentle waves, trying to bring her friend some comfort. Hanna sat there enjoying the relaxing gesture and after a few minutes, she spoke quietly.

"You can stop biting your tongue. Just say it, you knew he would hurt me."

Ava finally broke her silence. "Hey! Just because I was afraid he would hurt you doesn't mean it feels good to smear it in your face. It feels horrible that my instincts…," Ava broke off. "It feels horrible. Period."

Her open palm was splayed over her heart as if making a solemn vow. They had turned on their stools facing each other. "I'm sorry you're going through this Han. You didn't deserve that. I think Jacob's a complete asshole. You know that I'm here for you right? Whatever ends up happening with you guys, I'm here to help you get through it. In fact…," Ava gave Hanna a wicked grin. "Did you want me to help you start packing right now?"

Hanna smiled brightly at the wisecrack offer, but when her cheeks relaxed, she looked like she might have been considering it. Ava thought it would do Hanna some good to leave the house for a while. Jacob should have been home, at least trying to make amends for what a pig he'd been. Instead, he'd left before Hanna was even out of her pyjamas.

"Jump up! We're going to lunch! You're buying!" Ava commanded, then abruptly stood from her stool.

Looking discouraged, Hanna glanced down at her outfit for the third time this morning. She pulled at her T-shirt letting it billow back against her body. Ava pointed to the big T-shirt and her bracelets clinked together.

"Yeah! You're right! Get rid of that garbage bag and throw on a top."

Following Ava's orders, Hanna jumped up and scooted down the hall toward the bedroom. When Ava took charge, the best option was to obediently comply. Besides, it would be nice to get out of the house and take her mind off things. Hanna quickly brushed her teeth and washed her face. She threw her hair up in a bun and applied a bit of blush and a few sweeps of mascara. Ava was standing in the closet holding up a grey one-piece jumper when Hanna stepped out of the washroom. Hanna considered the outfit and decided not to question Ava's choice. She tossed on the jumper, over her bra and panties then headed to her jewelry box sitting on her dresser. She pulled out a pair of small dangling jade earrings and slid them into her ears. She glanced in the mirror and noted the small dark circles beneath her eyes.

Ava was watching her. "Don't say a word! It is literally impossible for you to look bad."

Hanna turned around smiling at Ava, " How do you know I wasn't thinking that I looked pretty good?"

Ava was pulling something out of her purse. "Here," and handed her a slim gold lipstick tube. "You look damn good but we both know that's not what you were thinking."

Hanna slid the tube of lipstick across her lips a couple of times and handed it back to Ava. "I'm ready."

Ava shot her a loving smile, then held her hand as they headed down the hall and out to Ava's car.

CHAPTER EIGHT

The best friends shared an early lunch at a popular pub called The Barrel. It was located on the west side of the city and was set up in the renovated basement of a large, converted historic hotel. The upper floors were dedicated office spaces with the restaurant situated below. Its high stone walls were pleasantly rustic while the lighting and decor gave it a cozy, lounge-like atmosphere. It was always busy and being Saturday it was especially hectic. Finding a place to park was proving to be problematic. Ava was on her second lap around the parking lot when Hanna spotted someone leaving.

"Over there!" she cheered.

Ava ended up getting to the spot at the same time as another driver. In a stand-off between a Land Rover and Ava's small zippy BMW, she had won the only available parking spot. To show their appreciation, the driver of the Land Rover thanked her with a high middle finger as they angrily sped away. Hanna thought of her tricky maneuvering SUV. "Something tells me we would have lost that one if I were driving."

Once seated, Ava ordered them each a glass of white wine and an appetizer to share. The waitress serving them was a young brunette with long wavy hair. She was wearing a short black mini-skirt and a low-cut top that accentuated her breasts. She was cheery and helpful but something about her irritated Hanna more than she could understand. Hanna watched the young waitress busily bounce around from table to table taking care of the bustling crowd. She tried to put her finger on what it was about the waitress that bothered her. She turned her attention to Ava who was speaking animatedly about her latest voice-over role as an evil cartoon bunny with long humanlike hair. Ava was spending four days a week in the network's sound studio but was working with the producers to allow her to record from her basement studio part-time as well. Hanna was happy for Ava and could tell that she loved her job.

"I'm so sorry Ava, The bunny sounds like she's right up your alley. I'm a little bit distracted! I'm still in disbelief that Jacob cheated on me."

Hanna knew as soon as she said it that she sounded like an old cliche. She hated Jacob for doing that to her. She already knew she felt like a clueless idiot, but now she sounded the part too. She told Ava about last night and how she took satisfaction in delaying Jacob's orgasm, hoping to give him *blue balls*. Ava's full lips curled up into a giant smile, and then she laughed. "Really?" She had trouble believing it but hoped it was true. "Well, I definitely like the way you're thinking, but sleeping with the guy isn't exactly revenge."

Hanna knew Ava was right. Besides giving Jacob a false sense of forgiveness, she hadn't accomplished anything. Hanna could tell Ava was wondering about something. "What is it?"

"Just curious. Was that one of those doorbell cameras I saw when I came in?"

"Yeah. Jacob didn't want the porch pirates stealing our parcels so I had my dad put it in for us as a deterrent."

Ava raised her hands, shocked that Hanna hadn't shared the findings from the night Jacob received his ride home from the stripper. "Did you check the footage from the night everything happened? What did you see?"

"There was nothing there. Not because it was deleted but because Jacob came in through the garage and not the front door. I could see lights shining across the lawn from when his car pulled in but that's it."

"Shit. That's unfortunate. Woulda' been good to have."

"I know. I would have liked to see if he was as drunk as he said and what she looked like."

They both sat there coming to terms with how close the camera had come to being useful.

Ava shook her head. "That's frustrating Han. You know, you should come and stay with me for a while. Some time apart might give you both some breathing room."

Part of Hanna wanted to jump at the offer as a means of retribution, but leaving the house, she shared with Jacob was a big step back from being engaged and living together. She worried that it might do even more harm to their now-altered relationship. They weren't the type to argue and rarely disagreed. If they found themselves with different opinions, the discussion was only ever a diplomatic, verbal sparring match that always ended with both sides agreeing to disagree. Why they ended up here, she didn't know. Hanna was supposed to be planning a wedding, not moving out or looking for any *breathing room.* The waitress stopped in at their table to top up their water glasses. After inspecting the waitress' long waves of hair, Hanna self-consciously pushed the wispy hairs that had escaped her bun back behind her ears.

"I should have done something with my hair," she said glumly.

Ava laid her hand on top of Hanna's, giving it a gentle squeeze. "Listen to me beautiful. Those sluts have nothing on you. Most of them aren't even that pretty."

At first, Hanna thought Ava was talking about the waitress, and glanced over to decide whether she would go as far as to call the poor girl a slut.

Ava carried on. "To qualify for stripping, you need fake tits, two inches of makeup and a bare ass. Without all that, no one would even recognize them." Ava glanced at Hanna hoping to see a smile. Realizing she was being overly loud, she leaned closer, adding quietly,

"Not even the perverts who stick money down their thong would think they had an ounce of natural beauty."

Hanna loved that Ava was trying so hard and it felt good to be called beautiful.

"Hmmmm," Hanna gave a faint smile, "you sound like you know one," then wondered if maybe she did.

Ava responded by smirking and giving her a sinful smile. They both sipped at their wine and Ava glared at Hanna as if she was considering something. "I think we should go," she said casually.

Hanna leaned over and began to pick up her bag, readying to leave the restaurant. "Yeah, I should probably check in with Ethan and Sh..."

She halted when Ava abruptly put her hand over hers. Ava's shiny bob-cut swayed as she shook her head. She spoke slowly and quietly with an expression of deathly importance. "That's not what I meant."

It took Hanna a second to realize what the conspicuous look and dramatic tone were for. Hanna released her bag and sat back up in her chair. Now understanding Ava's meaning, she wore a contemplative expression and the tiniest of smiles.

"You're talking about The Pink Pearl," she stated instead of asking.

Ava had always been the adventurous one. Before she turned nineteen, and was of legal age to drink, she would brazenly use Hanna's driver's license to get into the local nightclubs. Ava had persuaded Hanna to fill in the paperwork, reluctantly claiming she had lost her driver's license. At the same time, she applied for a replacement so that she would conveniently have two, one for Ava of course and one for herself. Moments after Ava was given entry, Hanna would line up and enter the same bar. Sometimes the bouncers checking ID at the door, would pause or give Ava a suspicious once over but they either didn't care enough to confiscate the ID or didn't catch on. It helped that the two friends looked so much alike. They were close enough in height and build, both with long light hair. Until years later when Ava started dying her hair a light shade of brown, they could have been taken for sisters. Once inside they would drink and spend all night on the dance floor. It was rare for them to leave before closing time. If a house party was going on after the bar had closed, they would finish off the night at a party. The hard and fast rule was that they arrived together and left together.

"Wouldn't you like to see just what goes on in there? What it is that men find so fascinating?" Ava asked quizzically.

Hanna wasn't taking the bait. "Didn't you already tell me what lures them? You said it yourself. Lots of makeup, fake breasts and a bare ass. Whyyyyy would I want to go there?"

"Are you telling me that you aren't at all curious as to who this Mandy person is?" Ava's impeccably groomed eyebrows were positioned in high upward arches.

Hanna said nothing, but her face said everything. The fact was that she *was* curious, irritatingly curious. She had wondered what the stripper looked like since she first found out that she existed. She had seen her naked backside in the Instagram photo, but she had no idea what her face looked like. She told herself she didn't need to know what she looked like. If she was trying to put the incident behind her and forgive Jacob, this wasn't the adult way to do it.

"Yes," Hanna sighed, "Naturally part of me is curious about her. But what good would it do me to go to The Pink Pearl and see what the perverts do there? What if I were to see a client? Or worse yet, what if I couldn't handle it? Seeing her in person might put me over the edge." Hanna imagined how painfully awkward it would be, coming face to face with the woman her fiancé had cheated with. She knew it would only stoke her newfound jealousy and shook her head confirming her decision. "I know you're trying to help but it's a bad idea. Sorry, Ave. Not happening."

Ava rolled her eyes and clicked her tongue quietly in disappointment. "Fine, but it doesn't have to be a definite *no*. Who knows, maybe it would give you some insight or closure. Just think about it."

Hanna paid the bill and Ava gave her a ride back home. She thanked Ava for coming to her rescue and for taking her to lunch. They'd made arrangements to meet up again in a few days. As Hanna made her way up the front walkway, Ava lowered the power window so she could call to Hanna.

"The next ones on me! And seriously, if you need to get away from Jacob and stay with me for a while, just come over!"

Smiling at Ava's dig toward Jacob, Hanna shook her head, waved at Ava through the open window and continued inside.

CHAPTER NINE

Jacob wasn't back yet. Hanna finished the laundry she'd started earlier that morning, tidied up the kitchen counters then moved on to the bedroom to make the bed. Since she hadn't showered before going to lunch with Ava, Hanna thought she'd take a long bath to relax.

Hanna and Jason remodelled the ensuite so that the bathtub overlooked the backyard garden. The bather could lay back in the water and enjoy the tall trees and flower beds. The garden design mimicked the one that her mother Pam had back home in Ingleton. It wasn't overly formal but the garden housed some rare, large-leaf hostas, a variety of Japanese maples and an ornate arbour with English ivy. Each hosta plant had begun as a small division from her mom's mature plants at home. That made the view of the garden that much more special to Hanna, especially now that Pam was gone. She turned on the tap and adjusted the temperature. While the tub was filling with water she grabbed the mini Bluetooth speaker, put on some Ed Sheeran, then sprinkled some scented bath salts under the running water. She grabbed a fluffy bath sheet from the linen closet and sat it on the small bench beside the tub. Finally, to add softness to her skin, Hanna went to add a drop of her vanilla-scented body oil to the water. When she went to grab it, she found it missing from the tray on the counter. She remembered it was almost empty and meant to order more online. Sometimes Jacob and Hanna liked to use the scented oil to give each other rub-downs before they had sex. It was especially arousing for Jacob as he loved the way the glossy sheen from the oil, covered the curves of Hanna's naked body. For Hanna it not only felt amazing to have Jacob's warm hands gliding all over, but the way his hungry eyes seemed to relish her body as he caressed her skin, made her feel completely sexy. It was an intimate ritual that they both equally enjoyed. Laying in the tub, Hanna thought about Jacob and the day they'd met. When she'd first met him four years ago she thought he was flawless. He was funny, smart and the most in-tune partner she could have imagined. Jacob was a gentleman in every way.

They'd met at a gaming trade show in Toronto where she was the booth designer for a couple of vendors. It was the day before the show was scheduled to open. Hanna was checking the progress of the booths and verifying that all signage and components were in place. She was up on a tall ladder making sure the vinyl banner was holding up. The client had ordered it way too close to the exhibit's opening day and she wanted to make sure the quality hadn't been sacrificed. Hanna glanced from side to side to get an overall look at the space. She was pleased with what she and the team had created. The booth was nearly ready to be handed over to the client, Nextech to install their product for demonstration.

"Nice!" she said out loud, looking side to side. "I think we're pretty good here."

"Yeah! Real good," replied a deep voice behind her.

It was Don, the electrical technician they hired to help complete the installation of the electrical hardware.

Hanna was relieved the huge banner was not only printed and delivered so quickly, but also her team was able to install it on time without causing damage or issues. There was a massive banner facing outward so visitors could see the brand. Despite that and the name and logo decorating every possible surface, the client decided last minute that they wanted a large, banner on the inside of the booth as well.

"I don't think this customer realizes that I almost fell short of getting them this custom sign. Usually, the turnaround time for something this size is two weeks. We were able to get it in two days!"

Don agreed with Hanna.

"Yeah! Who orders a last-minute, custom thirty-foot banner with their logo on it anyway?"

"Well," Hanna replied, "I guess if your name is Jacob Barber from Nextech you do."

She heard Don chuckle. Hanna was cautiously making her way down the ladder when Don appeared, walking from the opposite direction of the deep voice. Hanna looked around, realizing the deep voice wasn't coming from Don. It was coming from a good-looking, well-dressed man wearing a sinfully sexy smile.

"Oh!" was all Hanna said.

She could see the man was wearing an exhibit lanyard around his neck and appeared as if he wanted to speak with her. She crossed her fingers that she wasn't being delivered a message that '*Jacob from Nextech*' wanted to make more last-minute changes.

"Hi there! I'm Hanna Richards, can I help you?" She walked toward the handsome stranger and before she reached him, he held out his hand for her to shake. "Hi there Hanna. I'm Jacob Barber from Nextech."

Hanna wanted to climb back up the ladder and dive off. Instead, she smiled and stood there wallowing in the fact she had just mocked a customer while he was standing there listening. Jacob could see how mortified Hanna was and smiled at her adoringly. He had come to check the status of his booth and so far he liked what he was seeing.

"I wanted to let you know how much I appreciate you accommodating the late requests for the booth. I'm not sure what happened. Everything had been discussed at the office and somehow our marketing person missed the interior banner detail." He glanced at the banner. "My apologies and thank you."

Hanna had watched Jacob speak but when he was finished she had only comprehended a fraction of what he'd said. She was temporarily deaf after falling into the deep blue abyss of this stranger's entrancing eyes. When she came to and could hear again, she told him he was most welcome and that she was honoured they had chosen Richards and Co. to complete their project. On an unexpected, but very welcome whim, Jacob had asked her to dinner that evening. During their dinner Hanna and Jacob talked about their careers as business owners, what foods they liked and what aspirations they had for their personal relationships. They even touched on the topic of children and spirituality. When Hanna asked him about religion, Jacob explained that after his father had been killed in the Twin Towers, terrorist attack he was having trouble believing in any God.

"I was nine years old. How about you? Are you religious?" Jacob asked.

"My mom died a couple of years ago and part of me chooses to believe she's up there with all the other good-hearted people gardening and baking lasagna. Does that count?"

"I'm sorry to hear about your mom." Jacob kindly offered his condolences, and then to lighten the mood he asked Hanna what some of the important qualities were that she needed in a partner. Hanna contemplated the qualities with a whimsical expression while she traced the circular rim of her wine glass.

"I want someone who will make me laugh, make me feel like I'm special to them aaaand…" She searched for the right words. "Just honesty. I want to know that I can trust my partner. That's important to me. When you trust someone your heart feels home."

Jacob smiled and then nodded in agreement as he listened. "Fair enough. What about attraction? How high is that on the list?"

The immediate and intense attraction they shared for each other was evident.

"It's important." Hanna's cheeks had warmed significantly. "But if the critical things like trust, desire and compatibility aren't there, it's not enough to float you through."

Jacob gave Hanna a genuinely warm smile. "Float you through what?" he asked but knew what she meant.

"Through forever," she answered bashfully.

Staring at Hanna across the table, Jacob shook his head in disbelief.

"You are the sweetest creature I think I've ever encountered."

It was safe to say that Hanna had fallen for Jacob after that first day. She loved him still.

CHAPTER TEN

The relaxing bath had been therapeutic for Hanna. She felt refreshed and would be in the right mindset when Jacob got home. He wanted to take her to dinner tonight and she was looking forward to it. He had just texted her. *Reservation at 6 pm!*

She picked out an outfit and laid it on the lounge chair in the closet, catching a glimpse of herself in the dressing mirror. Usually, when Hanna stepped out of the shower and had a quick glance in the full-length mirror, she'd been, for the most part, satisfied and even pleased with her reflection. Her slim but curvy body looked just as nice naked as it did fitted with a sweatshirt and jeans. But today looking in the mirror, she had this nagging voice telling her that she wasn't as sexy as other women and the fact that her breasts were just less than a C-cup meant she was likely a write-off in the eyes of any male. Hanna felt like something she usually enjoyed had been taken from her. She had never suffered from self-esteem issues before. Jacob's explanation as to why he cheated had boiled down to, "I was drunk."

It hadn't occurred to Hanna that her physical appearance may have played a role in Jacob's mishap, or alternatively, that the other woman's appearance had. She felt naive for not considering that and stepped closer to the mirror. Every minor imperfection she'd ever noted about herself appeared magnified. The small group of almost invisible dimples on her upper thighs seemed deeper than she remembered and when she turned sideways she thought her knees looked knobby. *Had they always been knobby?* All of a sudden, it wasn't feeling like a good leg day so Hanna hung up the short dress she'd originally chosen and pulled out a pair of black fitted Capri pants. With the right top and shoes, the pants could be just as sexy as the short dress. Now that she was bathed and had settled on her dinner outfit, she could relax until Jacob got home. It was a perfect day outside. Late summer weather in southern Ontario was great for sitting outdoors on the deck with a book. She would be comfortable in the shade wearing just her bathrobe. Hanna grabbed her sunglasses, book and phone, then slipped out onto the private balcony off the bedroom. It was at the side of the house and was just the right size for two outdoor lounge chairs and a small drink table. Each time Hanna sat out there, it felt like she was in her personal, secret hiding spot. The tall, mature maple trees surrounded the balcony, giving it the feeling of a well-engineered tree fort. It was sheltered from the street view and all of the surrounding neighbours. There was one small break in the tree line that gave her a view into the immediate neighbour's backyard. The neighbours, Bill and Beatrice, were an older but active retired couple who liked to affectionately bicker back and forth at each other. They had come over to introduce themselves the day after Hanna and Jacob had moved in. They arrived at the door with a dish of turkey and rice casserole and an hour's worth of chitter-chatter. Because they were always speaking so loudly, Hanna figured they were both hearing impaired or believed everyone else was partially deaf. Hanna always got a laugh out of their colourful conversations. Bill liked to tell fictitious tales about the journeys he and Beatrice had been on over their many years of marriage. When he was finished speaking, Beatrice would give the less astonishing, factual version. Bill expected it every time but it never stopped him from further storytelling or wearing his bashful expression when Beatrice blew his cover. She would never interrupt while he was performing. It was as if Beatrice herself was impressed at how far from the truth Bill could venture. They were never more than three feet away from each other. Hanna thought they were an adorable team. She would often stop to chat with them if she wasn't rushing off to the studio or job site. One day Hanna had overheard them while they were in the back yard doing some late spring garden work. Bill was supposed to be pruning the shrubs and Beatrice was weeding the garden beds. Hanna was outside doing some weeding herself and was kneeling at the fence. She heard Beatrice gasp loudly.

"Oh for heaven's sake Bill! You've butchered my clematis!"

Hanna pictured her holding her garden-gloved hands on her cheeks.

"Your what?" Bill bellowed loudly across the yard.

"My Clematis!"

"What? What's a matter with your clitsmatis?"

Hanna wasn't sure if Bill had mispronounced the plant's name on purpose or not but Beatrice wasn't happy about whatever he had done to her *clitsmatis.*

"It's *cle*matis you old ass! Not that *other* word you said!"

Bill had harshly over-pruned the vine. Hanna then listened to Beatrice educate Bill on how the vine grows from its old growth causing the vine to look dead, when only just *dormant.* She told him that if he hadn't completely killed it, he would start to see the new growth in a couple of days or so. No one was outside in their yard today, so it would be a peaceful retreat. Hanna used the table as a stool and put up her feet for maximum comfort. She pushed her robe off her legs, letting the sun kiss her lower body for a while. She read a few chapters and then checked the time on her phone. It was after four-thirty. If Jacob wasn't home soon, they would be rushed for their dinner date. As she noted the time, she heard a car drive up, followed by a door slam. Judging the direction the sound came from, Bill and Beatrice had just gotten home from one of their *ventures.*

Mildly deflated that it wasn't Jacob, Hanna was no longer in the mood to read. As she stood to go inside, a series of horn blows rang out from Bill's large sedan. He must have accidentally pressed the panic button on his key fob, initiating the blasts. When the loud trademark bickering began and the horn blowing continued, Hanna firmly tightened the belt of her robe and rushed over to assist. She regretted not bothering to put on a bra or panties after her bath. Before Hanna could run through the house and across the lawn, Beatrice had the passenger door open and was bent over, leaning into the car. Bill had his arm around her neck and one leg hanging out of the car, resting on the ground. He was injured in some way and was relying on the help of little old Beatrice to get him out of the vehicle. One of them must have squeezed the key fob in the chaos.

"Oh, Jesus Beatty! Can we not turn off that damn horn?"

"I don't know how Bill!" Beatrice blasted back in a panic.

It was usually Bill that drove the two around on their various excursions. Hanna couldn't remember ever seeing Beatrice in the driver's seat before today. It was likely she wasn't aware that the key fob even had a panic button.

Hanna could foresee this going badly for both of them. She couldn't simply stand back and watch them get hurt. "Whoa! Whoa, Beatrice let me help you!" she insisted.

When the older woman glanced back, it was obvious she was relieved to see help had arrived. Bill was embarrassed and shook his head. "Oh cripes! Now look what I've done!"

Still in her robe, Hanna rushed toward the car to help Beatrice with Bill. Beatrice had forgotten she was clutching the car keys with her fingers. When Hanna noticed the dangling keys, she bent down and reached under Bill's, less-than-toned bicep and squeezed the red button, silencing the obnoxious horn. Then in a graceless push-pull effort, Hanna and Beatrice were able to extract Bill from the car.

"Oh, that's better!" Beatrice breathed a sigh of relief. "Thank you Hanna dear."

Bill quickly tried to make light of the ordeal and laughed one of his loud exaggerated laughs. "Bah ha ha! I should have a heart attack more often! It's the only way I get the attention of two pretty girls at once!"

"Oh! You ooold dog!" Beatrice countered, then opened the back door of the car and pulled out a small duffle bag along with her purse.

"Did you say a heart attack, Bill?" Hanna asked with concern.

She wasn't sure if she had heard him correctly. Besides needing help from the car, he looked fine and in good health. Beatrice told Hanna that Bill had suffered a very mild heart attack and that they'd kept him in for a while, just to be safe.

"He woke up feeling dizzy and by late morning he said he was getting chest pains so we called the ambulance."

Hanna was surprised that she nor Jacob had been aware that the ambulance had ever come and gone. She had been out of town for a couple of days so it was certainly possible she missed it.

"I'm sorry to hear that Bill," Hanna offered, "I'm really glad you're ok. What day did that happen?"

Bill took over speaking for Beatrice. She was upset and her eyes had become teary recollecting the incident. "Well, I guess it was just yesterday morning. Feels like longer doesn't it Beatty?"

Beatrice nodded her head in agreement but still looked confused. "It was whatever day you had the taxi cab over there. I saw it pull away when they were wheeling Bill out of the house on the stretcher."

Hanna had used a car service to get to the airport three days ago and again on her way home yesterday afternoon, not yesterday morning. Hanna was both impressed and sad that retirement required so little awareness of times and dates. She felt grateful for Beatrice that Bill had made such a quick recovery. Still in her robe, Hanna was now somewhat eager to get back into the house. She'd put on enough of a show for one day and was thankful nothing had popped out. Waving goodbye, she let them know she was just next door if they needed her help.

"Take it easy Bill! Just let me know if you need me!"

"Thank you, Hanna!" And they all waved goodbye.

CHAPTER ELEVEN

Shortly after Hanna finished getting ready, Jacob finally arrived home. She had poured herself a glass of wine and sat at the kitchen island waiting for him. She was dressed in her black fitted Capri pants and her gold top was an off-the-shoulder design with long fitted sleeves that complimented her slim arms. Jacob adored Hanna's shoulders and she wanted to showcase them tonight. Beneath her top, a strapless push-up bra drew attention to a subtle cleavage and delicate choker necklace. Her gold ankle strap heels were covered with tiny silver rhinestones and crisscrossed over the tops of her feet. She felt incredibly sexy.

Hanna had almost finished her glass of wine when Jacob came into the kitchen looking for her. When he found her sitting there, he stopped and stood behind her. Hanna turned around on her stool to see why he hadn't said anything. He was biting his lower lip, inspecting her with uninhibited desire. Hanna took the opportunity to enjoy the flattery. Usually, only her sleaziest lingerie could provoke a sexy lip-biting from Jacob. He slowly approached her and bent his head to kiss her lips, slowly moving downward to her neck and then her chest. He lightly rubbed his lips back and forth over the partially exposed tops of her breasts. Hanna knew that he wasn't going to stop unless she told him to. He kissed his way around to her back, laying gentle kisses on her shoulders and behind her ear. He then slipped his fingers down the back of her top to unclasp her bra, removed it and dropped it to the floor. After he made his way back around to her front again, he pulled down her top and delicately lifted each breast so they were resting provocatively over the top of her gold shirt. After taking a moment to enjoy the sight of her exposed breasts, he unclasped his belt and freed himself of his shorts. "It's time to take those tight little pants off."

The carnal look in Jacob's eyes compelled Hanna to immediately comply. His possessive hunger spoke to her desperate need to feel his appetite for her and her body. She removed her heels and then pushed her jeans down to the floor. Jacob bent, pulling the jeans and thong over her ankles for her. He lifted her upward onto the shimmering quartz island, and she gasped at the cold stone against her backside. She was quickly soothed when Jacob leaned down and took her nipple into his mouth, sucking it gently. When Hanna let out a soft moan, he raised his foot to the stool rung for leverage, grabbed the base of his cock and slid himself deep between her legs.

As Hanna lay back on the counter, Jacob continued with his thrusting. He was unaware that Hanna had done something she had never done before. After he sat her on the counter, she closed her eyes and envisioned herself as a late-night exotic dancer. She invited Jacob, her sexy customer into a dark, private room and allowed him to go all the way with her body. She imagined that the lust she evoked was enough to make even a veteran pervert unable to control himself. In her mind, she allowed him to live out his dirtiest desires. The fantasy was a complete turn-on, an ego soother or more accurately, an *alter* ego soother. She was an ultra-sexy, irresistible, off-limits vixen that he, her customer, just had to have. He laid her back on a round table that was meant for table dancing or resting drinks. Neon lights lined the edges of the tall ceiling above, giving off enough light to see her naked, glittery skin. Her white stiletto heels glowed in the purple light, and the dainty leather straps were tied in a bow around the upper backs of her smooth calves. With her long legs spread wide, she pleasured herself while he pumped his body deep into hers. Her fingers, with long, brightly painted nails, turned small quick circles around her clitoris. He loved that she was touching herself, showing him how turned on she was. His low growl-like moans, a telling testament to his approval and arousal. As they worked each other closer to climax, she felt the wet muscles between her thighs tighten around the length of him. Her throbbing was enough to set him off, bringing his body to climax almost in sync with her own. Knowing that the sheer squeeze of her body was enough to make him come, felt like the ultimate empowerment. Hanna savoured the ego-gratifying satisfaction for the short time it lasted.

Hanna's cruel mind had soon brought her back to reality and the glitter on her body had disappeared. The emotional pleasure she felt during their sex had instantly vanished like cold water had been tossed in her face. When she opened her eyes, she could see that her nails weren't brightly painted or even overly long and her feet were simply bare. She didn't exactly know what it all meant and couldn't even begin to explain it. Jacob kissed her once more before heading to the washroom to shower and get ready. "I'll be quick. We're already gonna be late for our reservation!"

Hanna put her clothes and shoes back on and went to the bedroom to freshen her makeup and tidy her hair. Looking in the mirror, her mood had drastically changed. During their impromptu quickie, she had imagined she was a stripper who had sex with her lusting customer in a dim room. Her mind then re-channeled. She suddenly wanted to know how she measured up to this Mandy woman. She wondered if Jacob himself had compared her to Mandy. Then another series of indecent questions about Mandy and that night began spinning through her mind. *What type of perfume did the stripper wear? Was that part of her lure? Did she have similar subtle dimples on her upper thighs? And why did Hanna want to know?*

If she decided to ask Jacob for answers to her perverse questions now, it would spoil their mood and their dinner out.

She left the bedroom seeking out her wine glass from earlier, wishing she could bring the entire bottle with her. She was taking a thirsty gulp when Jacob walked into the kitchen ready to leave.

"We better go! Ready?" he asked, then left, walking briskly toward the garage where his car was parked. Hanna wanted to backtrack from the direction her mind had gone. She sat the empty glass down, grabbed her purse and followed him down the hall. As Hanna stepped over the threshold into the garage she stopped. She stood on the step, glaring at Jacob's shiny black, sinister-looking car. She imagined herself lighting an industrial-sized match and tossing it into the car, making sure it landed right in the middle of the back seat. She took a deep breath trying to collect herself but still hadn't moved. Jacob stood at the open driver's side door after he noticed Hanna had abruptly halted. With his aviator shades hiding his eyes, Jacob stood nonchalantly, resting his forearms on the roof of the car. She looked at his wolf tattoo.

"What is it?" he asked, "What's the matter?"

It should have been obvious but instead, Jacob appeared to be unaware that Hanna, in a sense was looking at the scene of a serious crime against her. A crime he himself had committed. When she pictured herself sitting in the car, she couldn't imagine a more degrading position she could put herself in. Her fiancé had sex in his car with another woman and she was expected to sit in that car like all was forgiven or that it was perfectly normal. Standing in the doorway of the garage, Hanna looked disheartened, like she had become aware of something important.

"I think I need some time."

Jacob wasn't comprehending what Hanna was suggesting. "We're already out of time Honey." He glanced at his watch. "We've left ourselves six minutes to get there and the restaurant's almost a fifteen-minute drive."

Not a single word he said had registered. Hanna had already turned around and was heading for the storage closet in the hall. She pulled her suitcase down off the shelf, carried it into their room and slung it on the bed. She began adding clothing from several different drawers and shelves, briefly considering each piece. Jacob had followed her and was leaning on the door frame watching her with a small frown on his face.

"Are we taking a last-minute vacation?" He attempted to joke as if in denial, then cleared his throat after she ignored him. "Hanna, I know that I shouldn't have gone golfing today. I'm sorry for that. I was going to talk to you about it at dinner so that you knew how I felt."

When she only nodded in response, he walked over and stood beside her hoping she would acknowledge him. Jacob sensed Hanna wasn't looking to argue. The anger she demonstrated the night before in the living room wasn't there this time. She wasn't in a flustered hurry, just moving steadily. She grabbed her jade earrings, slipped them into her makeup bag and added it to the suitcase.

"Sweety look at me. Why are you doing this?"

Jacob was agitated that she wouldn't answer him. For Hanna, it wasn't just the golfing or the car and what happened inside of it. It was the mountain of new perverse questions from earlier she wanted to hurl at him. It was the fact that her self-esteem had been painfully downgraded and her mind had been so badly messed with, that the sex they'd had a mere twenty minutes ago had been so confusing she didn't know whether she had enjoyed it or should seek therapy. Knowing she would probably never fully trust Jacob again also deserved honourable mention.

"Hanna, are you really willing to throw away what we have? It was just sex!"

He was using his hands, trying to get his point across. Because it was only sex to Jacob and meant nothing to him, in Jacob's mind, that meant it should mean less to Hanna too. She had always thought those two words should never be spoken in the same sentence. To Hanna, sex would never be just sex. Sex was the intimate and physical act that set a friendship or casual encounter apart from a committed, exclusive relationship. If you still had the desire to have sex with other people then there was no point in getting engaged.

"I didn't throw anything away," she said quietly, responding to his question.

Hanna stepped into the closet and grabbed several items off of hangers, folded them, and sat them into the suitcase. Jacob was frantically running his hands through his hair.

"Hanna, can't we just give this some time? Please! If you give me a chance, I promise I will make this up to you!"

She wanted to believe him and part of her wanted to stay and let him prove that he could make it up to her. So far he had missed the mark by a long shot.

"We were supposed to have a wedding in a few months. It wouldn't be healthy or fair for either one of us to get married after what's happened between us. Don't you agree?"

When he didn't argue, she gave him a sad, mirthless smile and pulled the zipper on the bag. Her calm reasoning only put him more on edge. He picked up the suitcase before she could grasp the handle and held it out of her reach.

"Hanna, I get it! I fucked up royal! I'm sorry! Please stop! Just let me make it up to you! At least let me try. Please don't cancel the wedding and please don't take your ring off again. Maybe to give you time we can just…," he paused not wanting to say it, "postpone the wedding for a while." Pleading with her, he softened his voice, "and then when you're ready again…"

Hanna slowly took the suitcase from him, stood it on the floor and extended the long handle. She raised her hands, gently cradled his face and spoke softly and surely.

"I'm going to stay with Ava for a while and sort some things out. I can't promise that I'll ever be completely ready again, but I do know that I still love you very much and that I never wished for this to happen to us."

His expression changed at the mention of Ava's name and when he realized he'd failed to convince her to stay.

"Hanna, what does that mean? Can you at least tell me where we stand? When will I see you next? Are we still going to be talking to each other?"

"Of course we are. We both know that we can't simply stop talking or seeing each other. We still love each other. Right?"

She looked into the deep sapphire eyes she loved getting lost in. "We don't want a marriage built on a damaged, unsteady foundation. I think postponing the wedding might be a good idea."

Jacob looked at the ceiling, closed his eyes, took a deep breath and exhaled loudly. He knew that she wasn't being unreasonable. It was him, after all, that suggested delaying the wedding. A defeated "Fuck," was all he said.

Hanna didn't feel she needed to say anything else to make Jacob feel bad and left it at that. She slung her purse over her shoulder, then went to grab the suitcase but Jacob had already grabbed it, angling it to tow behind him. As Hanna walked toward the front door, Jacob followed slowly with the suitcase, looking as excited as a misbehaved student heading to the principal's office.

"Can I at least give you a ride? How are you getting to Ava's?"

Hanna pictured Jacob's black car. "Honestly, Jacob, I just don't find your car overly comfortable anymore."

After mentally agreeing that she had every right to feel that way, he nodded. "Point taken."

Jacob arranged a taxi for Hanna on his phone. It would be there in ten minutes. Hanna's unplanned departure was affecting Jacob in a way that almost made her change her mind. He didn't want her to leave and she didn't want to be leaving, so how was she so sure it was the right thing to do? If Hanna stayed she would have a new set of questions daily. *How happy would she be questioning herself and blaming him for her new and sudden self-esteem issues?* There were some things she had to settle and she couldn't do that while she lived in the same house as Jacob, bitterly resenting him. She owed it to herself to take the time she needed.

"This isn't what I wanted," she said sadly.

"Then why leave! You've got it in your head to punish me but…" Jacob broke off, without finishing his thought. Instead of further pleading, he leaned down to kiss her because he couldn't let her leave without feeling her close, once more. Hanna didn't stop him. Jacob's kisses had a way of sending her into a mild euphoria and maybe leaving on that note wasn't so terrible. When he was finished giving her a long slow kiss he made her a promise.

"That's not going be the last time I kiss those lips."

The taxi had pulled into the driveway. Hanna took one last loving look at Jacob and walked out the door.

<h1 style="text-align:center">CHAPTER TWELVE</h1>

Hanna's fifteen-minute ride to Ava's was emotional. Halfway there she almost asked the driver to pull into a parking lot so she could take a minute to be certain, by getting space from Jacob, she wasn't making a life-changing mistake. She decided to say nothing after she reminded herself that she wasn't the one who had put her and Jacob in this situation. When she arrived at Ava's small house, it occurred to her that she hadn't forewarned Ava that she was coming. Hanna wasn't overly worried because she knew Ava would be more than happy to see she had shown up with a full suitcase.

"If you want to get away from Jacob, just come over!" were Ava's last words. Hanna knocked on Ava's door, waited a minute, then went ahead and used the coded keypad to enter. She hadn't let herself in for a while and was surprised Ava hadn't changed the code since they had lived there together. As far as she knew, no one else knew the code but the two of them. Once inside, she sat down her purse and pulled out her phone. Her suitcase would be fine in the front hallway for now. Hanna called out for Ava but didn't get a response. There was an open wine bottle on the counter and soft music played on the stereo. Hanna knew that Ava must be nearby and hoped that she wouldn't be startled once she found her. It was Saturday evening and Ava was likely in her bedroom getting ready to go out. It would be out of character for Ava to waste a Saturday night by staying home. Hanna would be welcome to go along or more accurately *told* to go along to whatever affair, Ava was heading to. She helped herself to the wine on the counter and then gazed around, admiring the changes Ava had made to the loveable little house. It was a two-bedroom bungalow with an eat-in kitchen at the back of the house and a decent-sized living room at the front. The two bedrooms were down the hall, across from each other with a washroom at the end in between them. When the two friends moved in together after university the entire house had been painted in a tired dusty rose colour. The hard-nosed landlord wouldn't allow them to paint over the pink walls, so that's how it remained for their time as roommates. Last year, when the landlord mentioned that he was looking to sell the house, Ava told him she would like to put in an unconditional offer. Her grandmother had recently left her a generous inheritance, giving her a big enough downpayment for mortgage approval at the bank. The landlord was happy about not having to go through the hassle of preparing the house to sell and not having to hire a real estate agent. It saved Ava from having to move and she was excited about dipping her toes into the housing market. Painting the walls *Toasty Grey* was the first thing she did. It made the house feel more modern and stylish like Ava herself and no longer like a life-sized doll house. Hung on one wall was a collection of round boho baskets and a large abstract painting. Below the painting was a stylish cream-coloured couch paired with two low-profile leather chairs. Hanna had just stepped toward the hall to look for Ava when she heard a man's low throaty laugh. She froze with her wine glass in hand, processing the untimely predicament. Hanna had basically, broken into Ava's house while she was in her bedroom enjoying the company of a man. While Hanna was standing there frantically deciding which direction to flee, Ava appeared at the opposite end of the hall with a shirtless guest. She was wearing her short satin robe tied at her tiny waistline. Despite the obvious intrusion, she was pleasantly surprised to see Hanna standing there.

"Holy shit! You did it!" She held an empty wine glass in one hand and both arms in the air. She was as pleased as a parent, cheering for their baby who'd taken their first few steps. Looking from Ava to her man-friend, Hanna was relieved they were both at least, partially clothed. Ava grabbed her friend and hugged her carefully to avoid spilling the wine. When they had finished hugging, Hanna used her long eyelashes to gesture toward the other guest. Ava picked up on her signal. "Oh yes! Thanks," as if she had forgotten about her guest in the excitement. She then turned and walked right by him, disappearing into the bedroom. Hanna and the stranger looked at each other in confusion. A few seconds later Ava returned with a T-shirt and unceremoniously tossed it to the shirtless stranger. He frowned at it and held it outward.

"This isn't mine."

"Oopsy!"

Ava grabbed the T-shirt from him and disappeared again, returning a second later with a different shirt. As he was pulling the shirt over his rippled stomach, Ava thoughtfully thanked him for his services. "Thanks for coming over Nigel. It was nice meeting you." She walked him to the door and after side-stepping around Hanna's suitcase, he was gone. Hanna was deciding whether or not she was impressed at the efficient, and unaffectionate goodbye. Ava topped up their glasses and gestured for Hanna to follow her to the living room so they could talk comfortably. Both Ava and Hanna curled their legs up beneath themselves as they sat at each end of the couch. They looked like a set of slightly mismatched bookends, one with slightly darker hair. Hanna was curious about Nigel.

"So this is a fairly new relationship then?" she asked.

"Ha! Relationship? More like a badly botched booty call!"

"Botched booty call?" Hanna laughed at the term. "It kinda' sounded like you were enjoying yourselves." She sipped at her wine, hoping she wasn't prying.

"I told him he was under-qualified, and out of desperation, he was trying to prove me wrong. I was just coming out to the kitchen for more coping-juice." Ava clarified by lifting her wine glass a few inches. "I should be thanking you for showing up when you did. He was about as useful as a receipt checker at Costco."

Hanna smiled, admiring Ava's humour and iron-clad sense of self. She had only been in Ava's home for a matter of minutes and had already laughed and her mood was enjoyably lighter. She was relieved that she hadn't interrupted anything too important for Ava. She was, on the other hand, willing to bet that poor Nigel felt somewhat short-changed after her unexpected arrival.

Ava glanced over at the suitcase Hanna left standing in the doorway. "I'm glad you decided to take some time for yourself Han. I think you'll be able to think more clearly without being around Jacob." Hanna looked somewhat disheartened but was nodding in genuine agreement. She hoped that she was doing the right thing. Ava looked at Hanna and smiled widely. "I can't believe I have you here again! I'm getting nostalgic," she squealed, "It'll be just like in university!" Hanna was flattered that Ava was so happy just to be in her company and to have her staying with her for a while, even under the less-than-ideal circumstances.

"You're already planning ways to get us into trouble aren't you," Hanna assumed.

Ava admitted it proudly. "I am, but I know it might be harder now that we're supposed to be adults with careers, mortgages and all the other grown-up nuisances."

Hanna couldn't argue with that. "No kidding. As kids, we can't wait to be all grown up. Then we finally get here and realize it's not nearly as fun as we thought. On Monday morning I get to inform everyone who was supposed to play a role in our big day that we're postponing the wedding."

Ava raised her eyebrows and tilted her head in surprise, her drink fixed mid-air. Hanna hadn't mentioned postponing anything when she saw her earlier that day at lunch. When she saw Hanna standing there in the hallway beside her suitcase, she thought she was getting some much-needed space, to figure out her feelings and maybe send Jacob a very clear message. Before Ava could express her shock verbally, Hanna irritably began to explain.

"If I had done something like that, I would be suffocating with remorse. I would have wanted to tell Jacob the first chance I had, so I could get it off my chest. When I came home, he acted like what he did, hadn't affected him in the least. It hurts when I picture him with that woman, but the fact that he wasn't going to tell me and just carry on as if nothing happened? That stings even more." Hanna shook her head slowly. "I only found out because of Ethan. To be honest, knowing that I may have married Jacob without knowing, that really gets me."

Ava knew how blindsided Hanna was by Jacob's cheating. "Does Jacob know this is happening? The postponing of the wedding?"

Ava had never been team Jacob and when she questioned Hanna about her decision to postpone the wedding, Hanna was surprised.

"He knows. Why? Do you think I'm making a mistake by postponing? You don't even like Jacob."

"No definitely not! I just know that you've never made a big decision unless you were absolutely sure. You haven't really given yourself much time to think this over."

"I know. Your right. It doesn't seem like I've given it enough time but I'm going more with my gut on this."

Hanna was quiet for a minute, uncertain if she wanted to share her stripper fantasy. "Jacob and I had sex on our kitchen counter not long before I showed up at your house."

Ava nodded her head like it was an everyday occurrence and Hanna continued with her story.

"The whole time I had my eyes closed. I envisioned I was a stripper and Jacob was my *John*. What do I even make of that?"

"Hmm. Oookkkk." Ava was digesting the information. She didn't look overly alarmed, and if she was, she wasn't showing it. "Well, apparently it's natural to fantasize during sex, even about people other than your partner. I know because I've done it before when I was struggling to get there with this one guy I was dating for a while. I kinda liked him but in bed….," she broke off, shaking her head and rolling her eyes, "Agonizing. Anyways," she continued, "Everything I've read about it says it's fine unless you need to do it all the time or it's something illegal."

Hanna wasn't bothered by the fact that she had fantasized during sex. It was knowing she had put herself in the role of the person who Jacob had cheated with. "I don't like the circumstances around it. If I had come up with it on my own without any of this happening, that would be one thing but I feel like it's a symptom of something more problematic. What if I'm suffering from some sort of deranged Stockholm Syndrome?"

Ava snorted lightly and sipped her wine. "It might be a bit messed up but honestly, I think these are things you'll get over in time. I'm not a therapist or anything but if you want..." Ava started clicking on her phone. "I'll send you something. It's the contact info for someone who I think can help you. Her name is Lisa Price. She's a really good life coach." Hanna's phone made a buzzing sound as the contact info for the life coach came through. She glanced at the text from Ava and then set her phone aside.

"Thanks. I'll see how I feel on Monday after I contact all the wedding suppliers. Depending on how awful it is, I might need all the help I can get."

"Just remember that I'm here for you. I can even make some of the calls for you if you want me to." Hanna's eyes became misty and she gave Ava a grateful smile.

"Thank you." In sync, they raised and tipped their glasses toward each other. Ava's hazel eyes were now big and round with sudden excitement.

"We don't have to sit at home all night and mope. I say we go out!" Hanna expected nothing less from Ava. She glanced down at the outfit she had dressed in when she thought she was going out to dinner with Jacob.

"I guess, I'm ready when you are! I just need to freshen up a bit." Ava jumped up off the couch and started toward the bedroom to put on some clothes.

"Ok! Just let me get dressed. Wait! Let me see what you're wearing." Ava spun around to gauge what Hanna was wearing so she could match the vibe. Tipping her head side to side she assessed Hanna's clothing. "Soo kinda sexy but not slutty. Ok got it!" Hanna giggled at Ava's comment then ducked into the washroom to check her makeup and hair. When she finished putting on her wine-coloured lip stain, she checked her phone to see that Ethan had texted her. He wanted to know if she was doing ok. She knew he felt guilty for being the one to show her rather than tell her what Jacob had been up to. She texted back so that he didn't worry.

No worries buddy. Just staying with Ava for a little while. Thanks for checking on me!

Talk Monday! Xo

Ava appeared a few minutes later, having traded her housecoat for a short sleeveless dress and tall-heeled boots.

Chapter Thirteen

After a short ten-minute walk they arrived at Patty's Place, an Irish pub that featured live music on weekends. Patty's had a large outdoor patio at the rear of the building with golden lights strung high around the perimeter and large cascading hanging baskets on each corner of the deck area. The fenced patio backed onto a quiet one-way street with other small businesses. After they were seated at the inside bar they ordered a large share platter of classic pub foods and shamelessly paired it with a bottle of white wine. Both the wine and greasy comfort foods hit the spot. Now fed, Ava and Hanna were looking forward to the high-spirited atmosphere of the pub and live music. As the band set up and got ready to play, the pub filled with anticipating patrons. Hanna and Ava turned on their bar stools to chat while watching the band prepare their instruments. The lead guitarist and vocalist was strumming small chords of music on his guitar doing a last-minute tuning and speaking into the microphone for a sound test.

"Check check."

His deep bassy voice immediately commanded the attention of the audience. As he introduced each band member and then himself to the audience, Ava noted his lean muscular arms and the way his sexy ripped jeans fit his lower body. To complete his look, he wore a black v-neck T-shirt and black cowboy hat. He was clean-shaven with a nice face. It wouldn't have mattered if he was performing a tribute to The Spice Girls, Ava had already committed her complete undivided attention. Luckily the band wasn't trying to replicate the girl band but instead had a catchy sound that was a mix of rock and country. The cowboy singer, whose name was Jasper Barnes had a great-sounding voice that held the crowd and had Hanna tapping her knee while Ava bobbed her head to the catchy beat. After the band had finished their first song, both Ava and Hanna clapped and cheered loudly. When the bartender asked if they wanted anything to drink, Ava ordered two Malibu sodas with a splash of seven for sweetness. It was the *go-to* drink for both girls back in university. Ava had introduced the coconut rum drink to Hanna. She said it was hard not to like a drink that tasted like a tropical beach. "Not only that, it makes your mouth taste like candy," she claimed. Ava passed Hanna her drink. "For old time's sake."

Hanna thanked her with a couple of loud air kisses and promised to buy the next round. A waitress with a full tray of drinks made her way up to the low stage and sat a beer on the large amplifier beside the singer. He bent briefly to say a few words to the waitress then stood and tilted his head back to see above the crowd and over to the bar area. As Hanna sat watching him, wondering what was happening, she decided that he looked like a perfect movie star cowboy. Hanna turned to Ava to see that she was staring at the singer with a thirst she wanted to quench with something other than her beverage. Her botched booty call with Nigel had seemingly left her with an unfulfilled need. Hanna was sure that Ava had undressed the singer with her eyes already, likely removing everything but his hat. The cowboy then smiled appreciatively, raised the beer bottle to his lips and took a long thirsty sip, as if to thank the purchaser. His gesture didn't go unnoticed. Hanna thought she must be imagining it. "Did he just look at you? And...Did you just buy him…?"

"Yes and yes!" was all Ava said, unable or unwilling to pry her eyes off the sexy singer. Hanna thought Ava looked like a groupie and laughed quietly. She stayed silent, allowing Ava to enjoy the moment. Jasper sat the bottle down and grabbed the mic again. He spoke in his deep voice in the direction of the bar. "Mmmm mmmm. That's pretty tasty! I needed that because I gotta admit, it just got reeeally hot in here."

He was looking at Ava the whole time. She seemed to enjoy his attention. "Holy cowboy, that is one sexy man!"

Looking from the singer and then back to Ava, Hanna playfully teased, "Jeez. I'm starting to feel like I'm intruding."

The band had started to perform another song. This tune had a different, more classic rock sound to it. Hanna recognized the beat right away from her dad's collection of seventies records. The song was titled *Some Kind of Wonderful*. Apparently, everyone's dad had the same record because, by the time the band got to the chorus, half of the crowd was singing along. After a few songs and drinks later, both Ava and Hanna needed to use the washroom. They had hurried hoping not to miss out on much of the performance, but made the mistake of going together. When they returned, their sought-after bar stools were occupied by two older women who looked to be enjoying each other more than they were enjoying the band. Ava and Hanna looked at each other with the same annoyed face. Hanna was nervous that Ava would say something to them but instead, she shrugged and gestured toward the outside patio. "It was good while it lasted," she said, "I think I might have been starting to look a bit desperate anyway."

Hanna kept her mouth shut and only smiled. After working their way through the crowd, they found a spot at a high table with stools in the corner of the patio. The night had cooled off nicely and the sky had darkened, prompting strings of golden lights to illuminate. Despite the absence of the cowboy, the gentle breeze was a welcome change to the heat inside. The stereo music outside was loud enough to drown out the band inside creating a completely different atmosphere. A friendly waitress came by shortly after they were seated and delivered two Malibu rums with soda and seven to the table.

"Here you go, ladies! These are from Jasper!" She tilted her head toward the door. "Enjoy!"

As the waitress was turning to leave, Ava decided to ask. "Oh Wait! Can I ask how you found us?"

"Easy! Jasper said to take some drinks over to the two hotties that were sitting at the bar inside earlier."

Hanna didn't mind the flattery of being called a hottie and it was evident Ava liked it too, especially coming from someone she thought was a '*hottie*' himself. As they were enjoying the afterglow of the compliment, they picked up their glasses to cheers.

"It's official," Hanna said, "You're a groupie!"

"Don't I have to sleep with him first to qualify?"

"Does doing it with your eyes count?"

They both laughed and took sips of their drinks. Ava decided that somehow the drink tasted better having been purchased by a good-looking cowboy.

A moment later Jasper and the drummer for the band showed up at their table. Jasper had removed his cowboy hat to cool down. Now that he was close, Hanna could see that his eyes were dark brown and his hair which was light brown, was long enough to have a slight curl. Hanna checked Ava's mouth for drool.

"Do you ladies mind if we join you out here while we take a break before our second set?"

Hanna kept quiet letting Ava steer the conversation, which she did gladly.

"I think I'd mind more if you didn't." The wine and rum had given Ava an extra dose of friendliness and she gestured to the two empty stools.

Before taking a seat, everyone properly introduced themselves and thanked each other for their gifted drinks. The drummer's name was Noah. He was friendly, funny and easy to talk to. His blonde messy hair and blue eyes made Hanna think of a California surfer. She didn't mind playing wingman along beside him. Their conversation was easy and the more Hanna talked with Noah the more she liked him. He seemed like an all-around genuine person. Ava and Jasper also seemed to be enjoying each other's company and after a couple of minutes, Hanna noticed that Ava had placed her hand on Jasper's thigh. The twenty minutes went fast and before they knew it, Jasper and Noah were getting up from their stools to go back to the stage.

"Well, I guess we better get back to work, hey there Jasper?"

Jasper had to pull his focus away from Ava.

"Yeah, I guess that guitar isn't going to play itself, though that might be pretty neat to see."

Noah looked at Hanna. "Are we gonna see any more of you ladies tonight?"

Hanna felt like this was probably the right time to explain that she was engaged but Ava spoke in her smooth, silky voice before she had the chance. "You can see *all* of us later if you want to."

Noah and Jasper smiled shyly and nodded at the forward comment. "Great! We'll look for you two ladies later!"

Hanna's eyes opened wide in surprise. As she watched the two men walk away and into the pub, she spoke through a fake toothy grin. "Us? Aaaall of us? Isn't that giving them false hope?"

Ava laughed at Hanna's amusing reaction. "Relax. We don't have to give them anything if we don't want to. We're just here to have fun."

Regardless of what she said, Hanna knew that Ava had definitely wanted to give Jasper *something*.

Like any night out with Ava, time had gone incredibly fast. They had happily regained the rights to their original seats at the bar inside and had been there for much of the evening. If they weren't sitting at the stools, they were dancing nearby. Hanna was fascinated by the series of silent expressions exchanged between Ava and Jasper throughout the evening. The chemistry between them was soundless but anyone with two functioning eyes could testify to their long-distance foreplay. As it got later and the male patrons less guarded, Hanna and Ava had turned down several advances. After the third guy that evening pretended to accidentally rub against Hanna's leg, Ava gave him an evil stare-down and he rushed off like he needed the washroom. The band announced they were performing their final song and thanked everyone for being such a lively, supportive crowd. To close the night they played a song by Damon Lee Murphy called *Dusty Bottle*. It caused a similar reaction as the *Some Kind of Wonderful* song and a large portion of the crowd was singing along. Hanna and Ava had recognized that hit as well. When the song was over, Jasper told everyone to enjoy the rest of their evening, clamped his mic in its stand then gave a small bow. Ava had of course been watching Jasper's sign off speech.

"He manages to look sexy even when he bows!"

Hanna smiled and rolled her eyes. The band began packing up their equipment and when Ava and Hanna didn't join him at the stage, Jasper made a gesture for them to come over. Ava immediately ushered Hanna and herself in his direction. When they reached the stage Ava snatched Jasper's hat and sat it on her head. Judging by the smile on his face, he thought it looked better on her anyway. The band had finished packing up the sound equipment, and a majority of the patrons had cleared out of the pub. Hanna and Ava sat and chatted with Noah and Jasper while they finished their beer and said goodbye to their fellow bandmate leaving for the night.

"Looks like we're all packed up here, did you guys want to move the party somewhere else?" Jasper was talking to Ava.

Ava surprised everyone by apologetically declining. "No thanks, we're gonna call it a night. It's getting late and we've already called an Uber."

Both Jasper and Noah looked disappointed but chose to be gentlemen about it. Noah didn't want the rejected offer to be awkward for anybody. "Ok sure, no worries, maybe some other time."

Jasper rubbed his lower jaw with one hand looking uncertain. "Sooo Ava, if I wanted to take you out to dinner sometime how would I get a hold of you?"

Watching the interaction, Hanna thought it was sweet he was asking her out, in front of Noah and herself. They looked like kids at the playground asking for each other's names. Ava smiled, held up her phone and asked Jasper for his cell number. She texted him something and then put her phone away.

"There! You now have my cell number and I have yours."

They stared at each other, both hoping for a kiss goodbye. For the first time that evening, Hanna got out her phone and then walked away. She wanted to give them and herself some privacy. She figured that she should actually arrange an Uber before Noah and Jasper figured out Ava had fudged the truth. Hanna wasn't going to chance walking home. It was a safe enough area to walk during the day but too risky to walk at night. Before Noah had followed Hanna's lead in giving the love birds some privacy, he reminded Jasper that they both had to work in the morning.

"Don't forget about tomorrow morning buddy! It's the last Sunday of the month, and you know what that means!"

Hanna ducked into the washroom, set up an Uber, then went to stand at the bar next to Noah. She was hoping to buy Ava and herself a bottle of water. Hanna knew they would both be feeling rough tomorrow and figured they should get started on the water sooner rather than later. She also wanted to say goodbye to Noah, he was a friendly guy and Hanna didn't want him to think she was rude. When Hanna asked the bartender for the two bottles of water and attempted to pay, he sat them down and casually waved his hand. He told her they were on the house, reminding her what good customers she and Ava had been all night.

"Well Noah, It was very nice meeting you guys. You were awesome up there. Your rendition of *Some Kind of Wonderful* went over really well! I love that one. My dad used to play that one on his old record player."

"Thanks! You'll have to tell your dad he's got good taste!"

She thought back to what Noah said to Jasper as he walked away.

"Did I hear you say that you guys have to work tomorrow? Really? After a late performance?"

Noah was nodding his head.

"You got it! We're supposed to go in on the last Sunday of each month for a few hours to keep caught up. We're both millwrights for Maple Lane."

Hanna knew it was a large food distribution facility on the north side of the city.

"You two don't look like the type to just call in sick either."

He took it as a compliment then smiled as he imagined the recourse from the boss for calling in sick.

"Not a chance. I don't think Jasper's dad would like that too much."

Noah glanced over to where Jasper and Ava were standing. He didn't want to keep Hanna from leaving but it looked like she might have her work cut out for her. He gave her a genuine smile and then nodded toward Ava and Jasper.

"Good luck with that one. I've never seen Jasper like this before."

Hanna took that as a good sign for Ava. She was standing next to Jasper leaning against him, while his arm was wrapped around her waist. She was still wearing his hat which acted as a partial barrier. It was difficult to tell whether Ava was telling him a secret or kissing his neck. Hanna figured it was probably both and wondered if maybe Ava had changed her mind about leaving.

"Thanks, looks like I might need it. I'll see you later Noah!"

"Bye Hanna."

While Hanna made her way over, Ava reluctantly pried herself off of Jasper.

Hanna passed Ava one of the waters, and she took it gratefully. "Thanks! Should we get going?" Ava asked.

"Yep. Ready when you are."

"Ok, I guess we're outta here. I'll just give you this back."

Ava took off the cowboy hat she had borrowed earlier and sat it back on top of Jasper's head. Hanna was relieved she didn't have to stand there, waiting awkwardly. "Should we wait outside so our Uber doesn't leave on us?" she suggested.

"That's probably a good idea." Ava nodded, knowing she couldn't be trusted not to reattach herself to Jasper's body.

Hanna smiled at Jasper. "Nice meeting you Jasper. I have a funny feeling I'll be seeing you again sometime."

He responded to her comment but was staring intently at Ava. "Oh, you betchya will!"

Ava gave him a small wave and they left Patty's to catch their Uber. They waited just outside the door on the wide sidewalk. Ava was so cheerful after her blissful evening, that she attempted to sing the song that had ignited the crowd. Still feeling the effects of the wine and Malibu, her normally beautiful voice now sounded like a parrot, sorely putting forth its best effort to catch a mate.

I doe need a ho lotta money!

I doe need a nice big car

I gat eeevratheen that a

While Ava was serenading the small outdoor crowd, Hanna glanced around looking for their ride. She'd ordered an Uber Comfort that was supposed to be a black minivan. When she turned her head, she spotted a large black SUV turning the corner, and heading toward them. It was moving slowly so Hanna assumed the driver was probably looking for the pub. To stand out from the crowd of other pub-goers, she waved at the driver as if casually hailing a cab. The vehicle abruptly stopped, then as if in neutral it revved its loud powerful engine. After several, nerve-wracking seconds it sped directly toward them. Hanna had been watching the big SUV from the moment she had thought it was their Uber. When it wasn't slowing she grabbed Ava who was still cluelessly singing and screamed, "Look out!"

They both stumbled and ended up colliding with a man and woman who were also running for shelter from the racing vehicle. Most of the people who were outside lining the street had all lunged back away from the sidewalk. The SUV was initially on the opposite side of the street when it turned the corner. But it had crossed over, driving on the wrong side as if intentionally veering toward the people outside the pub. It had narrowly missed two young men who'd been sitting on the edge of the curb, waiting for their ride. The giant driver's side tire violently hit the curb of the sidewalk and bounced back from the concrete edge. The truck zig-zagged back and forth a couple of times and then eerily drove away on the wrong side of the road. Everybody was too shaken to have gotten a look at the driver or the license plate. Hanna noted the shiny sticker on the back window that looked like a silver X but the name beneath was too small to make out. Visibly distraught and enraged, the people outside the pub yelled obscenities down the road toward the terrorizing SUV, now almost out of site. Hanna rushed over to check on the two young men who came within inches of being mowed over by the lunatic driver. One of them had badly scraped his elbow when he was forced to do a backward stunt roll out of the path of the vehicle. Other than being thoroughly terrified, no major injuries were suffered by the bystanders. The friend of the fellow who scraped his arm was on the phone with a 911 operator who said the police would be searching the area for the vehicle, believed to be a Chevy Tahoe. The Uber that Hanna had ordered had finally shown up. It was a black minivan as stated on the app. There were a dozen other witnesses and thankfully, no serious injuries, so Ava and Hanna felt they were probably ok to head home.

CHAPTER FOURTEEN

On the ride home, they were quiet, taking in the events of the last ten minutes. The reckless driver at the pub had partially sobered them. Once home at Ava's place, they changed into baggy hoodies and comfy sleep shorts. Ava threw a couple of toaster strudels into the mini oven and put on the tea kettle. Hanna stared at the toaster oven. "Did I just see you put toaster strudels in there?"

The pastries were a staple food for Hanna and Ava in university and there were days when they'd eaten them for multiple meals.

"Yeah, you don't like them anymore?" Ava wiped her greasy fingers on the tea towel hanging on the stove then spun the dial on the toaster oven.

"Don't like them? I wish! I still eat them on rare occasions, but I've had to cut back ever since I put a down payment on a wedding dress that requires a ten-minute shimmy session to get into."

Ava had been there when Hanna picked out her dress. "Oh yeah." Ava smiled remembering her wiggling into the dress. "I forgot for a sec that you went with the sexy mermaid-style."

Ava looked at Hanna's slim form. "Don't worry Han, it'll fit you perfectly."

"I guess we'll have to wait and see if I even get to wear it." She glanced at Ava's physique. "You're my size. Maybe you can wear it when you and Jasper get married."

Ava pasted an expression of exaggerated contemplation on her face and tipped her head side to side.

"Yeah, it might work!"

She was teasing in retaliation for the premature Jasper remark.

Hanna was depressed at the thought of not having the chance to wear her carefully chosen wedding dress. But if she had to be ok with someone other than herself wearing it, Ava was the someone. She brushed aside further thoughts of the dress.

"You kinda, really like him don't you?"

Hanna watched Ava's expression hoping to get an honest reading. Ava was pouring the kettle water over the teabags in the mugs. She couldn't suppress her smile as she tried to focus on not burning anyone with the boiling water.

"Oh, could you tell?" she asked innocently.

"I was pretty surprised when you turned down Jasper's offer to party somewhere else."

"Well it was getting late and besides if we hadn't left when we did we would have missed out on the psycho driver."

She was kidding, but Hanna sensed Ava wasn't telling her something. They moved to the kitchen table with their tea. "I would have been happier staying till close like the good ol' days rather than having the near-death experience."

"You looked ready to go to me," Ava challenged.

Hanna had been blowing her tea lightly to cool it then raised her head in confusion. "I did? Seriously? I thought I was the perfect wingman. Noah was a sweet, nice-looking guy. It's not like it was a terrible task or anything."

"Han, right after we came inside from the patio you started fiddling with your engagement ring."

"Hmm," Hanna tried to think back. "Sometimes I just do that, out of habit."

She spun her ring side to side with her thumb to show Ava. "See?"

All Ava said was, "Oh," and then quietly sipped at her tea.

Hanna was both shocked and touched. "You thought I was thinking about Jacob and you were willing to leave your future husband so you could get me home? Oh my gosh, Ava! This is a tragedy. I feel terrible! You're going to see him again right?"

Ava tried to play it cool and waited a second to answer. "We'll see. I don't usually like musicians, but he did say that they only play on the occasional weekend. He has a day job. He works for his dad as a millwright."

"That's what Noah was saying. I guess it was lucky we just happened to catch them playing tonight then."

Ava was thinking about that as she sipped her tea.

"For what it's worth," Hanna added, "I thought both Jasper and Noah were nice guys."

Ava smiled dreamily thinking back to the sweet kiss she shared with Jasper behind his wide hat. She nodded her head slowly. "Yeah, I think there's a chance, they just might be."

They were both ready for bed after finishing their tea. Ava set Hanna up in the spare bedroom and then yawned sleepily.

"See you in the morning Han."

"Night Ave."

Ava flicked off the light and headed across the hall to her bedroom. Hanna fluffed the pillow behind her head and pulled the light duvet up over her chest. After three years she was back in the same tiny bedroom and small bed she had occupied fresh out of university. It was about a quarter of the size of the bedroom she shared with Jacob. It was humbling how quickly and drastically a person's situation could change. Yesterday morning, before Ethan's text had arrived, she awakened thinking that she was flying back to Toronto to be with the man of her dreams, who would be waiting for her in the house of her dreams. The house hadn't changed, but whether she would ever truly feel the same about Jacob was a dismal uncertainty. Hanna believed the rules of love and decency were clear and simple. If you make a promise, you keep it. If you love someone you show them. And if you make an honest mistake, you apologize promptly so the person knows you feel as badly about what happened as they do. When she asked herself if she would have preferred Ethan said nothing about his discovery, she told herself, *of course not*. But now, lying alone in the small bed, she almost wished she was still blissfully unaware that her life wasn't entirely what she thought. If Hanna had to choose between a loss of dignity and a small bed, the bed would win the competition. She reminded herself that the downgraded bed was only temporary and after several minutes she dozed off to sleep.

CHAPTER FIFTEEN

Sunday was, for the most part, a sleepy lazy day. It had started raining through the night and continued throughout the day. Both Ava and Hanna slept till around noon. After a snail-paced wake-up and a bowl of cereal, they decided to do nothing but watch romcom movies while painting each other's nails and wearing creepy-looking facial masks. Later in the day, they switched their movie genre to cheesy, almost funny horror movies. For dinner, Ava made a tasty, thick stew in the crockpot with chicken, potatoes and carrots. It reminded Hanna of home and how much she missed her mom and needed to see her dad. Ava's stew was the perfect dish for a rainy Sunday night. When it neared bedtime Hanna found herself thinking about Jacob. She longed to hear his voice and wanted to say goodnight but convinced herself to wait until Monday after contacting the wedding suppliers. She could give him an update on the vendors and wouldn't have to look desperate by calling him.

Ava was scheduled for a voice-over at the network in the morning and insisted she give Hanna a ride to work on her way. Hanna couldn't help but feel like a needy freeloader. She had not only invaded Ava's house, but Ava was now chauffeuring her around. Hanna tried to arrange an Uber that morning but Ava threatened to chase them away with a broom if a car service showed up. It would be nice to have her vehicle again. At least she wouldn't burden Ava with *that* for too long. She would check in with the body shop later on to see how her vehicle was coming along. They had originally told her it would be ready today.

When Hanna arrived outside her small studio, she glanced through the large street window. She could see Ethan sitting at his desk working avidly at his laptop. She admired the passion he had for his work and how dedicated he was to her and his career at Richards and Co. He was often the first one to arrive each morning. Hanna had hired him solely as a designer but Ethan quickly inserted himself, by choice, into other roles. He was now the office administrator, event scheduler, coffee barista and Hanna's loudest cheerleader. The front of the studio was set up to accept clients and was divided into two sections. There were four large modern desks arranged on one side of the studio and on the other side a stylish sitting area where clients could sit comfortably as they viewed the concepts the team had created. Toward the back of the building, through two swinging doors, was the workshop. This was Shauni's domain and if you were looking for her, she could be found by following the sounds of the power tools. When Hanna walked in the front door, Ethan looked up with a wide-eyed expression. "Hey! Happy Monday?" he asked cautiously. He waited for confirmation that Hanna was doing ok since speaking to Jacob. Despite her reassuring text, he wasn't sure how Hanna's weekend had gone. Ethan would want to hear all the details.

"Good morning!" she replied.

When she saw the look of concern, she waved her hand to imply she was managing. Hanna could hear Shauni's saw screaming in the background and some faint music on the stereo. In between the saw screams and wood banging, Shauni belted out the words to an Elton John song. Ethan sprung from his chair and as if it were an emergency, headed toward the coffee and tea station. He opened the cupboard, pulled out a tall mug and fixed Hanna a coffee. Hanna sat her purse on her desk and was admiring Ethan's sense of urgency when the workshop door flung open. It was Shauni. She was wearing goggles and earmuffs as she held a large wooden silhouette of the letter *R*. "Check this out, nerd!" Speaking to Ethan, it didn't matter to Shauni how distinguished he looked in his four hundred dollar sport coat. Shauni then spotted Hanna. "Oh hey, Hanna!"

Hanna walked over to see what Shauni was so proud of. A couple of weeks back she asked Shauni to make something decorative for the wall in the presentation area. Shauni crafted a wooden letter *R* identical to the one Hanna had used in the company logo. "That's awesome! Did you use that scary old jigsaw?"

Shauni pulled off her earmuffs and pushed her goggles up onto her head. Her denim overalls were sprinkled with sawdust. "Ha! Like that old bear trap would work. Our new CNC router got here this morning and I just finished setting it up. This was only a test piece."

Impressed by Shauni's letter *R*, Hanna ran her hand along the edge of the curved wooden letter. "Well, you would know better than me but it looks like it might be working perfectly. I love it! I can't wait to see what you make us next."

Ethan handed Hanna a tall mug of coffee.

"Thanks," she offered.

"You should have seen what she was going to make us *first*."

Judging by the tone Ethan was using, and how well Hanna knew Shauni, she only needed one guess. "I don't mind if she wants to express herself creatively, as long as she takes her *hardwood* home when she's done. We want to keep up the appearance of being professional around here."

Shauni was snickering at Hanna's pun while she helped herself to the coffee. "What? You think a big penis clock might offend someone? Once in a while, a pecker can be somewhat useful."

Hanna and Ethan looked at each other, said nothing then went to their desks. Hanna had a lot on her plate for the day and wanted to get started. "Do you guys want to have the *daily* now or are you both already working on something?"

The *daily* was the name of the mini-meetings they held each morning, ensuring they were all in sync and aware of the current projects on the schedule. Ethan was hoping to get an update from Hanna about Jacob after she had texted him and said she was staying with Ava. Shauni would be just as eager for an update as Ethan.

"I'm good now Hanna, if you and Shauni are." Ethan looked at Shauni.

"Yeah, we can do it now." Shauni walked into the workshop carrying the letter R. "Just let me grab my iPad."

Hanna pulled up the schedule on her phone while Ethan grabbed his tablet off his desk. Shauni reappeared and was tapping away on the screen.

Now that they were ready, Hanna began with the *daily*. "Ok, we've got ShopNShip signed on for a booth set up for the franchise exhibition in three weeks. They're going with our top-tier package. We're meeting with their marketing person in the studio here tomorrow to discuss design ideas, booth layout and expectations."

Ethan chimed in. "We've already got the digital files for their branding and colours. They sent them late Friday."

"Ok, glad to hear. That means we can get going on any large custom items after we talk with them tomorrow." Hanna made a quick note on her device.

Shauni remembered reading an article about them online. "Are they the ones making a push to get into all the grocery stores?"

"Yep! That's them." Ethan offered.

"Cool."

"We also have to start organizing suppliers and vendors for the sweet sixteen surprise party for the twin daughters of Amir and Zara Mahmoud. Their names are Amal and Aaida. Guest count is twenty-five adults and about a hundred teenagers."

Ethan was looking forward to the preparation of the sweet sixteen party. "I'm soooo excited about this one. The parents want to go aaaall out! The colour theme is metallic gold and soft turquoise! I can't wait!"

Shauni joined in the excitement by raising her hands and clapping enthusiastically. Her tongue was sticking out ever so slightly. Instead of being offended that she was lovingly mocking him, Ethan joined in by giving a couple of quick claps himself. Hanna smiled, watching Ethan speak animatedly from excitement over his job. But her mood soon fizzled when it occurred to her that those were the two accent colours she had chosen for her wedding. She would be contacting her first vendor for the delayed wedding after she was finished here with their update. She was still mentally preparing. "No issues with you taking the lead on that one Eth. It's all yours. Oh! Just remember, Kai likes at least a week's notice for cake orders, especially a giant tiered one."

"It's already ordered and in the queue," Ethan announced proudly.

"Nice, I think we're good then for today."

Instead of dispersing the way they normally did, Shauni and Ethan stood there as if they were waiting for something. Hanna knew they wanted and rightfully deserved an update on her situation. They cared for Hanna and would help and support her in whatever way possible.

"Ok ok," Hanna surrendered. She added a splash of coffee to her mug and then walked over to the presentation area so they could sit in comfort. Shauni didn't want to get the furniture dusty after cutting in the workshop, so instead, leaned back against the coffee counter. Ethan sat beside Hanna on the modern leather love seat eagerly awaiting the details. He was sitting upright giving Hanna his fullest attention. She felt like a kindergarten teacher about to start storytime, only the story didn't have the happy ending she hoped for. Looking from Shauni to Ethan she asked, "Do you guys want the long version or the short version?"

In sync, Ethan and Shauni answered, "The long version."

Hanna shared the entire painful story. She told them that she had struggled to get the truth out of Jacob and that when she went to the Instagram post for reference, it had been removed, making her feel like a crazy person. She explained that once Jacob realized he was cornered he agreed to share the story of how it started as a dinner for clients and ended at The Pink Pearl.

"And afterwards this Mandy person drove Jacob's car home for him because he was too drunk. In exchange for the ride home, he then ordered her an Uber to get her home." Hanna stared straight ahead for a second, still struggling to believe her own words and then finally continued. "He seemed so desperate for me to stay that I almost wanted to. I want to forgive him but I'm just so mad at him. I'm staying with Ava for now until I decide whether or not I can get passed it." Hanna was happy to share the details with Ethan and Shauni but was relieved she didn't have a large social circle because after today she never wanted to go over the humiliating details again.

Ethan was silent while Shauni looked angry and in disbelief. "Sorry. A ride home to your house? Brutal. No wonder you shipped out Han."

Ethan shook his head and then pushed his glasses up on his nose. "I can't believe he wouldn't come clean until he realized he was cornered. How disappointing."

Hanna nodded her head in agreement. "I know. It struck me too."

Shauni didn't need another reason not to trust men, and most days she was perfectly happy avoiding them. "I take back my earlier comment about peckers being useful. Hanna, please tell us you're done with him."

Hanna knew that Shauni had her best interests at heart. "I'm not sure what's going to happen. For now, we're postponing the wedding. That's my big job for today. I have over thirty vendors to contact."

As with all things, Ethan wanted to help. "I can make some of the calls for you. Are we trying to get any deposits back or is there a chance that this is just a date change?"

"No, it's ok. I'll handle it. I probably shouldn't expect any refunds and honestly hadn't even considered that. I think I've missed the cutoff dates for refunds anyway."

Shauni thought it was unfortunate that Hanna hadn't all-out dumped Jacob already. She didn't have anything else to offer to the conversation. "I'll be in the shop if you guys need me." She then disappeared through the swinging door.

69

<h1 style="text-align:center">Chapter Sixteen</h1>

Hanna had dreamed about her wedding day since her seventh birthday when she received a Wedding Wonders Barbie doll set. She was blessed to have grown up in a loving home where her parents were happily married. She believed becoming a wife and mother was the greatest privilege. Instead of getting updates from the many suppliers and services, organized for the wedding, she'd be calling to inform them that some important changes were being made. Life wasn't always fair, she knew, and right now it all out sucked. With a shaky voice, she had to explain multiple times that she and Jacob would be delaying their wedding. After making the first few calls to various suppliers, Hanna became tired of the redundant phone conversations. Fortunately, most of the vendors were sensitive and understanding of Hanna's difficult situation. When she reached out to the florist he'd been so warm and kind that Hanna had to fight back her tears.

"Is there a new date we can put down for you sweetheart?" the florist asked.

"No, unfortunately, we don't have a new date right now."

Not wanting to weep into the phone all day Hanna opted for an email she could copy and paste for the rest of the vendors. She was thankful she didn't have to face anyone in person and no longer had to hide her shaky voice over the phone. She would have broken down every time. She then typed out a separate more personal message for the sixty guests. When she had finished typing the guest email, her finger hovered back and forth over *save as draft* and *send*. She opted to save the email as a draft. She was having some trouble making it official. She knew her dad would be hurt and angry if she didn't tell him in person and instead had opted for an impersonal, mass email. She scheduled the email to auto-send in four days, giving herself a chance to visit her dad and tell him in person. She would use the delay to mentally prepare for the borage of calls or emails from concerned guests. Just after noon, Shauni went out and grabbed Thai noodles for everybody. They were eating together at the group of desks discussing the day's progress when a courier carrying a large bouquet walked in looking from Shauni to Hanna.

"Hanna Richards?" He took a chance and began walking toward Shauni. When she curled up her lip and pointed her finger at Hanna, he quickly corrected course and placed the wrapped flowers on the edge of Hanna's desk. He pulled out an electronic writing tool and held it out for Hanna to initial the screen. Hanna stood from her desk and scribbled briefly on the device. "Thanks!" she said graciously. The courier nodded and then vanished. Shauni watched Hanna's face light up with an affectionate smile as she pulled the cellophane off the bouquet. She was hoping Hanna wouldn't be swayed to go back to Jacob because of a superficial bunch of flowers.

"Ooooh la la!" Ethan had quietly carried his box of noodles to the front window hoping to get a quick glimpse of the courier's ass. He wore a pleased expression afterward as he walked back to his desk. The bouquet was a combination of crisp white roses and soft peach Gerbera daisies. Jacob knew white roses were Hanna's favourite and had sent them to her at the studio when they'd first met and each year on her birthday. When Hanna noticed the small envelope tucked into the side of the package, she fished it out and opened it.

"Oh." Hanna looked surprised and her smile faded as she passed the mini card to Ethan who scanned it immediately. He was more pleased with who the sender was than Hanna and excitedly read the card out loud.

"The booth was just amazing! The frosted window was such a great idea!

You and your team did a wonderful job! Thank you so very much! Janice and Stacey Lee"

It was the mother-daughter owners of BabyDreams from Halifax.

"This is great!" Ethan cheered. "They were happy with the baby booth! Shauni! Did you catch the window comment? We knew they'd love that!"

Shauni was smiling proudly but her mouth was full of noodles so instead of responding, she came over and gave Ethan the high five he was waiting for. Ethan sat the small card on Hanna's desk. She was finishing with the cellophane then went and sat the flowers on the glass coffee table on the other side of the studio.

"Let's be sure we send a follow-up to Janice and Stacey Lee. And we should check in with the people in Halifax to make sure the booth has been cleared out."

Ethan immediately clicked on his phone. "Consider it done!"

"Thanks, Ethan."

"No problem!" and returned to his desk.

Shauni knew that Hanna's mood had been downgraded after she realized that the flowers weren't from Jacob. She picked up the three empty noodle boxes and headed for the workshop. Using her back to push the swinging door open, she called out to Hanna.

"Hey!"

Hanna turned to acknowledge her.

"Let me know if you need anything." Shauni sounded casual but the extra second she took to stand in the doorway assured Hanna, that she knew what she was going through, hurt very much.

"Thanks, Shauni."

Shauni's kind words gave Hanna the small boost she needed to start the last half of her day. She still had invoices to send to clients and had yet to call the auto body shop to check on her vehicle. After she'd emailed a majority of the invoices she called the auto shop. They told her it would be ready for pickup before the end of the day. At least *that* was going as planned. She wouldn't have to count on Ava to drive her around again. Ethan overheard the phone conversation. "Do you want me to give you a ride to the body shop? Seriously, it's no problem. It's on my way, and even if it wasn't, I'd still be more than happy to."

Hanna shook her head wondering how other people without the support she had would even begin to get through such an ordeal. "You are truly amazing Ethan, I'd appreciate that. Thank you."

Hanna was sending out the last invoice when Ava sent her a text.

*How's it going? I know you weren't looking forward
to today and wanted to make sure you weren't ready
to flip your lid. I'm here for you and if you're sick of
me don't forget about Lisa Price. She seems to have
a way. See you tonight?*

Hanna texted Ava back to let her know that for the most part, she was keeping it together.

*Thanks for the check-in!
Holding up for now. See you tonight after I get my
vehicle from the shop, I'll make you dinner. xo*

CHAPTER SEVENTEEN

Hanna wanted to do something special for Ava in appreciation for letting her stay with her. She knew Ava loved vintage postcards and had even framed some to use as wall art in the bedrooms. She would shop for some unique ones online after getting more work done. Ethan had been busy joyously organizing the twin's sweet sixteen party and Shauni was hammering tall display stands together in the back. There were things Hanna needed to be doing too but for the third time today, she had caught a glimpse of the white roses across the room and it steered her mind to Jacob. She hadn't been expecting flowers from anyone but when she thought Jacob had sent her flowers to make amends, she was hopeful for their relationship. She had planned on reaching out to him to see how he was doing after she had notified the many wedding vendors but found herself delaying the call. She hated admitting to herself that she was, in a way, hoping he would have made the effort to reach out before she had the chance. It was silly but, each time she looked at the flowers it stung that they hadn't been from Jacob. Hanna figured that maybe if she sat the flowers in the back with Shauni where they were out of sight, her mind might be focused elsewhere. More specifically, back to her job. She stood up from her desk and walked toward the table with the flowers. Ethan was working on digital renderings on his laptop and noted Hanna's action. Without looking up, he spoke. "I was wondering when you were going to do that."

Hanna smiled apologetically. "I'm hoping for an out of sight out of mind effect."

As she was picking up the vase, someone triggered the digital door chime. When she turned to see who it was, her fingers went numb causing her to fumble with the bouquet. She was able to quickly regain a solid hold on the flowers just as Ethan had stepped over to rescue them.

"Here Hanna, I'll take those for you. Hi Jacob!"

Ethan took hold of the flowers. Unsure if Hanna had revealed him as the source of the photo, he disappeared into the workshop like a mouse being pursued by a cat. Jacob was standing in the doorway looking like the man of her dreams. The dreams that Hanna had over and over as a young girl and up until she had met him that day in the exhibition booth. He looked to be dressed for a meeting, wearing a collared shirt, navy dress pants and leather shoes. His deep blue eyes stood out vividly against his bright white shirt. It was as if Hanna were seeing him again for the first time. Jacob smiled one of his most tempting smiles, and as if hypnotized, Hanna started to step toward him. She stopped when she remembered that she had just spent the morning postponing their wedding because he had done something so awful, that she didn't know whether she would ever forgive him. She only knew that she wanted to.

"Hi," he said softly. Jacob waited for a reciprocal greeting but sensed Hanna was caught off guard, so went ahead. "Sorry, I didn't call first. I had to come this direction anyway so figured I would just stop in on my way by."

Hanna thought it was somewhat lovable that he tried to make up a reason for not simply calling because he wanted to see her in person. "I don't mind at all. It's really good to see you. I was going to call you today."

Hanna hadn't seen Jacob in two days. Despite being in good company with Ava and her dedicated work family, she missed him. Now that she was standing only a few feet away from him, she wished he would reach out to grab her, hold her against him and tell her again, how sorry he was. Maybe if he did that every day for a year, she would know just how remorseful he was and that he knew how deeply he'd hurt her. That was probably asking for too much, she knew. Jacob pulled his stare away looking withdrawn. Instead of responding to her small talk comment, he forged ahead. "I just wanted to let you know that Luke and I are flying to London, England this afternoon to meet with a potential client. We'll probably be gone for four or five days."

Hanna said nothing, reeling in surprise and waiting for Jacob to finish speaking.

"The flight's about seven hours alone and I know the different time zones make it tricky to talk so I thought I should let you know before I go."

Jacob wasn't making up an excuse to see Hanna because he missed her or wanted a chance to convey his love and remorse. He was on his way to the airport to fly out of the country on business for almost a week. Hanna felt naive and tried to recover quickly. "Oh! Well, that's exciting for you guys. It must be a big deal if you're willing to fly all that way."

"Yeah. We've been communicating online and have even done some Zoom presentations for them but before they sign a contract they want to meet with us in person."

Hanna knew the request, though last minute, wasn't rare or uncommon. "That makes sense. A lot of our clients like to come in to see who they're dealing with before signing on with us too. Your clients are probably putting a lot more capital at stake than ours."

Jacob nodded in agreement. "It's a long way to go for a shakedown, but it's just part of the game."

Hanna smiled at his *shakedown* comment. His eyebrows lifted slightly and he couldn't help smiling back at her. After a couple of seconds, Jacob broke eye contact. His expression had changed and he looked irritated. Hanna didn't know if it was because he had to travel to London, their current relationship situation or both.

"Thanks for letting me know. I appreciate that. I guess we can still text each other and still talk right? I'll just let you do the calling so I don't interrupt you when you're sleeping. Maybe when you get back from the UK we can get together."

He nodded and responded quietly, a stark contrast to his desperate plea just days before. "Sure. I'd like that."

"Ok, then I guess we'll talk soon then."

Jacob turned and left the studio, the door quietly chiming again behind him. Anyone who hadn't known their back story probably would have thought this was a new relationship and that they weren't yet at the comfortable hugging and kissing stage. Hanna turned around to find Ethan spying through the small rectangular window of the workshop door. He looked like a puppy dog eagerly waiting for his owner to invite him up onto the couch. Now that the coast was clear, Hanna waved him out. She stood at the window staring sadly at the busy street. The day was turning out to be as crappy as she expected with Jacob's announcement only adding to the pile. Hanna had taunted herself with the false assumption regarding the sender of the flowers, then believed briefly that Jacob had made up an excuse to come and see her. She had served herself enough false hope for the day.

"You ok Hanna?" Ethan asked.

She gave a small smile at how foolish she had been.

"Jacob wanted to let me know that he was going to be out of the country for a few days."

Ethan was shocked and knew that likely wasn't what Hanna wanted or needed to hear. "Really? Now? What country? What for!"

Hanna looked at Ethan. Trying to make light of the situation, she answered him in her prissiest British accent. "To England for business!" She turned back to the window.

Ethan sighed. "Of course he is," he said dryly. "That was a good accent by the way."

Hanna smiled faintly at the compliment. Shauni had come out from the workshop and overheard the conversation. "Why is this starting to feel like a hit-and-run? Again. Jacob gets caught cheating and then conveniently needs to leave the country for a few days. Is the guy for real?"

Shauni was holding a long, red licorice stick in her fist and chomped off a bite. Part of Ethan wanted to join in on the bashing but instead tried to be positive. "Well, he did stop by in person when he could have taken the easy route and just called or texted. If he had to catch a flight, maybe a quick pop-in was all he had time for."

Shauni had bitten both ends of the licorice stick and like a straw, used it to blow air into Ethan's ear. He tolerantly tilted his head away, knowing she'd be irritated that he wasn't grossed out or overreacted. He'd been practicing. When he didn't defend himself Shauni was annoyed. "Why would you stick up for him?"

"I wasn't sticking up for him. I just know that Hanna doesn't need any extra drama or negativity right now. I'm simply trying to give Jacob the benefit of the doubt."

"You shouldn't be giving him anything." She then whipped Ethan lightly with the floppy licorice.

Hanna was only partially listening to the bickering. She wasn't sure if it was entirely fair to be mad at Jacob or not. He had a chance to propel his business, so naturally, he would seize the opportunity. It had been so nice seeing his handsome face and hearing his voice but she had to admit, Jacob being halfway across the world, might not have the same effect on him or their relationship. He wouldn't be missing her from their home and consequently his life. If Hanna hadn't left and gone to stay with Ava, she would have been the one left living in their home alone. Jacob would be preoccupied, concentrating on building a relationship with his new customer and would have limited opportunity to think of her. She wasn't upset at him for trying to grow his business but she wasn't thrilled he was leaving when their relationship was teetering so precariously. Hanna would have to make the most of Jacob's time away and spend the time focusing on herself and the business. For now, she would take things one day at a time. She had to pick up her car and told Ava she would make her dinner. It was earlier than Hanna expected to leave, but after enduring the stresses of the day, it felt much later and she was tired. "Ethan, would you be able to drive me to get my vehicle now?"

"Sure thing. Just let me get my satchel and keys."

Hanna turned to Shauni. "Shauni you can call it a day too. We can all start early tomorrow morning before ShopNShip arrives to go over our design proposals."

Shauni finished chewing the last of her licorice stick. "Ok, you guys go ahead. I'm just gonna finish what I'm doing in the back. I'll lock up when I'm done. See you in the morning!"

Ethan drove Hanna to the auto body shop and after a fairly painless process, she had her vehicle again. Now that she had a means of transportation, Hanna could get a few things for the meal she had planned to cook up for Ava. She wanted to make fettuccine Alfredo with bruschetta bread and made a stop at the grocery store for the items on her list. She worked her way through the fresh section, then over to the store's bakery for the baguette she needed for the bruschetta. Next to a basket filled with baguettes in paper bags, was an older, grey-haired man standing at the glass cake counter. From behind, he reminded Hanna of Bill, her elderly neighbour. She wondered how Bill was doing since his heart attack. The man had his arm around his slim, much shorter wife. Hanna politely excused herself after reaching for the baguette that was so close to their personal space.

"Pardon my reach, sir. Just grabbing a baguette here."

As Hanna was pulling the bread from the basket, the woman poked her head out from around the man's body to glance in Hanna's direction. She looked about twenty-five years old, slightly younger than Hanna herself. That meant she was roughly forty years younger than her grey-haired companion. She was wearing bold makeup, fake lashes that looked like the bristles of a broom and beneath her long button-up shirt, a crop top that covered less skin than some of Hanna's sports bras. They both appeared happy, gazing at the desserts behind the glass. Hanna was trying not to judge, especially since they were smiling but couldn't help wondering what interests they would have in common. The girl looked college-aged while the man looked old enough to be her grandfather. As Hanna waited in the lineup to purchase the groceries, she wondered what the mismatched couple's conversations might consist of.

"Did you get your final grades back yet dear?

"I sure did Grampybear. Did you take all your heart medications today?"

Hanna told herself unconvincingly that it probably had nothing to do with sex on his part and nothing to do with money on her part. Besides it was none of her business. Driving home on the highway, she hit traffic and was stuck behind a dump truck spewing exhaust fumes. To avoid it, she changed lanes and then came to a dead stop again. She found herself beside a young mother driving with her baby boy in the back, buckled into his car seat. To entertain him, she was smiling and singing with her mouth wide, glancing up periodically into her rearview mirror to make eye contact with him. The mother didn't care how ridiculous she looked. The baby was kicking his tiny feet out of sheer love and joy. Hanna thought she would boil over with emotion at the sweetness of them. Instead, she breathed deeply and held the steering wheel like it was her lifeline. After several minutes, traffic started picking up speed again. She took the exit for Ava's house and passed a tall billboard sign on the side of the road, high up in the air. It had a bright neon pink background and centered in the middle was a silhouette of a woman's long legs in stiletto heels. At the bottom of the billboard, between the stilettos was a large open oyster shell with a 3D sparkling pink pearl inside. In the same sparkling finish, the billboard read, The Pink Pearl and included the address. Hanna knew the premium glittery sign would have been a costly upgrade. The owners knew the expense of the high-visibility advertisement would pay off quickly. She might not have given the racy billboard a second glance a week ago but looking at it now had risen her temperature a few degrees. She turned up the radio for the duration of the drive, trying to forget it. Hanna pulled into Ava's driveway and turned off the ignition. She almost wished that she didn't love Jacob anymore so she could walk away from him and begin to move past the pain and anger. She knew by the way she felt after seeing him in the studio, her feelings for him hadn't disappeared. It made her stomach ache when they acted as though they were only acquaintances rather than passionate lovers and companions. Hanna grabbed the bags of groceries along with her purse and went inside. She pulled up Ava's text on her phone, including the number of Lisa Price, the life coach and entered the number. A receptionist with an upbeat voice answered and kindly scheduled Hanna for an appointment tomorrow morning.

CHAPTER EIGHTEEN

Simply knowing she had the appointment booked had drastically lowered Hanna's stress level. By seeking some professional guidance, she had taken a step in the right direction. She could now change into comfy clothes, throw her hair up in a bun and start a tasty dinner for her and Ava. Hanna minced up the garlic and onions, added some olive oil and began to fry everything together in a large pan on the stove. After she had all the bruschetta ingredients diced and stirred into a bowl, she turned the dial on the toaster oven to let it preheat for the sliced baguette. Her dad, Dale had always said that the key to a perfect non-soggy bruschetta bread was to pre-toast the bread before adding the topping. Hanna loved to help her dad cook as a small girl and before she was even five years old she had her own child-size apron for when she would cook alongside him. When it was Dale's turn to make dinner he was always sure to get Hanna involved. He trusted her enough to pull a chair up to the stove and stir the ingredients for him. He would be proud she remembered his tip and could hear his voice now. He'd say, "One toasting before and one toasting after!" like he was an enthusiastic chef being videotaped for a cooking show. Years later he told Hanna that parents who cook with their children have a better chance of getting them to eat the meal afterwards. She laughed at his clever tactic and was happy for the memorable cooking classes he gave her. Dale had instilled a love of cooking and home-cooked foods within her. She would take a picture of the meal when it was ready to serve and text it to him. Hanna started the noodles in a pot and then added a brick of cream cheese into the pan with the onions and garlic. She was getting to know her way around Ava's kitchen pretty well but couldn't find the strainer for the fettuccine noodles. She kneeled as she looked in each low drawer and cabinet. Finally, it materialized in the back of the very last cabinet she opened. "Uh-huh! There you are!" she announced victoriously to the well-hidden strainer.

When she stood up to set the strainer in the sink, there was thick smoke coming from every possible opening of the small toaster oven. She peered inside but the smoke only allowed her to see a tiny flame near the back corner. The smoke had taken very little time to fill Ava's small kitchen. Without even knowing what her plan was, Hanna slid open the patio door, put on the silicone oven mitts and grabbed the toaster oven by its two handles. With outstretched arms, she hurried it outside and sat it down on the grass, where it continued to billow grey smoke. Hanna looked around, hoping that the neighbours hadn't been watching, then raced back inside to salvage the noodles and sauce. Just as Hanna finished straining the noodles, Ava appeared in the doorway of the smoke-filled kitchen, holding a bottle of their Pinot Grigio wine. She glanced from the stove to the open patio door. It was evident something had been burnt. Badly. Politely ignoring the thick clouds of smoke, Ava came to the stove to see what Hanna was cooking. "Mmmmmm. Smells great! What's for dinner, dear?"

Hanna rolled her eyes at Ava's phoney praise and put her lips together in embarrassment. "I'm so sorry! I don't know what happened! I was preheating the toaster for the bruschetta."

Unoffended, Ava reached up into the cabinet for two wine glasses and carried them to the kitchen table. "Don't worry about it! I know it'll taste awesome. Always does."

Hanna waved the hand towel, trying to usher out the smoke. "Are you talking about my pasta or the wine!" she joked, then coughed on the suffocating air.

Ava sat Hanna's glass of white wine on the counter for her then watched as she pushed the tray into the large oven.

"Let's hope I don't wreck two ovens in the same night," bringing the missing toaster oven to Ava's attention.

Ava lifted her chin, looking out the open window, eyeing the mini oven lying haphazardly on the back lawn. As Hanna pulled plates from the cupboard, Ava disappeared through the patio door to investigate and assess the damage. Hanna made a mental note to purchase Ava a replacement toaster oven. If she ordered one online tonight, it would probably be there in a day or two. She was grinding fresh pepper onto the pasta noodles when Ava stepped back inside. She was holding two small, charred items that she had retrieved from the evicted toaster. Upon first inspection, Hanna thought they were men's old leather wallets. In an effort to touch them as little as possible, Ava held them between her index fingers and thumbs. She began slowly turning her wrists back and forth, trying to figure out what the items could be or *used* to be. It then registered for both women, what the mysterious briquettes were. They were the late-night, after-bar toaster strudels they had cooked and forgotten to eat. They were wearing the same stunned expression with matching 'o' shaped lips.

Hanna broke the silence. "Oooooh yeaaah," she said quietly.

Ava was surprised that the strudels sat in the toaster for two days unnoticed. They hadn't used the toaster since that night, giving them ample time to forget about the greasy snacks. Looking down at the evidence, Hanna was embarrassed for both of them and scratched her upper lip.

"Suddenly those warnings about not drinking alcohol while cooking are making a lot of sense."

While Hanna was still pondering the dangers of drinking and cooking, Ava opened the under-sink cabinet, tossed the strudels into the garbage and closed the door. Hanna broke out laughing at their drunken misadventure.

"That could have been so much worse!"

Ava swiped her hands together, brushing off the crumbs and the incident at the same time. "Ah! What's a little evening kitchen fire? I'm forgetting it ever happened. I think the toaster oven might even be ok. We can bring it back inside after dinner and have a look. You wanna eat now?"

CHAPTER NINETEEN

Ava and Hanna sat at the table and enjoyed the home-cooked meal. Despite the rough start, it had turned out to be delectable. Ava moaned in pleasure after her first bite. Hanna had taken a photo of her fettuccine and colourful bruschetta bread beforehand and sent it to her dad. She figured he likely wouldn't see it or respond for a day or two. Dale considered his cell phone to be more of a burden, but the trade-off was that it allowed him to keep in touch with his daughter regularly. He would be pleased to see her photo.

During dinner, Hanna and Ava talked about their day. Ava spent most of her day recording a last-minute radio ad. The commercial was for an event called ScholarsNTech. The event is hosted yearly by a group of large technology companies that collaborate to create a series of scholarships for select students who show promise in the fields of engineering, technology, robotics or computer science. The scholarships are awarded in partnership with the most prominent technology schools in the country. A few of the schools participating in the event are McGill, Simon Fraser and Queens University. The benefactor companies pay all expenses for the students, in hopes that they will come work for their company after they are thoroughly educated and have graduated. Some of the sponsors are Riley Innovations, Google, Synoptex and a dozen other technology companies that want to have their company's image associated with doing good in the community.

The event is a formal gala held once yearly. This year it was being held at the Riley Event building on the north side of the city. Tickets were sold for the gala online and some tickets were given away by the organizers when it got closer to the event date. Attendees included the sponsors, the scholarship recipients, their parents, the Deans of the schools, and anyone else who wanted to attend the gala and could afford the three hundred dollar tickets. The radio ad that Ava had voiced was to promote online ticket sales. The event organizer in charge of marketing, Fiona Bergman, had come into the network to see how the ad recording process was going. She wanted a quick sample of what the ad would sound like. Ava was given the script and instructed by the director to read it out loud. Fiona was impressed with Ava's smooth voice and charismatic personality. She pulled two gala tickets from her large leather purse and handed them to Ava. "I think *that* voice will grab the attention of just about anybody. That earns you two free tickets. Hope to see you there!"

"Thank you!" Ava beamed graciously.

Ava thought she and Hanna should go for the free drinks and formal festivities. Ava loved getting dressed up and when she did, it was guaranteed that all heads would turn her way.

"We are definitely going, right? A free formal party! Come on, you love getting dressed up, just as much as I do. Besides no one's legs look better in a dress than yours!" Hanna accepted the leg compliment gracefully. "Thanks. I'll have to think about that one."

"Don't think too long, it's this Wednesday."

"Like in two days?" Hanna confirmed.

"Yep!"

Shifting gears, Ava asked Hanna about her day. Hanna told Ava how Jacob had stopped in briefly at the studio on his way to the airport for his business trip.

"After he left, I felt like my day had slid downhill so badly that I took your advice and made an appointment with Lisa Price for tomorrow morning."

Ava raised her eyebrows dramatically and then sipped her wine.

Hanna noted her expression. "I know. I don't feel right about Jacob's trip either. Shauni made the same face you did."

Before Ava had a chance to bad mouth Jacob, Hanna changed the subject. She didn't feel like dwelling on the day, especially since she would be discussing her rickety love life with the therapist first thing tomorrow morning.

"Enough of that. Have you been in touch with Jasper yet?"

Ava was twirling her fettuccine onto her fork then started to smile guiltily. Hanna took that as a yes.

"Nice! So what's the status? When are you seeing him next?"

Ava finished chewing her pasta. "Well actually, I invited him over tonight after dinner for a drink or two."

"Oh, really? That's great! " Hanna was excited that Ava would be seeing Jasper again. She felt terrible when Ava ended their pub night early because she had mistakenly thought Hanna was upset about Jacob. "I'll keep a low profile, I've got a client coming into the office, late tomorrow morning after my appointment with Lisa. I'll be finishing up their designs tonight. You might not even see me."

Ava frowned. "Oh please! Like I'm confining you to the bedroom. Just be casual. You can even join us if you like. I'll be asking your opinion on him after he leaves anyway."

"Thanks for the invite Ave. You're a sweetheart but I'm beat and I know I'll be in bed early. I'll say hello, just so he doesn't think I'm avoiding him."

After they tidied up the kitchen and brought the banished toaster oven back inside, they waited for Jasper out on the front porch with their wine. Before long, a large, shiny pickup truck pulled up to the side of the street in front of the house. Jasper appeared from around the back of the truck box carrying a long bouquet of mixed flowers.

Wearing a white T-shirt beneath an open plaid shirt and blue jeans, he looked just the same as both women remembered him. That night at Patty's Pub, Hanna had thought he looked like a Hollywood cowboy. Jasper might not have been a movie star, but he looked like one and by any standard, was a fantastic singer. After all the idiots that Ava had subjected herself to, it wasn't surprising that she had gotten so worked up over him and his wholesome nature.

"Hello, ladies!" Jasper called out in his deep unforgettable voice. He walked up the driveway and before he got to the steps of the porch Ava had skipped down and over to him. Jasper handed her the bouquet and she smiled bashfully as she inhaled their fragrance. Hanna stood feeling like she was encroaching. She would say hello, then get to work on her designs for tomorrow. As Ava held the bouquet proudly in her hand she led Jasper over to Hanna.

"Hi Hanna, how are you doin' today?"

His genuine smile had just the right amount of confidence. "I'm good Jasper! How are you doing?"

"I'm doin' pretty darn good thanks!"

"Glad to hear!"

Jasper waited politely for Ava to invite him inside for the drink she had promised him. Looking at Ava, Hanna found her already eyeing Jasper with the same hunger she had the night she watched him sing on stage. Ava made an earlier effort to convince Hanna that she wouldn't be in the way, but she felt it was time to disappear for a while. This was their first date and she didn't need to be right in the middle of it.

"Well, nice seeing you again Jasper but, I've got a lot of work to do so I'm gonna get to it. I'll see you guys around!"

Jasper gave a friendly smile. "Good seein' you Hanna!"

Hanna then disappeared into her temporary bedroom, where she spent the next couple of hours listening to music and finishing the ShopNShip designs. Ethan had done a thorough job on the designs during the day and Hanna only needed to verify the progress. After a few subtle changes, she was satisfied with the presentation. She then posted some photos of the BabyDreams booth on Instagram and Facebook. All she needed now was a glass of water before going to bed. When she emerged from the bedroom she could hear the TV down the hall, in the living room. Hanna hoped that Ava and Jasper weren't in a position that might embarrass anyone. To Hanna's surprise, there was no one in the living room, and after getting her glass of water from the kitchen she realized they weren't in there or even outside enjoying the warm summer night. That only left Ava's bedroom. Hanna snorted lightly and smiled as she imagined Ava putting the moves on Jasper and then compelling him to go to her bedroom in such a hurry she hadn't bothered to turn off the TV. Hanna tapped the power button on the TV, carried her water to her room and brushed her teeth. Now that the house was quiet, Hanna could hear the music coming from Ava's bedroom. Just then, a deep muffled yelp from Jasper was followed by a contrasting high-pitched giggle from Ava. Hanna was genuinely happy for Ava but at that moment, she felt like an intruder and wished she could beam herself home for the night. The thought of sleeping alone in the big bed she usually shared with Jacob wasn't comforting either and she quickly brushed off the thought. Hanna turned on the table fan to drown out any sounds from the neighbouring bedroom and fell asleep.

During her deepest phase of sleep, she dreamt of dark-haired men and passionate sex. In the dream, Hanna had erotic sex with a stranger while Jacob was tortuously made to watch. Hanna and the man enjoyed every sexual act they could imagine. With unnatural strength, Hanna's dark-haired lover lifted her, spread her legs and brought her to him, entering her with his sex-ready body. He began a slow blissful rocking, in and out. Maintaining his rhythm, he was able to bend his neck downward, taking her nipple into his mouth, sucking it ever so gently. To prolong and delay their orgasms, he sat Hanna down and she bent to her knees while he slid himself into her mouth. As the two strangers took turns sucking and kissing each other, a higher power made Jacob stand there pinned at their bedside and unwillingly observe the entire hedonistic act. It drove Jacob crazy to watch her with the other man and he was yelling at her to stop. Hanna defiantly moved her naked body in sync with the stranger. The more it infuriated Jacob, the closer Hanna climbed toward climax. Straddling her dream lover, she pleasured them both with her grinding motion. When he used his hips to push upward deepening the sensation, she began to pulse and squeeze around him. No longer mindful of Jacob's protests, she came blissfully and euphorically. Hanna awoke with both hands clenching the sheets and had thoroughly moistened her underwear. She hadn't enjoyed a wet dream since she was a teenager. Her orgasm was so intense it caused her to sleep through her alarm. When Hanna glanced at her phone and realized how late she was, she showered, dressed quickly and headed out to the kitchen before leaving. Ava had made coffee and was standing in the kitchen at the sink.

"Good morning!" Hanna said as she hurried to put on her shoes, "I'd ask you to tell me about your night with Jasper but I'm running late. Sorry, Ave!"

"No worries! We had a good time." Ava was smiling like she had a secret. Hanna grabbed a travel mug and poured herself a coffee for the drive. She gathered her purse and keys and told Ava to wish her good luck with the appointment.

"You won't need luck, Han. Lisa is amazing! You're going to love her!"

Hanna opened the door and turned to Ava who was watching her.

"See you tonight Ave! and hey! Tell Jasper good morning for me! Glad it went well!"

After Hanna winked at her and shut the door, Ava wondered how she knew Jasper had a sleepover. She then looked down at the rug in front of the door and spotted Jasper's boots sitting in the entryway.

She smiled proudly to herself then scampered back into her bedroom with two cups of coffee.

About halfway to Lisa's office, Hanna found herself thinking back to the sex dream with the faceless lover. It was indecent that Jacob had been coerced to spectate, but what Hanna felt afterwards, didn't exactly feel like suffocating guilt. She asked herself if sleeping with someone else would settle the score between her and Jacob. He would learn how painful and humiliating it felt. *Would that make it easier for Hanna to move forward with a life together with Jacob?* She felt shamefully petty for even considering the perverse scenario. *What's wrong with me?* Hanna shook off thoughts of the dream and cast aside the mental debate about the revenge sex. She arrived a short time later at the address of Lisa Price, the life coach. Lisa's office was on the main floor of a tall, early nineteen hundreds red brick home that had been converted into a large studio office. There were wide concrete steps up to the door and a large arched window at the front. The building reminded Hanna, of a New York Brownstone. She rang the doorbell and after several seconds was greeted by a petite woman with dark hair, cut in a short pixie style. She invited Hanna inside and introduced herself. "Hi there Hanna!" She had a warm smile and a friendly voice. "I'm Lisa. Nice to meet you! How are you doing today?"

"Hi, Lisa. I'm ok, how about you?" Hanna hoped she didn't look as nervous as she felt.

"I'm fantastic. Thank you!" Lisa closed the door and gestured for Hanna to enter the main room, where they could sit and talk. Lisa wasn't like the therapists Hanna was used to seeing on TV with the collared button-up shirt and reading glasses. She reminded Hanna of a life-size, talking TinkerBell in jeans and a T-shirt. Aside from a few framed degrees on the wall and a large antique desk in the corner, the space didn't look all that different from Hanna's living room at home. Two long modern sofas with a matching love seat were arranged in a U shape. Opposite the smallest sofa were two plush chairs, finished with button trim. In the centre of the furniture arrangement was an ornate wood coffee table with a tray holding a few glasses, a water pitcher and a tall potted orchid. Lisa invited Hanna to make herself at home wherever she liked. Hanna glanced around briefly and then chose one of the plush chairs. Lisa poured them each a glass of water, sat one on the small table next to Hanna, and then took a seat herself on the nearby sofa. Lisa started by asking a couple of basic questions to get Hanna talking and to allow her some time to relax and settle in. Hanna was pleasantly surprised by Lisa's down-to-earth, casual presence. She noticed Lisa wasn't holding a notebook for taking notes on their session. It was as if Lisa had read Hanna's mind. "Please don't be offended that I don't take any notes. I prefer to write a summary of our discussions afterward. I find that note-taking during a session only tends to distract everybody. We're just going to talk and get to know each other a bit."

Hanna respected Lisa's explanation for her streamlined practices. Besides Hanna felt her situation was sadly, pretty commonplace. *Boy cheats on girl, girl now has issues and doesn't know if she can move past it.* Lisa may have been small in stature but had a big way of quickly connecting with her clients. It allowed Hanna to feel at ease talking with her. After Lisa asked what had led to their meeting that day, Hanna explained how it all happened. She told Lisa about the relationship she shared with Jacob and omitted none of the details. They'd touched on the topic of their sex life, how they'd first met and of course Jacob's infidelity. Now that Lisa knew the entire situation, and Hanna had become more comfortable, she wanted to ask Lisa about her recent curiosity regarding revenge sex. "Lisa?" Hanna asked hesitantly.

Lisa nodded her head, encouraging Hanna to proceed.

"Do you think the things we dream of, say something about who we are? As people?"

Lisa shook her head and scrunched up her pert nose. "I don't put a lot of stock in dreams, but I do think they can tell us a bit about our fears and maybe our fantasies."

"I'm not overly proud of this but since I can be honest…" Hanna glanced at Lisa, deciding whether she wanted to admit her perverse desire or not.

"Sure!" Lisa encouraged.

Hanna prepared herself for the shame that would surely follow her question. "Sometimes I can't help but wonder if sleeping with someone else, would take away some of my anger. I don't think Jacob will ever fully understand how low I feel until he's felt the same pain that I have."

Lisa didn't make Hanna feel shameful. "Revenge may provide temporary satisfaction, but, long term, it will likely only result in disappointment." Lisa suggested that if Hanna truly loved Jacob and planned to continue the relationship, she would feel negative about it in the future. After Lisa and Hanna continued talking for a while, Hanna wanted to ask another question that had been weighing on her mind.

"Will I eventually forgive Jacob?" she asked reluctantly. "I don't want to be angry about it for the rest of my life."

Lisa gave her a compassionate smile. "As partners, we have natural expectations. We hold those we love to a higher standard and don't expect to be wounded by them. When they let us down, the array of emotions we experience can be completely bewildering. We might feel confusion, sadness, physical pain, and even rage. These are all normal responses to the stress of betrayal. It can take some time to process all of these feelings. But if we want to be truly happy again, we not only have to forgive the person but unfortunately, we have to take a chance at trusting them again. That part takes time too."

Hanna sighed, knowing she wasn't there yet, but knew Lisa's statement was probably true. She glanced out the tall arched window framing the row of oak trees along the sidewalk.

"What if I can't trust him again?" Hanna asked sadly.

Lisa studied Hanna's childlike expression with a mixture of admiration and empathy. "In time, do you think you'll want to forgive Jacob?"

Lisa waited for Hanna's delayed answer. Hanna only let out another deep sigh.

"Ironically," Lisa offered, "Forgiveness is a choice. It's something we do for ourselves."

Hanna looked at Lisa with an expression of mild surprise. She thought it was ironic that Lisa was suggesting that the solution to her unhappiness had to be implemented by herself, the injured party. Despite being mildly irritated by the suggestion, she made a mental note to mull that over later. Lisa was the professional after all. Their time was up and Lisa began to stand. She walked behind her desk on the far side of the room, scribbled on a pad of paper and then walked back to Hanna wearing a warm smile.

"Here," Lisa said. "You've got homework," and passed Hanna a small piece of paper.

Hanna was expecting some lengthy online reading assignment, or maybe an antidepressant prescription. Instead, in fancy scroll writing were the two words, *Have Fun* and an exclamation mark that followed. This wasn't the first time during their session, that Lisa had caught Hanna by surprise.

"Spoil yourself and take care of yourself! In time everything will get sorted out." Lisa threw her two hands up and added, "It's going to be a beautiful summer night, you should go out and enjoy it!"

Lisa then guided Hanna easily toward the door. Everything Ava said about Lisa was true. She didn't necessarily give Hanna an instant solution but her positive outlook was refreshing. Talking with Lisa felt like a soft light at the end of a dark tunnel.

CHAPTER TWENTY

After leaving Lisa's office, Hanna started on her drive to the studio. She spent several minutes, going over what Lisa had said. It didn't feel right, the part about choosing to forgive someone for the sake of ourselves. It had been put on her to offer Jacob forgiveness. Hanna thought forgiveness was something you awarded someone who hurt you after they had genuinely atoned for something they'd done. *Why was it so difficult to forgive Jacob?* She had almost flung herself at him the day before when he'd stopped in. He then left the country for four days. *How were they supposed to rekindle or rebuild trust when he was out of the country?*

She would be at the office in a few minutes but was running late and cutting it close for the presentation with ShopNShip. With any luck, Ethan would have started without her if she had to arrive a little late. A week beforehand, a woman from the marketing department named Viara, sent over a wish list and the digital logo files for printing. Beyond the stated requirements, she said that Hanna and the team had permission to create a booth they thought best suited the goals of ShopNShip. After researching competitors and profiling potential customers, they created a sleek booth design that would mimic the shipping outlets set up in the grocery stores. When Hanna arrived at the studio she entered through the back door, into the workshop. This gave her a second to put her things away and catch her breath from her hurried jaunt from the car to the building. Peeking through the narrow workshop window, Hanna saw a young, slim woman holding Ethan's iPad. Her overly long nails extended well beyond the ends of her fingers. She wore heeled boots and a slim-fitted dress that rested mid-thigh. Her long straight hair was dyed the same colour as the black onyx paperweight sitting on Ethan's desk. Overdressed for the occasion, Hanna decided that Viara was a diva.

Hanna was somewhat irritated she would be joining the meeting late. Being late was a *never-do* for Hanna. She hated being late so badly that for a second, she considered skipping it and letting Ethan handle the entire presentation. Ethan was standing beside the woman pointing animatedly at the tablet in her hand while Shauni held a large sample piece of black glassy acrylic. Shauni was rarely involved in this part of the process and Hanna had to wonder what was happening. Shauni's facial expression signalled she wasn't participating by choice. A second later when Shauni spotted Hanna through the window, she cast her large eyes up to the ceiling. Every once in a while there was a client that needed some finessing and it looked like the marketing person for ShopNShip might be one of them. Hanna swung open the workshop door and quickly moved in for the rescue. "Good morning everybody!"

Ethan and the young woman turned to acknowledge the new arrival. Hanna extended her hand to give Viara a proper and friendly greeting. Looking relieved, Ethan said good morning while the woman looked at Hanna blankly waiting for an introduction.

"Hi, I'm Hanna Richards! You must be Viara from ShopNShip. How are you today?"

After giving Hanna a slow, visual once over, the woman finally extended her hand. Hanna shook the woman's hand, careful not to impale herself with any of her long nail extensions.

"Actually, I'm Monica, Mr. Antonio's executive assistant," she purred arrogantly.

"Oh! Ok great! Are you standing in for Viara today? Or are we still waiting for her?"

Monica wore an insolent smile. "I'm here in place of Viara. I'll be going over the proposal and reporting back to Mr. Antonio directly."

Despite the multiple questions going through Hanna's mind, like, *since when do young executive assistants step in for the marketing team?* She attempted to proceed as professionally as possible. "Sure! I don't know how far into the presentation we've gotten so far Monica, but maybe you can tell us what you think of everything so far."

"Well, I think there's too much black."

Shauni and Ethan made discreet eye contact for support, while Hanna acted as though the blunt statement hadn't surprised her. The head office had emailed the team photos of the look they wanted for the interior of the store outlets. The entire service counter was made of a shimmery black acrylic. It was ultra-modern and chosen to allow the white and red logo to stand out boldly. The marketing person, Viara would have known this. Hanna could see this was going to take some time and patience. Shauni was already backing away slowly making her escape, leaving Hanna and Ethan to deal with Monica alone.

"You're right Monica, it is a lot of black. This was actually a corporate design decision we were asked to adhere to. But despite the dark colour it looks modern and is a great backdrop for the company logo."

Hanna referred to the digital drawing on the iPad.

"The acrylic counter doubles as a digital screen that allows ShopNShip's current ads and promotions to be showcased."

"Oh, that's neat!"

Hanna was happy to be making headway. "It's pretty innovative, isn't it? Some companies have found it to be a great marketing tool. If it's busy in the shop, customers can watch it while waiting in line to be served. My dentist has her reception area finished in a large white model. It's sleek and people seem to be impressed with it."

Monica thought for a moment. "Maybe I want one in place of my desk."

Now that Ethan could see Hanna was working her magic, he cheerily asked if anyone wanted a coffee or water. In sync, both women asked for coffee with cream and sugar. By the end of the discussion, Hanna had Monica convinced that she was happy with the concepts and designs. Monica threw on her expensive-looking sunglasses, tossed her ebony locks off her shoulder then strutted out of the studio proudly, like she'd accomplished something of utmost importance.

"Nice meeting you Monica! Looking forward to working with you!"

After Monica had waved and walked out the door, Hanna went to the window and watched her walk to her car. Instead of feeling proud the way she normally did after a successful presentation, she felt cheated. Monica was young, beautiful, wore short dresses and had long painted fingernails like a badger. According to his JobLink page, her boss, Stefan Antonio was none of those things. Besides her pleasant physical attributes, Monica had no endearing personality traits and was clueless about design. Hanna couldn't help speculating.

"Is it always about sex with men? Or am I just becoming completely jaded?"

Shauni was coming out from the back and piped up from behind her. "Yes to the sex part!"

Ethan and Shauni had come over to get one last glimpse of Monica from over Hanna's shoulder. Ethan too was genuinely puzzled. "What on earth do you think the story is there? How does the executive assistant get in a position to override the marketing person on the company's marketing projects?"

Shauni offered her worthy opinion. "It sounds like she probably gets into whatever position Mr. Antonio wants her to."

Ethan couldn't argue with the statement and nodded in agreement. Hanna had been patient and professional with Monica but now that she was no longer in her presence she could express her frustration. "What if our presentation had sucked or what if I allowed her to bully me into all the ridiculous changes she was suggesting? Was the CEO of the company willing to have a mediocre booth for the sake of sex? What about our reputation?"

Without warning Hanna was overcome with a distracting curiosity. It wasn't to do with Monica and Stefan Antonio, but instead, the woman named Mandy who inspired her fiancé to cheat, caused the delay of her wedding and ultimately put her into a therapist's chair first thing this morning. *Just who was this person that Jacob was willing to alter their lives for? Didn't Hanna deserve to know what she looked like?* Hanna shook her head and marched toward her desk. Shauni and Ethan had watched Hanna walk away and were still regarding her with concern. She was tapping at her laptop like she was entering the codes to disarm nuclear missiles. She was so focused that she was barely registering their presence. Hanna found herself Google searching word combinations like Mandy and Pink Pearl or Mandy and Stripper, but the search only provided images of pearl necklaces and canned paint strippers. She then tried Facebook and Instagram and found several strippers named Mandy but none of them were local. Without Mandy's unique user name, Hanna knew she was wasting her time. Mandy might not even be her real name. It could simply be her stage name. According to every Hollywood movie that ever involved a stripper, they always had made-up names they used while working the pole. Hanna quickly slammed her laptop shut in humiliation. Reaching into her purse, she pulled out her phone, tapped a couple of buttons and then sat it down again. She reopened the laptop and pressed a few more keys, getting back to work on her nuclear codes. When Hanna looked up briefly, she found Shauni and Ethan watching her.

"Everything ok Hanna?" Ethan asked.

"You need help with anything?" Shauni offered curiously.

Hanna's eyes shifted to her laptop, then darted back and forth at the screen in a panic.

"Yes! No! Shit! How do you *unlike* something!"

Ethan and Shauni ran over to Hanna's desk and crouched on either side of the chair to help. Shauni and Ethan stared at Hanna's screen. A close-up video of an award-winning twerk played on a loop. Hanna's entire screen was covered by a set of naked, well-oiled ass cheeks. Ethan was appalled.

"Oh lord, please make it stop!"

Shauni reached over the keys and *unliked* the video, then as Ethan requested, she put a stop to the shiny gyrating ass. She had simply closed the tab, but not before getting a glimpse of the words in the search bar. Everyone was quiet for a second. Hanna either had to confess that she was trying to find out what Jacob's stripper looked like or had to convince them she had a sudden urge to run over to her laptop to watch x-rated twerk videos. Thankfully she didn't need to explain anything. It was clear what steps Hanna's mind had taken after the Monica woman left.

"I don't blame you," Shauni offered. "I would want to know who she was too. I can get you images of her if you want them."

Hanna appeared to be listening intently so Shauni kept talking.

"I know a guy. He works for this drone company but on the side, he does private investigator jobs for people. We know where she works right? He could set up in the parking lot and when she came out he could get some pictures. He could even find out where she lives if you want."

Ethan frowned with a look of concern. "Well just from my experience, nothing good ever comes from, *I know a guy*. What exactly are you getting Hanna into?"

"Relax Mother, I'm not getting her into anything. I'm just letting her know about a useful service that's available if she's interested." Shauni wasn't a criminal, but she kept a large circle of friends and a couple were somewhat questionable regarding their character. Hanna wasn't waiting any longer. This woman had managed to get her fiancé to have sex with her and Hanna wanted to see what Jacob had found so tempting about her.

"Thanks, Shauni. I appreciate the offer. I actually just texted Ava and told her that she's taking me to The Pink Pearl tonight. I might see Mandy in person for myself."

Shauni and Ethan looked at each other with large eyes. Ethan didn't think that going to see the woman your fiancé had cheated with was such a good idea. There was no way it was going to make Hanna feel better. It would only hurt and humiliate her. If Hanna had any hope of repairing her relationship with Jacob, this was the worst thing she could do. Ethan had to wonder if maybe this time, Shauni's *guy* was the better option.

"You really think seeing her in person is better than just getting a couple of pictures Hanna?"

Ethan had the same panicked expression as someone who just stank up the washroom and was fearful someone would rush in after him.

"Part of me just has to say, be careful what you wish for."

Hanna thought about Ethan's words briefly. "I know that you're right. It'll probably be a total disaster. I love you for caring so much, but I'm still going."

Hanna looked somewhat dismayed but at the same time determined. She'd made up her mind after watching Monica strut out of the office. The ordeal had awakened her curiosity and when her online search proved fruitless, she decided she needed to see this home wrecker with her own eyes. Shauni respected Hanna too much to say anything else negative. Ethan grew frustrated picturing Hanna at the well-known strip joint. The Pink Pearl may have been the gold standard at one time but it had become increasingly seedy in recent years. He was worried Hanna and Ava might be in for a scary surprise. "Maybe Shauni and I will come with you two."

Shauni turned her head to look at Ethan. He'd just signed her up to visit a female strip joint. It was no secret that Ethan was gay and preferred men over women but he was still a perfect gentleman and didn't like the idea of Ava and Hanna putting themselves in such a position. Not to mention, Hanna would likely need moral support after she saw the Mandy woman in person. It wouldn't matter what the stripper looked like. It would make Jacob's one-time lover a flesh and blood human and would reopen a deep wound for Hanna. He would be willing to go for those reasons. Hanna knew Ethan wasn't offering to go for enjoyment.

"You don't think Ava and I can handle The Pink Pearl alone? You guys know Ava Williams right?" Hanna asked sarcastically.

Ethan continued to argue his case. "Trust me. It's not the kind of place you want to be. Not to mention, you and Ava are good-looking women and you'll be in a dark bar with hard and horny, drunk men. You don't see the danger in that?"

Shauni walked closer to echo Ethan's warning. "Trust me, it's shady as hell, and if you two go, you might want us there."

Hanna admired their concern for her and Ava's well-being but had doubts they were available on such short notice. "You two are welcome to join, but we plan to go tonight, sometime after dinner. That probably doesn't work for you guys."

Shauni and Ethan looked at each other and shrugged. "I hate to disappoint you my love but that works fine for me!" Ethan said proudly.

Shauni was slightly less enthusiastic as she would be missing a Taekwondo class. "I'm in," she said dryly, "what time are we leaving?"

Hanna sighed and rolled her eyes, feeling like a childish fool. Ethan and Shauni might not have needed to see the front side of Mandy the way Hanna did but they were willing to humiliate themselves for the sake of Hanna's safety and support. Hanna was biting her lip, her standoffish tone now cast aside. "I have no idea. I've only known that I've been going for two minutes myself. I'll have to see what Ava says. Maybe we can meet there or meet at Ava's. Can I text you two, when I get home?"

Satisfied with Hanna's suggestion, Shauni walked toward the workshop. She stopped halfway and yelled back to Hanna. "And don't conveniently forget about us!"

Mirroring Shauni's threat, Ethan jokingly glared at Hanna, pushed up his glasses, and went back to work at his desk. Now that Hanna had decided to get a visual on Mandy, she needed to refocus her energy on work. She was busy working on a booth design when Ava called, wanting to confirm her sincerity about the hastily hatched plan. Hanna had originally told Ava that going to see Mandy was a bad idea. She still held the same opinion but was going anyway. After Hanna irritably admitted that she was, without a doubt serious, she added that Ethan and Shauni would be chaperoning them. Ava chuckled into the phone, then said sarcastically, "What? They don't trust me? I won't get you into any trouble."

Hanna nodded slowly in accord but was thinking the opposite. *No, not you, maybe just your mouth.*

Then Ava added chipperly, "I'm glad they're coming. The more the merrier! I'm excited!"

"Yeah, I knew you'd say that."

They planned to talk later when they were home from work, then said a quick goodbye. Hanna focused on helping Ethan pull together some more ideas for the Sweet Sixteen party, worked on the finer details for an exhibition design and placed orders for materials they needed for upcoming projects. Hanna kept herself busy but thought of Jacob several times throughout the day. She hadn't heard from him since he stopped in on his way to the airport yesterday and wondered how his presentations were going. When Hanna wasn't focused on work, she was thinking of Jacob. She missed his voice, his comforting embrace and those beautiful deep blue eyes. The current time difference would make it about eight o'clock in the evening for Jacob. Hanna figured he and Luke were likely out at dinner with their clients. She wondered if he missed her, or had even thought of her. Maybe he would call when he finished for the night and was back in his hotel room. Hanna would miss her opportunity to hear Jacob's voice if she was at The Pink Pearl hoping to quench her curiosity about Mandy. Thinking about the time change again, she figured they should still have a chance to talk before she left. *If* he decided to call.

CHAPTER TWENTY ONE

It was after four o'clock and time for everybody at Richards and Co. to go home for the day. Everybody made their way out to their vehicles and agreed to meet at Ava's for around seven. When Hanna got home to Ava's she began feeling antsy about her last-minute plan. Maybe if she could somewhat change her appearance, she could feign confidence, disguising not only her identity but her frazzled nerves at the same time. The reality of it all was starting to set in. Questions she should have asked before planning The Pink Pearl visit now circled her mind. *What would happen if she saw Mandy and she was more attractive than Hanna herself?* Hanna's self-esteem might never recover. The next time she had sex, she would wonder if Jacob was comparing her body to the stripper's body. *Would seeing this half-naked woman give her the closure she hoped for? Would it give her anything? Maybe she should just cancel the whole crazy plan.* Before she could change her mind, Shauni and Ethan arrived together at the door. When Hanna opened the door, everyone threw their heads back and laughed. Ethan opted to wear contact lenses instead of his dark-rimmed glasses. He was dressed in a billowy dress shirt with long cuffs and had opted to leave the top few buttons open, baring part of his chest. His hair was gelled back and so filled with hair products, that it looked wet. He paired his top with wide-bottomed pants and leather, pointed-toe shoes. Ethan reminded Hanna of a good-looking seventies movie gangster. Shauni had put her hair in a high ponytail and wore a short dress topped with a baggy satin varsity jacket. Her platform tennis shoes had given her a couple of extra inches of height and her eye makeup was so heavy and dark that Hanna barely recognized her. When she smiled her bright signature smile, there was no question as to who she was. Ethan and Shauni had been thinking the same thing as Hanna. No one would recognize any of them. After getting a good look at their disguises, Hanna put her palms on her cheeks, blaming herself for their ridiculous get-ups. "Oh, good God. What have I done to you guys?"

Ethan looked Hanna up and down. "The better question is what have you done to yourself? Where is your beautiful hair!"

Ethan was mortified when he thought Hanna had cut off her long shiny locks and then died them an inky brown.

"It's ok Eth! It's just one of Ava's pricey wigs."

Shauni inspected Hanna's unrecognizable look. Her wig was a short dark bob and her round-framed glasses looked like heavy goggles. Her outfit consisted of a knitted turtleneck, a frilly mini skirt and a pair of buckled shoes. "Were you purposely trying to look like the brainy Scooby Doo girl?"

Hanna glanced in the entryway mirror at her reflection and smiled. "No." Hanna knew who Shauni was referring to. "But she was my favourite as a kid, so maybe I was subconsciously inspired. I just don't want anyone to know who I am."

"No fear of that," Shauni reassured her.

"Good!" Hanna laughed, feeling relieved.

They made their way inside and into Ava's kitchen, where they once again admired and shared comments about their dramatic transformations. Hanna mixed everybody a drink of their choice and was sure she made them doubles. They made their way outside to the deck and a moment later Ava arrived. She looked from Ethan to Shauni and lastly Hanna. She grinned and nodded her head.

"Aaaaahhhhhh! Looky looky, the gangs all here!"

She couldn't help but laugh at the mismatched group of characters. It looked like they were pre-drinking for a Halloween party in August. Hanna gave Ava a small wave, preparing for any comments to follow.

"Well Hello there Velma! You look lovely this evening. Will we be solving any mysteries tonight?"

"I'm hoping to."

Ava knew Hanna's nerves would be ready to unravel, and she walked over, placing a quick kiss on the top of her head. "Sorry, I'm late. I stopped by the bakery to grab us some magic brownies for tonight." She grinned at Ethan and then Shauni. "Hey, you guys! How's it going?"

"Hi, Ava!"

"Would Harley Quinn or Mr. Seventies Disco like a magic brownie?" Ava held a small pie box and slid it onto the patio table.

Shauni and Ethan both stood and gave Ava a quick hug. Not bothering to wait for Hanna to serve up the brownies, Shauni flipped open the box lid, grabbed one of the brownies and devoured it before returning to her chair. Ethan was looking at the box, thoughtfully considering a brownie. "Sooo, when you say magic brownies, do you mean, like marijuana-infused brownies?"

Ava smiled and swung back from the doorway. "I sure do!" she boasted, "and they're very strong, so be careful! I'll be right back after I'm all changed. I won't be long."

Hanna gave Ava a weak smile as she walked away, then glanced at the empty glass in her hand. Even after her stiff drink, her jittery nerves were still unsettled. She looked over at the box of brownies on the table, while Ethan observed.

"What are you thinking about over there Hanna?" he asked.

"I'm thinking about having another drink and eating that entire batch of brownies."

Ethan raised his eyebrows. "Well if they're as potent as Ava says they are, maybe we should just share one."

Since Shauni had already delved into one, Hanna glanced over to ask her how the brownies rated. Shauni was sitting comfortably, wearing a small whimsical smile, hinting that her brownie was already beginning to work its '*magic*'. Something was making its way through her small system.

"How was the brownie Shauni?"

Looking thoroughly subdued, Shauni looked around admiring her surroundings.

"It was great but I'll be honest, I also took a little weed gummy before I left home." She held her thumb and index finger up for size. "I don't feel so bad about missing my taekwondo class anymore."

She then reached over and closely examined the leaves of a climbing vine, growing up the corner of the deck. She looked as though she hadn't seen plant leaves before, and had just discovered they were fascinating. Ethan was nervous for Shauni and decided he and Hanna didn't need a whole brownie to themselves. The last time he had ingested a marijuana gummy he thought it wasn't taking effect and ignorantly ate a second. About thirty minutes later he was unable to feel his legs which triggered an unpleasant and long-lasting panic attack. "Hhhmmm," he pondered cautiously, "I think I'm ok with just a half."

"Me too!" Hanna agreed.

Ethan picked up a brownie, took a large bite, then handed the other half to Hanna. Hanna was eating the remainder of the brownie when Ava reappeared. She was wearing a red chin-length wig and had fastened on some fake lashes. She pulled tall heeled boots over her skinny jeans and wore a long-sleeved bodysuit with a see-through mesh upper portion. She reached into the box grabbed one of the brownies and popped it into her mouth.

"Well, I'm ready. How about you guys?"

Ethan stood from the patio chair and held out his hand to assist Hanna in getting up.

"Ready Hanna?"

"No, but I'm hoping the brownie will help once it hits me."

Chapter Twenty Two

By the time they had arrived at The Pink Pearl, everybody's brownie had begun to kick in. After emptying the Uber, Hanna began to giggle as if she was either seeing everyone's altered appearances for the first time or was on edge about what she was about to do and who she would see. When she finally got control of her laughter they went to stand in the short line, waiting to get in. A few of the other men standing in line took the liberty of having a thorough examination of the three women. Ethan knew the men weren't admiring their outfits and when he had protectively given them a sideways glance they reluctantly looked away. A large bouncer in a black suit then checked everyone's ID. He ushered them inside where a woman in a shimmery tube top behind a high counter was collecting the cover charge fee. On the wall behind her and continuing down the hall, there were framed posters of half-naked women who would have been the club's regular dancers. Hanna searched but failed to find one that read *Mandy* beneath the photo. Loud dance music thumped from down the long hallway, leading to where Hanna presumed, Jacob had met Mandy. Hanna paid the cover charge for everyone as promised and then they followed Shauni who bravely started down the hall and then made a turn. Once around the corner, the dimly lit club opened into a large lounge-style area with comfortable chairs and low round tables. A balcony above encircled the upper floor. Hanna wondered if those were the VIP rooms up above. A large ornate chandelier hung from the centre of the ceiling and was draped with a million pink pearls. Shauni began down a clear wide ramp trimmed in lights, leading to a sunken carpeted area. She chose a table that was further away from the main stage.

"What? You don't wanna sit in pervert row?" Ava jeered.

Surrounding the table was a padded, high back, bench and two tub chairs that were angled slightly, toward the main stage. Ava and Shauni each sat in one of the chairs so Hanna and Ethan could have the clearest view of the club and the dancers. Within a few minutes of sitting down, a cheery waitress appeared and asked what everybody wanted to drink. "Did you want to give me a card so you can start a tab with us tonight?"

Taking a second to consider the offer, Hanna remembered Jacob said his card had likely been over-swiped that night at the Pearl. She then received a gentle tap on the side of her foot coming from the direction of Ava's long leg. When she looked toward Ava, her eyes were big and round and she was mouthing the word '*no*'. Hanna looked back at the waitress. "No thanks. I think we'll be using cash tonight."

It was likely a lot easier to sneak purchases onto credit card tabs when more than two or three people were drinking. The number of drinks ordered might become more of a blur after you'd been served a few and had several people charging to the same card. Not to mention the card had Hanna's name on it. She wasn't looking to have anyone from the strip joint know her or her name. Everybody ordered a drink and the waitress disappeared with the order. Having visions of the bouncer escorting them out for failing to pay for their drinks or not purchasing enough lap dances, Hanna figured she better go to the ATM and make a withdrawal. There was a machine conveniently located inside the club and another twenty feet away from that one in the wide hall to the washrooms. Walking the length of the strip joint, full of revved-up men to access the bank machine would normally seem unnerving to Hanna. But with the help of Ava's brownie and the fact that all eyes were dedicatedly fixed on the strippers, Hanna walked steadily across the club to the bank machine. While she waited for the machine to count out the bills, she glanced over to the main stage where a pink-haired maid with a feather duster danced seductively. She had dropped the top part of her dress revealing her large breasts and used her duster to tickle herself across her nipples and beneath her short apron. She then made her way to the edge of the stage and used her feathers to tickle the face of a customer who looked overjoyed to be there. He rubbed his face briskly back and forth on the feathers and inhaled deeply as if trying to get a thorough whiff of whatever she was offering. He then tossed several bills onto the stage in approval. His thick gold wedding band implied that he was married, and probably not to Molly maid. Hanna wondered what his wife would think had she seen him throwing money at the feet of the young, bare-titted stripper. Some couples had open relationships and some wives told themselves that it didn't matter where their husband's appetite for sex came from as long as he *ate* at home. It was a misogynistic philosophy that Hanna figured was contrived by some self-serving husband. It mattered to Hanna where her lover acquired his appetite. *If she hadn't been the inspiration for her lover's sexual hunger, then he was welcome to satisfy himself with his hand.* Most of the patrons were men in groups of varying sizes but there were also a few couples who had come in hopes of heating things up, adding some spice to their night. Hanna made it back to the table just as the waitress had arrived with their drinks. Hanna paid with the cash and sat down again on the bench. A few dancers were performing lap dances in plain view and several dancers were working their way around the patron's tables, soliciting for lap dances or attempting to coax customers up the wide spiral staircase, to the VIP rooms. Hanna watched a well-dressed middle-aged man descend the stairs from the VIP areas. He looked smug, as if pleased with the service he had received. When he returned to his table, where there were three other men, he received an enthusiastic high five like he'd had a victorious win. Hanna compared the scene to a group of university frat boys. Shauni had glanced toward an older man sitting a few tables over enjoying the company of one of the dancers. The topless dancer was sitting sideways on his lap. She had her arm around the back of his neck as if she were his close friend listening intently to what he was saying. Other than the fact that she had her double D breasts completely exposed, it looked more like they were deep in conversation rather than negotiating a sex act. Shauni looked away unfazed still enjoying the glow from her gummy and marijuana-infused brownie. Ava weighed in on the scene.

"Pretty sly aren't they? The strippers are like pretend therapists. Once they hone in on some unmet emotional need of their customer, they act as if they can fix or fulfill it. She's probably telling that old guy how sexy and important he is."

Shauni partially agreed. "Oh yeah. I'm sure she thinks his *cash* is important." She then laughed animatedly at her joke. Hanna was partially listening but mostly she was scanning around waiting for a glimpse of the dancer named Mandy. Ethan had been watching the brunette dancer who just finished her set on stage. She would be making her rounds on the floor any minute. Hanna wondered what it was, Ethan had found so intriguing about her. She knew she couldn't have been Mandy because she wasn't nearly as curvy as the woman she'd seen in the photo with Jacob. Before Hanna had the chance to ask him, Ethan had thrown his head back and chugged what was left of his drink then briskly sat his empty glass down on the table. "Hanna! Give me a hundred bucks quickly and please don't ask any questions. And you two," He looked at Ava and Shauni with a warning in his eyes that was meant to be intimidating. "Don't say anything! It's Nightqueen346."

Smirking, Ava and Shauni looked at each other and then laughed at Ethan's intended threat, not comprehending who this Nightqueen person was. Hanna reached into her purse and passed Ethan five twenties, just as the dancer he'd discreetly summoned over, arrived at their table. She was a petite, brunette woman wearing thigh-high boots and red vinyl booty shorts that zipped at both hips. Her swaying nipple tassels matched her silver suspenders and tall boots. When she arrived at the table she smiled at each of them.

"Hi! How's everybody tonight?"

Shauni and Hanna were slightly wide-eyed while Ava looked unfazed, admiring the woman's flashy outfit. The dancer wasn't looking to waste precious time but remained friendly. "Are you guys looking for a table dance or a lap dance?"

Ethan answered smoothly, not sounding at all like himself.

"Actually, I was wondering if you could take me somewhere more private."

He had rested his hand on her hip. When she looked at his hand and saw that it was grasping Hanna's wad of twenties, she held out her hand for him to hold. "Sure. I know just the place." Her voice was suddenly a soft and cunning purr.

When Ethan stood up from his chair, the dancer gave him a once over, smiled then guided him up the stairs in her tall boots to the VIP area. Hanna, Shauni and Ava all watched as Ethan was led away to the great unknown of the upper floors. Hanna stared in the direction of the spiral staircase as if Ethan had gone off into the woods with a bear. "Remind me to give that man a raise."

Ava didn't understand how Ethan had earned a raise by getting private services on his boss' dime. "Can someone fill me in? What's happening? I thought Ethan preferred men. Is he just making sure?"

Some of the dancers were sexy but everybody knew Ethan didn't suddenly decide that he wasn't gay. Hanna rolled her eyes at Ava's sarcastic question."Noooo, he's not just making sure he's gay. Nightqueen is the name of the influencer on Instagram that posted the picture of Jacob. He must think she knows something."

Ava turned her head toward the spiral staircase hoping to get another glimpse of the Instagram influencer. Instead, she saw a young man coming down, looking like he'd just been laid for the first time. "I think someone just got lucky."

Hanna felt guilty thinking that Ethan was subjecting himself to something undesirable for the sake of her curiosity. Shauni knew Hanna didn't need to worry about Ethan. It was out of character for Ethan to let anyone do anything he didn't want them to.

"Don't worry about him! I'm sure whatever that dancer does to or for him, won't be that bad, besides a hundred bucks might not get him much more than a couple of dances and maybe a quick pull."

Hanna wasn't sure she knew what Shauni meant by that. "A pull?" she asked.

Shauni made a quick gesture with her hand that looked like she was shaking formula in a baby bottle.

"Oh!" Hanna then understood.

The DJ started a new song and loudly introduced the next dancer as Miss Emanuella. Speaking energetically, he fused the prefix and name making it difficult to understand what he said. Hanna, Ava and Shauni turned to see who the new dancer was. A curvy dancer with long brown hair had strutted onto the main stage. Her top, a sleeveless button-up was tied just below her large breasts and her white micro-skirt glowed electric purple in the UV light. In pace with the beat of the music, she made slow, dramatic, hip-swaying steps toward the center of the stage. She bent down into a crawl position, and like a prowling cat, crept along on hands and knees, graciously giving her audience a premium view up the back of her skirt. She then spun and sat with her knees bent in front of her body. With her chin tipped upwards, she leaned back seductively on the brass pole and used both hands to grasp it above and behind her head. Still holding the pole with her arms raised, she briefly spread wide then closed her legs together again, teasing the onlookers. This generated loud excitement from the groups nearby, followed by an ear-piercing whistle. She then pushed herself into a standing position and effortlessly began twirling, performing gravity-defying moves around the brass pole on stage. From a fitness perspective, Hanna was impressed with how graceful the dancer appeared, going from a seated floor position to standing upright. The dancer looked to have done the move a million times, still Hanna was sure it must have been physically demanding. She was somewhat annoyed and admitted to herself, that she was impressed with her ability. The dancer seductively slid her splayed hands, up and down her body, from the top of her chest, over the mounds of her breasts and down to the front of her pelvis. With her swaying, toned body, Hanna decided the dancer was equal parts seductress and talented gymnast. A few men had moved closer and stood near the stage as they sat bills at her platform heels. When she came to the edge of the stage to entice her admirers, a young man reached up and inserted a rolled bill beneath her elastic thigh belt. She paused briefly allowing him to secure the bill for her and then gave him an appreciative smile. When she raised her long fan-like eyelashes, Hanna could see her striking, dark chocolate coloured eyes. She didn't think she'd seen the girl before but something about her was strangely familiar. With her long hair and dark eyes, she was exactly the type of girl Hanna would playfully tease Jacob about when they watched movies. Jacob had many of, what Hanna called, *TV girlfriends*. If the actress was young, beautiful and had big brown eyes, she qualified. He would never deny it and even smiled when Hanna announced the movie had one of his girls. Whenever Hanna and Jacob would watch a movie starring one of his '*TV girlfriends*' Jacob had no trouble holding his attention. On occasion, Hanna would notice him doing a funny, upper-body adjusting thing when they first appeared on screen. Depending on what the actress was or wasn't wearing, Jacob would sometimes reposition himself through his pants as if his penis had twitched in excitement and he needed to tell it to settle down. Accepting that it was innocent and even funny, it had never bothered Hanna. As of this moment it did. Hanna received a heavy injection of stabbing jealousy. Behind her thick glasses, Hanna's eyes were fixed on the young, brown-eyed woman. She had no doubt this was Mandy, the woman who had derailed her life. Hanna took a couple of deep breaths, trying to hide the effects the adrenaline had on her breathing. Shauni couldn't help but notice the way this dancer held Hanna's sudden interest. "Hanna, you either have a big crush on little miss brown eyes up there or….," Shauni paused. "You think that's her don't you?"

Hanna nodded her head up, then down. Ava looked to Shauni who was in slightly less of a trance than Hanna. "Did the DJ say E-maaaan-uella?" Ava had spaced the syllables for clarity.

Shauni got up from her chair and slid into the bench beside Hanna. They sat there gazing at Mandy with deflated facial expressions. Mandy was much prettier than Hanna would have hoped. She had soft features and big brown eyes that didn't require much makeup to stand out. The second song of her routine had started and Mandy had now removed her top, revealing her large round breasts. They looked authentic which only added to Hanna's stinging irritation. She wasn't sure what she expected Mandy to look like. She just knew, now that she'd seen her, she felt terrible about herself and everything in existence. Shauni put her hand on Hanna's thigh. "We can leave whenever you want Hanna. You just have to say. Ok?"

Hanna nodded again. She looked injured but wore a brave face, refusing to be emotional. "As soon as Ethan comes back I'll be ready."

Ava looked at the stage watching the fresh-faced dancer, thinking she looked like a teenager. "That girl looks too young to even be in here. That can't be her."

Just then the chipper waitress came over with another round of drinks and sat them on the table. Ava reached into Hanna's purse, paid for the round and gave the waitress another bill. "Can you make sure Mandy gets this for me?"

"Sure! Do you want me to just toss it on the stage or..?"

Ava had a mischievous gleam in her eye. "Can you wait till she's done on stage? And make sure you tell her it's from Hanna."

Hanna promptly reached for the closest drink and slung it back as if she were in a drinking contest. She then considered drinking the vodka the waitress had brought for Ethan but knew he'd likely need it just as much as she did, once he finally came down the stairs. Shauni and Ava weren't all that different when it came to looking for trouble and speaking their minds, but even Shauni didn't think it was cool that Ava was being so juvenile. Hanna stared at Ava as if she had just turned into a poisonous snake, sitting proudly coiled in the chair across from her. Hanna was so unravelled, that when she spoke it sounded more like a squeal. "What in the actual fuck? Did you miss the part where we all wore disguises because we didn't want anyone to know our names or recognize us out in the real world? Your voice-over career allows you complete anonymity, I don't have that privilege!" Hanna's raised eyebrows dropped into a frown. "And why would you give that woman any money?"

The alcohol and marijuana were wreaking havoc on Ava's judgment. Hanna swallowed and took a breath trying to calm down. Ava looked so relaxed and unaffected that Shauni too figured it had to be the brownies working overtime. She was envious of that and wished they'd brought the brownies along with them. Ava waved her hand making light of her actions. "Relax Han. Trust me."

Ava reached for her drink on the table and her glamorous red wig shimmered in the light from the pink chandelier glowing above. "The waitress thinks Hanna is *my* name, not yours. And besides, now we know. That is definitely her. That's Mandy. Nobody has any reason to know you or your name. Am I right?"

Avas's hazel eyes watched and waited as Hanna went over the logic. Hanna considered Ava's theory and relaxed slightly as she realized the unlikelihood of someone at The Pink Pearl knowing who she was. She had worn such a ridiculous disguise and looked so different from her usual self that it didn't matter if someone here had learned her first name. Hanna was embarrassed for being so paranoid and losing her cool. Seeing Mandy had completely flayed her nerves. "You're probably right. I really wish the brownie would have had the same effect on me as it did on you."

Mandy's second song had ended and she had moved to a different, smaller stage, further from where they were sitting. The men who had been watching Mandy at the edge of the first stage followed her to the next platform where they could continue to ogle. Hanna wondered if Jacob and his clients had stood at the stage handing money to the dancers. The more clothing Mandy took off the more desperate Hanna was to leave. Hanna decided to sit in one of the chairs, where it was difficult to see the two stages. She didn't need to see Mandy anymore. As soon as Ethan came down and finished his drink, she planned to leave promptly. The club had filled significantly and it seemed there was a dancer at every other table, including theirs. Ava had been approached by a dancer who had asked if she wanted a lap dance. The dancer had introduced herself as Daisy. She was shy and sweet with a chubby round face. Ava felt bad for her after she watched her get turned down by every customer she had approached. Nobody could deny, the spandex outfit she wore wasn't the best look for Daisy. The thong she had on was so snug that what few seams it had looked ready to separate upon the first bend. Ava surprised everybody earlier when she went out of her way to mention Hanna's name, and she'd surprised them again when she took Daisy up on her offer of a dance. Hanna wasn't looking to get up close and personal with the dancers and was utterly annoyed. Feeling as uncomfortable as Hanna, Shauni picked up the tall glass of vodka soda that Hanna had been saving for Ethan and took a big gulp. She passed the rest to Hanna, who finished it gladly. Figuring Ethan would be back soon, Hanna left to use the washroom so she'd be ready to leave once he was back and to avoid being witness to Ava's dance from Daisy. Ava had a much smaller and lighter frame than Daisy. The lap dance would have to be more of a slow-paced, makeshift hover grind. Once Daisy began her dance, Ava smoothly injected casual questions about Mandy. "It must be hard for Mandy's boyfriend when all those men are drooling at her feet like that."

Daisy delayed responding while she focused on her laboured movements. "Well, if she has a boyfriend, he'd be pretty jealous about the things she does here at work."

Daisy didn't seem to mind conversing while she danced, so Ava pressed on with her questioning. "What's the worst thing she's ever done?"

Daisy turned around to twerk briefly, ran her hands down her legs then turned back around. "Everybody knows some of us do extras for certain customers but about two weeks ago she all-out left with a customer for over an hour and a half. I thought the guy abducted her. She paid her nightly fees to the club already and everything. I guess she was willing to lose business for him. Maybe he made it worth it."

"He must have been a special customer," Ava prompted.

"He's special to her alright. He dresses nice, has money and has these big pretty blue eyes. We all call him Mr. Blue Eyes. Nobody gets to dance for him but Mandy."

Out of the corner of her eye, Ava could see Hanna was heading back to the table. Question time with Daisy was over for now. For her dramatic finishing move, Daisy put her hands on the ground and performed a perfect handstand in front of Ava. With her strong arms supporting her body, Daisy lowered her legs so her feet, one on either side of Ava's head, rested on the extra wide, upholstered chair arms. Hanna stood back to avoid getting kicked by Daisy's chunky platform heels. Shauni would have been laughing had it not been for Daisy's response to Ava's last question. She was speculating about who Mr. Blue Eyes was. Daisy then geared up and shook her ass side to side with Ava's head centered between her spread thighs, all the while avoiding any physical contact. Ava's eyes were peering out over the humps of Daisy's butt while she prayed, for Hanna's sake, this was the last act. After Daisy had completed her dance and stood to take a bow, Ethan appeared at the table. Hanna hugged him immediately, needing his comfort after the stress of seeing Mandy. Ava smiled at Ethan looking relieved to be done with Daisy's dance. She thanked Daisy graciously and passed her a few bills. "Thanks Daisy! I loved it! Keep onna' shaken it!"

Daisy folded the bills a few times and then shoved them into her bra. She took a long appreciative look at Ethan, gave a tiny wave and walked away. Everyone in the group waited for Ethan to share whatever he'd learned from the woman who'd posted the photo of Jacob. When his straight face revealed nothing, Shauni decided she couldn't wait. "Sooo? What did the Night Queen say?"

Ethan looked perturbed. "Nothing. She wouldn't tell me anything."

Shauni wondered if he was lying and was slightly offended. "C'mon. Are we supposed to believe you were just up there spending some quiet time together?"

Ethan ignored her question. "Can we just get out of here, please? Hanna, are you ready to leave?"

"I was ready to leave ten seconds after Mandy came out on stage."

Ethan turned toward Hanna at the mention of Mandy's name. He gave her a questioning glance waiting for her to elaborate.

"Yeah," Hanna answered. "We got to watch her take her clothes off and everything. Ava even tipped her."

Ethan glanced at Ava to see her half-smirking, then focused again on Hanna. He could tell by Hanna's expression that seeing Mandy had undoubtedly upset her. He anxiously asked for details. "Shit. You saw her? Are you ok Hanna?"

Ava knew if Hanna started talking about it, she would start crying. Before she could answer, Ava and Shauni stood up in preparation to leave the club. Shauni swung her jacket over her shoulder and motioned by tipping up her chin.

"If we leave right now, you'll get a chance to see for yourself. She just sat down on some old guy's lap. Over there, to the left."

Not giving anyone a choice or even a moment to think about it, Ava strutted out ahead of the group. Shauni followed close behind Ava, who walked with the confidence of a cranberry-haired queen. Ethan walked beside Hanna, clasping her shaking hand. From her seat on the older man's lap, Mandy noticed Ava immediately. Her dark eyes, wide with alarm, followed Ava as she made her way through the club. Ethan had witnessed the entire scene, noting the dancer's remarkable brown eyes. Disheartened by Mandy's unexpected beauty, he squeezed Hanna's small fingers for support. Just as Ethan began to look at Hanna to offer a reassuring smile, Mandy diverted her focus toward Hanna and her round glasses. Hanna, refusing to glance in her direction, stared straight ahead and hadn't noticed the recent attention. Mandy suspiciously stared at Hanna for a moment, then went back to inspecting Ava like she was trying to spot the difference between identical twins. Ethan looked away, able to appear unaffected as he and Hanna passed by, leaving the building. Once outside, Shauni and Ava set up two separate Ubers and waited for them to arrive. The cool, fresh air was a much-needed change to the raunchy air in the overheated strip club. Hanna's teeth had begun to chatter and she was shaking despite not being cold. Shauni took off her jacket and carefully put it around Hanna's shoulders. Hanna shook her head from side to side. "I thought I could handle seeing her but I can't. I was wrong. It hurts." Hanna continued speaking through quietly clanking teeth. "Sh she's pretty, isn't she? I'm n-not surprised, it's not like Jacob's an ugly guy. Anyone would w-w-want him."

It pained Ethan to see Hanna in such a state. She was smart, creative, confident, and the best boss he'd ever had. Not to mention beautiful. Mandy might not have been ugly but she'd had sex with someone who had promised themselves to his boss and very dear friend, Hanna Richards. In Ethan's mind, that put her in the bad books. Hanna didn't deserve what Jacob had done to her. Ethan knew going to The Pink Pearl would only hurt Hanna, the reason he insisted on going along. If he had more time, he would have tried harder to talk her out of it. Knowing what he knew now, all he could do was hug her. When the Ubers arrived, Ethan helped Hanna into the first car and buckled her in. "We'll see you in the morning, Honey. It hurts now but it'll be ok. I promise." He gave her a quick kiss on her cheek and closed the car door.

The car ride to Ava's had settled Hanna's nerves to the point where her teeth were no longer chattering. She spent most of the ride remembering Mandy's painfully entrancing face. It would be impossible for a man to join bodies with her and simply not remember, no matter how drunk he was. Jacob lied to Hanna about the details in an effort to not cause her further anger and pain. That didn't mean he didn't love her, regret it and still want to marry her. She was stupid for going out tonight and for selfishly subjecting her friends. She'd taken a step backward instead of figuring out her feelings and moving forward with Jacob. Hanna didn't know why she was so curious to see the woman and now that she had, could say with certainty, she wished she hadn't.

The Uber had just pulled away from the curb in front of Ava's house when Hanna's cell phone began buzzing. She looked at the screen to see that the caller was Jacob. She hesitated for a minute before answering. Maybe if she spoke to him and heard his voice, she'd somehow feel better. Maybe, he was calling to tell her that nothing was more important to him than she was and that he was taking the next flight home to be with her. Hanna's finger hovered once again over the button. Not wanting to disturb Hanna's conversation, Ava blew her a silent kiss, tossed her wig over the kitchen chair then headed for her bedroom. Hanna answered the phone quietly.

"Hi."

There was a couple seconds of silence as Jacob gauged the sound of Hanna's voice. "Hi. What are you up to? Are we ok to talk?"

Hanna had never lied to Jacob before, but there was no way she was telling Jacob what she'd been up to. "Yeah. I'm fine. Ava and I actually just got in. We went out for a few drinks."

"Oh yeah? Just you two?"

For the sake of his ego, Hanna thought he was making sure there hadn't been any of Ava's male entourage out with them. She didn't need to lie about that. "Shauni and Ethan came with us."

Jacob was silent. He normally got along with both Ethan and Shauni. There was minimal interaction when he'd stopped in at the office the day before, but no reason he should have been bothered by Hanna's choice of company.

"Oh, so there were four of you?"

"Yep."

"Hmm. How are they? Besides the quick Hello, I didn't get much of a chance to talk to either of them the other day."

"They're ok. Shauni just got her new CNC router, so she's excited about that."

"Oh yeah? You mean like a computer router?"

"No." Hanna thought she told Jacob about it when she was ordering it. "Not that type of router. It's a tool that can cut and carve into wood and thin metals."

"Right. I think I remember that now. Sorry."

Hanna figured it was her turn to be courteous. "How is it going over there? Are you close to closing the deal?"

"Yeah, they love it. We're meeting again today to go over some more things."

"Today?"

The time difference between Toronto and London made it just before five am for Jacob.

"Oh wow! So this is more like a very early morning wake-up for you then?"

"Yeah, something woke me up and I couldn't get back to sleep."

Hanna told herself that *she* was the something. "Anything to do with us?"

Jacob was quiet for a second then sighed through the phone. "Yeah, you could say that."

Hanna pictured Jacob lying there bare-chested, unable to sleep, thinking of her. How nice it would be to run her hands over the soft hairs while she cuddled up to him.

"It feels good to hear your voice," she said quietly. Hanna thought she could hear him tapping on his phone.

"It is nice. Can you send me a selfie?"

Usually, when Jacob asked for pictures of Hanna, he had a slow, sexy, compelling quality in his voice that made Hanna want to undress and look as sexy as possible. Their conversation was going well and she didn't want to lose the rhythm by inquiring about his technique in asking. One selfie couldn't do any harm. Hanna had thrown off the terrible thick glasses long before but hadn't had a chance to remove anything else. She flung the dark wig off to the side and removed her sweater, leaving her with a lace bra and short skirt. She shook out her hair, letting the long layers spill over her shoulders. She held her phone out as far as possible, captured the image and sent it to Jacob. It was quiet for a second or two. Hanna presumed it was taking some time for the photo to reach him.

"Nice bra. That's my favourite. You look sexy."

She was basking in his compliment when she heard Jacob make a sound like he'd discovered something unfortunate. "Hmmm, just curious. What's the red thing in the background?"

Hannah glanced at the photo she took, then over her shoulder to where Ava's cranberry wig was draped over the arm of the chair. "Do you mean over on the chair there?"

"Yes. What is that exactly?"

The wig looked a little creepy hanging there. The deep red locks of hair without a body or face.

"It's just a wig. I don't think it can hurt you." Hanna tried to sound playful.

"Very funny. Which one of you was wearing that?"

"Ava was."

He was quiet for a second. "She's pretty damn brazen isn't she."

Jacob didn't sound nearly as playful as Hanna and was making a blunt statement rather than asking a question. Hanna wanted to keep the mood light and hoped his curiosity about her night out was appeased. "That's Ava alright. As my dad would say, *more balls than a juggling clown.*"

When he didn't laugh, Hanna knew Jacob was done talking about Ava and her balls, so changed the direction of the conversation. "Did you and Luke get a chance to visit Buckingham Palace yet?"

"Ha! No, but I've heard the pansy gardens are beautiful this time of year."

Hanna smiled at his comment and pictured Jacob doing the same. They spent the next fifteen minutes talking casually and even joked a few more times. It felt good to be talking amicably with him, helping to bridge the distance between them.

"Maybe we can talk again tomorrow? Will you have some time?" Hanna asked.

"Yeah! I'll see how the day pans out. I should be able to."

Realizing he sounded condescending, Jacob tried to be more reassuring. "I'll make sure we get a chance to talk tomorrow. It's great to hear you laugh........I miss you."

The sincerity in his voice felt like a warm hug and she ached to see him. She wished she could look into his handsome face and have him hold her all night.

"I miss you too."

Hanna would have spoken longer but was just happy to end the conversation on a positive note. "I guess I'll talk to you tomorrow then."

"Yep. I Promise."

They signed off the call with Hanna feeling much better. Despite her unpleasant outing earlier, the light conversation with Jacob did wonders for her mood allowing her to sleep soundly. In the morning Ava and Hanna shared a coffee before heading off to work.

"So. How is Jacob doing? Just thought he'd check in at five in the morning?" Ava's voice held a bit of a snarky edge.

"He said he couldn't sleep."

"Was his guilty conscience keeping him awake?"

Instead of defending Jacob, Hanna leaned over and kissed Ava on the forehead. "Thanks again for taking me in. But I do have to give you shit for giving me false hope that she'd be ugly."

"Who? Oh! You liked Daisy then! She was pretty cute, wasn't she? That last move she did, with her two round…" Ava was holding her two hands up as if she was about to catch a beach ball.

Trying not to laugh, Hanna interrupted Ava's theatrics. "Stop! You know who I mean. Besides, I prefer redheads."

They both looked over at Ava's cranberry wig, still hanging there from last night.

"I don't think Jacob liked your red wig very much."

Ava frowned from behind her coffee mug. "What? How did he even see it?"

"He asked for a selfie and it was just in the background."

Ava tilted her head slightly, going over that in her mind. "The wig was in the background and it made its way into the conversation?"

"Yeah, he saw it and asked about it."

Hanna's smile had faded slightly and she didn't know why Ava thought that was so strange. She was somewhat relieved when Ava got up from her stool to leave. Ava either wasn't willing or didn't have time to elaborate on her thoughts, which Hanna knew weren't good.

"Ok, I've gotta get going to work."

Ava tossed the last bit of coffee into the sink and put her mug in the dishwasher.

"Oh hey! That tech gala is tonight. If you aren't going, try to let me know before lunch."

"Ok! I probably won't be going though. Jacob is supposed to call and I don't want to miss him. I'll see you here after work though."

Instead of making a rude sexual gesture like she wanted to, Ava grabbed her keys, gave Hanna a Cub Scout salute and walked out the door.

Chapter Twenty Three

There was no shortage of women seeking the privilege of being Isaac Fletcher's sexual conquest. A few of his past ladies had proudly bragged online about his bedroom talents which only added to the enthusiasm. Last month it was rumoured he'd been seen leaving a downtown nightclub with Eliza Morgan, a beautiful sports model blowing up the internet and one of the youngest athletes to grace the cover of Let's Get Fit magazine. It hardly hurt his feelings when she told him she couldn't see him anymore, claiming her gymnastics schedule was *too busy*. Isaac had the heart to let her believe she was the one, breaking it off but they both knew it was he, who had already moved on. A week before she called to inform him, he had taken Ryan Vance, his COO and a few friends on a guys-only vacation to Hawaii. While vacationing they enjoyed some heavy sampling of alcoholic beverages throughout the day and provided companionship to the local ladies till dawn. One of the guys on the trip had posted a short video selfie online, costarring a beautiful, sparsely dressed, young Hawaiian woman. Both with a drink in hand, they were cuddling while the girl slowly tickled his bare chest, calling him '*sexy paniolo*'. Eliza Google translated the term, discovering, in English, it meant '*cowboy*'. Slightly blurred in the background was a man with an astounding likeness to Isaac. Sitting on his lap was a dark-haired '*wahine*' of his own. Behind his Ray-Ban sunglasses, the man wore a sly sexy smile and had turned to whisper something into the pretty girl's ear. Whatever he'd said, she found it amusing and was giggling shyly at him. Eliza wasn't overly surprised a video like that had surfaced. She had known going into the relationship that Isaac wasn't one for commitment. Still, she held hope that she might be the one to fasten the reins on this extraordinary man's heart.

At thirty years old, Isaac was six foot two with a dark Clark Kent haircut. When on the longer side, it was just another one of his many pleasing, physical attributes. Some might say that Isaac was built the way a woman would design a man if she could create him all herself. He was athletic and his many extracurricular activities kept him fit and in good shape. He had nice wide shoulders, in perfect proportion to the rest of his wonderful form. When he walked, his strong legs maintained a stride that proclaimed confidence, an undeniable sexual magnetism and the insight of a man prepared for whatever was around every corner. He was the CEO of Skyfleet Robotics. A company specializing in Remotely Piloted Aircraft Systems, commonly referred to as drones. Isaac founded the company while attending university. He graduated with honours from Queen's University in Kingston, Ontario with a degree in Mechatronics and Robotic Engineering. During his final year of university, Isaac submitted his commercial drone business model as a project for one of his classes. His professor suggested the model was unlikely feasible, but despite the discouragement, Isaac pursued the idea further anyway. He built several custom drones with upgraded cameras and audio recorders. He started small by acquiring contracts with upscale real estate agents who needed aerial footage of their property listings. His client list grew when he began getting work orders from other businesses and corporations that would benefit from having an eye in the sky. Later he approached news networks with his *news finder* business model. Isaac set up a website where locations of breaking news could be entered by anyone with a computer or cell phone. A drone was then dispatched to that location to collect video footage. News and social media outlets paid decent money for the footage and in turn, Skyfleet quickly became mainstream. As the Skyfleet drones became more sophisticated and agile, Skyfleet won contracts with delivery companies, online retailers, insurance companies, government agencies, and land survey professionals. The video quality and data reporting were so astounding that he quickly caught the eye of the armed forces, one of his newest clients. Isaac's straight-talk approach when negotiating contracts and explaining the technology had been a welcomed change from the other smaller less sophisticated drone operations trying to win space in the market. His client base was now anyone who wanted an aerial view of just about any location on Earth.

Where Isaac's personal life was concerned, he was sure not to promise anything he couldn't guarantee, like marriage, love or even monogamy. Though a lasting, faithful relationship wasn't an option, open honesty was something he had never faltered with. If the relationship got to a point where questions were being asked of him or someone felt expectations of him weren't being met, he was quick to set the record straight, which undoubtedly meant ending the romance. Consequently, Isaac had never had a relationship that lasted longer than a few months. His career ranked first place before all else and after this latest stint in Hawaii, it was evident Isaac wasn't changing his recreational habits anytime soon. Isaac's reputation as a Casanova wasn't a secret. One might even say he was proud of the way he avoided commitment with the opposite sex. It was easier for everyone that way and made it less likely for anyone to become confused or hurt when the relationship ended. His conscience could fall back on the fact he'd been upfront from the start. Sometimes he would even find himself recycling the same lines he'd use on his long-term hopefuls. "Let's be honest here. We both knew this relationship was based solely on our sexual attraction to each other. Aside from that, our lives aren't heading in the same direction."

Because Isaac was always forthright with his partners, he could convince himself that he wasn't the selfish bastard they'd often accuse him of being. It made for a guilt-free farewell and the most part, a clean and easy break. According to his sister Sadie, it also made him a total dog.

Of course, Sadie still loved him though. The relationship Sadie shared with her brother was unconventional but special. Sadie was six years younger than Isaac and their relationship tended to resemble more of an overbearing father-and-daughter bond instead of a typical sibling friendship. Isaac wasn't shy about overstepping where Sadie was concerned. He felt he had to protect his romantic, disillusioned little sister. They could laugh, joke and hang out comfortably but if Isaac thought for a second that someone didn't have Sadie's best interests in mind, a short exchange with the offender would occur. Their friendly banter was something they both greatly looked forward to. It wasn't a normal conversation for them, without the typical teasing from both ends. They lived in the same building and met once a week for lunch or dinner if their schedules allowed. Isaac was diligent in asking if Sadie needed money or wanted anyone investigated. She had gone on a date recently with someone she met online and told Isaac about him over the phone.

"Oh my god Isaac! You're still doing that? Is that even legal?" She could almost hear him smirking through the phone. "Isaac, you need to focus more on what's going on in your own love life, and not mine. I don't have commitment issues like some of us do!" she mock scolded him.

"Maybe that's the problem, Honey. You're willing to commit way too easily. You can afford to be a hell of a lot pickier than you have been. You're letting these guys do the crime without putting in the time. Most of the guys you find would rather have their balls in a sling than commit." He pictured her rolling her eyes and smiling her beautiful wide smile.

Sadie laughed at his comment. "Yeah. You'd know!" she teased.

"Well, I haven't tried one yet but…"

"Isaac! Gross! I don't want to think about your b…"

He interrupted before she could finish.

"I meant the commitment part you pervert!" he defended himself.

Of course, his sister knew what he meant. Sadie hounded him regularly about his apparent incapability to commit. And he hounded her about her romantic disillusionment about....everything. She loved her brother and wanted him to find that special person who made him want to share himself, his true self. Sadie feared the temporary relationships that Issac engaged in were satisfying his ego and body, but didn't necessarily award him genuine or lasting fulfilment. For the most part Isaac liked it that way.

"Well, there may be hope for you yet!" Sadie professed. "You've said the word commitment twice in five minutes."

"Don't get your hopes up," Isaac laughed, "But I promise you'll be the first to know if I decide to try the sling."

She wasn't going to give him the satisfaction of rattling her again. "Sounds good! You know, you'll probably really like it!"

He smiled and ignored her. "Are we still on for today at Bernard's?" He could hear her talking quietly to someone in the background.

"Sorry just helping these guys pack up an order."

"Sounds like the home staging business is keeping you busy."

"More than you know. Beth's gotten me at least ten gigs this month. She's offended that you don't do the real estate side of things yourself anymore."

"Ha! I'm sure she is! She's lucky I never brought sexual harassment charges against her the way I could have."

"Oh please! she's fifteen years older than you and crazier than a cat in a dog park."

Isaac had to laugh at her analogy. If it had been the other way around and he'd been the one groping his client, he'd have been slapped with a lawsuit and half a dozen mixed versions of what happened would be floating around on social media. It was a double standard he knew but the touchy real estate agent had pushed dozens of large clients in Sadie's direction. She was happier than she'd ever been. If it meant taking some minor, on-fabric ball rubbing to help out his sister, he'd be willing to oblige. *Once.*

"So noon then?" he confirmed, trying to shake off the unwelcome image in his head of Beth molesting his crotch.

"Yep!" She answered. "I'll be there!"

"Ok! See you then."

And with that, they hung up and met at Bernard's for noon.

Bernard's was a restaurant that Isaac liked to call an upscale hole in the wall. It served the best New York strip steak in the city. The interior consisted of two long rows of bench seating with an aisle in the middle that led to the back kitchen. Each table had an elegant chandelier hanging above and a single-lit candle on each table. For its small size, it was luxurious and had great ambiance.

"What's for lunch baby girl? Are we going with the Cab Sauv today or the Grigio?"

Baby girl, had been Sadie's nickname ever since she could remember. Isaac didn't care if other people didn't like it, he didn't even care that Sadie didn't like it. Whenever he would use it in public, she would open her big bright eyes and give him a comical stare down, half smiling of course. He especially liked to use it over their lunch dates, being sure to use it endearingly in front of the young waitresses.

"Just water for me please." Sadie pretended to check the early time on her non-existent watch.

"Then Grigio it is. He said smiling confidently into the waitress's eyes."

"Sure," the waitress offered seductively, "I can do that for you."

She then slowly pulled her gaze away from Isaac's charming face. Isaac briefly watched the waitress strut off for the wine, then turned back to Sadie, already looking forward to her lecture.

"You can't keep calling me baby girl!" she whispered loudly. "People will think we're together. Won't that be bad for your…. *love* life?" she asked sarcastically, hiding a smile.

Isaac grinned and patiently explained his theory to Sadie as if she was a young child. "Yes, you would think being with another woman would impede my chances of scoring. However, it doesn't seem to work that way. In fact, women seem to find it a turn-on when they think they've poached a man away from another woman."

Sadie shook her head and her long dark ponytail swayed back and forth. "What shameless floozies."

She had to give him credit for being partially correct. She did know that women could be competitive and some women considered it a victory if they could *poach* a man as Isaac called it. "A woman that goes after a man who's already promised himself to someone else isn't a woman worth having."

Isaac agreed with her on that point. "I think you're right, but I don't have to tell them that," he said lightly with one of his playful smiles.

Them? It was like he considered all women, advocates of the enemy army. *Is that how her charming brother viewed all members of her sex? Why did he hold them in such contempt?* She adoringly glared at him wondering if he was hopeless where love was concerned. She decided she loved him too much to consider him a lost cause. Sadie knew it would be tough, but there was no reason Isaac shouldn't be able to find someone who checked the many boxes on his wish list. If he decided he wanted to.

"You know, one day you'll meet a girl you really like and you won't even know what happened to you. She'll steal your heart and you won't get it back," shaking her head and wearing a bright smile, she added, "I hope I'm there to enjoy every minute."

The waitress returned with the white wine and a platter of baked appetizers. Isaac took the bottle and filled his glass right full. While holding up his glass in a motion of a toast he promised,

"If a woman comes along and somehow steals my heart, I promise to literally wear a ball sling."

Sadie laughed at his toast and her eyes sparkled with glee at his promise.

"Perfect! I'll start shopping for one now!" And together they sipped their drinks.

CHAPTER TWENTY FOUR

Hanna was still in a good mood after talking to Jacob the night before but during the drive to the studio, she kept thinking about Ava's suspicious reaction to Jacob's interest in the red wig. During her first therapy session, Lisa told Hanna that if she loved Jacob, in time, she would forgive him and want to take a chance at trusting him again. She did still love him and that was what she decided she was going to do. She pulled into the back parking lot, grabbed her phone and purse and headed inside.

Neither Shauni nor Ethan were back in the workshop. Judging by the fresh aroma in the air, they would be out front fuelling themselves with coffee. As Hanna went to push on the swinging door, she could see them standing shoulder to shoulder hovering over a cell phone. Ethan was holding the phone horizontally just under his chin. It was on speaker so that both Shauni and Ethan could hear the caller. A familiar voice was coming out of the phone. It was Ava. She was speaking loudly as if still in her car, driving to work.

"I just don't believe it's a coincidence that he called for the first time in days, just after we'd left the strip joint. I wanted to see if I'd stir anything up by throwing Hanna's name out there and it looks like I did. *And* he asked about the friggin' red wig he saw in the background of a selfie she sent him? C'mon!"

Ethan shook his head. "Please! A straight guy with a sudden interest in women's hair fashions?"

"I kinda hinted it was weird that he asked about it but she didn't see it. Mandy probably called him in a tizzy right after we left. If she knew Hanna didn't normally have red hair she might have mentioned that. I'm thinking they're still in contact with each other."

Ethan and Shauni had no idea Hanna had entered the building. Shauni responded candidly to Ava's comment.

"Holy shit! Thaaat prick! I never even considered that!"

But Ethan had. After he'd seen Mandy eyeing them as they walked by, he knew the name and the person named Hanna was problematic for her. "Did you two see her staring as we left? She kept looking back and forth from you to Hanna."

Shauni had to point out the obvious. "You did give the waitress money to deliver to Mandy. I'm sure the waitress then pointed you out. Your red wig was pretty memorable."

Ethan remembered the look on Mandy's face. "No. Uh uh. It seemed more personal."

Shauni leaned inward toward the phone. "Well, I get why she was confused. No offence, but you two don't look that different, and you were both wearing a similar wig, too."

"Totally not offended Shauni. We've heard it many times," Ava admitted.

The sound of several horn blasts came through the phone followed by Ava shouting, "Let's go ya dildo!"

Shauni and Ethan were running out of time.

"We better let you go, Ava. Hanna will be here soon."

"Ok. Talk soon guys!"

When they turned around Hanna was standing there looking pale and confused. They both thought she was going to be ill. Ethan wanted to shrivel up and hide beneath the closest rock he could find and Shauni was now contemplating some early morning drinking. The three friends shared equally horrified facial expressions, like they'd stepped in gum with their new shoes. Everyone was silent as Hanna walked calmly to her desk, put down her purse, and went to fix herself a coffee. Ethan and Shauni were weary at how unaffected Hanna seemed to be. She'd just overheard her best friend speculating with her two employees about her fiancé. They were waiting for Hanna to acknowledge them, so they could explain and apologize. Hanna took her phone out of her purse and sat it on her desk.

"You two can stop waiting for something messy to hit the fan. I'm not mad at anyone, just a little caught off guard."

Ethan usually made a big deal out of preparing and delivering Hanna's first coffee in the morning, as he genuinely enjoyed it. "Are you sure Hanna? You even went and got your own cup of coffee."

Hanna gave Ethan an affectionate smile and spoke self-assuredly. "I'm just going to call Jacob right now and prove that, what you three think happened was just a result of your much-appreciated, overprotective, friend instincts working overtime. He called me because he couldn't sleep and he missed me. You'll see." She smiled at them again and took a sip of her coffee.

"And if I'm wrong we're going to crack open that bottle of Crown Royal, Shauni has hidden in her cabinet."

Shauni gasped in surprise and gave a guilty smile. "You know about that?"

Hanna winked at Shauni, inhaled deeply and dialled Jacob's cell phone number. Ethan and Shauni proceeded to the workshop so Hanna could have some privacy. Jacob's phone rang several times before he answered.

"Hey. Everything ok?"

Hanna didn't know if Jacob would have any time to talk. "Good morning, am I interrupting anything?"

"No, you have good timing. Luke and I just finished a late lunch. I needed to pop back into my hotel room for a bit. I dropped some sauce on my shirt and came back to change and see if I could save it. I was just thinking about calling you."

Instead of having the pleasure of having Jacob reach out to her, she'd called him with a ridiculous question. She was about to ask him if the reason he called her last night was to ease the mind of a stripper following a visit from Hanna and her friends. Chances were slim she would be able to casually work the question into the conversation. It would be pretty embarrassing if he had no idea what she was talking about.

"Really? I'm sorry. I should've waited. I just had the urge to call."

"No worries. I'm glad. Like I said, I was just gonna call you."

"Are you and Luke meeting with the clients again this afternoon?"

"Luke and I are going to meet up in a bit to go over some things, and then later tonight the clients want us to take them to The Gong. It's a bar slash lounge up in The Shard."

Hanna had heard of The Shard, the tallest building in London, renowned for its angled glass shape and reflective surface. The unique design and brilliant facade captured the changing colours of the sky as well as the lively cityscape. Over the years, The Shard had been the recipient of several design awards.

"Wow! Lucky clients! I hear there are some neat restaurants and bars up there. "

"It was the spot they chose, so we just thought we'd accommodate them."

"You'll have to let me know how it is."

"We'll likely be a bit late getting back so unfortunately I don't think I'll be able to call you afterwards."

"That's ok maybe you can just send me a goodnight text so I get to see it when I wake up in the morning."

"Sure. You gonna do the same for me?"

Hanna loved that he was asking sweetly for a goodnight text. She hadn't sent Jacob a text in several days. It was difficult having gone cold turkey on their communications and now she knew, Jacob had been affected by the sudden absence of their texts as well. Their conversation was stiff at first but had started to feel just like it used to. Hanna began talking in her flirty voice.

"Sure! Maybe I'll even send you a sexy pic or two."

He made a quiet growling sound, expressing his pleasure at the thought. "I sure hope you do."

"Well, I'll do that then."

Hanna knew that sometimes Jacob had a hard time sleeping in hotels when travelling so she thought she would ask how that was going. "Have you been able to get your beauty sleep over there?"

"Ha!" Hanna could tell he was smiling. "Yeah, the bed and the pillows aren't too bad so I've been getting some decent sleep. As long as I don't get any more four am wake-up calls."

Each end was silent as they both registered the implications of what he'd just said. A dreadful feeling flooded Hanna's body like a dark storm cloud appearing out of nowhere.

"You hadn't mentioned it was a phone call that had woken you last night."

"Oh," he cleared his throat, "I just meant that my phone made a noise."

Hanna was under the impression that Jacob had been laying there awake missing her, after thoughts of her had stirred him awake.

"I'm......." Hanna paused, second-guessing herself then forged ahead with her question. "Jacob?"

"Yep," he clipped.

"I need to ask you a question and if you ever want me to fully trust you again, I'm asking that you pleeeease answer me honestly."

Jacob took a couple of seconds to answer as if he wasn't sure he should agree to Hanna's request. He sighed as if he knew what was coming.

"Ok."

Hanna swallowed a painful clump of fear and began to speak in a calm and quiet voice.

"What was the initial reason you called me last night? Did you get a call from someone shortly before you called me?"

Jacob was instantly annoyed and defensive. "What are you talking about?"

These were the exact words he'd used in their bedroom when she'd asked him who Mandy was. After she'd provoked the cold familiar reaction, Hanna knew she was justified in asking but humiliated for needing to. She continued in her soft voice "You said someone called you at four am. Who was it that called you?"

"I called you because I wanted to hear your voice. Christ! I thought everything was going well."

"Me too. Our talk was really nice. But I'm not sure you answered my question. I just need to know that you're being completely honest with me. Always. Are you going to tell me who it was that called you?"

Jacob grumbled a few choice swear words and spoke.

"Ok!" he agreed, but to Hanna, it sounded more like 'Fine, you asked for it!'

Hanna waited for Jacob to tell her that it was Luke who had called him and that she was just being overly suspicious.

"*Someone* from my past called me because they were paranoid that you were out to get them or something. I told them you weren't like that and that was it. I then told them not to call me again."

Hanna listened to Jacob speak anonymously about the caller he only referred to as *someone* and *them*. All the while, she'd been picturing the curvy young woman with the hair that swayed opposite her hips when she walked and of course her memorable brown eyes. Remembering her face was as pleasant as a full body waxing, but what Jacob said had hurt even more. She had to replay it in her mind and say it out loud to make sure she had it right. "I think you just told me that Mandy called you and said she saw me out with my friends. You then called me to see if it was true. What I don't know is why she had your cell number, and how she knew my name or what I look like. I don't think I like that at all. Maybe I should be the paranoid one."

Jacob was taking his time answering. Surely he knew he would have to say something.

"Hanna I just need you to understand that I will never see or talk to her again. I wouldn't have even answered the phone, if I'd known it was her. I made a mistake. I'm sorry."

When he knew he had to say something, he'd confessed and then apologized immediately following.

"She had your number, Jacob. And something tells me you had hers too. Did you call her back right after we laughed and talked, to let her know I wasn't out to get her?"

Jacob didn't want to lie and he didn't want to admit it either. As Hanna waited for an answer, she looked at the small framed photo of Jacob she had sitting on the corner of her desk. It usually made her smile. Hanna took the picture the day he'd asked her to marry him. She had wanted to remember that day forever. She stood up, turned around and faced the wall behind her desk. After an unnerving amount of time had passed and Jacob still hadn't said anything, Hanna began to feel an unrelenting sting in her eyes. Promising herself she wasn't going to cry, she tried to blink it away. She had a business to run and work to do. It was time to get off the phone.

"I'm gonna have to let you go for now Jacob. Be safe over there."

"Wait! Hanna!"

Jacob had started to plead, trying to keep Hanna on the line but she ended the call before he could finish. Hanna had never hung up on anyone before. She felt childish for not giving him a chance to finish what he was saying and hoped she was warranted in her reaction. *Why couldn't he answer her question? Did he call the brown-eyed stripper after they'd ended their call last night?* When she turned around Ethan was at the coffee machine holding up the pot, offering to top up her coffee. Hanna looked at the pot and then called out Shauni's name.

"Hey, Shauni!"

A second later, Shauni swung open the workshop door, appearing from the back as if she were a secret service agent being summoned for protective duty. She was carrying a crown-shaped bottle of whiskey and three glasses. Ethan and Hanna watched Shauni set the items down on the counter with utmost efficiency. Shauni looked at Ethan with bright eyes, expecting him to compliment her on her speedy service. Ethan couldn't resist the opportunity to tease. "What no ice?"

Shauni stared at Ethan with the usual cat-like glare she gave him whenever he tormented her. "Ice is for babies."

The idea of a stiff and numbing drink was more than tempting, but all Hanna wanted, was a heart-to-heart talk with her friends. "We don't need any ice or alcohol. As much as I want to, I'm not going to.

I need a clear head right now. Not to mention, we do have work to do, we can't be all wasted."

Shauni picked up the bottle, disappointed that the prospect of day drinking had evaporated. "Crap. I was looking forward to that."

Ethan grabbed Hanna's mug, topped it with coffee and handed it to her.

When Shauni returned from putting the liquor bottle away, Hanna summarized her conversation with Jacob. "Ava was right. Mandy called him right after we left the strip joint. She was worried that I was coming after her."

Shauni gave Hanna a surprised look. "So she knew it was you? What? Even in the wig? But..... why would she know what you look like and know your name?"

"I think when Ava sent money over with the waitress and gave my name, it drew attention to us."

Ethan was struggling to hide his frustration at Hanna's denial. "But Hanna, that doesn't explain why she had the slightest idea who you were. Is she asking for all the names of her customer's wives and girlfriends then making sure she knows their faces in case they come after her?"

Shauni was examining the framed picture of Jacob on Hanna's desk, noting the memorable blue eyes. "Well, depending on how many wives and girlfriends she screws over, her job might have some occupational hazards. Maybe she's right to be paranoid." Shauni sat the frame back down. "What did Jacob say when you called him?"

"We were having a good conversation then when I asked how he'd been sleeping, he let it slip that someone had called and woke him up. I knew it was her because he didn't want to tell me who it was. When I asked why she had his number he quit talking." She paused briefly, feeling guilty. " I kinda hung up on him."

Hanna looked rueful, thinking about Jacob's unfinished sentence and wondered if he was about to say something that would explain everything.

Ethan couldn't stand there and let Hanna torture herself. The possibility that Jacob only called last night because Mandy wanted to know if Hanna had been at The Pink Pearl was beyond maddening.

"You aren't the one who needs to feel guilty Hanna. Your fiancé cheated on you and naturally, you wanted to see who she was. She shouldn't know your name, your face or anything else about you. That orifice of a fiancé needs to step up and explain that to you!"

Shauni was surprised at how to the point Ethan sounded. She was so impressed that she clapped a few times for him.

"That was awesome and even kinda sexy."

Ethan had surprised himself with the outburst. He rolled his eyes in Shauni's direction and cleared his throat. "Well, it felt weird. I'm sorry if I sounded rude. Maybe I should lay off the coffee."

Hanna appreciated Ethan's honesty. "You weren't rude. You were just telling it like it is."

Without having the opportunity or desire to ask Mandy about the relationship she had with her fiancé and Jacob sitting mute, Hanna was in the dark. Just when she began to feel a flicker of hope for her relationship with Jacob, she became aware, that Mandy not only knew her name and what she looked like but also felt comfortable enough calling Jacob on his cell phone. It wasn't difficult to look someone up online and find a photo or contact number. And maybe that's all Mandy did. Jacob said she was paranoid, but he didn't say how she knew Hanna's name. *Did she look that up too?* Most of the logical explanations were disheartening but Hanna wanted the truth. The ball was in Jacob's court now. He could reach out when he was ready to make sense of everything if that were even possible. Hanna reached down and turned over the picture of Jacob so it was facing downward. The stripper played a role in damaging her relationship with Jacob but Hanna wasn't giving her the power to ruin anything else. "How about we all move on to something else for now? Let's do our *daily*. Ethan, did we start gathering everything for the sweet sixteen?"

Ethan was fine with changing the subject if it took Hanna's mind off of Jacob.

"Yep, I've got all the bins in the back room, loaded and labelled. The tent, cake, dishware, and tables are being delivered to the location the morning of. The DJ and the mentalist have confirmed as well."

"Ok! Sounds good. We're on site tomorrow prepping for the home renovation show so we should make good use of our time here today. We also need to touch base with GlassScapes and confirm what time we're meeting in the morning."

"They're aiming for about ten," Ethan offered.

"Ok, thanks!" Hanna made a quick note on her iPad."Shauni did we end up getting the tint-safe window cleaner we had last year?"

"Yep! Two litres. It's all packed in tomorrow's bins with the shammies already. "

"Perfect. I think that's all I've got."

Ethan situated himself at his desk and Shauni walked into the workshop holding two thumbs up. "Sounds good!"

Hanna began working at her desk on her laptop and a few minutes later her phone buzzed. Ethan glanced over at Hanna to see if it was Jacob trying to explain why Mandy had his cell number and how she knew who his fiancé was. Hanna shook her head so Ethan would know it wasn't Jacob. It was Ava texting.

Hey! Did you decide if you were going to the charity thing with me tonight?

Before leaving for the office that morning, Hanna told Ava that she probably wasn't going to the gala that evening because she didn't want to miss Jacob's call. Since speaking with him that morning she'd had a change of heart. Now that her pride wouldn't allow her to sit and wait for Jacob to call, she was free to go along to the gala. Lisa had prescribed a dose of *Have Fun!* By accepting Ava's invitation, she could also convince herself she was taking the advice of her therapist. Ultimately she was relieved she had something to distract her, at least for one night anyway. Hanna picked up her phone to reply.

I'm coming. When are we leaving?

Yaaaay! We don't need to be there for the scholarship part, so let's aim to leave at 8

Ok see you at your place tonight, you'll have to lend me a dress.

No problem! I've got lots!

Hanna focused her attention on a booth design for the upcoming home renovation exhibition. The client, GlassScapes, a window manufacturer, participated in the show every year. This year, they wanted to showcase their new line of windows that automatically adjusted the glass' level of transparency, depending on the intensity of the sunlight outside. In addition to reducing the purchaser's cooling bills, the window's privacy level could also be adjusted. It was a product sure to get some positive attention at the Exhibition. Hanna wished the innovative windows had been around when she and Jacob renovated the Tudor. For Hanna it didn't seem to matter what task she was working on, everything seemed to steer her thoughts to Jacob. She knew it was pathetic. She was still willing to hear Jacob's excuse for calling Mandy to reassure her, that Hanna wasn't planning any revenge. He hadn't said it, but his silence made it obvious. He called the dancer after saying his goodnight to Hanna. She'd be fooling herself if she didn't admit the idea of them speaking over the phone, didn't infuriate her. Hanna wished she would have had a better hold of her nerves, the night before at the strip club. The thought of giving Mandy a reason to fear her a little was certainly appealing. Hanna wondered if she may have even enjoyed herself, had she known the moment the waitress handed Mandy the money and said Hanna's name, Mandy was instantly fearful. Hanna wasn't violent and wasn't seeking revenge, but part of her still liked the idea that Mandy had to worry that she might be. At least until Jacob had so valiantly called her back to reassure her that Hanna wasn't a threat. He was probably surprised when Mandy told him, that a red-headed Hanna showed up at The Pink Pearl and sent her money via the waitress as if saying *hi*. It was Ava who had sent the money and announced the name but Mandy thought it was Hanna. Jacob's Hanna.

Hanna had truly hoped that the time she and Jacob spent apart would give them both a chance to realize how much they meant to each other. She hoped to repair their relationship before their wedding so that going into the marriage they would both know it was right. For Hanna, the distance was also meant to be a time for healing and self-reassurance that she could trust Jacob again. She needed to believe that the reason he'd ended up sleeping with someone else wasn't because she'd failed him in any way but because, as he said, he'd been incredibly drunk. Hanna couldn't imagine ever being so drunk that she suddenly thought it was a good idea to take her clothes off for someone other than Jacob. She just missed what they had and wished there was a way to get it back. Most of the day was hectic for Hanna, making final arrangements with GlassScapes and helping Shauni find a couple of extra labourers for tomorrow's booth setup. GlassScapes had their own team of window installers but they needed to work in sync with Richards and Co. for placement and layout within the booth. They had always been a dream to work with. Glen Daniels, the owner was a rough and tough, fifty-something country boy who had built his window empire from the ground up. He was the type of businessman who liked to meet each of his customers personally and would thank them genuinely for their business. Most people who met Glen underestimated him. It was Glen himself and his wife who helped create the thermochromic window design. Hanna was fond of Glen and his work methodology. He didn't mind getting his hands dirty and made a point of working with his crew on every window installation. Hanna always looked forward to seeing him and his team at the exhibition setups. Glen would never fail to deliver a cheeky joke, which brought out his East Coast accent. Hanna hoped Glen would be around for the setup tomorrow at the expo so she could tell him she appreciated his loyal business.

Later in the day, Shauni and Hanna loaded up the company van so they would be ready to start first thing tomorrow morning. Hanna had briefly forgotten that she agreed to go along with Ava to the gala tonight and when she remembered, she hoped Ava wouldn't keep her out too late. Booth setups could be exhausting with all the running around and an extra long day was usually expected. Starting the day already tired was just asking for trouble. If she wasn't careful she could even end up with a wretched migraine. Toward the end of the day, Hanna still hadn't heard anything more from Jacob. She knew he'd be busy with his clients, drinking in luxury, up in The Shard as mentioned and likely couldn't call. Even a short text from him would have done wonders for Hanna's sagging mood. She was relieved she had plans for the night and wouldn't be sitting around by herself feeling crappy about the call she'd ended with Jacob.

Finally, it was time to finish up for the day. Ethan had left moments before, for an appointment and Shauni was throwing in a few extra battery packs for the drills into the van. She was driving it home for the night and would drive straight to the exhibition in the morning with everything they needed.

"I'm locked and loaded. You ready to jet?"

As Shauni slammed the two rear doors of the van, she noticed Hanna looked tired and sad. "So where are you guys going Han?"

Hanna pulled on the back door of the building and twisted the key in the lock.

"Ava was given tickets to a charity gala from someone she did voice-over work for. There's no way she was going to waste them. You know how she likes to get glammed up!"

Shauni raised her eyebrows and pursed her lips. "Ooh! So, this is a formal black-tie affair. Mmmmm, I love a man in a tux. There's just something about it that makes me wanna throw em' on the floor and just…..arrgh!" Shauni trailed off, squinting and hungrily biting her lip. Hanna smiled at the X-rated tuxedo fantasy. Shauni jumped up into the high seat of the van, started the engine, and opened the window. "Bye, Hanna! No one's gonna blame you for shagging one of those sexy James Bonds! See you in the morning!"

Hanna waved back at Shauni, then drove off toward Ava's. They would have lots of time to eat dinner, get ready, and, as Ava called it, do some pre-gaming. Hanna was looking forward to that part. After a full day of overthinking about why Jacob made no effort to reach out, she felt like an overtightened guitar string. Yes, she had hung up on Jacob, but only after he wasn't willing to admit he contacted Mandy after speaking with her. Instead, he'd gone completely silent. Hanna wanted to believe that couples who were working through their problems were denied the privilege of *pleading the fifth*. Just thinking about it got her nerves fired up again. Jacob should have called her back today. He should have stopped her from leaving when she packed up her suitcase. He should have come to her and explained that he'd made an awful mistake and felt the need to tell her immediately because he couldn't bear keeping it from her. If he only knew what a difference his efforts would have made for them both.

Ava pulled into the driveway a few moments after Hanna. She was excited that she was getting a second season as the voice of the evil, cartoon bunny *Grenna* and figured tonight could be an impromptu celebration. Hanna was happy for her and didn't want to pollute her good mood by sharing any of the Jacob drama with her. While they waited for their dinner to bake in the oven, they went into

Ava's closet to find something to wear. Ava slid the hangers back and forth looking expertly at the row of dresses. She had a dress for every occasion. Finally, she stopped, looking at a short-length, white knit dress with long slender sleeves. The dress overlapped at the front and had a tie-up belt at the waist. Hanna looked longingly at the dress knowing it would look awesome on Ava. Everything looked awesome on Ava.

"Here!" Ava grabbed the dress and handed it to Hanna. "You need to wear this tonight."

Hanna held up the dress, still on the hanger. "Oh! It's for me? Thanks! Will it fit me?"

Ava had already moved on, now searching for a dress for herself.

"One of these days you'll learn to trust me, Han. Sometimes I just know things."

Ava sounded pretty sure of herself so Hanna didn't argue. The dress fabric was slinky and lightweight and had a gold sheen woven into the fabric. It would match Hanna's heeled shoes perfectly. Ava knew this too of course.

After they'd eaten Ava's baked chicken dinner they started getting ready for the gala. The dress Ava had chosen for Hanna fit her exquisitely. The bottom hem rested mid thigh showing off her smooth, toned legs, and the low cut, crisscrossing front, drew attention to her round breasts. For herself, Ava chose a long satiny pink spaghetti strap, low cut, cowl neck dress. The lower portion of her dress had slits up to her mid-thigh on both sides revealing her long shapely legs. She straightened her blunt bob for a glamorous look while Hanna scrunched her locks, creating loose, natural, long waves. She completed her outfit with her silver and jade earrings. They each picked out an evening purse to match their dress, then stocked them with lipsticks, phones and their gala tickets. Ava glanced in the doorway mirror. "Damn. We look good!"

Ava took a selfie and then instructed Hanna to stand beside her so she could get a photo of them together.

"I'll send it to Jasper. He asked me to send him a picture."

"For sure!"

Hanna suddenly felt like Ava's plus one should have been Jasper.

"No need to feel guilty now, Jasper's out of town. He comes back tomorrow."

"Oh!" Hanna wanted to make sure she captured Ava and her pink glamorous appeal.

"Well, let's get a good one for him then!"

For best lighting, they went outside where Ava pretended to lean back seductively against the deck railing. She extended both arms at her sides and rested her hands on the wide railing. With one hip slightly bent to show off her curvy waist, Ava looked like a hazel-eyed movie star ready for the red carpet.

"I gotcha!" Hanna gushed.

"And I got you, babe! Stand here and I'll get some of you now!"

Hanna traded places with Ava and let her snap several more photos. On the car ride to the Gala, Hanna sent her dad one of the photos that Ava had taken. To her surprise, he responded almost immediately.

Beautiful Honey! Where are you going?

To avoid getting into anything regarding Jacob, she answered,

A charity gala

Enjoy yourself, Honey. Be safe!

She would have to make the drive home to visit him soon. It had been several weeks since she last visited and she had yet to tell him about the postponement.

Ok, Dad! Love you!

The ScholarsNTech gala was at the Riley Event Building on the north side of the city. With its deep amber glass and silver steel exterior, the building had an ultra modern appeal. Once inside, Hanna and Ava were invited into the elevator and chaperoned to the fourteenth floor where the event was taking place. The large ballroom had a stage at one end of the room with plush, floor-to-ceiling curtains and on the opposite end, a long bar stretching the length of the space. There were dining tables covered with crisp white linen, topped with large floral centrepieces and formal brass dining chairs. Several bar-height tables with stools were situated near the bar area and large artificial trees were placed near each high table and throughout the room. An extravagant chandelier hung from the center of the ballroom and several identical, smaller versions, hung over each table. Now that the scholarships had all been awarded, the lights had been dimmed subtly, and the volume of the music had been slightly elevated. Hanna and Ava were both taken by how elegant the banquet room was. Hanna noted the heads in tuxedos and dresses turning to catch a glimpse of her and Ava as they walked into the hall.

"Wow! This is more elaborate than I expected."

Hanna spoke quietly, attempting not to draw more attention to herself than she already had. Ava wasn't wasting any time checking out the offering at the bar and Hanna didn't bother objecting. The pre-gaming they hoped for before leaving Ava's place, didn't happen. When Ava went to open a bottle of wine for her and Hanna to drink as they got ready, she regretfully found the cabinet void of alcohol.

"Let's go over and check out that bar!" Ava suggested.

"You read my mind."

A tall, bow-tied bartender was located in the center of the bar and another was at the far end. Both bartenders were busy pouring and stirring mixed drinks for the guests. Ava and Hanna naturally, chose the closer location to gravitate toward. While they waited for the bartender to finish up his current request, Hanna was deciding what she wanted to drink. If only there was some magical elixer that could take her far away for a while. She could forget temporarily that her relationship felt as if it was on the brink of being over. Ava wanted to be ready to order when the busy bartenders asked what they'd like to drink.

"What'll it be sexy?" Ava asked Hanna.

"Well, normally I'd say a glass of Pinot Grigio but you know what? I'm looking for some more nostalgia this evening."

"Hey, who can blame you? Malibu-soda and a splash of seven then?"

"Yes please."

"Ok, I'm on it."

It was like old times yet again, both women dressed to impress, standing at the bar, enjoying each other's company. Not long after they'd enjoyed a few cocktails, servers dressed in formal white shirts came around, serving ornate appetizers that looked like creamed cheese roses swirled onto circular crackers. Hanna and Ava each had a couple to see if they tasted as good as they looked. Ava was pleased that Hanna was out enjoying herself instead of sitting at home alone thinking about Jacob. Ethan had texted Ava to let her know that her hunch about Jacob was correct. As far as Ava was concerned, Jacob was an absolute write-off. She wanted the best for Hanna and that wasn't Jacob. Looking around the hall, Ava was assessing some of the men, not for herself, but for Hanna. Some were the underaged recipients of the tech scholarships, but besides that, there looked to be a good assortment. Using the lower-pitched tone she used for her evil bunny character, Ava noted, "There are some very nice specimens here tonight," then did her bunny character's evil little laugh.

Hanna laughed at Ava's rendition as she glanced curiously around the hall. "I'm still engaged Ave."

"Yes, you're wearing a ring, but you're not married. Thankfully. Not to mention, I just saw you do some scanning around. You're curious. Enjoy yourself, Han! Have some fun! Talking with some of these guys will do wonders for your self-esteem!"

Hanna sipped on her cocktail while she covertly considered Ava's suggestion.

"The last time we mingled with other guys, you ended up kissing one of the band members at Patty's Irish Pub."

"Exactly! Jasper's a great guy! Speaking of Jasper, I can get you Noah's number too if you want! He thinks you're amazing!"

Hanna smiled demurely. "Noah is a very nice person and I'm sure you're right. There are probably lots of nice-looking men here tonight. But right now I'm just looking to have a nice night with my favourite gal and take my mind off things."

"That's admirable but I want you to know that if you wanted to nail every guy in this room for some revenge sex, I wouldn't judge you and I definitely wouldn't blame you. I'll even be your wingman."

They said cheers and clinked their glasses together. After a couple more cocktails, both Ava and Hanna needed to use the washroom. It was large and busy which caused them to lose track of each other. Hanna figured if she returned to their original perch at the bar they were bound to sync up again. When she returned to the bar Ava was speaking with a tall, slim woman in a stylish pant-suit. The woman was holding a tablet, signalling she had a role other than attendee. Hanna was feeling the buzz of the rum and was nervous they were being cut off at the bar. As embarrassing as it was, it wasn't the first time she and Ava had been told they'd had enough. Just then, both Ava and the woman erupted into laughter. Ava introduced her associate to Hanna as Fiona Bergman, the woman who had given her the tickets for tonight's gala. Hanna shook hands with Fiona and thanked her for the considerate gesture. As Ava and Fiona continued their conversation, Hanna kept a slight distance and ordered herself a drink. Looking around at some of the men standing around the hall, Hanna couldn't help but think of Shauni's comment from earlier. Shauni wasn't wrong. A man in a tuxedo did have a certain dose of sex appeal. The right man in a tuxedo might just inspire you to climb up on top of him as Shauni had suggested. As Ava continued her conversation, Hanna pretended to challenge herself, to visually find a man, she would consider sleeping with. In the past, Hanna would have felt that browsing for other men was a mild form of cheating but for the moment she allowed herself the liberty. As she scanned the men in the room, she locked eyes with a man with dark brown hair, dressed in an impeccably fitting tuxedo. Hanna thought he was so attractive, that she let out a tiny gasp and quickly looked away. To shake off his effect, Hanna attempted to rejoin the conversation with Ava and Fiona.

From across the banquet hall, Isaac casually watched her. He wasn't trying very hard to hide the fact he'd been fixated on this woman since he first saw her over an hour ago. Standing in a small group of women, she was mingling sociably and drinking cocktails. Her hair was the colour of warm brown sugar and honey as it rested just above the center of her perfect but natural, he happily noted, breasts. She was wearing a crisscross-style dress that Isaac thought, hugged her curves deliciously. It was held closed with a slinky belt that rested around her tapered waistline and hung in a loose bow. He knew it wouldn't take much to pull it loose and have it untie, bearing her seductive curves. *I know what I'd like to use that little string for,* he thought, then slowly shifted his eyes downward to her slender wrists. He was curious as to what shade of pink her nipples were. *Was her skin creamed gold or was it fair and sensitive to the heat of the sun?* He couldn't help but wonder what secret treasures he might find under that dress. Standing among the small group of guests with his rye glass in one hand, Isaac might have looked as though he was listening to the men in his circle with interest.

"Isn't that right Isaac?" Ryan Vance, one of the men, asked curiously.

"Oh, for sure, definitely," Isaac replied, only half-turning and not knowing exactly what it was he was so definite about. He then raised his eyebrows and nodded, the way he'd been doing every so often to fake interest. With each sip of rye, he took the opportunity to allow his partially sheltered eyes to linger longer than some might consider decent. He didn't care much, what anyone thought or whether he was being decent or not. This whole charity gala wasn't his idea, not because he wasn't charitable but because he wasn't in the mood for this kind of party. Vance the company COO had suggested that Skyfleet partially sponsor the event, for good publicity and public perception of the company. Isaac had to admit, when he caught sight of the huge banner with the company name, hung above the central bar, it did give him a sense of satisfaction. But not nearly as much of a thrill as the sexy young woman standing beneath it. Up until that moment, Isaac assumed the night would be another small talk, high school prom he would rather not attend. He'd settled in at a bistro table with a full whiskey glass hoping to keep a low profile. The table was tucked beside a tall potted palm tree on either side. In hopes of making the night tolerable, he requested the young waiter, visit him and Vance regularly and passed him a few folded bills. "See you again soon my friend." The waiter nodded his understanding and then disappeared, scurrying eagerly toward the bar. A short while later, after Isaac had finished his first glass, he'd lifted his chin and glanced around to see if his waiter friend was on the way with another drink. That's when he'd spotted the sexiest pair of legs he'd ever seen. He was pleasantly surprised when he scanned upward and discovered they were attached to a delicious body and a very pleasing face. He hadn't seen the woman before but he knew he planned on seeing her again. Despite Isaac's best efforts to be invisible that evening, several young men had gathered around the bistro table hoping to get a few minutes with the executives of Skyfleet. He'd been hoping to avoid that part of the evening or better yet, all parts of the evening. He had just returned to the city that afternoon from a tech conference in New York. His vehicle had been stolen a few days ago and while flying home from the conference, the airline had lost his suitcase full of clothing, a laptop and a bottle of Johnnie Walker Blue whiskey. Isaac treated himself to the whiskey when he popped into the specialty liquor shop next to his hotel. He was going to shake off the loss with a few stiff drinks and a damn good look at this very pretty lady. He let Vance handle the chitchatting while he got his tenth better look at the woman beneath their banner. How perfect it would be to take her home and have his way with her and her body for a few hours at the end of the night. He imagined the different ways he would make her moan under his sheets. Once given the chance he would tease her until she begged him to finally let her come, again. He wondered which sex positions she liked best. Did she prefer it from behind where he could reach forward with his long arms and rub that little sweet spot for her? Or maybe she liked it on top where she had control and could slowly rotate her hips, grinding her body against him until she finally found her release. There were countless ways but he would happily take her any way she wanted him to.

Isaac was now surrounded by industry associates hoping to collaborate with Skyfleet on contracts. He might have had these stooges fooled but Vance, who was watching him closely, knew his attention was fixed elsewhere. Ryan Vance wasn't just Isaac's right-hand man, he was Isaac's closest friend. He knew Isaac wasn't the slightest bit interested in hearing any more business proposals tonight. Reluctantly, peeling his eyes off the sweet thing across the room, Isaac turned to one of the men. "Thank you, gentlemen. Why don't you leave us your contact info and we'll set something up. It was nice meeting you."

Taking the hint, the men walked away feeling hopeful they'd be hearing from the executives of Skyfleet in the somewhat near future. Isaac could finally get some peace. He took a minute to enjoy the short-lived silence.

"She's married my friend," came the amused but sympathetic voice of Ryan Vance. When Isaac seemed to have ignored him he added, "Her name is Hanna Richards, the wife of Jacob Barber, the CEO of a digital payment company called Nextech."

Isaac exchanged his empty glass for two full glasses from the waiter's drink tray and handed one to Vance. He was smirking as if he'd just become aware of some important and pleasing news. Isaac knew of the so-called husband, Jacob Barber. The last time he heard mention of *Mr. Nextech,* he became aware of the news quietly circulating that the cash app executive had recently cheated on his pretty fiancé, *not* his wife. It was in New York while attending the technology conference that Isaac, involuntarily overheard the gossip. The two young women seated diagonal to Isaac were in disgusted shock, that the poor woman chose to stick with her fiancé after the cheating dog he'd been. "She should've completely called off the wedding! I would have," the one woman had pleaded, then added, "She's so pretty and that slut he screwed in his back seat...." When the woman turned her head and saw Isaac sitting there looking amused, she was surprised and embarrassed. Isaac gave her a reassuring friendly nod. She seemed to like that. Isaac didn't care who Jacob Barber was screwing in his car. But he was mildly curious who the *pretty* wounded fiancé was, who'd stood by his side. She had certainly won the loyalty of the two young women at the technology conference. Isaac lived by his own twisted rules, he knew, but convincing someone you would be faithful to them, and then cheat behind their back was outside, even his moral realm. Jacob and Isaac didn't move in the same circles very often but it sounded like Jacob moved in the same circles as the women at the conference. It was only chance, that Isaac had overheard the women that day and an even bigger coincidence that Hanna Richards was here, in the same room as him tonight. Isaac was more than happy to set the story straight for Vance. "Actually, no, they aren't married."

Isaac continued to steal glances at the beautiful woman standing across the room.

"Well, they might as well be," Vance retorted. "Do you see that big glittery ring on her pretty little finger? Apparently, the guy spent over $50k on it."

"Hmmm, impressive," Isaac responded thoughtfully. He didn't think, that was too much money to find out how sweet she tasted.

"I bet she's worth it," he quietly wagered, then sipped again on his rye.

Vance's eyebrows slowly formed into a perplexed frown, as he stared curiously at his friend. He had to glance over at this woman again, to see what it was about her, that his friend had found so mesmerizing. The last time he'd seen his friend so enthralled, was during the testing of their drone cloaking technology. Skyfleet's testing was successful and allowed them to proceed with the latest contract, a huge victory. Vance couldn't argue. She was certainly a pleasure to look at, but Isaac had always been abundantly lucky with the ladies so it wasn't like he was hard up for sex or companionship. Vance knew that once Isaac had decided on something, it could take effort to change his mind. He wasn't the type of man to shy away from a challenge or let obstacles intimidate him. Isaac looked around and wondered if the cheating fiancé had come along with Miss Richards this evening. So far there was no sign of a male companion anywhere and he hoped she had left him at home. He then thought what a simpleton this Jacob guy would have to be, to cheat on someone that looked like her and then let her go out without him, looking that incredibly sexy. The honey-haired woman had caught his eye from across the room, and the minute he saw her, he wanted her. Isaac knew that usually any worthwhile investment paid off with a little patience. He could be patient if he needed to. He'd shown his face long enough at the gala but wasn't leaving without being introduced to Miss Hanna Richards.

A couple of Fiona's associates had now come over to join the group. Ava's stunning looks and her *Life of the Party* personality had always drawn both men and women. Hanna wasn't surprised when their group of two, had grown to be five women and two men. The two women most recent to join the group, seemed only half engaged in the conversation and kept stealing curious glances over Hanna's shoulder. Hanna had been drinking steadily and hadn't noticed or stopped to check who had been standing there behind her. Judging by the masculine voices, there was now a group of men who were standing a couple of feet away from her. With her back toward them, Hanna couldn't see what they looked like but wondered if that explained the keen interest coming from Ava's newest friends. Hanna was instantly more intrigued by who was behind her, rather than in front of her. With a threatening undertone, one of the men had quietly spoken to the other. When he was finished, Hanna heard the other respond by repeating a saying that her dad always said to her when she was having a bad day. "Well my friend, you can't have a rainbow without the rain, can you?"

Not only did the comforting phrase from her childhood send a quick warm ripple over her nerves, but the deep masculine voice who said it, caused the fine hairs on Hanna's arms and neck to stand. It was like a magnetic force had been triggered from within, pulling her toward him. Curiosity overcame her and the alcohol further encouraged her to turn and see the face of the man, from which this tempting, deep voice had originated. Hanna glanced up toward the high ceiling as she turned around, trying to look inconspicuous. When she had turned enough to see who was there, she found two tall, well-built, nice-looking men in tuxedos. One of the men was the good-looking stranger she'd locked eyes with earlier. He was leaning casually against the bar holding a highball glass in his hand. In his white tuxedo jacket, black bow tie and classic Clark Kent hairstyle, he could have been the most striking James Bond character, there ever was. His companion looked slightly less relaxed and had raised an eyebrow at his friend in the white jacket as if sending him a silent warning. His stylish, slicked-back hair was almost black, complementing his dark eyes and all-black tuxedo. Both men looked between thirty and thirty-five years old. They had pivoted in Hanna's direction after she had turned around to peek at them. The man leaning on the bar then smiled at Hanna so warmly, that she felt an instant flash of feverish heat not only in her cheeks but in places she was thankful to have concealed. Then in the same voice that had repeated her dad's time-honoured phrase, he spoke to her in a familiar, calm and pleasant manner. "Well, Hello there."

It was like he'd known her his whole life and was pleased to have seen her after a long absence. His friend with the slicked hair glanced at Hanna, smiled politely, gave a quick nod and then walked away as if he'd been given an invisible cue. Hanna now stood there alone with the handsome stranger. She was trying to regroup from her internal flustering and the only thing she could respond with was a high-pitched, "Hi, I'm Hanna."

Looking slightly amused at her discomfort, Isaac stood up straight and held out his hand so he could properly introduce himself. Reaching out with his large warm hand, he gave what Hanna thought was the perfect handshake. Firm enough to feel but not a contest of strength, the way men often do. "Hi Hanna, I'm Isaac Fletcher. It's nice to meet you."

Hanna was taking in the shape of his bright eyes and inviting smile.

"Would you like to have a drink with me Hanna?"

She wanted to. He'd only politely asked if she wanted a drink, but the invitation felt devilishly forbidden as if saying '*yes*' would have life-changing consequences. Saying yes to one drink wasn't the same as agreeing to sex or anything else. Hanna glanced over at Ava as if she needed to check in or ask for her permission. Ava was smiling ear to ear in Hanna's direction as if someone had just set a cake full of lit candles down on a table in front of her. Fiona was still busy clucking incessantly toward Ava's ear and hadn't even noticed the thumbs up that Ava had gestured in Hanna's direction. One of the newest women in the group was now walking away as if she was no longer interested in who had been standing over Hanna's shoulder. Ava had discreetly but enthusiastically given Hanna her blessing to proceed. When Hanna turned around, Isaac was holding a fresh cocktail for her. "The bartender must like you. He remembered your drink."

Hanna gave Isaac a sheepish smile and took the drink from his outstretched hand. *How embarrassing*, she thought. He returned her smile, admiring her honest and humble reaction. For a flash of a second, she wondered if he had noticed her engagement ring during the handoff, then shook off the needless concern.

"Well," Hanna said after taking a quick sip, "you know you've probably almost had enough when the bartender has your drink memorized."

Isaac smiled at her comment and tried to ease her a little. "Naah. I think the real threshold is when they start calling you by name."

Hanna appreciated his effort to reassure her that she wasn't being overindulgent at the bar. Just then the young waiter who had been busy serving Isaac and Vance drinks all evening, came up with a fresh rye on his tray. "Here you are, Mr. Fletcher."

Feeling like he'd been called out by the young waiter, Isaac smiled proudly, picked up the drink from the tray and gave Hanna a comical *so what* expression. Hanna again, couldn't help noting his dazzling smile. They clinked their glasses together and laughed easily like close friends. Now there was no denying they'd both had their fair share to drink this evening. The earliest part of their conversation was typical, commonplace small talk, yet nothing about their interaction felt common in the least. Hanna explained how they had ended up at the gala in thanks to Ava's voice-over career and Fiona's gifted tickets. She told Isaac that she designed and planned exhibition booths as well as organized special events for a living. She made honourable mention of Ethan and Shauni, her two special employees and close friends. Isaac explained that he worked for a company called Skyfleet. When Hanna heard the name she thought it sounded kind of familiar. "I think I've heard of that before." She was trying to remember where she'd seen the name.

"Have you now?" he asked somewhat sarcastically.

At first, Isaac thought she was joking with him, then realized she was oblivious that she was standing beneath an enormous banner reading Skyfleet's name.

"It's possible you've heard of us. Or you might just recognize the name from our company banner here tonight. We're one of the sponsors."

He felt minutely guilty for teasing her but was having too much fun to stop just yet.

"Oh!, Maybe that's it! Where is it?"

Hanna glanced around, looking toward the several small banners across the room, hanging below the stage.

Without answering, Isaac reached out, gently taking hold of her slim arm. When she didn't object, he seductively ran his finger down the inside of her forearm, sending a shiver throughout her entire body. She watched as his finger slowly slid the length of her arm then down over her wrist. He took her hand and with absolute care, slowly folded all of her fingers, except the index, and lifted it slightly so that it pointed to the ceiling over her head. Now mildly hypnotized, Hanna's eyes followed the direction of her finger. She was staring at the banner stretched high above and across the length of the bar. When she saw the massive logo that read Skyfleet in big bold lettering, she rolled her eyes at her complete lack of observation. She and Ava had been too busy sprinting to the bar to notice what name appeared on the banner or that there even was a banner.

"Ooooh! You mean thaaat Skyfleet!" she professed, as if she had just remembered that she was familiar with the name after all, and knew the banner had been there the whole time. Hanna then shook her head at how ditzy she must have looked and felt.

"Ok, that's it! I'm cutting myself off," and took a big contradictory sip of her drink.

Isaac chuckled at her good-humoured handling of the situation. "Don't feel bad about it." His voice became soft and intimate. "I almost missed it myself, until I saw you standing beneath it."

Hanna glanced up from her drink. There was no doubt, his eyes were overtly conveying his desire for her. She then wondered what her own eyes were saying. She didn't know what she should say or do, or if she should even say anything. She'd only been in the company of this stranger for a short time and already she felt a warm indescribable bond between them. To be fair to them both, she needed to explain that she was engaged. It wasn't a big deal. It would simply clear the air and no one could accuse her of being a flirt or as Ava would say, a '*cock tease*'. Before she could think of a way to slip it into the conversation Isaac spoke again in that intimate way.

"What would I have to do to convince you to come home with me tonight Hanna? I'll make sure you don't regret it and that you have a safe ride home afterwards."

Hanna had never had casual sex before and if she wasn't mistaken, this was what Isaac was offering her. He'd even told her he'd make sure, she had a safe ride home when they were done. *Had she heard him correctly?* She needed to clarify his meaning. "Usually when someone asks you to come home with them, it's so that they can have sex with you."

Isaac smiled at her upfront explanation of how a hook-up was usually arranged.

"That's right," he said easily. By agreeing with her statement he was admitting that if she left with him, he planned, or at least hoped to have sex with her.

Guys had hinted at it in the past but this was the first time someone had been so blatant about it. It was a little surreal. *Was this how one-night stands were typically arranged?* Her mind cast her away and she wondered if Jacob had been this upfront when he made his arrangement with Mandy. If asked, she was sure he'd have said he couldn't remember. She was angry for letting her mind even go there. She'd been enjoying the flirty, exhilarating company of this, not only physically impressive but charming man who made her feel abundantly wanted, even if his ultimate goal was only to have sex with her. Instead of feeling guilty for discussing the verbiage of hooking up with a stranger, thoughts of Jacob had only intensified her motivation for leaving with Isaac. Hanna couldn't believe she was considering his offer. There was no way she could be having this conversation with this stranger right now. She was sure Ava had somehow arranged the meeting. "Ava put you up to this, didn't she? Because she doesn't like Jacob?"

Isaac was amused with her inner struggle. Most women didn't have to debate the offer this long, but this particular one didn't trust him. *Who would, after being cheated on by the person you promised your life to?* Isaac had known before he walked over, that persuading Hanna would be enjoyably different.

"Who's Ava?" He looked sincere and Hanna knew she'd falsely accused him. Isaac glanced toward Ava and her group. "Your friend over there in the pink dress?" He blinked slowly and shook his head briefly. "No one put me up to anything Hanna. I saw you standing here and I just wanted to meet you. I was deciding on the least cheesiest way to introduce myself and then you turned around and saved me the trouble. You know what they say about never getting a second chance to make a first impression."

Hanna was familiar with the statement. The thought of him deciding the perfect pickup line was somehow admirable and she was shamefully flattered. With his looks and wicked charm, Hanna had to remind herself, that this likely wasn't Isaac's first crack at a hookup. On second thought, maybe it was. He was probably used to women pursuing him so often that he hadn't had a chance to brush up on his *first impression* pickup lines. Even if she hadn't been engaged, she knew Isaac was not husband material and likely not even boyfriend material. Still, Hanna had to admit, she was impressed by him in many ways.

"This is a game for you isn't it?" she asked. The corners of Isaac's mouth turned up. "And I bet you win every time."

Isaac admired her bright and sparkly green eyes that matched the small earrings dangling from her ears.

"Am I winning now?" Smiling playfully, he dared her to answer.

If Hanna hadn't been engaged she would have found it impossible to say no.

"You'd probably give yourself extra points if I cheated on my fiancé wouldn't you?"

She hadn't meant for it to sound so snotty and was relieved that Isaac wasn't sensitive enough to let it offend him.

"I don't care about your fiancé. If he's naive enough to let you around me, he deserves whatever he gets."

Hanna was pleasantly curious to know exactly what he meant by that. "If a man's fiancé is at risk, just by simply being around you........ maybe you should tell me what it is you'd do to me?"

He looked at her, smiling at the thought of her reaction if he'd said, just what it was, he would do to her, given the chance. "There are things I wanna do with and to you, that might not be appreciated by all members of our crowd here tonight."

Hanna took a sip of her drink to cool down. Isaac was certainly outspoken in his technique. She wanted to call him arrogant or egotistical but the fact was, he was just being boldly honest. After the lies she had endured lately, his approach was surprisingly soothing. She was more than curious now and wanted to know just how honest and forthright he'd be. "What is it, that you want to do to me at your place, that you can't do to me here?"

Isaac shook his head and let out a low throaty laugh revealing that tempting smile again. "I'm sorry. If you want to know my secrets, you'll have to come and find out for yourself."

He was sexy when he smiled but even sexier when he laughed. This man was as smooth as they came, both inside and out and Hanna was pretty sure he knew it. Hanna stared at him, painfully contemplating his offer and desiring him so deeply that she was frightened of never finding out just how incredible, one night with him could be. *Would she regret her decision if she went home with him? Or would she regret not going a whole lot more?* All she had to do was say no and walk away. She was engaged to someone else and leaving with another man was so very wrong. Maybe after spending the night with Isaac, she'd feel like she'd regained whatever it was she lost that morning she found out Jacob had cheated. Hanna glanced at her phone to see that besides several work emails, there were no calls and no texts. As if that had influenced her final decision, she slowly let her arm fall back down to her side and looked at Isaac with a blank expression. "I'll go tell Ava I'm leaving."

Regardless of how attractive Isaac was, leaving with a stranger from a charity gala wasn't something Hanna could have imagined herself doing only a week ago. It simply wasn't woven into the fabric of her character. If a psychic had told her she would partake in a one-night stand, she would have laughed at how crazy that was and shrugged off the impossible prediction. But at the same time, she wouldn't have believed them if they said that Jacob would do something that hurt her so deeply that it caused her to have thoughts about things completely foreign to her. Hanna's entire world had been flipped upside down by the person she trusted and loved more than anyone else. That was more than enough to cause even a good person to act totally out of character, even if just for one night.

Chapter Twenty-Six

When Hanna woke early morning in Isaac Fletcher's bedroom she tried to flee. The swiftness with which she was dressing into last night's clothing, was an obvious sign she was ready to get the heck out of there. She was fumbling with her clothing so badly, it reminded Isaac of a rookie firefighter gearing up for his first blaze. Glancing at her bulky engagement ring quickly thrust him back to reality. This woman was engaged to be married. She'd come back from an event with a stranger, had sex with him and now completely regretted it. He couldn't help but think of the irony. He'd been in that position before, more than a few times. Isaac had made countless early morning exits and for the first time, someone had spun the table on him. It was 2023 and women no longer had to be timid about their freedom of sexuality. If a woman was promiscuous it was no longer a black mark against her reputation. Thanks to the array of popular online hookup sites, women were just as entitled and comfortable with having casual sex as men were. Compelled to delay her exit, Isaac sprang from the bed, walked around to where she stood and offered quietly, "Hanna, please," he paused, "you don't have to leave."

Still focused on her tangled garment, Hanna didn't seem to hear him. Because of the hasty technique Isaac had used to remove her clothing the night before, the arms of her dress were inside out and seemed impossible to put the right way. Hanna let out a long slow sigh and kept pulling at the fabric. She had managed her thong and bra minutes earlier but the troublesome dress gave Isaac a chance to survey her wonderful curves for a few seconds longer. He felt like a heel watching her struggle in such an uncomfortable situation, but he couldn't waste the opportunity to enjoy the spectacular view, one last time. It was the second time this morning, he'd found himself stealing glances at her. He'd awoken a couple hours earlier, after he'd dozed off for about an hour and when he awoke he thought he'd had a wild dream. When he'd spun his head around to check, his eyes were greeted with a beautiful curvy body, partially draped in his sheets. His king-size pillow cushioned a head of shiny, dark blonde hair. Hanna was lying there in his bed, sleeping soundly beside him. Normally Isaac would politely request that his late-night guests head out before morning. "Sorry, really early flight in the morning," he'd sometimes say, but last night he'd been drinking more than usual and too satiated from the amazing sex to ask for anything, but one last, slow kiss, before unintentionally dozing off. He didn't know how Hanna would react if he tried to help her into her dress. She might take it as a hint to leave more quickly and for the meantime, Isaac was more than content being in the presence of Miss Hanna Richards. As mind-blowing as it was, it had not been a date. It was an unplanned hookup that had resulted in the most satisfying sex Isaac had ever had. Even still, he knew there would be no assumptions they would now be expected to hook up or even talk again. He glanced at the small clock on the bedside table, a few feet from where they were standing. "Hanna, it's early morning, can I get you some breakfast?" Before she could answer he added, "You're probably hungry." *All that incredible sex surely worked up an appetite.*

"How about some coffee?" he suggested.

The words sounded foreign to Isaac and he had to ask himself if he'd ever invited a sleepover guest to coffee before. *He'd never had a sleepover guest before, not one that he wasn't eager to usher out before morning.* Hanna tried unsuccessfully to tie the belt around her waist. As she fumbled, she realized she was still mildly intoxicated. "Thank you, but I have to get..."

She then swayed slightly before she could finish her sentence. Isaac's strong arm instinctively wrapped around her waist, preventing her from falling. He held her against him, their faces practically touching. "To bed?" he jokingly finished for her.

Hanna looked up into his eyes with an expression of helpless embarrassment. Isaac felt both, relieved and guilty when it registered that this wasn't something she made a habit of doing. He walked her over to the wide upholstered bench at the end of the bed and carefully helped her to sit. She sat for several silent minutes with one hand held to her tilted head and the other grasping the edge of the bench. Isaac disappeared briefly and returned with two small pills and a glass of water. "Here take these," he gently coaxed, holding out the pills and water.

Hanna angled her head and glared at the pills, making sure she could trust them. This was a total stranger after all. Well, not a *total* stranger. She recognized the small pink tablets. They were good old-fashioned ibuprofens or really good counterfeits. Hanna took her chances, swallowed the pills and slowly drank the water, avoiding eye contact the entire time. She couldn't remember the last time she'd woken up still dizzy and hungover from the previous night. Hanna felt like a teenage adolescent, not like the grown woman she was. *How much exactly did she drink the night before? Oh yes, that much.* The thought of the Malibu rum and sodas made her want to cry. She couldn't think about that right now. The dizziness was a minor inconvenience compared to the ice pick lodged in her temple. If she could just keep it together until the pills kicked in, she could call an Uber and get back to Ava's. Back to Ava's and out of this man's bedroom. A bedroom she noticed, that was ample in size and tastefully decorated. It was like a modern boudoir from one of her Pinterest boards.

Hanna had fantasized about having revenge sex with a stranger, but the dream had never continued into the next morning. In the fantasy, it was just supposed to happen then she'd quickly slip away feeling like she'd regained whatever she'd lost the morning Ethan showed her the photo of Jacob in his car. Needless to say, the night hadn't gone as planned. "I'm sorry," she said quietly. "I'll be out of here as soon as I can. I just need a few minutes."

Isaac scoffed, taking the empty glass from her. "You don't need to apologize for anything."

Hanna thought, maybe if she slowly opened her eyes, the dizziness might subside and she could find the strength to walk out of there, the ultimate walk of shame. When she opened her eyes again, he was still standing there in front of her. Wearing only the bottom half of his pyjamas, he looked like a sexy loungewear model waiting for the photographer to hurry up and take the picture. He was undoubtedly a very welcome sight to his other ladies but instead for Hanna, the intense heat building in her face set her back. Hanna closed her eyes and delayed attempting to stand. She'd adjusted herself so both hands were now grasping the edge of the bench, praying she wouldn't throw up. A few silent moments had passed and she assumed he'd left the room. She'd partially opened her eyes to find him watching her. Just casually watching her.

"It's a migraine isn't it?" he confirmed.

Isaac stepped a few feet closer and firmly grasped each side of Hanna's head in his hands. It was as if a pulse of energy had transferred from his body to hers, sparking brief flashes of the night before in Hanna's mind. She was in no condition to bolt and his caress was so hypnotic, she was now pleasantly paralyzed in place. In sync, his thumbs began to rotate and press the muscles around her temples, while his fingers worked the tissue behind her ears. The instant effect was similar to the relief she'd felt after taking high heels off at the end of a long day. Migraine headaches had been a part of Hanna's life since puberty. They were intense enough to cause nausea and vomiting but, by leading a healthy lifestyle, exercising regularly and sadly, with help from a couple of prescribed medications, it was possible to carry on with daily life. If a migraine began to creep in and she couldn't get to her medication in time, she would miss a day's work and spend hours in bed. Her triggers had to be avoided, and for the most part, she was doing just that. For Hanna, several events could trigger a headache. They included PMS, stress, heavy perfumes, missing a meal or the obvious one, staying up till dawn, and drinking with a beautiful stranger. Isaac's head massage was unlike anything she'd felt before. Even her massage therapist hadn't achieved the instant wave of relief she was currently appreciating. Completely unaware, Hanna allowed her head to lower forward, coming to rest on Isaac's midriff. His hands adeptly worked their way down to the back of her neck, then out to the curved edges of her shoulders. It was as though he was skillfully drawing the pain out through his expert fingers and palms. She took in a deep slow breath and involuntarily let out a soft moan. Isaac's hands paused briefly at the quiet sound, then began working again at a slower pace. Hanna could have fallen asleep, sitting there, and had even started to dose off. Her head rolled slightly to the side and she startled awake in a panic. She awoke with her head pressed to a warm, muscular stomach lightly covered in dark, soft hair. Isaac's hands were still grasping the sides of her head. He delicately tilted Hanna's face so she was looking up into his eyes. Now in the daylight, she noticed they were a pretty, unique shade of grey. Not simply grey, but instead a beautiful mosaic in shades of green, blue and grey. The only word she could think of to describe them was spellbinding. *What am I still doing here?* Hanna had never done anything so irresponsible in her life. She was telling herself that every minute longer, she stayed in this man's bedroom, made her more of a bad person. She'd done what she thought she needed to and now it was time to go. "Last night-never-happened," she mumbled as if, trying to convince herself.

Staring down at this beautiful woman, Isaac offered no reply, but instead a tiny humoured smile. It was a line Isaac had heard muttered before. Not from any of his lover's mouths but his own. This insanely intriguing woman had come home with him and awarded him the most satisfying sex of his life. To his surprise, she'd spent the night in his bed and then told him to forget that it ever happened. Isaac could only describe the ordeal as a mild version of an out-of-body experience, coupled with an unfamiliar feeling of having just been used for sex. He smirked lightly at the thought, then gave himself a minute to let that set in. Feeling slightly underdressed, he walked over to a large dresser against the wall and pulled out a shirt. He threw it on, turned around and leaned back against the dresser, his arms crossed at his chest. Isaac managed to look even sexier now, wearing a plain grey T-shirt with his slightly tousled hair. Hanna hadn't looked at another man since she'd met Jacob. She considered it to be against the rules of dating decency. Now, she'd not only slept with this man, she'd given him a very thorough visual inspection as well, and he'd seen her doing it. Isaac's cell phone had been charging at the edge of the dresser. It lit up and began buzzing, then finally stopped. He stared at Hanna as if he hadn't heard it. He smiled into her eyes with a warm yet uneasy expression. "I need to see you again, Hanna." He then frowned like he was uncomfortable with what he said. *I bet you do!* Hanna thought and then began to stand. She'd been a total sex maniac and he was hoping to get another taste. Hanna shook her head at the thought of seeing Isaac again. They'd had an amazing night of sex. She couldn't deny that. Growing up, Hanna led a fairly non-promiscuous sex life. She wasn't exactly a virgin when she'd met Jacob, but Hanna was happy to admit that all of her sex partners were men she'd been in a relationship with. She didn't mind being a little old-fashioned. She lived by the philosophy that, sex was meant to be intimate and exclusive. The night with Isaac would technically be her first and only one-night stand. It wasn't going to happen again. Whatever he was hoping to get, he wouldn't be getting from her. Her dizziness had subsided and her head was, for the most part, pain free. It felt like a migraine miracle. Hanna couldn't believe it. She didn't have her medication with her and the ruthless stabbing was gone. He didn't know how thankful she was for that.

"Isaac." Hanna swallowed uncomfortably, like she'd just eaten a spoonful of sand. "We both need to pretend that last night never happened."

"You mentioned that," he replied dryly, leaning against the dresser. Only now he was staring down at her ring. She glanced at the gem on her finger, fighting another urge to throw up. "You'll forget it and….," she paused then added quietly, "so will I."

With a tiny frown, Isaac tilted his head in a doubtful, *yeah-right* gesture. "Hanna, we both know that neither one of us will be able to forget about what happened here last night."

Again he looked at her with this intimate familiarity and those spellbinding eyes. They had shared a single night but the connection between them felt deeper and more natural than Hanna could fathom. Isaac was right, she would never forget the night they shared. She felt that she at least owed him acknowledgement of that. She looked at him apologetically for trying to downplay her enjoyment. Hanna didn't need to say more. Her facial expression was admission of the night's imprint now on her memory. It was now out in the open. They both enjoyed or rather, *loved* last night. He was frowning less and Hanna could see that his wounded ego was partially soothed. She found it surprising, this player needed to hear that his latest lover had enjoyed herself and that the night would be forever stored in her memory bank. Neither of them would forget the events that went down, in Isaac Fletcher's bed. Not to mention, his leather bench, the one she was currently standing beside. Hanna would try to convince herself that the night was, as Jacob put it, *Just Sex.*

CHAPTER TWENTY-SEVEN

The early summer sun was threatening to rise, reminding Hanna that it was time to leave. She glanced out the window and then at her evening purse where her phone was. Following the direction that her eyes had gone, Isaac walked over to the small purse that had been heedlessly thrown aside in last night's heat of the moment. Hanna sat back down on the bench to put on her shoes. How strange it felt to be putting on gemstone stilettos while on the verge of a new day. As Hanna clumsily fiddled with the tiny glittery straps, Isaac placed the small purse on the end of the bench and then sat down beside her. "Would you like some help with that?" he offered kindly, pointing to her toes. Hanna was comforted by that and angled her foot so he could help. Isaac then proceeded to take over the task of fastening her shoes. It wasn't just his kind offer that she appreciated but also his voice when he spoke to her. The same commanding voice that had sent a wave of pleasure down her spine at the gala, had gotten her again. She glanced down at him while he worked at the miniature buckle. She looked at those able hands, his strong shoulders and then at the back of his neck. When he finished and straightened up again, Hanna stared blankly at the wall as if she didn't want to look at him anymore, or being this close to him made her uncomfortable.

"I can give you a ride home if you want." Isaac's offer of a ride snapped her out of her daze. Hanna shook her head and reached inside her purse for her cell phone to call herself a ride. "That's ok, I'll just call an Uber."

Hanna expected him to insist he drive her home but thankfully he refrained.

"Here let me help you then." Isaac held out his hand and after she entered a five-digit code, Hanna surprised herself by passing him her cell phone.

"What's your destination?" he asked.

"Twenty-six Pinedale. No! Sorry! I mean Eighteen twenty-five Lawson Road."

Isaac held up his finger, patiently waiting in case Hanna changed her mind again. When she didn't, he smiled at her, tapped on the screen for a moment and then passed her back the phone. His calm, patient nature should have put her at ease but when he gave her that sweet smile a second ago, her cheeks began to heat again and she stood, trying to escape it. She didn't know how much longer she could stand being in the same room with him before she burst into flames.

"You've got about six minutes," he answered.

"Oh!, I guess I should go out now then. I don't want to make anybody wait for me."

"I'll walk you out. I just need to grab some shoes."

Hanna didn't argue. They left the bedroom together and walked through the large, high-ceilinged living area. Isaac stopped briefly at the door to slip on the dress shoes, he'd hastily kicked off the night before. They continued out into the beautifully decorated hallway and elevator area. Hanna figured that the building was either brand new or had been recently renovated. The poshy hallway furniture was like an extension of Isaac's apartment, details she was too distracted to notice the night before. Hanna figured the rent would be crazy in a place like this and that Skyfleet must pay their employees abundantly well. The elevator finally opened and an attractive young brunette stood there looking from Isaac to Hanna, her long dark ponytail swinging energetically in sync with her quick back-and-forth glances. She was dressed for a workout in yoga pants, runners and a fitness bra. A sweatshirt was tied at her slim waist and a mini backpack was slung over her shoulder. Hanna presumed she was planning to use the gym in the building. The woman gave Hanna a friendly but curious once over then turned back to Isaac. She looked genuinely happy to see him and unfazed by Hanna's presence or evening wear.

"Hey!" She said cheerfully.

"Good morning," Isaac responded curtly. His arms were crossed as he waited for her to exit the elevator so that he could get in. It was obvious that they knew each other and Hanna wondered if the woman was one of Isaac's little darlings. The woman's sunny expression changed to surprise at Isaac's cool, impersonal greeting. Her wide eyes looked at Hanna again, down at the time on her watch and finally back to Isaac. She quickly noted his casual outfit and then glanced down at the polished dress shoes that had no business being paired with the pyjama pants he was wearing. Now donning a big smile, she stepped energetically out of the elevator and twirled around. Isaac and Hanna had stepped inside and Isaac had promptly pressed the ground floor button trying to make an efficient getaway. Just before the door began to close, the young woman asked in a cheery voice, "We still on for lunch this week?"

Instead of answering her query, he stood there glaring at her with a tiny smile, trying not to crack at her troublemaking antics. "Enjoy your workout, Sadie."

The young woman gave Isaac a dramatic wink, then smirked as she stared down at his out-of-place shoes. With the door now closed, Hanna couldn't help but wonder what the relationship between Isaac and the woman could be. Hanna reminded herself it was none of her business and attempted to look unconcerned. As if sensing her interest, Isaac shared the identity of the lively young woman.

"That was my sister Sadie. She lives two floors below me and comes up to work out in the gym each day before work."

Incidentally, his statements only added to Hanna's curiosity. She had noted the young woman's smiling face before the door had a chance to close. She had the same thick dark hair and grey eyes as her brother. "She's beautiful."

The elevator took several more seconds to reach the ground floor. As the doors slid open, Isaac let out a deep sigh and watched Hanna walk out of the elevator and into the lobby. Her hips had a natural, hypnotic sway that reminded Isaac of a slow swinging bell, a bell he wanted to ring again and again. He was now familiar with the masterpiece that hid beneath the dress and found himself reminiscing about the night before. Isaac wanted to coax her back inside the elevator, undress her slowly and kiss her the way he had, right before they'd fallen asleep just hours before. When Hanna turned back around, it prompted him to leave the elevator and join her at the double glass entry doors. He had about two and a half minutes before the Uber would arrive. There wasn't enough time to convince her to see him again. And he knew that if he tried for the second time this morning, he'd only look pathetically desperate. All he could say to this woman in the current situation was what she wanted to hear, *'goodbye'*. He had one hand on his hip and the other on the back of his neck, unintentionally declaring his disapproval of her departure. He looked like a little boy who'd just been told *no* by his mom, to the candy he'd cleverly sat up on the counter in the grocery store. Isaac swallowed his pride and cleared his throat.

"It was," he paused, regretting that regardless of adjective, it would be sorely inadequate, "very nice meeting you Hanna."

Hanna looked at Isaac intending to give him a simple but courteous farewell. When she looked up into his eyes she knew it would be impossible to forget them, their unique and magical array of green and grey. Moments earlier, she was trying to flee his bedroom, feeling like a sleazy tramp overstaying her welcome. He told her she didn't need to leave and that he had wanted, needed to see her again. Compelled by a force too powerful to ignore, Hanna laid her hand on Isaac's face. She went up on her toes and kissed him. He instinctively wrapped both arms around her waist and gave her the warmest, most gentle kiss. He was savouring her like it would be the last intimate kiss he may ever share with a woman. He had never suffered that fear before this morning. From the corner of her eye, Hanna saw a car pull up and stop in front of the glass doors. When she went to break the kiss, Isaac brought his hands up so he could cup both sides of her face. He laid one last kiss on the center of her forehead. As Isaac stepped back, Hanna opened her eyes and had one more look at Isaac's handsome face. She then turned, pushed open the door and disappeared into the backseat of the car.

CHAPTER TWENTY-EIGHT

The morning Uber ride to Ava's house was a dreamy, soft pink haze. Hanna watched sleepily through the side window, as the sun slowly made its way over the horizon. As it crept upward, its radiance cast shadows over the trees and buildings creating black silhouettes against a warm, fluorescent-pink background. The pink profusion made Hanna think of a saying she had heard several times, about a *pink sky morning, and sailors taking warning.* The early morning array occurred when a low-pressure system moved inward and stormy weather was an imminent threat. It was also a threat for Hanna as these low-pressure weather systems could mean an excruciating migraine and half a day in bed. At the moment, aside from being a little tired, she felt at peace and sedated, both body and mind. She should have felt ashamed or guilty. The full scope of the evening's events had yet to set in. Her small evening purse containing her phone sat in her lap. Notifications to both Isaac's phone and her own had been ignored during their time together in his bedroom. There would be plenty of notifications, she knew. Hanna closed her eyes and sighed at the thought of the backlog. As she inhaled deeply she could smell a subtle, clean, masculine fragrance. Traces of Isaac's cologne had transferred to her face and body during their intimate night of passion. The man smelled as good as he looked and felt. Mental images of the previous night then began to pleasantly seize Hanna's mind. Hanna recalled first taking in the scent of Isaac as she kissed him, the moment they'd stepped into his bedroom. It was Hanna who made the first move. They helped each other to quickly undress as if on trial to see who was fastest, intermittently stopping every few seconds to deepen their kisses. Articles of clothing lay spread from corner to corner of the room. At last, they were naked, standing at the foot of the bed where a large, low bench was positioned. Hanna turned to face the headboard, inviting him to enter her from behind. Instead of delving at the offer and encouraging her to bend over, Isaac delicately pushed her hair to the side, baring the back of her neck and sending pleasant shivers over her nerves. He leaned down and laid feathery kisses from one shoulder and over to the other. When Hanna thought his tender touch would be her emotional undoing, she bent her knees to the bench and laid her hands out on the bed in front of her. She knew he would be a greedy lover, ensuring they both came but nothing more. Isaac stepped closer and without entering, pushed his upward-pointing erection against her most intimate, moistened crevice. Hanna thought he was asking for permission to proceed. "I'm ready," she whispered.

She waited for him to thrust himself inside of her, but rather than plunge into her, he took both of his hands and slowly caressed the feminine curve of her hips and behind. He took a moment to thoroughly enjoy her smooth skin and the arousing shape of her. After letting out a low quiet growl, he finally slid himself deep inside and held himself there within, savouring the pleasure. His grasp on her hips tightened and then void of any thrusting, she felt several powerful, internal throbs. He was finished before he had even moved.

Isaac Fletcher was even more selfish than she had imagined. After the intense anticipation, Hanna was justified in her disappointment. Unexpectedly, he began to push himself deeper, using long, slow, intentional movements. Her pleasure was immediate and his deep, controlled thrusts had Hanna joining him in a backward swaying motion. Her nipples tightened in arousal and she became wet around him, loving the intensity and feel of his size. His positioning and the way he filled her lusting body, was enough to begin a quick, heavenly build. Hanna grasped tight handfuls of the duvet for support while he clamped her hips securely on either side. She would hold nothing back. She released one hand and began desperately circling her fingertips where her clit pulsed, begging to be touched. She could feel her inner muscles begin to work, tightening around him. She was going to come any second now. He felt amazing.

Without warning, his rhythm slowed and he pulled himself out of her warmth. She felt him press against her, this time without penetration. He lifted himself, letting it drop on her ass cheek making a quiet slapping sound. He felt just as substantial coming down against her bottom as he did when he'd been inside of her. He was preventing himself from coming before her. He reached down to reinsert himself and began his long thrusts again. She had never been so filled or so desperate to finally come in her life. He increased his pace like he was close, then slowed again, this time stalling halfway inside of her. He wasn't delaying his climax. He was simply torturing her, the bitch! She looked back to see him smiling coyly. He was making it clear that if she wanted to finish what she started, she would have to come and get it from him. She wanted his body and he wanted to watch her take it from him.

"Show me," he encouraged softly.

Instead of being frustrated at the disruption, the sensual authority in his voice made her more wet with pleasure and she accepted his challenge. With both hands pushing against the bed she drove her hips backward, hard against Isaac's firm body, allowing every blissful inch of him to glide inside, as deep as her body would allow. His hands were engaged as he appreciatively caressed her curves but his hips remained still, fixed in place. His stillness prompted Hanna to continue her thrusting, allowing her control over his body for her pleasure. As Hanna drove her hips toward him, she provided Isaac with a front-row seat to her luscious body and the erotic hunger she wanted him to fulfill. A need that went deeper than simply physical. A night of sex with another man would prove she had the worth she'd been robbed of. She would do everything he asked, and take everything he gave. She would be a greedy lover and at the same time a yielding lover. She could have easily orgasmed and teetered on the brink multiple times but wouldn't yet allow herself the pleasure. She gave one last meaningful thrust toward him then turned around so that she sat on the bench. As he stood in front of her, she took him hungrily into her mouth, giving him the deepest throating possible. He once again made masculine sounds of pleasure, conveying his enjoyment. Isaac knew Hanna would bring him to climax quickly but he still had an important hunger to satisfy. The *ladies first* philosophy was not one to be dismissed. He took another moment, enjoying the sight of himself in that sweet mouth then lowered his eyes slightly. There was no escaping the added sensation that Hanna's sensual profile awarded him. He looked down at her face, past the feminine curve of her shoulders and breasts to her curvy legs that were seductively spread to accommodate his stance. This goddess of a woman was a sight to behold. Isaac had never been so hard or so aroused in his life. He needed to make her come before he could no longer contain himself. "You're beautiful Hanna." Isaac used his finger to push her hair back, allowing him to see more of her profile. "Let me make you come now." He spoke softly and she felt her nipples tighten again in response.

Hanna rose from the bench and Isaac bent his head seizing her mouth with his. Treasuring her lips with his tender and thorough kisses, she felt truly cherished. Hanna thought she could have stood there kissing him all night. How wrong she'd been to think he would be a selfish lover. When they broke the kiss they looked into each others eye's, both hungrily wanting to continue.

"I want you in my mouth again," she said quietly.

If Isaac's erection had lost any girth, it rebounded full strength after Hanna's statement.

"Let's see if I can please us both," he suggested.

Isaac held her hand and led her a short distance to the side of the bed. He laid back and gestured for her to straddle him. Lying down the way he was, made it easy to survey Isaac's impressive, naked form. Hanna took a moment, slowly running her eyes down the long length of Isaac's firm, muscle-covered body. She wanted to explore every inch of him. Two strong arms and a well defined chest sat above rows of rippling stomach muscles. His strong legs made her want to run her fingertips, gently down over them, testing his reaction to her tickly touch. Waiting for her, he remained hard and ready. Not wanting to delay any longer, Hanna climbed on top and straddled his hips. Isaac smiled unsure if what he was about to whisper would put an abrupt end to the erotic game they'd been playing.

"Should you turn around? Would that give us both what we want?"

Isaac was pleasantly surprised when Hanna nimbly turned around, approving of his idea. They both wanted to feel the other inside of their mouths. Once in position, Hanna slowly ran her tongue up the long length of him, then took him deep into her mouth again. After surprising himself with a gasp of enjoyment, he followed her lead, mirroring her actions. Their bodies had melded together, like the ancient Chinese philosophy symbol, Yin and Yang. In sync they pleasured each other with their tongues, mouths and hands, inching each other closer and closer to climactic eruption. With perfect pressure and placement, Isaac licked and sucked on Hanna's most secret of places. His strong hands grasped her round behind, pulling her deeper into his mouth, giving her the immense pleasure she wanted and needed from him. The more intense it became for one lover, the better and deeper it felt for the other. Hanna's sensitive nipples moved against Isaac's hardened stomach each time she brought him deeper into her mouth, adding even more pleasurable stimulation. It was one of the sexiest encounters that Hanna had the pleasure of experiencing. When she felt herself at the edge of orgasm, she pushed Isaac as deeply as possible within her throat. His pelvis jerked slightly and he pushed himself deeper into the blissful wet heat. As Isaac released the first hot burst into her mouth, Hanna moaned in pleasure. Several more pulsing bursts followed as Hanna then enjoyed the blissful ecstasy of her powerful orgasm, sucking and moaning at the same time. The pressure from Isaac's mouth had gentled and he finished with long, slow, licks, savouring the taste and feel of Hanna in his mouth as the final pulses of her climax slowed and then faded. Hanna rolled to her side taking a second to catch her breath. Isaac left the room and returned a few seconds later with a glass of water for her. She drank several sips and set the glass on the bedside table. She would be expected to leave shortly, an expectation that harmoniously aligned with her exit plan. Isaac then climbed back into the bed and laid so close beside her that the lengths of their bodies were touching. He then reached out to touch her face and leaned in to kiss her. Contrary to her assumption, Isaac Fletcher wasn't ready for her to leave yet. He broke the kiss to speak but held his face so close she could feel the heat from his mouth on her lips as he whispered. "Let me make you come again Hanna."

The sound of his voice was like silk against her nerves. He took her silence as permission and lightly touched the side of her face. Even in the dim light, she could see the intensity in his eyes as he watched his hand, gliding with carefully measured gentleness to the side of her jaw, down her neck, chest and finally to her breast. He opened his hand grasping the roundness as he brought his mouth to her nipple. He took the soft skin into his mouth and sucked so pleasurably that Hanna had swollen again with need. With her free hand, she explored his dark hair then moved lower to his upper shoulder, holding him to steady herself through the jolts of sheer pleasure. He ran his hand slowly down her side, over the curve of her hip then forward to the small wet space between her legs. Hanna lowered her back to the bed allowing his warm mouth access to her other nipple, and his hand, entry to her wet opening and pulsing clitoris. It was hot and slick where he circled the tips of his fingers. He then slid them inside, obligingly tending to her building need. As he pleasured her in this erotic, intimate manner, hushed sounds of pleasure escaped Hanna's throat. Isaac's body instantly reacted to her quiet moans allowing Hanna to feel his arousal against her thigh, throbbing with need for her. She wanted to surround him with her hunger. "I want to feel your body inside of me," she pleaded in a whisper and watched as he gave her a small sexy smile. His expression was just as effective at getting her wet as his hands were. After a few more finger circlings and blissful sucklings of her nipples, Isaac obliged and raised onto his knees, positioning himself above Hanna's body. Taking a second to enjoy her beautiful curves from above, he then opened her legs and brought them upwards so that her feet rested on his chest, beneath his collarbones. As he ran his hands appreciatively up the length of her legs, his hardened cock stood out proudly, centred between her knees. A bead of clear cum sat at the opening of his penis in anticipation. Hanna stared at the arousing sight of him, loving the way her skin looked against his. She watched him hungrily as he reached beneath her bottom, lifted her slightly and pulled her effortlessly toward him. Isaac then grabbed hold of himself and slowly but intently entered her. His eyes narrowed as he enjoyed the intense pleasure that being inside her awarded him. He brought his fingers to her clit and began the blissful circling once again. A gasp escaped Hanna's lips at his touch and she felt him pulse inside of her at the sensual sound she'd made.

They locked eyes and watched as they worked each other to orgasm. Isaac's fingers were masterly in their technique and Hanna began panting as her body trembled around him. Her fists clenched the pillow tightly on either side of her head, anticipating an absolute shatter of control. Each pulse of Hanna's body, stroked Isaac's pleasures and he too began to climax, bringing them both to orgasm in a powerful synchronized release. Isaac soon collapsed beside her on the bed as if every ounce of energy had been expelled during his powerful orgasm. He laid on his side so he could face her where she rested. Hanna finished the glass of water from earlier and waited for him to hint at her exit or maybe even request another round of sex but all he wanted was to kiss her. His kisses were gentle and sweet, prompting Hanna to open her lips, welcoming more of his sensual tasting. The combination of rum from earlier and Isaac's tender kisses made Hanna feel far away, as if in a pleasant dream. Lying in the comfort of Isaac's warm arms, she unwittingly drifted off to sleep. A few hours later she awoke in a panic and began looking for her clothes.

CHAPTER TWENTY-NINE

The Uber had now arrived at Ava's house and Hanna attempted to shake off the vivid images of her and Isaac from the night before. When Hanna stepped into the house, Ava was starting her morning routine, pouring water into the back of the coffee maker. "Oh my god, you're back!"

As Hanna entered the kitchen, Ava watched her excitedly awaiting a report of her shared night with the good-looking stranger. She inspected Hanna, checking her for damage, the way a parent would a teenager who failed to come home the night before. When her quick inspection was complete and Hanna still hadn't said anything, Ava prodded. "Sooo? How did it go with Double 'O' Sexy last night?"

Hanna grinned at the appropriate nickname Ava had given Isaac. She allowed herself a brief recollection of the way he looked in his white tuxedo jacket, complimenting his broad shoulders and chest. She filled herself a glass of water from the sink, took several thirsty sips and sat at the table where Ava immediately joined her. Hanna didn't know where to begin and strangely didn't even know how she should feel. She only knew it would be a challenge, trying not to think about the night before and the exquisite man she'd shared it with. Hanna looked at Ava nervously and confessed.

"I did something very wrong that felt amazing and wonderful."

Ignoring how severe Hanna appeared, Ava's eyes lit up with glee and she let a faint squeal escape. When Hanna's expression didn't soften, Ava tried to persuade her to look at things factually. "Come on Han. You need to stop making that face. It's not like you planned for it to happen or anything."

Ava was right. Hanna hadn't planned on having an impromptu affair with another man but she had fantasized about it and even had a wet dream about it. Lisa had told her not to put a lot of stock in her revenge dream. She also told Hanna if she acted on it, she would feel remorseful about it later. Lisa would be disappointed that she hadn't taken her advice. The coffee maker beeped, prompting Ava to jump up and pour them each a coffee. She stirred in some cream and sugar then sat one of the mugs on the table in front of her friend. Hanna picked up her mug and took a sip, waiting for Ava to say something to ease her guilt. "Hanna, please don't feel guilty. Your fiancé cheated on you. You didn't deserve that. You're practically a nun."

Hanna looked dazed. "I don't feel like a nun. I did something crazy out of anger. I might have just ruined all chances of things ever being good again, between Jacob and I."

Ava was irritated at the mention of Jacob's name. "There was a chance it was never going to be good again, even before last night. Maybe part of you knows that and that's why you did what you did." Ava shook her head in frustration at Hanna's self-blame and forged on. "This is on Jacob. You are not the one who needs to feel guilty. You were doing your part and Jacob wasn't." Ava couldn't resist, "He was doing someone else's parts." She put her lips together waiting for the repercussion, but when Hanna looked at Ava's silly expression she didn't protest. Ava took the opportunity to get back to their conversation about the man from last night. "I wanna know about your night! Who is this guy?"

Hanna told Ava about Isaac, who he worked for and lastly about their steamy night of sex. "I don't think I was expecting it to be so..." Hanna searched for the most accurate words. "Intimately erotic? I was only expecting a bump and run but I got something else. He savoured every moment and every inch of me."

Hanna remembered Isaac's genuine desire to satisfy her. "It was the best sex I've ever had."

"Wow!" Ava was fanning her grinning face with her hand. "When do you think you'll see him again?"

Hanna thought back to the bashful expression on Isaac's face when he said he needed to see her again.

"I won't be. I'm still engaged, remember?"

Ava tried to hold her tongue but didn't know how. "Yeah, being engaged didn't seem to stop Jacob though." She knew she had gone too far this time and regretted her comment. The kitchen was silent for a minute while they both sipped their coffee.

"Shit. I'm sorry Han. Forget I said that."

Ava rose from the table before she could say anything else and went to top up her coffee to drink on the road. "I've gotta get to work. You here tonight?"

Hanna was rubbing her tired eyes thinking about her busy day ahead. She remembered that Ava said Jasper was back in town tonight and figured they would probably appreciate some privacy. "Probably not. I might go home for more clothes and check on things. I might even sleep there."

"Ok. Sounds good! Just let me know."

She could also check in on Bill and Beatrice to see how they were doing while she gave Ava and Jasper some alone time. Hanna finished her coffee, showered and then tried to psych herself up for a hectic day at the renovation show. After throwing on a short-sleeved top and linen shorts, she grabbed her medication in case a migraine tried to creep in again. So far she had already checked off multiple boxes on her headache risk assessment list and wasn't chancing it by not having her medication. She sent off a few emails and then made the trek to the renovation trade show. Ethan, Shauni and the extra crew members had arrived at the convention center shortly beforehand. Everybody grabbed an item and began to make their way into the back of the building. Shauni wanted to hear about Hanna's night at the black-tie gala. "How did you and Ava do at the gala last Night? Did either of you get cozy with a man in a tux?"

Not only was it impossible to pretend that last night never happened, but Hanna felt confessing her actions to someone who didn't all-out hate Jacob might give her another perspective. "I met someone and I went home with him."

As soon as she said it, Hanna felt lighter and could breathe more easily. Expecting Hanna to answer with nothing but a smile, Shauni and Ethan spun their heads in Hanna's direction to see if she was joking. She wasn't. Hanna couldn't elaborate when the carpenters were present and the GlassScapes team would arrive momentarily. "I'll have to tell you guys about it later."

Ethan and Shauni looked at each other in disbelief that they would have to wait to hear about Hanna's night and who she'd met. Shauni was wearing a knowing, prideful smile and whispered loudly to Ethan. "I'm telling you. Men in tuxedos. They're dangerous!"

Ethan nodded in agreement. "Apparently. Remind me to buy one."

The crew from GlassScapes had arrived just after the Richards and Co. team. As hoped, Glen the owner had come along, allowing Hanna to thank him for his loyal business.

"It's a true pleasure, ma lady, and to prove it, I've even got wunna ma bad joke's for ya."

Hanna grinned upward at Glen, admiring his loveable character. Being a master joke-teller, Glen raised his paw-like hands for dramatic effect.

"Where do ya find all the trees down in Newfoundland?"

Hanna raised her eyebrows and waited for his punch line.

"Between de two's and de fours!"

Hanna chuckled and nodded her head, more at Glen's contagious laugh than his silly joke. The two teams worked harmoniously for a good part of the morning. It was nearing lunch and functioning on only a few hours of sleep, Hanna was just happy to be upright. Her phone then buzzed. She glanced to see it was from Mani, the neighbouring tenant who ran a sign and print shop beside the Richards and Co. studio. Mani's unit had a heavy leak in the ceiling, and he was kindly letting Hanna know it could be affecting her unit as well. He had notified the property manager already and was expecting them later in the day. Thinking of the tools, furniture and computers at risk, Hanna would have to go check the status of the studio. Shauni had set up two cameras in the studio but they faced the two entrances to the building. They were installed to alert Hanna of intruders and not uninvited water. Shauni and Ethan had gone out to get everyone lunch, so were unaware that Mani had texted. They would be back any minute. Hanna grabbed her purse and texted Ethan to let him know the situation and that she'd left for the office.

With any luck the studio wasn't affected and she could come back to the expo after her quick inspection.

CHAPTER THIRTY

When Hanna arrived at the studio she discovered a puddle on the floor near the desks from a leak in the ceiling. One of the ceiling tiles was bowed and discoloured from the wetness and weight of the water above. She was deciding what her next step was when she noticed a mini puddle of water on her desk. It had destroyed the photo of her and Jacob, taken on the day they were engaged. The photo was now just a blurry muddle of colours sitting behind spotty glass. Their images were no longer recognizable. The water must have been coming down, making direct contact with the picture. Hanna picked up the frame, about to throw it into the garbage then stopped. She brought it close, had one last look at the ruined photo then finally tossed it, making a loud thrash as it landed in the pail. Her lack of sleep was catching up with her and she sat down in her desk chair to rest for a minute. Since meeting Isaac Fletcher, Hanna had been in a state of emotional disarray. Driving to the convention center this morning, she thought she'd felt a pang of vengeful retribution toward Jacob, then imagined his handsome face and instantly felt ashamed. Each time Lisa's words about regret and disappointment floated through her mind she was filled with guilt. Her mindset would then quickly flip-flop when she pictured Jacob beneath his exotic dancer, leaving her feeling vindicated for her night with Isaac. It was like a scene in a movie where a miniature shoulder angel whispers words of reason into the protagonist's ear and is then challenged by a miniature red devil of equal size on the other shoulder. When she wasn't feeling guilty about where she'd been the night before, Hanna replayed the immensely pleasurable moments she shared with Isaac. She told him she would forget about their night together. They both knew she was lying. If she didn't get up and start moving she would fall asleep sitting there in her chair. Hanna headed to the workshop for the mop, bucket and some towels. She would mop up the floor, wipe the desk and set up a bowl to catch the water drip until the leak could be fixed later that afternoon. While she was grabbing the mop from the closet, the door chime chirped and she glanced through the workshop window to see who it was. She hadn't locked the front door behind her and had only been relying on the light from the window. Hanna didn't need much light to know who the tall, dark profile belonged to. She received an instant dose of excitement when she realized Jacob had flown back early and came straight to the office to see her. Too ecstatic to consider releasing her cleaning tools, she swung the workshop door open and rushed toward him, the mop and bucket clanking in sync with her stride as she tried to reach him as fast as possible. As he shifted his focus from the puddled floor to where the commotion originated, it became clear that the man standing in the studio wasn't Jacob. When Hanna realized who it was she tried to slow her speed. She wasn't able to stop until she was only a foot from where he stood. He pulled his hands from his pockets and raised them in case he needed to catch her in her urgency and prevent her from falling. To Hanna's surprise, Isaac Fletcher was standing in her studio. He was grinning, admiring her wide-eyed shock at his mere presence. Clearly, he wasn't the person she was expecting. When Isaac could see that Hanna wasn't going to fall, he broke the silence. "If you're hoping to chase me out of here with a couple of old towels and a mop, it's not going to work."

Hanna glanced down at the mop, realizing how threatening she must have looked, flying at him in the dim light with a weapon in her hand.

"Sorry about that. I have a leak."

Isaac flashed her a smile and then looked her up and down.

"Do you now?" He asked, even though he'd already made note of the puddle.

She returned the smile and clarified her meaning. "My ceiling has a leak and I was just about to mop it up."

Isaac pulled his gaze away and looked up at the ceiling, briefly surveying the damage.

"There's probably not enough insulation on the air conditioner's condensate pipe."

He looked side to side at the water-logged ceiling tiles. "Those ceiling tiles are going to crumble and fall once they're fully saturated." Isaac looked down to see where they would land once they fell. "Do you want me to push that desk out of harm's way for you?" he offered, pointing to the desk.

Not looking forward to a water-damaged desk or fried computer, Hanna took him up on his offer. "I'd appreciate that."

Avoiding the puddle, Isaac rolled the chair out and away from the desk then unplugged Hanna's computer. He stretched out his arms and laid his two hands on the edge of Hanna's desk. He bent slightly and heaved the desk several feet from its original location, his strong upper body easily moving it across the floor. Hanna had watched him intently the entire time. She wondered if his clothes were custom-made or if everything just happened to flatter that physique of his. He looked sexy wearing regular jeans and an untucked T-shirt. After he straightened, Isaac brushed his hands together, rested his hands on his hips, and turned to Hanna. "There, how's that?"

Happy to have been able to help, he smiled brightly. It was his most powerful weapon against her restraint. Hanna worried if he made even a subtle hint of a move, she would want to give in instantly.

"That was perfect. Thank you."

Just then, the slow drip coming from the ceiling turned into a much quicker drip. Isaac glanced at the puny container that Hanna had carried out with the mop.

"I'm afraid that's not going to cut it. It's humid out there today. The hotter and more humid it is outside, the more fluid you get. That'll be full in less than an hour. You're better off shutting it down and using a big garbage bucket. Is there one around?"

Hanna knew Shauni had one for wood scraps in the workshop. She quickly turned off the AC at the thermostat and then went to the back to get the bucket. Stepping through the door she discovered it was full of lumber cut-offs. Isaac then appeared from behind her. "Oh, perfect."

Hanna thought after finding the bucket full, he was being sarcastic.

Isaac glanced around. "Where's your garbage bags?" He was switching his plan.

"For the water?" Hanna asked concerned.

Isaac was trying not to laugh at her adorable, fearful expression. She was giving him the benefit of the doubt, despite knowing, that his bird-brained plan to catch dripping water in a garbage bag was about as clever as pruning a tree with a butter knife. He was giving her that disarming smile again. "The bag is for the wood. Unless you're ok with me dumping it out on the floor."

Hanna was embarrassed at her train of thought and tried to be useful. "I'll go get the garbage bag."

Flooded with relief at learning Isaac had a healthy, full-sized brain after all, she then wondered if perhaps it was she who had the brain of a bird. Hanna was sleep-deprived but maybe she just couldn't think logically with Isaac Fletcher nearby. After dumping the scraps of wood into a large garbage bag, Isaac carried the tall rubber bucket out to the front and lined it up beneath the leak near Hanna's desk. Hopefully, it wouldn't overflow before the cause of the leak was fixed. Now that *they*, Isaac had done everything possible to minimize damage to the Richards and Co. studio, it was time to politely address his impromptu visit to her place of work. Hanna didn't want to sound ungrateful. "Thanks for your help. It sounds like I would have been shopping for a new desk and a computer if you hadn't come along. Thank you."

"My pleasure," Isaac offered softly.

Hanna found herself gazing at his mouth. Somehow Isaac's simple, two-word response sounded like dirty talk. His voice was working her nerves again and she wondered if he knew the effect he had on her. It was evident that she wasn't able to be near him without having impure thoughts. She hadn't expected to see him again and here he was standing in her studio helping her with a maintenance issue. Just then her phone rang. It was Ethan's custom ringtone. He was likely giving her an update on the booth.

"Hey, what's up?"

Hanna held the phone out from her ear a few inches to quiet Ethan's hysteria. Isaac stepped away to give her some privacy but could still hear the one-sided dialogue.

"Calm down. Nobody abducted me."

"Exactly. That's why I texted you to let you know I was heading to the studio for an emergency. We've got a leak in the ceiling."

"I did, check your texts."

"Really? That's weird. You sure?"

Hanna put Ethan on speakerphone and held out her phone while she scrolled her recent text history.

"The last text I sent........hmmm."

She was confused when she saw that the number she had texted about the ceiling leak wasn't Ethan's, but rather an unfamiliar number. She texted the same mystery number at five am this morning. About the same time Isaac had used her phone to arrange the Uber for her. Hanna glanced at Isaac standing at the window, looking out toward the street.

"My apologies Ethan. I think I know what happened. My mistake. I'm at the studio and yes I'm fine. Sorry about that. Are you guys able to hold the fort with Glen and the team, while I deal with," she paused a second, "the situation here?"

Isaac half turned and smirked at her reference to him as *the situation*.

Hanna hung up the phone and crossed her arms over her chest, trying not to smile. She was waiting for him to apologize for overstepping by texting himself from her phone so she would, not only have his cell number, but he'd have hers.

"I'm sure that most women are begging you for your number but I didn't ask you to do that. Is that why you came in and saved the day so I couldn't be mad at you? Or are you just here to offer me another round of sex?"

Isaac was humoured by her accusation. "I hadn't even considered sex, but I'm not against the idea if that's where your head's at."

Hanna had to admire his shameless, clever twisting of words. She spoke quietly, hoping for an honest answer. "That's not what I said." She stepped closer to him. "Isaac, why are you here? And please don't say you have an upcoming exhibition or you're planning an event."

When he finally turned to face her, he was wearing the same expression he wore at the gala when he uncomfortably admitted he'd simply wanted to meet her.

"I actually just came in to ask you to lunch. Since you aren't mad at me for sneaking in that text to myself from your phone, I'm hoping you'll take me up on my offer."

His tone was light and innocent as if one lunch would be harmless. They both knew very well what happened when they were in the same room together. Trying to convince her he added, "If I inquired about your services, we could call it a lunch meeting."

The good angel from earlier was telling her to decline his offer. But the little red devil was telling her she had every right to have lunch with this man. It would do no harm. No *further* harm anyway. "I'm supposed to be at the convention center with my team. I'm only here because the neighbour next door texted me about the leak."

Isaac thought back to the panicked individual on the phone. "It sounded like they had everything perfectly under control."

Hanna shot a sideways smile at his smoothly delivered sarcasm. Isaac wasn't giving up easily and tried an alternate angle. "Ok fine. What if we just went out for a coffee? You can even choose the place."

A cup of coffee sounded less dangerous. It would be easy to get up and leave if things got awkward or uncomfortable. Surely she was capable of having an innocent cup of coffee with him.

"Ok. We can do coffee." Hanna lifted her chin toward the street. "There's a place not far from here."

She draped her light cardigan over her arm and pulled out her phone to update Ethan and Shauni. Looking pleased, Isaac reached into his pocket and pulled out a set of keys. "I'll drive!"

Hanna glanced up from her phone smiling at his enthusiasm then group texted the team.

Hey guys, be back in about an hour. Quick impromptu meeting

Ethan, who knew every detail of the business, couldn't help but probe.

With 'The Someone' from last night?

James Bond?, Shauni asked.

Hanna responded simply with, *Later!*

Ethan and Shauni seemed to be encouraging her to continue.

Ok! We got this!

Take your time!

Before leaving, Isaac peered into the tall bucket he sat beside Hanna's desk to check the water level.

"I'm guessing you've got about four hours of drip time but now that you've turned it off it should slow down some."

Hanna crossed her fingers on both hands and held them upwards. "Cross your fingers for me then."

Isaac was willing to do much more for Hanna than cross his fingers, but for now, he'd settle for just coffee. They stepped outside and Hanna locked up the front door of the studio. After a short walk, Isaac held up his key fob and aimed it outward, unlocking the doors to his vehicle. The taillights belonging to a shiny black Chevy Tahoe lit up red, declaring itself as his. Hanna realized that Isaac's vehicle looked the same as the one that nearly mowed a group of people down, that night at the pub. She could have shaken off the coincidence, had it not been for the metallic *X* sticker on the rear window. The same one she'd noted that night, as the black SUV eerily drove away. Hanna stopped abruptly on the sidewalk and asked herself what the chances were, of Isaac owning the same vehicle with the same silver sticker on the back.

She pointed to the metallic sticker, which she now realized was a top-view image of a drone. "Are there a lot of those silver X stickers out there?" Hanna asked curiously.

Isaac focused on the rear window of his truck. "My Skyfleet sticker? I highly doubt it. How come? You want one?"

He almost sounded excited that Hanna had asked about it, not realizing his answer didn't bode well for the situation. When he noticed she was no longer moving, he stopped and turned to see what the hold-up was. Hanna looked to be frozen in a state of fear. He half smiled at her stunned reaction. "Is the sticker, really that bad?" he shrugged casually, "I only put it there so I could tell my truck apart from the other hundred just like it at the airport parking garage."

Hanna didn't know what to make of the upsetting information. This was the vehicle that had swerved toward and almost killed her and a group of innocent people. She was scared to ask but desperately needed to know. "Isaac? Did you happen to drive down Auckland St. just after midnight last Saturday?"

He peered at her, trying to understand why she was asking him about his whereabouts as if the answer was of utmost importance. He then folded his arms over his chest.

"Why? Were you there? Did you see my truck driving in that area?"

He wasn't being defensive but was avoiding the answer, and Hanna was losing patience.

"I can't get into that vehicle until you explain to me why on Earth, you swerved your truck toward a crowd of people including Ava and I! I don't drive with people who drink and drive."

Instead of denying the accusation he stepped over to the vehicle and opened the passenger door. He opened his hands and positioned his arms like a hired driver inviting her into a limousine. He then partially explained. "Unfortunately, yes, it was probably my truck."

He was admitting it!

"But no, I was not the driver. I wasn't even in the vehicle. If you come with me I can tell you the whole story."

Isaac still had his hands out toward the open door, hoping to convince her to listen to his explanation and join him for coffee. Hanna wanted to believe that, despite being a whiskey-loving playboy, Isaac had nothing to do with the vehicle that nearly ran her over. She looked into Isaac's grey eyes and knew he wasn't lying. Hanna poked her head inside the truck, did a quick interior inspection and then jumped up into the SUV. Pleased with her decision, Isaac winked at her and carefully shut her door. After hustling around to the driver's side, Isaac started up the Tahoe and pulled away from the curb. Hanna gave him directions to the coffee shop and waited for Isaac to begin the story.

"Ryan Vance and I, you might remember him from last night at the gala, the tall, dark, intense guy. He's my COO."

Hanna nodded her head, picturing Isaac's intimidating but handsome companion.

"We were hanging out at his place, drinking with......" he cut off, clearing his throat, "friends. Anyways, It got a bit late and I ended up spending the night because I was drinking and didn't want to drive."

Hanna shrank in her seat remembering her earlier accusation.

"About five thirty a.m. I got a phone call from the police asking if I was the owner of a black Chevy Tahoe with a license plate number that matched mine. They told me, my truck had been stolen, but not to panic because it was safe and now in their possession. When Ryan and I arrived at the police station half an hour later, the guy who'd stolen my truck was sitting there in a chair, passed out, slumped over on his side, reeking of booze. His hair was greasy and shaggy and his beard looked like he groomed it with a switchblade. I couldn't understand why his boots were so worn when his clothes were the complete opposite. On his feet, he was wearing the dirtiest, holiest pair of hiker boots I'd ever seen. But his suit looked clean, decent and even on-trend. When I asked the cops who he was and what his story was, they said they weren't allowed to tell me his name but told me he was homeless with no fixed address. The crisp white shirt and designer suit made no sense. Then it became glaringly obvious to me that he was wearing all three of my freshly starched shirts along with the suit I'd picked up from the dry cleaners the day before and had hanging in my back seat."

Hanna had to cover her mouth to avoid bursting with laughter at Isaac's comical misfortune. After stealing a quick peek at her sparkling eyes, he started to laugh himself. "Yeah, kinda funny now I guess. The guy must have thought my truck would be a nice place to sleep for the night but to his delight, found half of my freshly pressed wardrobe hanging there and beside it, two full bottles of the hard stuff. I meant to take the alcohol into Ryan's place with me and forgot. The guy couldn't resist himself. He threw on my clothes, *all of them*, and cracked into the whiskey. When he realized he was all dressed up with nowhere to go he took the big girl out for a joyride. I had about twenty bucks worth of change in the cup holder so he scooped it and went through a drive-through for dinner. There were burger wrappers and pickle slices everywhere."

Still half smiling, Hanna shook her head in disbelief. "My god. How did they catch him?" she asked.

"Before he was done cruising the town, he'd completely polished off the one bottle and had gotten started on the second. He must have been completely sloshed. The police had been out looking for him but couldn't find him. As luck would have it, or I guess bad luck for him, he passed out right in front of the cop shop. Thinking it was some kind of terror plot the cops called in the swat team and surrounded the idling vehicle. They finally opened the driver's door to find the suspect passed out at the wheel. They hadn't told me that he'd almost hit a bunch of people, only that he'd taken my truck out for a nice long drive. They asked me if I wanted to press charges against him." Isaac shook his head recalling the situation.

"I felt kinda bad for the guy. I said 'no' and let him keep the clothes. It's not like I'd ever want to wear them again, though the suit was one of my favourites." Isaac held out his hand pointing to the dash. "I had an interior detailing done the next day."

Hanna looked around noting the sparkly clean, fresh interior, then glanced at Isaac's profile. He was just as attractive from the side as he was from the front. The corners of his mouth turned up and he arched an eyebrow when he caught her checking him out. Hanna quickly circled back to the story. "So he's still out there somewhere, sporting your fancy suits?"

"Yep! He's elevated his wardrobe, that's for sure."

Hanna took a second to digest the whole crazy story. She did have a couple of questions, not because she didn't believe him but because she was curious.

"How was he able to steal the truck in the first place? Doesn't that require a copy of the fob?"

Isaac pulled his focus from the road to briefly shoot Hanna a guilty grin. "Not if you don't lock the doors and the dealer never told you about the third fob in the glove box."

Hanna gazed at Isaac in disbelief. "Wow! You're lucky you got it back unharmed."

"I know. My insurance company wouldn't have been too happy about the key fob being left in the vehicle. Ryan doesn't even live in a rough area. But I guess it's not exactly Carriage Lane either."

Hanna reflected on the city's increasing homelessness and car theft problems.

"I don't think it matters where you park these days. It's a pretty big issue for the city now. Any idea what happened to the homeless fellow?"

"I'm not too sure. The cops called me crazy. I tried to give the guy some money but he wouldn't take it. He wasn't well. He looked even younger than me." Isaac paused briefly. "You just wonder why and how he ended up there."

He looked genuinely affected by the young man's situation.

"Anyways," he sighed as he drove, "I'm very sorry about the role my truck, and I played in scaring you and Ava. I'll be making damn sure I lock my doors from now on. I've also got a new tracking device that notifies my phone when the truck is on the move, in case something like that happens again. I'm just relieved nobody got hurt."

Isaac almost missed the parking lot thinking about the scary possibility of Hanna getting hurt or worse, with his stolen vehicle.

"Oh, we're here!" Hanna announced.

Isaac wheeled into the parking lot of Cafe Amis and expertly parked the Tahoe. Inside, the coffee shop Hanna and Isaac were greeted by a petite waitress who invited them to seat themselves. Hanna asked that the waitress bring them two large coffees with some cream and sugar.

For a coffee shop, the place was larger than Isaac expected. It was more like a social lounge with antique couches and ornate lounge chairs. There were more decorative crystal chandeliers than he could count and the walls were finished, floor to ceiling with intricate carved panelling. In sync with its name, the cafe was decorated with French Parisian furniture and light French music played on the sound system. Hanna chose a corner consisting of a small Florentine drink table and two tall, lavish, upholstered chairs that sat across from each other. A large antique portrait of a young girl holding a Pekingese dog was hung on the wall next to their French chairs. Mindful of the delicate table, Isaac felt like a bull in a china shop. He cautiously shuffled around it and into his seat, knowing it would have snapped, had it made contact with his foot. He felt ridiculous in the fancy chair but thought Hanna looked like royalty in hers. The waitress delivered the two mugs of coffee and a small bowl of creamers and sugar packets. "Will you be needing lunch menus today mes amis?" She was focused on Isaac. He lifted his chin and looked across the table at Hanna, allowing her to decide and answer. Staring at him, she hesitated then politely said, "No thanks. Just the coffee."

The waitress took one more long peek at Isaac, smiled, and then strolled away. Isaac looked around taking in the busy atmosphere of the cafe. It was filled so densely with gilded frames and decor pieces that it reminded Isaac of an Old Montreal antique shop. Hanna wondered what he was thinking. "Admiring the decor?"

He snorted lightly. "I'm waiting for Marie Antoinette to appear and join us. She'd probably prefer a cup of tea over the coffee though."

Hanna smiled brightly at his comment and nodded in agreement. "Touché. The decor is very French Rococo. You'd almost think you were sitting at a sidewalk cafe in France! I love it!"

"Oh really, France?" he asked, "Have you ever been?"

Jacob had promised to take Hanna to Paris on their honeymoon. She sighed at the thought of not going but quickly pushed the displeasure aside.

"No, not yet. But if I ever do, my first stop is Chateau de Versailles."

Isaac was staring at her with a small relaxed smile on his lips. Hanna wasn't sure if he was attempting to not look bored or just feeling the effects of their sleepless night.

He was certainly feeling something but it wasn't his lack of sleep. He was aroused after thinking back to how good it felt when Hanna climbed on top of him and took him deep into her mouth. They'd been sitting in the cafe for less than five minutes and his mind had already gone there. The truth was his mind hadn't left *there* since he'd seen her at the gala, standing beneath his Skyfleet banner. He needed to get a hold of himself if he didn't want to show off the awkward bulge forming beneath his jeans. Isaac turned his focus to learning more about Hanna. "Did you grow up around here or did something else bring you to the area?"

Hanna wanted to shake her head at how silly it seemed, going from a crazy night of sex with this man to what felt like an unnerving first date. If Isaac could set aside thoughts of last night for the duration of their coffee, then surely, so could she. She finished stirring cream and sugar into her coffee and then obliged by answering. "Actually, I grew up just north of the city in a very small town called Ingleton. It's just off Highway Twenty-six."

Not once, had Hanna met someone that had heard of, or been to Ingleton. She waited for Isaac to ask where the heck Ingleton was.

"Oh! I know where Ingleton is," he said enthusiastically.

Hanna eyed him with skepticism but was smiling politely. "Really? You've heard of Ingleton? Population five hundred, blink and you'll miss it, Ingleton?"

Isaac chuckled at her doubtful expression. It was starting to feel like he was developing a soft spot for all of her expressions. Still grinning he continued. "Yep. I've even been there. And forget blink and miss, I almost missed it with my eyes wide open."

Hanna needed to hear, why on earth Isaac Fletcher had been to her microscopic hometown, an hour outside of the city. "When were you in Ingleton?"

"Well," he glanced at Hanna, looking forward to sharing the story, that would back up his doubted claim. "I was eighteen years old, and in my last year of high school. My neighbour was selling his old pickup truck, so I told him I wanted to buy it. He wouldn't let me give him any money and told me to save up for university. It only needed a few parts to certify, and I knew I could fix it myself, so I found the parts online and drove up to..."

In sync, they said the name of the auto wreckers where Isaac found his parts.

"Ivan's of Ingleton."

Hanna was instantly charmed and took a second to enjoy Isaac's brilliant eyes. It was obvious he was doing the same. It was a silly fun fact that Isaac had once visited Hanna's hometown, but it quickly broke the ice and paved the way for further, more relaxed conversation.

"So you're a small-town girl?"

Hanna smiled apologetically. "That's meeee."

Isaac thought Hanna's voice sounded like a happy little jingle and he couldn't help smiling. "So you would have had to venture away from home after high school to attend university or college."

Hanna finished sipping her coffee.

"I did. I studied art and design at Shelton. That's where I met Ava. We were in the same residence."

Isaac's memory flashed back to the woman in the pink dress giving Hanna the thumbs up. Hanna had mentioned that Ava didn't like Jacob.

"She seemed like a nice person," Isaac offered.

Hanna was just as curious about Isaac as he was about her. "What about you? Where did you grow up?"

"Whitehill. Down by the water. My sister and I were raised there by my aunt Diane. I lived there until I left for university. We're all still close so Sadie and I go and visit her on holidays."

Hanna couldn't help but wonder what the circumstances were around Isaac's birth parents and his childhood guardian. For fear of prying she stuck to safer questions.

"Where did you go to university?"

"Queens in Kingston. I'm an MRE graduate."

Most Queen's programs were difficult to get into and required mid-nineties for acceptance. Hanna took a second to think about what the acronym was short for. She wouldn't be able to surprise Isaac by knowing what he had studied the way he surprised her when he'd heard of, and even been to rural Ingleton. "Sorry, am I out of touch if I don't know what that is? I know you work for a company called Skyfleet, but honestly, I don't know what they do."

"To answer your first question, you are not out of touch. And unless you're into robotics and engineering, you likely wouldn't recognize the acronym. It stands for Mechatronics and Robotic Engineering. I'm trained in electrical engineering, mechanical engineering and artificial intelligence.

Our company, Skyfleet specializes in remotely piloted aircraft systems or Unmanned Aerial Vehicles. Most people just call them drones."

Hanna knew that drones had become extremely popular in recent years. She had seen a young man on her street using a drone that he controlled with his phone and Shauni had offered to put Hanna in touch with a *'guy'* who secretly investigated people using tiny spy drones. With the dangers that the flying devices pose to airspaces and humans alike, it became a legal requirement for drones over two hundred and fifty grams to be registered with Transport Canada.

"We have contracts with retailers, large agricultural facilities, as well as mining and construction companies. We're growing all the time."

Thinking again about Shauni's *guy*, Hanna was curious. "Does Skyfleet ever do anything that's top secret or Mission Impossible?"

The corners of Isaac's mouth turned up. Hanna had either hit a sensitive spot or he was humoured by her choice of wording. "One division of our business is professional drone services and aerial surveying. Corporations or individuals will hire us to complete sight surveys or investigate for them. We also have our sales division. We only offer sales of our products to the Canadian Armed Forces and the US military."

Hanna thought that sounded somewhat ominous. "Oh. Is that by design?"

"It sounds like a foolish business move but for the sake of the West's security, we convinced them to be exclusive purchasers. We have some proprietary technology that makes us unique and more advanced than others in the industry. Thankfully the good guys were willing to come on board with us. They didn't want anyone else having access to our technology and honestly, neither did we."

Hanna was sure she looked like a deer caught in headlights. She wanted to ask what technology was so important and what Skyfleet would have done had those governments not been able to come to an agreement with them. She then decided maybe she didn't want to know and quickly changed the subject. "So what's your role at Skyfleet? What do you do there?"

"I'm an engineer. I work on the design and inner workings of the drones."

Hanna was impressed but not all that surprised that Isaac wasn't just a pretty face, not to mention good with his hands. She found herself staring at those warm, capable hands of his. The ones that had massaged away her headache and taken hold of her hips as he slid himself inside of her. Holding back a shiver, she refocused and pressed on with her gentle quizzing. "Did you always know that you wanted to build things when you were growing up?"

Isaac had sobered slightly as he thought back.

"When I moved to Whitehill to live with my aunt. I was…" Isaac paused briefly, "a bit lost. I never had a father figure so when I met Ray, my aunt's neighbour, I was enthralled by him. Ray was always fixing things out in his garage, small motors, electrical devices, you name it."

Isaac wore a tiny smile as he recollected his youth. "If I looked over and saw his garage door open, or his garage light on, I would go over to see what he was working on. I tried to soak up every bit of knowledge he offered. I wanted to absorb everything he could throw at me."

Hanna pictured Isaac as a young boy, his brilliant eyes watching his mentor, eagerly learning, then later, putting that knowledge to use in his career.

"Any more interview questions for me?" Isaac challenged playfully.

Hanna felt guilty that she was giving Isaac a one-sided grilling, but the truth was she had thoroughly enjoyed learning about him.

"Sorry. I'm being rude." Hanna shook her head in embarrassment.

"Not at all," he countered, "I'm enjoying it." He was being sincere. Isaac finished his coffee, set his mug aside and waited cooperatively for her next question.

Instead of further probing, Hanna paid him a compliment. "It sounds like you must have absorbed a lot, from your neighbour Ray. He's probably really proud."

Isaac accepted her compliment graciously with a single nod and small grin. He didn't need to spoil the mood by announcing that Ray had passed a year and a half ago. Their Florentine table then started buzzing. It was an incoming call to Isaac's phone. He turned it over and glanced down to see who was calling. He lifted his finger.

"Excuse me." He then tapped a button and brought the phone to his ear. "Mr. Vance. What can I do for you?"

A loud masculine voice came through the phone prompting Isaac to hold his phone outward, away from his ear. If Isaac was on the clock while he sat at Cafe Amis with Hanna, then his boss had every right to be looking for him. After several seconds Isaac responded calmly and sarcastically.

"Sounds about right."

Hanna wondered how Isaac was able to act so casually while the caller continued to spout off into the phone.

"We've only got today to complete the project so it doesn't leave us a lot of choice. The kids gonna need a backup."

Further, slightly quieted yelling followed. Again, Isaac calmly responded.

"I'd say it's a perfect job for Adam but he's off having surgery." He paused briefly. "Ok. Let Josh know we're working on a solution and in the meantime he can carry on. He can work in shorter intervals to keep it from overheating."

Isaac tapped the phone to hang up and sighed. Hanna realized their coffee break was coming to an end and Isaac was being beckoned back to work. She figured it was likely for the best anyway. Isaac then looked at Hanna with a hopeful smile. "You wanna go for a boat ride?"

Hanna smiled at Isaac's accurate reference to his hulking SUV. She picked up her purse and sweater preparing to leave. "Sure. We can get going if you like."

Isaac looked puzzled but at the same time happily surprised. "Really? You'll go with me?"

Hanna assumed this was the part where he took her back to the studio where he'd found her, but his expression said something else.

"We aren't talking about the same thing, are we?" she asked. "When you said boat ride, did you mean an actual boat ride?"

Isaac looked less excited, now that he realized Hanna hadn't been eagerly agreeing to go with him after all.

"I did," Isaac smiled, admitting he was asking to extend their visit. "I have to deliver some batteries to a job sight that's a bit…" Isaac paused and rubbed his chin, attempting to casually downplay the location he finished. "Remote."

Hanna stared at Isaac, contemplating the invitation. Each time she looked into his eyes, a feeling of serene calmness washed over her. She'd willingly gone home with him just the night before and when he'd stopped in unexpectedly at the studio to ask her to coffee today she again, agreed. Isaac was now inviting her to go on a boat with him, to who knows where. Isaac tried one more time to convince her.

"Seems a shame, we have to cut our time short. Not to mention, I don't think you were quite done interviewing me just yet."

Hanna's cheeks warmed at his teasing. He was admitting that he had enjoyed their conversation and wanted it to continue.

Whether by car or boat, Hanna would be lying if she tried to say she didn't want to go with him.

Feigning contemplation, Hanna asked casually, where it was they would be going.

"Renaissance Bay. Up near Rutherton." Isaac glanced down at his watch. "If we leave now I can likely have you back on land before dark."

Hanna wasn't scared of being in the dark with Isaac but appreciated his respect for her safety. Sensing the urgency, Hanna answered, "Ok. I'll come. When do we leave?" Isaac shot her a victorious smile and stood as he glanced around for their waitress.

"Right now."

Isaac tossed a few bills onto the table and waved goodbye to the waitress from across the cafe. Hanna was now bemused with herself as she walked beside Isaac to his truck. It was the same frightening but exciting feeling she had when she'd signed the lease to the studio. While en route to the marina, Isaac had made several phone calls to various people. The first call was to the marina staff, requesting the readying of the boat for their journey. Another call was made to arrange for someone to meet him at the marina with a series of items and the backup equipment he would be delivering to one of Skyfleet's drone pilots. In between calls, Isaac explained to Hanna, that a fellow employee, a drone pilot named Josh, was recording aerial footage, that their client would be using in a commercial. Josh had completed half of the filming when the drone's battery started overheating. "It can happen as the batteries get older. Josh forgot the drone's extra backup batteries. It's the client's busy season and they don't want the facility to be utilized longer than one day. That's what makes it kind of urgent."

Hanna wondered why the client wouldn't have arranged to film the commercial footage during the off-season.

Chapter Thirty One

When Hanna and Isaac arrived at the marina they walked down the dock and were met by Ryan Vance. Hanna recognized him from the gala. He was wearing a collared shirt, long shorts and casual shoes. His hair wasn't slicked back like it had been the night before, softening his intimidating look. With his eyes covered by his sunglasses, it was difficult to read his straight-faced expression. He was the person who'd given Isaac an earful over the phone.

"Mr Fletcher," he nodded, and Isaac returned the gesture.

"Hello, Mr. Vance. This is my friend Hanna Richards. Hanna this is Ryan Vance, COO at Skyfleet."

Hanna held out her hand for Ryan to shake. "Hi Ryan, nice to meet you."

He surprised her with a warm smile to accompany his handshake.

"Hey there Hanna. Nice meeting you."

Ryan then turned to Isaac. "You're all set for your journey. They've topped up the gas and untied all but the last line. Everything you need is already on the boat. Batteries are in the crew quarters below."

"Thanks Ryan. Don't wait up. I'll see you bright and early tomorrow."

"Safe travels my friend."

Ryan then walked down the dock, toward the marina and out of sight. Hanna realized Isaac's boss wasn't so terrible after all. Isaac made sure Hanna was able to get on board safely then joined her on the lower platform at the rear of the boat. Watercraft had never been an interest but after glancing around, Hanna thought that the boat was surprisingly impressive. There was a large upholstered lounge area that was trimmed with chrome accents and a high gloss wood dining table was bolted in the center. Isaac gestured for Hanna to follow him up the narrow wood steps leading to the upper area of the boat. "Come on up to the flybridge."

Hanna followed, not knowing what the flybridge was. On the upper deck, there was a covered lounge area with another table and at the other end a large captain's chair at the boat's control center.

"We can start up here and if it gets too hot, we'll go inside and use the inner control's where it's air-conditioned. You can even have a nap down below if you want."

Still taking in the boat's many features, Hanna answered distractedly. "Ok! Sounds good."

Hanna was impressed the boat could be controlled from two different locations. Isaac was more than comfortable and Hanna could tell that he had captained before.

"Does Skyfleet get you to take the company boat out often? You seem to really know your way around."

Isaac hesitated for a minute. "Yeah, sometimes Ryan and I take clients out for a cruise when business calls for it."

That made sense. Especially now that Hanna knew what methods men were willing to use to forge profitable business relationships and convince their clients to work with them. Isaac went to take a seat at the helm and Hanna gazed around at the luxurious boat once more. There was another chrome-trimmed lounge area with a table consisting of cup holders for drinks and an additional bench seat was located slightly further up and across from the boat controls. This seat would be perfect for allowing a passenger or two to converse with the captain while cruising the waters. Hanna claimed that seat by setting her purse and sweater on it. Isaac stood in front of the control panel, flicked a couple of switches then keenly worked a small joystick in the middle. He glanced over the edge of the boat to make sure the small lever obeyed the command and was pushing them away from the dock. Now that the boat was out a few feet from the edge, Isaac swiftly made his way around the outer edge and pulled up the four dock fenders. Hanna sat at the bench seat so she'd be out of the way. Now seated comfortably, she watched him from behind her dark sunglasses. He was an incredibly sexy man and was just as distracting dressed in his casual clothing as he was in a tailored tuxedo. Hanna's mind had begun to picture him in his jeans and no shirt, then pictured him in nothing at all. *Good grief!* The August summer heat and minimal sleep were affecting her yet again. A moment later Isaac was back at the helm. This time he reached for the the throttle and pushed it slowly forward, toward the bow. They were finally setting sail. Once they were out of the harbour and far enough from the no-wake zone, Isaac could increase their speed. He looked down at the boat's navigation screen to give Hanna an update. "According to our GPS, we should arrive in just under two hours."

Hanna acknowledged that the two-hour boat ride there and back would account for the longest stretch of time they would spend in each other's company, awake.

"Quite the cruise. You'll be tired of me before we get back."

Sitting at the wheel, wearing that sexy smile of his, Isaac shook his head in disagreement, then slowly mouthed the word '*nope*'. Even with his sunglasses hiding his eyes, it was clear, he was conveying his desire for her. As stylish as Isaac's glasses were, Hanna was bothered she might have to go the duration of the cruise without seeing those eyes of his, a beautiful kaleidoscope of grey and green. A breeze then came off the water, lifting her from her daze. The city skyline was now fading into the distance and the further they were out on the water, the more the breeze blew. Hanna hoped it would help to keep her awake. She knew she needed to touch base with her team again and give them an update. They would tell her that they had everything under control. She also needed to ask Mani if someone had come to rectify the leak and replace the ceiling tiles. If they hadn't been there yet then she'd have to send Ethan or Shauni to empty the garbage bucket that Isaac set beneath the drip. She sent a quick text to Ethan warning him of his probable task. He responded immediately.

No problem, heading back to the studio
at the end of the day anyway to put the
tools back. Things are moving along
quicker than expected here!

Ethan's last statement surprised Hanna. Booth setups usually took a full day to complete, not to mention they were missing a set of hands. *Hers!* She felt guilty but reading Ethan's encouraging text eased her mind. It wasn't every day that Hanna was shirking her business duties to go out for coffee and a boat ride with a man who was technically a stranger. Admittedly, the more time Hanna spent with Isaac the more he felt like a close companion. So far their conversations were easy and enjoyable. Now that the journey was underway, Isaac wasted no time starting the conversation. "Shall we continue with the interview process Miss Richards?"

Hanna didn't know why but she immensely enjoyed his use of her last name. She attempted to hide a grin as she sat there and watched him. Standing at the wheel of an expensive boat, Isaac looked like he could be a rich and famous movie star. The wind blew lightly at Isaac's hair and his muscular arms grasped the boat's polished wood steering wheel. Aside from his good looks, Hanna admired Isaac's absolute confidence. He wasn't arrogant or self-righteous, just pleasantly confident in the most casual, sexiest way. Women likely flustered themselves over him all the time, just the way she had when she first laid eyes on him. It hadn't occurred to her until now that she could be sailing down the lake with someone else's boyfriend or worse, fiancé. Hanna asked Isaac the question. "Am I stepping on anybody's toes by accompanying you today?" She tried to sound innocent but was uneasy asking. The last thing she wanted, was to be *the other woman,* no matter how hot the sex was or how beautiful the man's eyes were. How awkward it would be, if he answered yes, now that they were so far out on the water. Isaac gave a small smile but remained focused on the water ahead, tormenting her by delaying his answer.

"Are you asking if I'm involved with anybody right now?"

"I'm asking if I'm playing a role in breaking some innocent girl's heart, should she happen to find out about last night or that you're here with me now?"

Isaac thought a minute and then casually responded.

"What if I was? What would you think of me?"

Hanna found herself instantly infuriated, not only at the thought but at his avoidance of an answer. The thought of inflicting the same pain onto someone else, that she had been made to feel, brought tears to her eyes. "I'd think you were a cruel, lying, selfish, unforgivable cheat."

Isaac raised his brows then made a big dramatic '*o*' with his lips in surprise at Hanna's venomous unleashing. When he looked at Hanna, she was making a similar face. Hanna was just as surprised at her words as Isaac was and wondered if she'd made a big mistake today by getting on the boat.

"I'm sorry! I shouldn't have said that! You didn't deserve that!"

Isaac reached for the throttle and pulled it toward him to slow the boat. He then lifted his glasses and glanced around for other vessels on the water. There was no one else in sight. The boat would be harmless drifting slowly for a minute. Isaac went to kneel beside Hanna's bench. He raised her glasses so she could see his eyes and fully comprehend his sincerity. "If I were doing that, I would say that I agreed with you. All of those things you said are absolutely true. If someone makes a promise, they should keep it." Isaac leaned in and placed a soft kiss on Hanna's lips. His kiss brought about a sudden sense of calm, assuring her that she wasn't playing a role in hurting an unsuspecting woman. Hanna sighed deeply, wanting to pull him close and lose herself in him all over again, the way she had the night before. Instead, she took advantage of the opportunity to gaze at his eyes for a moment. It was as if he understood where her overreaction had stemmed from. It felt good to hear that someone else felt the same about keeping promises as she did.

"Thank you," she said quietly.

He gave her a reassuring smile and then carefully pulled her glasses back down over her eyes for her. Isaac lifted his chin and glanced across the waters, then back to Hanna."Are you getting hungry? I haven't had anything since this morning. I'll grab us a snack from the kitchenette." He then disappeared down the small steps to the middle cabin of the boat. He was only gone just over a minute when he returned with a prepared platter covered in a clear plastic dome. The tray had a variety of sliced meats, cheeses, crackers and veggies. In the center of the tray was a bowl of creamy dip. Isaac sat the platter on the wood table in front of Hanna, then popped off the clear dome lid. "Help yourself!" he offered, then bent down opening the door to a refrigerated cabinet and pulled out two bottles of water. He turned off the cap and handed one to Hanna. "Is water ok?"

Hanna smiled and nodded as she took the water. "Thanks."

Isaac piled a few pieces of cheese and meat onto a cracker, popped it into his mouth and returned to the control center. Still chewing, he glanced over to shoot Hanna a quick smile and pulled down his glasses to cover his eyes. Finally, Isaac pushed the throttle forward again, setting them back on course. Keeping the mood light and his conversation going with Hanna, Isaac lifted his hands and briskly rubbed them together. "Ok! Sooo, great first question! Whatta ya got for me next?" Hanna was thankful for his tolerant attitude and sense of humour. Most men would have considered throwing her overboard after her explosive response. Instead, Isaac surprised her by coming over to gently kiss her. He told her that he felt the same about promises as she did, then went to fetch them a platter of food. Hanna had to wonder if this was some sort of trick. *Could a man be this good-looking, great at sex and easy to talk to?* It was clear that it would take a lot to fluster him. So far he had only smiled and seemed humoured with her curiosity. "Why are you being so accommodating to my questions? You're even encouraging it?"

Isaac was sitting in the captain's chair, with one hand on the wheel and the other resting casually on his thigh. He shrugged. "I don't know. Maybe it's because your inquiries tell me just as much about you as my response tells you about me."

He was admitting he wanted to know about her. Hanna then looked slightly uncomfortable when she considered what her questions might have revealed about herself. After her reaction to his hypothetical question, it was obvious she didn't take lying or cheating very well. She then felt ridiculous when she realized what a hypocrite she must seem. She was still engaged. She had no right to judge anybody on cheating after everything she'd done with Isaac the very night before. Isaac then interrupted her thoughts with a proposition. He spoke light-heartedly. "I'll make you a deal. You can quiz me for the duration of our journey there. And on the way back I get to ask all the questions. No pressure and neither one of us is obligated to answer unless we want to." Hanna thought it sounded like a perfectly fair proposal. Especially if no one had to promise anyone an answer. *What would be the harm in getting to know Isaac Fletcher at Mach speed?* Later, if he asked her anything she wasn't comfortable with, she could opt out of answering. "Ok! Deal!" Hanna agreed.

"Deal. We have an agreement then?"

Hanna answered by smiling and nodding. Isaac invited her to begin. "Great! Bring on the questions then." Hanna felt that a weight had been lifted now that they had both agreed to allow each other to inquire openly about the other. Isaac had the perfect answer and reaction to Hanna's first question. Let's see how he handled her next question. She wanted to know how he felt about strip joints. A man who liked sex as much as Isaac, would certainly see the perks in visiting a place with such low-hanging fruit. It would be easy to walk away from him after he admitted he wasn't all that different than Jacob and his business associates. Maybe she wouldn't feel so bad that Jacob had been to The Pink Pearl after Isaac admitted he too visited those places. "Ok," Hanna swallowed uncomfortably, "can I ask what your take is on strip joints?"

Isaac gave a small shrug. "Strip joints? I don't have a take on them. They don't do anything for me."

Hanna found that hard to believe. "Are you backtracking on our deal?" she teased.

"Not at all," he said casually.

He was trying to tell her that he wasn't into watching naked women dance seductively around a pole or grind bare assed on his lap. He was comfortable with casual sex. *Wouldn't he be comfortable with a casual blowjob or quickie from a stripper in the VIP suite?* "You don't frequent those places?" Hanna asked surprised.

"No," he scoffed, then smirked, making Hanna wonder if he was being truthful.

"What's so funny?" She tossed a cracker at him, that flew up in the air and then instantly disappeared over the edge of the boat. He ignored it, knowing she would miss him. Hanna sipped her water while she watched Isaac over the top of the bottle. Isaac's dark hair blew wildly as he turned slightly to answer.

"I'm laughing because you automatically assume I go to strip joints. Just because I like sex doesn't mean I'm ok paying for it."

It didn't seem like money was an issue for Isaac. "Why not? Pride?" She was curious to get his take on the topic.

"I just don't see the value in paying someone I don't find attractive to pretend to be sexually attracted to me and then leave me with a..," He paused to rework his word selection. "in an uncomfortable state of frustration. I can get that for free. And besides...," The corner of his mouth turned up. "I hear the drinks are way overpriced."

Knowing that wasn't his reason, Hanna chuckled at his joke. She thought back to the ridiculously expensive whiskey, Isaac had been drinking at the gala, then again later at his apartment. She knew his preferred brand, Johnny Walker Blue, cost more than a full day at the spa. "What about your male clients? I thought it was a routine method of building business relationships."

He looked more serious now, his smile fading. "No, not for me. If they want to be desperate perverts, they can do it on their own time."

Hanna inwardly marvelled at the contrast between Isaac's approach to business and her fiancé's. She kicked off her sandals and stretched out her long bare legs, lengthwise on the bench.

"Has this always been your philosophy?" she asked, "even before you were hooking the big fish?" She was referring to the exclusive government contracts he mentioned at the coffee shop.

Isaac glanced over, did a quick double take, and then down at Hanna's brilliantly displayed legs. "Yes ma'am," he answered slowly, then gave her legs one more thorough scanning. Even behind his sunglasses, Hanna knew where his mind had gone and to avoid a boat crash, she redirected the topic.

"So how much further is this place?"

"GPS says forty-five minutes."

The large coffee from the cafe had worked its way through Hanna's system and was tweaking her small bladder. She wished she had more knowledge about where they were going and if there would be a washroom she could use once they arrived. It was so much easier for men. They could discreetly aim themselves out into a bush or over the side of a boat if they had to, all while keeping their prized possessions somewhat concealed. Hanna thought back to the horrifying time she had peed her pants as a child. A child that was much too old to be wetting her pants. The stress of remembering the ordeal must have been apparent on her face.

"What are you thinking about over there?"

Hanna's eyebrows were drawn inwards. "I'm remembering the time I had an accident at Funland."

Isaac grinned, anticipating a humorous story. "What kind of accident are we talking about?"

Hanna didn't think there was any way to say it gracefully. "I peed in my pants."

Isaac then broke into a chuckle and Hanna watched his chest shake as he tried to hide his laugh. When she didn't continue or join him in laughing, it occurred to him that she might have been hinting at something. "Oh! You need a washroom?"

Hanna gently placed the palm of her hand over her bladder. Isaac felt silly he hadn't given Hanna a more thorough tour of the boat before leaving the dock. "There's literally three different washrooms on the boat. I never gave you the tour. I'm sorry. I was just so focused on getting the journey underway."

Hanna was relieved to hear there was an actual washroom on board. Isaac went over to Hanna's bench seat and held out his hand for her to grab. Hanna grasped it and in one steady motion, Isaac's strong arm pulled Hanna upward. She now stood vertically on the bench, her eyes slightly above Isaac's head. Isaac tilted his face, taking advantage of the moment to admire Hanna's eyes. She bent her neck downward to meet his gaze. When she thought he would steal another kiss, he grabbed the sides of her waist and carefully lifted her down and off the bench.

"I can't leave the wheel right now but it's just down the stairs, through the glass doors and off the bedroom." It sounded like there were several steps to remember so Hanna got going, hoping to find it quickly. She was thankful to have guessed the correct door on her first try and had never been so happy to see a compact toilet in her life. When Hanna was finished in the washroom, she began to make her way back to the flybridge. As she passed through the lounge area, she noticed a small sidebar. Sitting on the bar was an Art Deco-style table clock and a detailed wooden sculpture of a pot-bellied old man, overly happy to be holding what Hanna assumed was a liquor bottle. It was a great piece. She wondered if the carved sculpture was the work of Quebec folk artist Adalbert Thibault. Her dad had a couple of very small carvings created by the same artist that he kept on his bookshelf at home. He would be impressed at the larger size of the carving. When Hanna turned the sculpture to confirm her hunch about the artist, she found the Initials S.F. carved into the back. She'd been wrong about the artist. It wasn't the work of Thibault after all. Hanna repositioned the wooden man and began climbing the stairs again, her bladder beyond relieved. When Hanna returned, Isaac was holding his cell phone, talking to someone on video. A woman could be heard giggling joyously. She spoke in a high-pitched voice.

"I knew it! I told you it would get you eventually!"

Isaac was shaking his head but didn't sound angry. "You don't know anything, little sis."

His sister's finger came up and was wagging teasingly into the screen. "Oh yes, I dooo! That's why you were acting so weird in the elevator! When do you ever wear…"

Isaac ended the call when he saw Hanna cresting the flybridge, preventing Sadie from finishing her sentence. As Hanna reclaimed her seat on the bench, she wondered what Sadie would have said next. "I didn't mean to interrupt your call. Sorry."

Isaac waved his hand casually shrugging off his abrupt disconnection.

"Ah! Don't worry about it. I'm sure I'll be punished for it later. It was my sister. We have lunch once a week and she was seeing if we were still on for this week."

Hanna admired that the siblings were so close. Isaac had mentioned Sadie a few times since they'd met and Hanna had witnessed the curious interaction between the two, as they exchanged places in the elevator.

"That's really nice. You live in the same building and you meet once a week? You must get along well. That's kinda special."

Isaac nodded his head. "Sadie definitely adds colour to my life but she's the most naive twenty-five-year-old alive. I can keep an eye on her a bit, now that we live in the same building." Isaac seemed to be protective of his younger sister. Hanna thought there was something admirable about a man with paternal instincts toward his family. Hanna wondered if he struggled to convince her to be his neighbour. From what Hanna witnessed during her brief encounter with Sadie, she seemed pleasant and chipper.

"How much younger is Sadie than you?"

"Six years. But it feels more like twenty. She just started a home staging business. She's doing really well at it."

"That's a great business to be in right now. The real estate agents are keeping all the home stagers busy. Good for her!"

Isaac waited for his next question. His earlier mention of colours made Hanna think of the previous night when he'd used her dad's rainbow phrase. It was none of Hanna's business what Ryan Vance had said that prompted Isaac's response but really, what was her business? She'd known Isaac for less than twenty-four hours. If they hadn't made their deal involving the questioning of one another, she would never have asked.

"At the gala, you told Ryan that you couldn't have a rainbow without the rain. Can I ask what that was in response to?" Hanna didn't even know why she cared. Maybe it was because Ryan had looked so perturbed and in contrast, Isaac was leaning nonchalantly against the bar. Maybe her instincts were telling her that somehow it had something to do with her. She hadn't even met them yet when

Isaac's voice had teased her ears. Isaac looked less enthusiastic about answering this question. He spoke with a straight face. "Ryan knew I wanted to meet you and he was worried you'd break my heart."
Hanna knew he was only kidding, not to mention eager to change the subject. He didn't want to share what had been said between them so Hanna didn't press him further. Isaac was waiting and wanted to hear the rest of the Funland story.

"I know it's still technically your turn to ask the questions, but you've piqued my curiosity. What happened at Funland that was so bad it made you pee your pants?"

Hanna now wished she hadn't mentioned it at all. She was thankful to be wearing her sunglasses. "If you make me tell you the story I'll up the ante on the personal questions that I've got for you."

He was smiling coyly, challenging her. "I'm ok with that. But just remember, you don't have to tell me. This is for fun."

Hanna worried that if she didn't share her story, Isaac might not be as generous or open when it came time for him to answer future questions. So far she knew that he was being fairly forthright and honest with her. That felt good. Hanna then sighed deeply. "Ok, but you can't judge or hold it against me."

The only thing Isaac wanted to hold against her was his hard naked body. "Ok, I won't judge. I promise." Isaac's sincere expression convinced Hanna to begin her story. She took a sip from her water and then began to speak. "I was eight years old. My teenage neighbour Krissy, who I adored like an older sister, invited me to go to Funland with her and her boyfriend Tim. I said yes, of course so they picked me up in her mom's Buick and off we went. She loved me and wanted to completely spoil me. That included buying me a lunch of my choice. Shortly after we got there we each had a burger, fries and the biggest cup of iced tea I had ever seen. It was in a fancy plastic cup and I drank the entire thing!"

"Uh oh," Isaac said sarcastically.

Hanna nodded in agreement and continued with her story. "Krissy wanted to take me on the Wild River Canyon ride. It sounded like fun at the time, and I guess everyone else thought so too because the lineup had a few hundred people, all waiting ahead of us. Each raft held five or six people, so Tim thought the line would move fast. It didn't. My giant iced tea soon made its way to my mini bladder and I needed to pee. We'd been waiting in line for what seemed like an hour and there was no washroom in sight. I didn't want to disappoint Krissy by forcing us to get out of line to go look for one."

Isaac held his smile and kept quiet, listening to Hanna tell her story.

"By the time it was finally our turn to board our raft, it was really starting to hurt me. The ride itself was over ten minutes long and I knew I wasn't going to be able to hold it until after the ride was over."

Hanna glanced at Isaac, trying to read his expression. He looked sympathetic, wearing a small saggy smile. He was imagining her as a young girl, tormenting herself about not wetting her pants. The ride was designed to give one lucky passenger in each raft, a complete soaker every time. It was unavoidable and whoever got wet would depend on who's seat happened to end up beneath the waterfall as the raft floated under it.

"Our raft was bobbing and spinning as it made its way down the rapids and I wondered if I was the rider who was going to get drenched by going under the waterfall. I told myself that If I was the one who went under the falls, I would be soaked for a while anyway." Hanna glanced at Isaac to see if he was following. He was. "I figured, I could relieve myself while beneath the waterfall and it would just blend in with the water from the ride. As luck would have it I was the chosen one. Soooo that's what I did. The heavy waterfall poured down over me and that's when I just let it go."

Hanna raised her palms upwards in a form of confession. "And there you have it, I peed in my pants, something I have never confessed to anyone before."

Hanna shrugged then chuckled, quietly remembering the event. When she peeked over at Isaac he was wearing a tiny smile, staring at her intently.

"In the end, it wasn't so bad, I guess. The sun dried the water quickly and we carried on for the rest of the day. Krissy sat beside me on every ride and poor Tim had to sit there like a gimp, riding solo for the day. He was crazy about Krissy and I think he was happy enough to do it."

Isaac was still watching her. "Whatever happened to Krissy and Tim?" he asked.

"They got married after high school and had five kids."

Isaac's eyebrows appeared briefly above his sunglasses. "I guess some of us do have happy endings!" Isaac seemed to be less talkative now that Hanna had confessed. He'd glanced around the water a few times but said nothing else.

"Are you grossed out?" Hanna asked nervously.

"No. I'm thinking, how cute and smart you were. Honestly, I probably would have done the same thing."

"Wouldn't you have just hung it out into some bush?"

Isaac smiled wide at her suggestion. "Not if I was an eight-year-old girl."

Hanna laughed cheerfully at his logical remark, and Isaac laughed at himself for loving the heartwarming sound so much. Hanna's questioning seemed to dissipate after her Funland story. She took a minute to check in with Mani who told her that the landlord had planned to have someone there within the next hour. She could stop thinking about it now. The next while was spent contently conversing about Hanna's dad and even her amusing neighbours Bill and Beatrice. Hanna told Isaac that she hoped to check on them soon. He thought they were pretty lucky to have her as their next-door neighbour. Isaac looked at the boat's GPS screen and glanced around the water. He pulled out his phone and Hanna thought he had likely texted someone.

"Well Miss Richards, we are officially in Renaissance Bay. Home to the beloved Blythe Castle. Have you heard of it before?"

Hanna raised slightly from the bench and looked around, hoping to see the castle. It was like remembering a dream she once had as a child. "Blythe Castle? Are we seriously going to see it? I know some of the history around it, but I've never been."

Isaac could see Hanna was excited just having the opportunity to cruise by the castle.

"Would you like to come over here and steer us for a couple of minutes? You can tell me the history of the castle while we slowly make our way toward Ever Island."

Hanna remembered the endearing name of the island that housed the enchanting castle.

"We're going to Blythe Castle? Oh my gosh."

Isaac stood and waved Hanna over to the control center. "Come on! It's your turn! I'll be right here the whole time."

Hanna stood from the bench, stepped over and reluctantly tucked herself in front of Isaac at the wheel. The narrow space between the captain's chair and the wheel caused her back to press snuggly against the front of Isaac's body. The intimate proximity to him and his body was hypnotic and Hanna wondered if Isaac was sharing the same physical response. As if waiting for something to happen, she stood there in a trance. After a few seconds, Isaac surprised her when he brought his hands up from behind her and gently sat her limp hands on either side of the wheel, patting them in place.

"This is the wheel right here." He joked quietly into her ear as if Hanna wasn't aware the wheel was the boat's steering mechanism.

"Thanks," Hanna said ruefully. She felt silly for assuming that Isaac couldn't simply stand behind her without being able to contain himself.

"Are you going to tell me the story about the castle?" Again, Isaac spoke softly near Hanna's ear. She tried brushing off the physical sensations that Isaac's proximity invoked and began to speak.

"My mom told me about it a long time ago when I was little. Part of me thought it was just a story. When I looked it up online years later, I realized it was true. Mom said that my Grandpa, a carpenter, had been hired in the early eighties to help refurbish the inside of a castle on the water. It had been sitting vacant for decades but had been purchased by a private equity firm from the estate of the man who had originally built it, or I guess started to build it. The man, Mr. Blythe, who must have been very, very rich, wanted to build the castle as a monument of love for his wife. The castle was well underway, almost complete actually, when something terrible happened. His wife had been killed in a horse riding accident. There were dozens of tradesmen all working on the castle when they received news of the tragedy. The tradesmen were ordered to halt whatever they were doing and to leave the island immediately. The castle was close to being finished but Mr. Blythe never did complete it. I think Mom said that he never set foot on Ever Island again."

Hanna paused. "Isn't that sad?"

Isaac took a moment to answer. "Yeah, that is a sad story. It would have been a worse tragedy if it had never been restored. Sounds like it would have just completely rotted away."

"I can't believe I'm going to see it after all these years."

"You can do more than just see it if you want. We'll go inside for the tour."

Hanna was giddy at the news and did a quick multi-bounce shake, forgetting momentarily that she would be rubbing vigorously against Isaac's front side. When she remembered, she went still, wondering if he noticed. Isaac bent his head so his lips were touching her ear, then spoke slowly and quietly.

"If you do that again, I'm going to embarrass myself."

It felt like a tease more than a threat. Hanna felt guilty for causing Isaac discomfort but was humoured and even relieved that he'd finally demonstrated his lack of restraint toward her. If they weren't so close to where they were headed, Hanna might have turned and kissed him, letting it lead wherever they wanted it to.

The boat was now approaching a narrower part of the water and Hanna could see trees and cottages on either side of the waterway. The lake had dozens of small islands scattered across the water, some with cottages erected and boats or canoes docked at the edge. Isaac slowed the throttle and began to navigate toward the castle. With his increased hand maneuvers, Hanna returned to her original seat on the bench and angled herself slightly, hoping to see the castle as it came into view. The boat was coming to an area of the lake where tall granite cliffs towered out of the water, posing as a gateway to something mystical. Isaac steered the boat gradually to the left preparing to round the one rock mass. When they cleared the rocks, a majestic stone manor, unlike anything Hanna had ever seen, appeared, situated on an island. Hanna stood at the edge to take in the best possible view. "Ooooh wow, it is real."

Hanna was so taken by the vision before her that she found herself short of breath. The mere sight of the castle was as moving as the powerful love story entwined with it. The castle was a fair size and was easily five or six stories. Several steeples covered in green-aged copper stood out prominently against the warm grey stone of the building. As the boat drifted closer to the dock, Hanna could see how much attention to detail had been paid to its design and creation. She was soaking in the sight of it, for fear she'd never see it again. The grounds were manicured with beautiful gardens, trees and flowering plants. Rows of short, groomed, boxwood hedges lined the pathways around the castle and large fluffy, snow-white blossoms covered the many hydrangea shrubs. Several large concrete urns were placed at the entrances to the castle and spilled over with lush summer florals in shades of white and purple. In the distance, an elaborate garden arbour was covered with pink climbing roses. It made sense to Hanna now, why the owners were only willing to allow a single day for filming. The venue would easily yield a hefty price for couples dreaming of an island-castle wedding. Hanna wondered how she had not been here before.

"Well," Isaac said, " It's no Chateau de Versailles but it *is* a castle on an island." He teased her by downplaying the castle. He could tell how taken Hanna was with the castle's beauty and admitted that he was too, by letting out a long whistle. "That is *one* impressive sight."

Isaac slowly brought the boat around to the other side of the island so he could secure it. Even the dock had been thoughtfully decorated, finished with large cast iron light posts, ornate metal benches and large moss hanging baskets, flowers pouring from all sides. Isaac worked the boat controls gently, bringing the vessel lengthwise against the long dock. He then turned off the engine, helped Hanna exit safely, and then worked quickly tossing down the fenders. Hanna gazed around while Isaac worked quickly to tie the lines. "This place is a dream!" Hanna took in the surroundings and stared longingly at the castle.

"I won't be long." Isaac knew how eager Hanna was to look around. "I'm just finishing up so our ride's still here when we're ready to leave."

When Hanna realized Isaac was rushing for her sake she looked back apologetically. He shot her one of his sexy smiles, then returned his attention to his task. As Isaac was bent securing the boat's lines to the dock, Hanna spotted a young skinny man holding some kind of controller. He appeared from behind a group of shrubs and slowly made his way toward the dock. Hanna presumed this was Josh, Isaac's fellow employee who was capturing footage for the commercial. Josh was walking casually toward the boat and when he realized who it was tying the lines, he clumsily shoved the small controller into the pocket of his cargo shorts. He then hustled to the edge of the boat to assist with the docking process. "Hey there, Mr. Fletcher!" Josh gave Hanna a meek smile, then turned his attention back to Isaac. "I wasn't expecting to see you here."

Isaac turned to acknowledge Josh. "Hey buddy." He stood and gave Josh a quick fist bump.

"Castle visits weren't originally on my calendar today but I heard you needed some extra batteries."

Josh looked like he was waiting to be reprimanded, but his face quickly registered relief when he wasn't. "Yeah! I was getting some amazing footage then my controller signalled low battery and I realized I was in trouble."

Isaac leaned into the boat, grabbed what looked like a camera bag and handed it to Josh. "There's three extra batteries in there, all fully charged."

"Perfect, that should keep me going the rest of the day. Thanks for bringing them!"

Isaac glanced upward at the castle. "Is anyone around that would care if we took a quick tour inside?"

Josh looked toward the group of shrubs. "There's a security guard just passed the first garden and one or two people inside, but otherwise, I doubt anyone would even notice. The place is huge!"

Isaac was eager to give Hanna the tour he promised. "Ok Josh, we'll let you get back to work. I'll check in again when we're heading out."

Isaac held out his hand as if inviting Hanna to lead the way. "Shall we, Miss Richards?"

Hanna accepted the invitation by turning and walking up the stone pathway. The security guard that Josh mentioned, was standing there, distractedly laughing into his phone watching a video. He was easily six foot four and looked like a bodybuilder. When he noticed Hanna and Isaac, he stood up straight, trying to look serious and professional. Isaac and the security guard nodded in sync before the security guard spoke in the most gravelly voice Hanna had ever heard.

"Hey there. You guys here with the filming guy?" He lifted his chin in the direction he'd last seen Josh.

"Ten-four boss. I see you've mastered that poker face."

Hanna didn't think insulting the large, intimidating security guard was their quickest ticket into the castle. The guard squinted his eyes and glared at Isaac. He then lifted his eyebrows and a big bright smile covered his face. "It's Isaac Fletcher! Holy cow man!"

"Mr. Tyrone Bossman! How's it going, big guy?"

Isaac met Tyrone during their first year in university. They liked to play poker in their dorm room with a couple of other guys who lived on the same floor. Tyrone left university after the first year when his girlfriend Tessa became pregnant. Tessa's family was very traditional and Tyrone didn't want her to be looked down upon by her family. He married her the summer after his first year and Tessa's father helped him start a security business. Isaac and Tyrone came together for a quick embrace then separated to converse again.

"I'm good! I'm good! Tessa and I have two kids now. We just moved to North Crest to be closer to her parents. I started my security service when we found out Tessa was pregnant. I guess that was almost nine, maybe ten years ago now. So what are you up to? Did you put that engineering degree to use?"

Tyrone glanced at Hanna who smiled at him, and then back to Isaac.

"I did," Isaac answered, "I work at Skyfleet, the company hired to get the aerial footage of this place. We also build and design drones."

Still smiling, Tyrone shook his head.

"Oh man, that's awesome! Good for you!"

"Hanna this is Tyrone Bossman. Tyrone, Hanna Richards."

"Hi Hanna!"

"Tyrone and I went to Queens together. We stayed in the same residence."

Tyrone looked as if he were remembering the brief period fondly.

"Hanna and I are just here delivering a few backup batteries and were hoping to get a look at the place."

"Absolutely! As long as you're talkin' the self-guided tour. I'm supposed to stay out here and make sure no undesirable guests visit the island. The place is stacked with valuable antiques."

Isaac didn't expect Tyrone to take him on a guided tour, nor did he want him to. A private tour with Hanna was the preferred option.

"Works for me! Do we just let ourselves inside then?"

Tyrone held up his giant finger, pointing toward the castle's front walkway.

"Go right in!"

CHAPTER THIRTY TWO

The main entrance to the castle featured a gigantic solid wood door with iron hinges and a large lion head door knocker that looked to be a hundred years old. Encircling the knocker was a crisp white rose and ivy wreath, foreshadowing the opulence and luxurious splendour within the castle. Isaac pushed the heavy door open, revealing a large cathedral entryway adorned with an enormous sparkling crystal chandelier hanging above. The floors were finished with large slabs of ivory-coloured marble. In the center of the entry was a pedestal table with a wide silver urn holding several dozen, large white roses. Laying beside the urn, was a brass pen with a feather end and a guest book for wedding guests to sign. The inside of the castle was just as breathtaking as the outside. It was like having a peek into an impeccably decorated wedding venue before any of the guests or bridal party arrived. Clawfoot furniture was placed against the walls and gold-framed, painted portraits hung high on display. A wide staircase with scrolled iron balusters wound its way to the upper floors of the castle, and classical music played on an invisible sound system. Summoning to Isaac and Hanna, the castle begged to be explored. For fear of causing an echo within the open castle, Isaac spoke in a quiet tone.

"Where would you like to begin the tour?"

Hanna was drawn to the painted portraits hung on the stone wall and instead of responding, stepped forward to get a closer look. Isaac watched her curiously then joined her in examining the artwork. The antique painting was of a pretty young woman sitting outside in a plumed back wicker chair with a water view behind her. After a moment Isaac spoke quietly."This was Mrs. Elaina Blythe in 1879. She was thirty-five."

Hanna looked at Isaac in amazement. "Really?" she whispered, "I wondered if maybe that was her. How did you know that?"

Isaac playfully arched his eyebrows and dramatically focussed his eyes sideways, encouraging Hanna to follow his line of sight to the small brass plaque beside the painting. Hanna had been standing so close that she hadn't noticed the plaque stating the info and dating of the portrait.

"Oh! Sorry," Hanna said timidly.

Isaac smiled into Hanna's eyes. "My Aunt Diane used to say that if your nose is pressed to the canvas there's a chance you'll see less. Would you agree with that Miss Richards?"

Hanna inwardly smiled, stepped away from the painting and slowly made her way to the scrolled staircase. Isaac followed, taking the opportunity to admire the natural sway of Hanna's hips as she moved slowly up the stairs. He loved the angle more each time he had the privilege of viewing it. Hanna continued to talk as she walked.

"Yes. Based on my recent oversight, I would have to agree with your aunt. I just wanted to get a good look at the woman whose love had inspired the creation of this wonderful castle."

Isaac had to contemplate her comment. "Does she get all the credit?" he asked lightheartedly, "What about the besotted husband who wanted to show his incurable love and devotion?"

Hanna tipped her head to the side. It was her turn to do the teasing and maybe some testing. She turned around just as Isaac was slowly pulling his eyes upwards away from her hips. Instead of trying to hide it, feigning innocence, he shamelessly continued with his scanning. Hanna's ego enjoyed provoking the reaction from him and she smiled. "Maybe it wasn't her love at all, that inspired him. I've learned that men can certainly be salacious creatures. Maybe it was lust that inspired him. Or," Hanna looked mildly irritated, "maybe he was trying to atone for something that he'd done to hurt her."

Isaac sobered slightly at the comment. "It would have to be one hell of a mistake to attempt smoothing things over with a castle build. But," Isaac paused to look at Hanna, "if he truly loved her and broke a promise to her then he should be doing everything in his power to make it up to her."

They walked down a wide hallway with more gold-framed paintings and a large circular window at the end. Large brass sconces with softly lit bulbs graced the walls, illuminating the way. Hanna stepped out of the hallway and into a room with double doors that had been left wide open, enticing her inside. It was a massive boudoir with a king-size, four-poster bed, centered against the wall. On the opposite wall, a large arched window allowed views of the lake and grounds. Plush comfortable chairs were placed on either side of the window and a small table with fresh flowers and heavy silver candle holders sat in between. Hanna thought it was the perfect spot for enjoying morning coffee with your lover. A connected dressing room was off to one side and a large-sized en-suite washroom was located through the dressing room. Isaac walked to the window and admired the view. "The man was certainly trying his best if he was attempting to make up for something. This view is stunning."

Hanna joined him at the window taking in the landscaped gardens and stone path leading to the water's edge. "Sadly, some mistakes can't be smoothed over. Not even with a castle on the water."

Isaac turned to Hanna and gazed into those pretty eyes of hers. He wanted to touch her and taste her mouth.

"True," he agreed. "Some things can't be forgiven. But sometimes people make mistakes that can lead to something unexpected, something better."

With yearning eyes, Hanna invited him to show her what better was. Isaac bent his head, bringing his lips to hers. She brought her hands up, threading her fingers through his hair the way she'd yearned to, each time the wind blew it wildly on their boat ride over. His soft and sensual kisses, combined with the alluring scent of him, engaged Hanna's senses like a potent elixer. Fulfilling her fantasy from earlier, of Isaac in just his jeans, Hanna pulled Isaac's T-shirt over his head, baring his brilliantly toned upper body and steely abs. Hanna wished they had all day and night so she could stop intermittently to look at this perfect, masculine body. For fear of being interrupted, Hanna whispered for Isaac to lock the door.

"Sorry," he apologized, "there's no lock. I checked when we first walked through the door."

Hanna glanced at the lockless door and then smiled at Isaac's naughty admission. His smile was devilishly sexy and it made her want to kiss him again. Isaac reached for her hand, led her into the large dressing room and shut the door behind them. Brass clothing rods with black satin, padded hangers and fluffy white bath robes hung high on each side of the closet. Beside the door, there was a king-sized chair, upholstered in deep purple velvet. At the other end of the dressing room, a brass-framed, full-length, mirror stood stately against the wall. Light from the adjoining washroom window offered a soft illumination, allowing them to see each other as dream-like shadows. Isaac pushed the chair slightly so that one of the heavy legs would impede the door from opening, should someone attempt to enter. Their remaining clothes were urgently removed and Isaac, now naked, sat down in the thronely chair. His legs were spread slightly and his cock pointed upward, hard and ready. Sitting nude, Isaac looked so immensely sexual that Hanna had to take a second to scan and appreciate his body and powerful erection. When she delayed another few seconds, Isaac feared she was doubting her actions. "Would you care to join me?" he offered, almost whispering.

Hanna pulled Isaac's discarded jeans over with her foot and knelt down between his knees on the makeshift padding. She leaned forward and gently ran her hands downward over Isaac's chest and nipples, then down over the ripples of his stomach before resting them on his thighs. Isaac laid his head back and made a low sexy sound of approval. Using her warm, wet tongue, Hanna licked him up and down then sucked him as deeply and pleasurably as possible. Watching the way her lips and mouth worked his body was the complete fantasy. Her breasts pushed against his thighs and her gentle fingertips reached up to tease his sensitive nipples. The sensual sucking combined with the sweet touch of her fingers was an intoxicating combination. Isaac could have exploded after mere minutes but wouldn't have had the pleasure of experiencing this arousing woman's moans of pleasure before he had. He was forced to hide his excitement once in the French cafe then again on the boat when Hanna had bounced cheerily against him. Making Hanna come, played as much of a role in his intellectual satisfaction as it did his physical satisfaction. Her sweet sucking was more than he could handle.

"Careful there Honey," he warned lightly. "You're going to get me to the finish line before the race has even started."

He caressed her head and pushed her hair aside, allowing himself a better view of her face. Hanna took deep satisfaction in knowing this man was savouring her body and the things they were doing together, rushing the last thing on his mind.

"Come up here, Hanna."

She knew how aroused he was by how hard he was in her mouth. Hanna used her tongue to tease and pleasure him another minute, then stood up from between his legs. She looked at Isaac's face and leaned down to kiss his lips. He returned her kiss, and at the same time, put two of his fingers, softly inside her, drawing a surprised and pleasured moan. After a moment, he withdrew his slick fingers and slid them carefully front to back hitting all the sensitive parts of her clitoris, bringing further soft moaning and more warm wetness. Her nipples responded to his touch by tightening and she wished that he would ease them with his warm mouth and tongue. He sat both hands on her hips with care and laid several soft warm kisses across her stomach. The gentle gesture was sensually intimate and she couldn't help reaching for his head of dark hair. He tipped his chin up to suck softly at each nipple, then slowly guided her hips in turning so she was no longer facing him. He was asking her to ride him in the velvet chair, giving her command of the rhythm and an uninhibited view of their erotic affair in the dim castle dressing room. Hanna turned around and spread her legs slightly then using his thighs for support she lowered herself, sliding down over the hardened length of him. Her backside came down and rested on his lap. Isaac was so overwhelmed with the pleasure of being inside of her that he had to press his head back against the chair, bracing himself for further bliss. Watching his reaction in the mirror compelled Hanna to give him more of what he wanted, more of what she wanted. With Isaac deep inside, Hanna began to grind in a slow, erotic motion. The mirror, with its heavy brass grandeur, called at Hanna to watch herself in its reflection. The grand size allowed a full, graphic view of both Hanna's bare body and the masculine parts of Isaac not covered by her naked image. The way he tilted his head to see more of her and how his eyes appreciatively peered at her reflection, made her feel incredibly sexy and self-assured. Hanna noted the shadowy outline of her curvy body as she moved. It was feminine and beautiful just as it had always been. Her breasts were round and full, above her stomach and her slim waist accentuated her round hips. Watching him, intently watching her, Hanna had never felt sexier. Isaac's hands explored her body from behind. He ran his hands softly down the sides of her neck, across her shoulders and arms then down to her hips. He slowly circled the shallow dimples at the bottom of her back using the pads of his thumbs. His touch was like a warm drizzle of honey on an already decadent dessert. Hanna slowly increased the rhythm and pressure, heightening Isaac's pleasure in sync with her own. His hand then reached over her hip and began tantalizingly rubbing his fingers in quick, tiny swoops between her legs. The deep and thick penetration of him, combined with the teasing of his fingers was sweetly and unbearably arousing. Hanna's entire body tightened and every cell within, buzzed with torturous pleasure. She watched herself edge closer and closer to orgasm. Her body began to move in faster, harder thrusts and her inner muscles squeezed and pulsed tightly around his thick throbbing length.

The uninhibited view of Hanna's writhing body, and sweet, quiet moaning, overpowered Isaac's constraint, igniting his orgasm. Sensing his powerful body, she too was consumed by the searing bliss of orgasm. She watched their bodies move together in the mirror as they lost control over themselves, overtaken in unison. With his hands grasping her hips, Isaac finished his climax in powerful, upward thrusts accompanied by several low sexual moans. Hanna savoured the arousing, masculine reflection and the gratifying sounds she drew from him as he came. Watching your lover, entrust you with the ultimate surrender was the most empowering, erotic experience two lovers could share.

Hanna's legs were weak and shaky and her breathing remained heavy from the blissful exertion. She rested by leaning back against Isaac's chest as he sat in the velvet chair. They stared at each other in the reflection, their bodies still joined and naked while they recaptured their breath. Isaac then unexpectedly gave the side of Hanna's head a gentle kiss and whispered into her ear. "You're beautiful."

The quiet sound of his voice and the heat from his breath sent pleasant shivers across her body. Hanna watched, waiting for him to say or do something to wake her from her fantastical dream. Instead, he remained perfectly still, staring back at her as though she were a newfound marvel. Thoroughly satiated, Hanna could have fallen asleep sitting on Isaac's warm lap but they both knew, under the circumstances, it was time to get moving. They collected their clothing, briefly used the en-suite and then vacated the boudoir. Isaac again, invited Hanna to lead the way as they continued their castle tour, occasionally stealing glances at her swaying hips. The most memorable room, aside from the dressing room, was the two-story library with the upward-arched ceiling. The deep mahogany bookshelves stood the full height of the room and were filled with antique linen books, their titles all stamped in gold. Resting at the end of one shelf was a sliding ladder for accessing the high, out-of-reach collections. When Hanna stopped briefly to check the state of her appearance in a mirrored wall panel, she unknowingly stepped on the trigger to a secret passageway. As her shoe compressed the small wooden peg, the mirrored panel made a *click* sound and popped open, revealing a hidden gateway. The narrow stone hallway led to several different rooms in the castle as well as the top-floor outdoor balcony. Isaac concluded that it was built as a secret escape in the event there was ever an intruder. A beautiful glass solarium off the kitchen was arranged with couches and furniture for gathering and lounging. This time, noticing the wall plaque, Hanna read that it was originally designed to house vegetable and herb plants for the cooks who would have prepared the castle meals, had the family ever had the chance to reside there. When they felt they had toured most of the castle, Isaac thanked Tyrone again for allowing them to view the inside and then exchanged contact info with him. Josh still had a few more hours of filming to complete but insisted that he help Isaac untie the boat. Josh explained to Hanna that he would be driving back to Toronto after water taxiing off the island to his van on the mainland. Josh admired the boat as he helped Isaac pull up the last fender. At the back, in small cursive letters, its name was inscribed.

"That's a great name for a boat. *Ray of sunshine*!"

Josh stared at the lettering expecting Isaac to share the origin of the boat's name. Isaac must have thought it was self-explanatory and didn't offer any insight.

"Thanks Josh, maybe I'll see you tomorrow!"

"Thanks again for bringing the batteries, Mr. Fletcher. Safe cruise back!"

Isaac helped Hanna step onto the boat and through the sliding glass doors to the enclosed interior. He would captain from the middle deck for their early evening ride back to the harbour. He knew Hanna was exhausted and would be more comfortable in the air-conditioned cabin and out of the sun. As she walked through the enclosed sitting area, she took a second to admire again, the funny wood man she'd examined earlier. It was a neat piece and she wondered who the artist was with the initials S.F. Instead of the co-captain's chair, Hanna chose a seat across from the control station so she could see Isaac's face during the voyage home. If they decided to stick to the arrangement they'd made on the ride over, it would now be Isaac's turn to do the interviewing. Isaac then appeared through the sliding glass door and delivered Hanna a wink and a smile. After flicking some switches and adjusting a couple of levers, he pushed the throttle forward. She admired his expertise in maneuvering the small yacht. It wasn't your typical job perk, having the opportunity to cruise around on the luxurious company boat. Hanna wondered what something like it would even be worth then thought about the vessel's name, *Ray of Sunshine*. She was curious as to why Skyfleet's owner, whoever he was, had chosen that name. There was nothing wrong with the name but Hanna knew that often a boat was named after someone or something personal to the owner. *Maybe the owner's name was Ray? Didn't Isaac say that his idol-neighbour was named Ray?* Hanna was now compelled to do a little online research about Skyfleet and clicked the search app on her phone. The boat was now slowly moving outward, away from the castle on Ever

Island. Isaac sat casually at the wheel watching Hanna.
He wore a content grin as he recalled their explicit rendezvous in the softly lit closet.

"Well Miss Richards, we have officially begun our travels back to the city. Do you plan to uphold your end of our bargain?"

She surprised him when she lifted her eyes from her phone looking wounded.

"Of course, I plan to uphold my end of the bargain. I wouldn't want to disappoint the CEO and founder of Skyfleet Robotics."

Isaac stared blankly, nodding his head slowly in defeat. Using the same sweet tone that Hanna had used to apologize, for being a small-town girl, Isaac tilted his head and responded sarcastically. "That's meee!"

Hanna sighed deeply, looking at his regretful expression. His senseless withholding affected her more than he knew. He'd had multiple opportunities to tell her that he was not only the CEO and owner of the company he worked for, but also the likely owner of this valuable boat. The boat, she assumed had been named after his beloved neighbour, Ray.

"What reason could you possibly have for not telling me that you were the CEO and founder of Skyfleet?"

Isaac lifted his hands off the wheel and shook his head in confusion at his actions. He wasn't able to give her an answer. "I don't know. I'm sorry."

Hanna didn't think she could handle any more vague answers from people about their reasons for lying or withholding information from her. She had curiously asked Isaac about the boat earlier and he had implied that his boss had instructed him to use it to deliver spare batteries to a coworker. Sounding distant Hanna responded to his weak answer.

"You don't owe me an apology. You hardly even know me. Why would I expect you to trust me with something as precious as the truth?" She felt awkward and out of place. "Did you say there was a place to sleep down below? I'm pretty tired, would you mind?" Isaac glanced side to side, out the windows, then at the screens for water traffic. He pulled the throttle toward him and drastically slowed the boat. Isaac then stepped over to Hanna who was already standing, looking like she wanted to jump overboard. He raised his arms to embrace her but she rejected him by backing out of his reach.

"Hanna please don't do that. This is new territory for me. I wanted to tell you, I just wasn't ready."

He ran his hands through his hair in frustration. "In the world of dating, once you've flashed your CEO card, women…." He paused for a second. "They aren't looking at *you* anymore, it's just different."

"You're calling this dating?"

Isaac raised his eyebrows, looking surprised and offended at Hanna's query.

"You wouldn't? Ok, What would you call it?"

Hanna looked down at her engagement ring, then out the window at the water, avoiding eye contact as she answered numbly. "Sex. Just sex."

Isaac slowly shook his head at her baseless comment. "It's more than that Hanna. You know that it is."

She allowed him to pull her gently against him and hold her in his arms. "I don't exactly know what to call it, I just know I want more and more. I know that it's difficult for you to trust me, Hanna."

His statement was more accurate than he knew. She wanted to tell him about the status of her relationship with Jacob, and what happened so he would understand her sensitivity to his secrecy. Hanna lifted her head from Isaac's chest, looking into his irreproachable eyes.

"It isn't fair to expect you to understand my trust issues if you don't know why I have them."

Isaac knew exactly why it was difficult for Hanna to trust him. If he said nothing, he would be committing an offence just as deceitful as lying. He would be repeating the same mistake he made by not telling her, upfront that he was the CEO and owner of Skyfleet. He wanted to tell her she didn't have to justify anything to him. Isaac held her tighter, and his eyes looked saddened beneath his down-turned brows. "I think I do understand."

Hanna could tell by the expression on his face that there was more Isaac wanted to say. "You think you know why I have trust issues?" She looked doubtful and searched his eyes for understanding. Looking remorseful, Isaac watched nervously, waiting for Hanna to grasp what he was implying. After a few more seconds it registered what he was trying to tell her.

"Who told you?" Hanna's eyes then grew round when it occurred to her that it may have been her closest friend who had spilled the beans. "Oh my g-"

Isaac shook his head and interrupted her.

"It wasn't Ava."

Hanna searched his eyes for the answer. "Then who?"

The photo of Jacob had briefly been on the internet but it was unlikely that Isaac was following the dancer with the username Nightqueen346 and saw the post. Speaking calmly, Isaac began to explain.

"I was at a tech conference in New York, sitting there, when I happened to overhear a couple of women talking loudly about him. Jacob Barber? That's his name isn't it?" Hanna nodded and Isaac continued. "Then at the gala, when I couldn't stop myself from staring at you, Vance thought he should tell me you were married. When he said the name of your fiancé, I remembered it from the conference, so I told Vance that he was wrong and that I knew otherwise."

Hanna watched Isaac speak, taking in his story. She had no idea the details of her private life had reached as far as New York. "New York? Ryan knows Jacob? Really? What?" Hanna frowned slightly and shook her head in bafflement. This was a lot to take in. "What were the women saying?" Hanna looked surprised and humiliated enough as it was and Isaac didn't want to add to her torment.

He shrugged his shoulders. "Do you honestly care what some strangers were saying?"

Isaac hoped that Hanna would decide she didn't want to know. He'd been looking forward to his turn at playfully quizzing her and enjoying her company on the ride back.

Hanna then asked herself if she did want to know. "It's ok. You can tell me what they said."

Now irritated with the unexpected turn their amazing day had taken, Isaac cut loose, verbally slamming Jacob. "They said that he was a cheating pig and that you should've called off the wedding." His blank facial expression concealed his brief satisfaction at the stab, only to have self-disgust quickly replace it. Hanna now humiliated, looked down miserably. Why had it not occurred to her that Jacob's infidelity would be circulating beyond her small, close circle of friends? All it took was one dirty photo on the internet. The news was a tremendous shock, not to mention, an uncomfortable and sudden awakening. She hadn't shared the fact that Jacob had cheated on her. Since meeting Isaac she had pushed almost all thoughts of Jacob completely aside. Being with Isaac had been a welcome escape from the anger and loneliness she'd had to endure. Jacob's cheating had mangled her self-esteem and somehow being with this sexy, witty man she had fought to resist, felt like therapy. Finding out that Isaac had been aware of her circumstances the whole time, felt like a violation. It was as if she'd just realized that the protective disguise she thought she'd been wearing had long since fallen off without her knowledge. Hanna turned around no longer able to face him. Isaac raised his hands and caressed the tops and sides of her shoulders hoping to ease her. "You don't need to hide from me, Hanna," he said softly.

Part of her wanted to turn around and immerse her body within him, forgetting the world around them. She wanted to think of nothing but the pleasures this man's body, touch and companionship had awarded her. She wished that Isaac hadn't known about Jacob when he'd met her at the gala. She thought back to the easy confidence he'd shown when he first said *hello* to her. Speaking with her back to him she asked,

"When you saw me at the gala, were you seeing me for who I was or as someone who was desperate after her fiancé had just cheated on her with a stripper?"

Isaac's hands halted at the mention of the stripper. He hadn't heard either woman at the conference mention that abhorrent detail. It was clear, why Hanna had been so intent, regarding the topic of strip joints on the way over. Isaac could only imagine how degrading the news must have been for her. "That shouldn't have happened to you Hanna." Isaac slowly brought the side of his face to Hanna's head to feel her soft hair and speak quietly into her ear.

His arms were overlapped at her waist, holding her safely against him. "I was never thinking about how vulnerable it made you. I was only selfishly thinking that it no longer made you his."

Hanna sensed the genuine truth in his voice. Her eyes filled with tears at his tender words and she was thankful she was still turned away from him. It felt incredible to be wanted by a man like Isaac and at the same time, the sad reminder that her heart should perhaps, no longer belong to Jacob, hit too many nerves at once. The clash of emotions overpowered her, bubbling over into streams of tears. Hanna allowed Isaac to hold her, enjoying the warm and steady comfort of his arms. Moments later, her tears had subsided and she took a deep breath to steady herself. Despite feeling soothed, she was weak and tired now. The revving of a boat engine that had been in the distance was now growing louder. A ski boat with several cheering teenagers raced by causing small waves behind its lively wake. The boat rocked gently, causing Hanna to sway slightly. Isaac slowly turned her around, wiped the tears from her cheeks and rewrapped his arms around her. "I'm going to get us a snack so we both don't faint of hunger and have our boat drift out to sea."

Hanna was grateful for the offer, and after letting out a small giggle at his joke, she gracefully accepted his suggestion with a small nod of approval. Isaac helped guide her to sit in one of the high-back captain's chairs, then stepped over to the mini kitchen and opened a sleek door that concealed a small fridge. He reached in pulling out several sandwiches wrapped in deli paper. Tilting his head to see the stickers he read Hanna the options. "We have turkey, assorted, and vegetarian."

Slightly embarrassed at her recent fit of tears, Hanna pointed shyly at the turkey sandwich. Isaac unwrapped it and set it on a plate he retrieved from another cabinet. Hanna ate half of her sandwich and then immediately drifted off to sleep. She slept next to him in the co-captain's chair with her head leaning on his shoulder. When she woke a while later and checked the time on the boat's navigation screen, she realized they'd been on the boat for well over two hours.

"Are we lost? She asked sleepily.

Isaac smiled endearingly at her. "No, not lost."

Hanna looked through the front window at the dark summer sky. There were boats nearby with safety lights guiding their way and high-rise buildings, lit from within, sparkled upon the distant shoreline.

"Where are we?"

"You fell asleep and I didn't want to wake you. I've been circling the outskirts of the harbour letting you get some sleep. I wasn't able to keep my word about having you back on land before dark. Sorry. I did have you back in the harbour though."

Isaac leaned down and laid a small kiss on the top of her head and began to head toward the marina's tall dock lights. It was an overly thoughtful gesture, driving aimlessly so that your passenger could continue to sleep while you fought to stay awake yourself.

It was the type of kindness that you might show toward your child or partner. The quick kiss Isaac gave her was given with such tender familiarity that it caused Hanna to contemplate the direction her affair with Isaac might be heading. She hadn't yet stopped to consider that. Their boat tour was over and she didn't know when they'd see each other again. She only knew that when she was with him her problems seemed far away. It felt natural in Isaac's arms like she was meant to be there. Hanna could see how easy it would be for someone to fall in love with him. Until now she didn't know she could want someone so desperately and still have such deep feelings for someone else. According to romance movies and novels, it was a predicament that occurred all the time. Hanna thought about the mess of feelings she still had for Jacob, and had yet to sort out. They were still engaged and she'd been wearing her ring the entire time. He made her promise not to take it off before she left for Ava's. She sighed and looked down at the light pink gem on her finger. The happy butterflies that usually came to life whenever she glanced at it, weren't dancing today. Isaac noticed her studying it.

"I wouldn't pass judgment if you wanted to take it off."

Hanna said nothing and discreetly tucked her hand beneath her thigh where it was out of sight. Moments later they had arrived at the marina. When Isaac was finished lining up the boat with the dock, Hanna got up from beside him and turned, expecting him to rise from his chair. He delayed as if in thought, and then finally got up. After helping Hanna off the boat and onto the dock he began busily tying the lines. Hanna was quiet, groggy, and more confused about her feelings now than ever. Isaac had stopped only once to glance in her direction. He shot her a half smile and looped the last knot around the metal dock cleat. "Would you like me to drive you home Miss Richards?"

Nothing sounded better to Hanna than going home to sleep that very minute. Unfortunately, she still had to pick up her vehicle from the studio. Traffic on the highway was light and Isaac had Hanna back at Richards and Co. within fifteen minutes. They were both tired and their conversation was kept light and minimal. The contrasting mood between the boat ride to the castle and the current quiet car ride was comparable to the excitement of picking up a dearly missed loved one from the airport, to the longing for more togetherness when it came time to catch their flight home. Hanna sensed that Isaac felt the same. He'd been withdrawn since he docked the boat. A subtle and soundless event on the voyage home triggered them to reflect on the events from the last twenty-four hours. After their night of erotica, Hanna never expected to see Isaac again. When he'd shown up at her office to ask her for coffee she was surprised but not disappointed. They'd gotten to know each other a little over a coffee, then enjoyed an impromptu boat cruise to Ever Island where they explored a breathtaking stone castle and made indescribable love in a purple velvet chair. It was an incredible day that Hanna would forever remember.

She knew Isaac would want to see her again and if he asked, she wouldn't be able to say no. She sat awkwardly deciding how best to tell him she needed some time and likely wouldn't see him again for a while.

Isaac pulled the truck into the parking lot around the back of the building and turned off the engine. When Hanna looked over to thank him and say goodbye, he was sitting there wearing a subdued expression. Expecting him to be smiling, Hanna figured it was the long boat ride or the truck's dark lighting, skewing his handsome appearance. Isaac spoke before she had a chance to.

"Well, we've officially come full circle. I enjoyed your company today. Thank you for coming with me."

There was an unexpected, impersonal quality in his voice. Hanna wanted to tell him she appreciated that he'd brought her Mom's castle story to life, but instead, she listened to Isaac explain that he would be tied up for the next several days.

"I'll still be here in town but Vance and I are working on a project that will need some extra attention. Some long days and late nights. Maybe we can meet up again sometime afterwards."

Isaac had just delivered a casual brush-off and tried to use *I'm busy with work* as a disguise. Hanna went from feeling guilty because she needed time to disentangle her emotions to feeling sorrowfully rejected.

"Oh!" She frowned slightly then quickly exchanged it for a small smile. "Important, top secret government projects?" she joked lightly. Isaac smiled and she was relieved he hadn't noticed her frowning.

"Yeah, it's important." He answered quietly, not confirming the government's involvement.

Hanna had just reached into her purse for her keys when the back door to the studio flew open and Shauni and Ethan emerged from the building. They stopped when they saw the unfamiliar vehicle in their small private parking lot with two shadowy figures within. Hanna could see their needless alarm.

"It's Shauni and Ethan. They don't know it's me."

Ethan was already rummaging in his satchel for his pepper spray and Shauni stood frozen with alarm. Hanna jumped down and out of the vehicle so they could see it was only her and wouldn't be scared. Isaac surprised her by taking off his seat belt and jumping out of the truck with her. Ethan abandoned his desperate search when he caught sight of Isaac's non-threatening, arresting appearance. Shauni was getting her own thorough look at the tall handsome stranger. When it registered it was Hanna with whom the good-looking stranger had arrived, Ethan quickly pulled his hand out of his bag.

"Oh, thank goodness it's you!"

Ethan exhaled forcefully and put his hand over his chest. Shauni looked down at Ethan's satchel and then to his face with a humoured expression. Because Hanna had announced she'd met someone at the gala and hinted she was with him again when Ethan called her today at the office, there was no need to guess who the mystery man was.

"Hi there. Isaac Fletcher. Nice to meet you."

Isaac held his hand out to Ethan, who was excited to take it.

"Ethan Shepard, my pleasure Isaac!"

Ethan continued to size up Isaac's pleasing physique as Isaac then courteously leaned over to shake Shauni's outstretched hand.

"Hey, Isaac. I'm Shauni."

"Hi there Shauni."

Listening to Isaac greet her coworkers in that arresting voice of his, sent an unexpected shiver through Hanna's body. She quickly tried to shake off his effect and then looked at her employees wondering why they were only just leaving the office after eight o'clock.

"I'm kinda scared to ask, but what are you guys still doing here? Did it go ok today?"

Ethan allowed Shauni to answer. "It went great! We finished up at the booth, went out for a bite to eat and came back here to ditch the tools. Oh! By the way, the ceiling's all fixed. Good as new. They told Mani that they added some insulation around a pipe or something."

Hanna was relieved that the leak in the ceiling was fixed. Isaac's assessment was bang on. "Thank goodness! That's great news. Thanks for taking care of the booth setup today. Sorry, I never made it back to help."

Ethan waved his wrist in front of him and glanced at Isaac. "No worries at all Han. It turned out great! I'm just glad you were in such able hands."

Flattered and humoured by Ethan's statement, Isaac gave a small nod and smiled as he glanced at Hanna. Shauni side-eyed Ethan after his cheeky comment, then changed the subject. "It was no trouble! We were fine! I think Glen was happy with the way the booth turned out. We took a bunch of pictures for you."

Ethan and Shauni didn't mind handling the booth setup on their own. They had handled everything the way Hanna would have herself. Shauni nor Ethan knew exactly where Hanna had been throughout the day but they'd now seen the attractive man with whom she had shared it. They supported the new connection and encouraged Hanna to go with Isaac that afternoon. They now wondered when or if they would see the intriguing man again.

Looking from Ethan to Shauni, Isaac felt it was time to let Hanna return to her life and him to his. "Well Miss Richards, I should get going. I've got an early meeting in the morning." He paused briefly. "Thanks again for coming along with me today."

Standing there only a few feet apart, Hanna wished she could embrace him for a moment and kiss him goodbye. Their quiet car ride and the current audience made it awkward and she opted to hold off.

"Thanks for inviting me." She smiled remembering her day, then downplayed their time together at the castle. "It was quite an adventure."

Looking at Hanna, Isaac didn't allow the two-person audience to discourage him. He reached out putting one hand at Hanna's waist and the other carefully cradled the side of her face. He bent slightly and laid a long, slow, gentle kiss on her lips. After the heavenly embrace, Isaac broke the kiss and subtly brushed his lips across her ear, causing another quick jolt of pleasure. Hanna's eyes had been closed for the tender kiss and when she finally opened them, they glistened with uncertain emotion. Looking into her eyes, Isaac gave Hanna a small reassuring smile. He then stepped away and walked toward his vehicle. He looked back briefly offering a quick friendly wave to Ethan and Shauni. "Nice meeting you both."

He jumped into the vehicle, backed out smoothly onto the street and drove away. Hanna, Ethan and even Shauni stood staring regrettably in the direction Isaac had left. Ethan broke the silence. "That-was-one-beautiful-man."

Shauni hadn't voiced her opinion but the fact that she hadn't disputed Ethan's comment could be construed as a rare show of unity. Ethan and Shauni expectantly waited for a rundown on the night before and the day that had ended with the most romantic display of affection either of them had seen in a long time. Hanna was now beyond tired but at the same time, she desperately hoped to clear her mind and emotionally recalibrate by sharing the accounts of the last day and a half with her two close friends. She looked up at the dark summer sky and slowly released a deep breath.

"What am I doing?"

Shauni walked over and rested her hand on Hanna's shoulder.

"I warned you about those damn tuxedos." She glanced in the direction that Isaac had driven. "If I'd seen Double O Seven Inches last night I would have done exactly what I hope you did."

It was some much-needed comic relief, prompting one of Hanna's big and bright smiles. Hanna then recounted the events from the gala, up until the return boat ride from Ever Island when she'd had her moment of reflection. Ethan was quick to defend and support Hanna's uncharacteristic actions. "I'm certainly not holding you accountable for anything. As far as I'm concerned, you did nothing wrong. You're not even sure that you're staying with Jacob. No one should expect you to miss out on an opportunity with someone who might be the love of your life. The *loyal*," he clarified, "*love of your life*."

It was clear where Ethan stood. And that was wherever Hanna stood. Hanna looked to Shauni to get her take on the situation.

"You may not be certain if you can trust this Isaac guy but, sorry Han, you know without a doubt, that you can't trust Jacob. It's pretty easy to understand why you left with a stranger."

Hanna didn't know if she would be able to trust Jacob again, but she knew that referring to Isaac as a stranger felt wrong. Shauni then asked if Hanna had spoken to Jacob recently.

"No." Hanna shook her head, wearing a blank expression. "Not since I hung up on him when he wouldn't admit to calling Mandy back."

"And no texts either?" Shauni asked, looking surprised.

Hanna only shook her head again in answer. "I don't even know if he's back from London yet." Ethan and Shauni looked at each other with a bleak expression. Hanna's phone then lit up and she turned it to face upward. It was a calendar reminder that read *wedding postponement email goes out tomorrow*. She had forgotten that she still had the daunting ordeal to look forward to. Hanna looked unimpressed as she read the reminder. "Perfect. My postponement email reminder. I've got less than twelve hours." Hanna knew that once the email had been sent, she could expect a full day of taking calls and answering texts or emails from curious and concerned friends and family regarding the announcement of her wedding postponement. She blinked slowly and laid her hand across her cheek. "What would I be missing if I took Friday off?"

"Tomorrow?" Shauni asked, then looked expectedly to Ethan who likely had the team's schedule memorized for the next full year.

"Not too-too much I guess. I'll be finalizing the plans and purchasing lists for the retired teacher's reunion and the birthday party for Rex the retriever. We then have a large delivery just after lunch."

Shauni wasn't sure if she had heard him correctly. "When you say retriever, do you mean a golden retriever? We're planning a birthday party for a dog?"

Ethan, who was trying to conceal his excitement, nodded proudly. "Yes, I dooo!"

Hanna knew Ethan would be blissfully submersed in the planning of the dog party and Shauni could happily torment him while he did so. Besides, Hanna could still be available by phone, text and email if they needed her. Her laptop would give her access to files or documents if she wanted them. "Ok, it's settled. I'm taking a personal day." Hanna immediately started toward the studio door to grab her laptop. "I need to go and see my dad. He has no idea what's going on with me and if he gets the postponement email before I get a chance to talk to him, he'll be pretty upset. I don't want that."

When she entered the studio, she saw that her desk had been pushed back into its regular position and Shauni's scrap bucket had been returned to its place in the workshop. She glanced up at the newly replaced ceiling tile. It was almost as if the incident had never even happened. Hanna grabbed her laptop and charge cord then left, locking the back door to the studio. She hugged Ethan and Shauni goodbye and then headed to her vehicle. She pulled up her phone and quickly checked the doorbell app to see that a parcel had arrived but had yet to be brought inside the house. The vulnerable parcel left outside likely meant Jacob wasn't there. Hanna started her engine and for the first time in almost a week, she headed toward her own home. Her assumption about Jacob was correct. When she arrived at Twenty-six Pinedale she could tell he hadn't been home in days. It was both a relief and a stinging reminder that Jacob hadn't been home missing her company but in a faraway country catering to a new client, too busy to think of her. She knew she had no right to complain after she'd spent the day with another man. After retrieving the parcel from the porch, Hanna walked down the hall and into her bedroom. When she laid eyes on her beautiful king-size bed she wanted to crawl into its luxurious comfort and open one of her new books, the parcel left at the door. She mentally scolded herself and went into the closet to locate her gym bag. This would be a quick clothing grab and nothing more. She grabbed her bag off the shelf and added a couple of T-shirts, some shorts and a sweater. Opening the drawer, she noticed the crumpled receipt from Jacob's jeans she eyed so suspiciously the morning he went golfing. She'd forgotten all about it. She absently glanced at it, grabbed a few more items and shut the drawer again. Hanna took one more quick look around the house, locked the front door behind her and got back on the road toward Ingleton. She turned on the windshield wipers and then the radio to keep from getting sleepy while she made the dark, rainy drive home. The pink sunrise that mesmerized her early that morning had been an accurate predictor of the rainy weather to come. The evening proved a very stark contrast to the unimaginable sunny day she'd shared with Isaac.

Chapter Thirty Three

As the city faded in the rearview mirror, Hanna tried to imagine what her dad would say or think, once she explained that she and Jacob had hit an unexpected bump in the road. Dale liked Jacob. The two of them would laugh and joke back and forth whenever they were together. Hanna knew that in today's scary world, her dad was relieved she'd found someone that made her happy. It was Dale who had lovingly taught Hanna to cook, read and tie her shoes. He had instilled the values within her that made it so difficult for her to understand and accept what Jacob had done. Dale was a kind and friendly man who would help a stranger if they needed him, but he could also be unforgiving if someone crossed him. Hanna remembered the time her mom took in a puppy after Dale had made sure everyone, Pam and Hanna, knew of the firm *no-dog rule* at the Richards' house. One day while Hanna was studying for her high school exams, the neighbour, Mr. Wright, had dropped by with a soft, sand-coloured ball of fluff. He said the puppy was free and handed it to Pam. Dad wasn't home to dispute the gift and Pam was too in awe of the cuteness to hand the baby dog back to him. Mr. Wright had told Pam that the puppy was the last remaining from the litter and nobody wanted her. He said the puppy would stay small, likely getting no bigger than a cat. That night, Pam and Hanna worked hard trying to convince Dale that the puppy would be a good little friend and addition to the family. After what seemed like years, Dale finally softened toward the dog, they'd named Barbie. He even built a miniature staircase that Barbie could use to climb onto Hanna's bed and sleep with her. But he never forgave Mr. Wright for going against his wishes. Mr. Wright owned a dog kennel and years before he'd hypnotized Pam with the puppy, Dale had specifically asked him not to show up at his house with any puppies. Dale knew that Pam wouldn't be able to resist the little creatures. He would be surprised when Hanna told him that she was postponing the wedding, and if Hanna told him the reason, he would consider Jacob's cheating a personal betrayal. Hanna wasn't sure what advice he would give her if she ended up telling him the full extent of Jacob's misstep. To Hanna, her dad's opinion would always be treasured, whether it was difficult to hear or not. After a forty-minute, lonely and rainy drive, Hanna finally drove up the driveway of her parent's home. The white, three-bedroom bungalow sat on several acres with perennial gardens and a large workshop in the back. There were only a few dim lights on inside and Hanna knew, now that it was after eleven o'clock, her dad would already be sleeping. Even now that he'd retired from his job at the township, Dale had made it a habit to be in bed by ten. Hanna hoped she could sneak in quietly to avoid waking Barbie and instigating a full-out bark-a-thon. Barbie considered it her life's work to broadcast every entry into the Richards' house. Whether it was her owner returning home after work or an uninvited mouse, Barbie announced it loudly and proudly. Dale referred to Barbie as the smallest and most efficient guard dog in the world.

Hanna used her key to let herself into the house and headed straight down the hall toward her room. When she was within steps from her old bedroom and thought she'd victoriously made it in without waking anyone, she heard the quiet jingling of metal dog tags. She turned to see not only Barbie's skinny legs standing there but also beside her, the large silhouette belonging to her father Dale. Pam often said that Dale looked '*a bit like Harrison Ford, only thicker*'. Not expecting anyone this evening, he was wearing his boxer shorts and a T-shirt. Hanna reached into the room and flicked on the light, partially lighting the dark hallway. She had shown up late at night without notice and without her future husband.

"Hello, Sweetheart," Dale offered quietly.

Hanna cautiously attempted a whispered, "Hi."

When Barbie heard Hanna's hushed voice she quickly pranced over and stood at her feet waiting for some affection. Hanna bent down to scratch Barbie's ears and without warning a tear fell from her eye and onto the floor. After she'd wiped it, Dale disappeared and returned wearing his housecoat and glasses.

"I'll go put the kettle on."

Hanna sat her bag down in the corner of her room and then headed out to the living room, Barbie trailing close behind her. She sat in one of the big recliner chairs beside the brick fireplace and waited to tell her dad why she'd shown up without giving him the pre-visit notice she usually offered. Dale appeared a few moments later with two steaming mugs of tea, handed one to Hanna, and sat in the other recliner. Barbie jumped up into Dale's lap, circled once then sat down. Hanna avoided eye contact with her dad for fear she'd cry again, once she saw the concern in his eyes. She was struggling as it was. "I'm sorry I showed up so late. I hope I didn't scare you guys too much."

Dale and Barbie would survive the late-night scare. "That's ok Honey. We were probably gonna' get up to pee again soon anyway. Barbie started needing a second nightly pee about the same time I did."

Barbie quickly turned her small head and looked up at Dale as if he'd just betrayed her by divulging her secret. Dale and Hanna both smiled in sync at the laughable little animal. Petting Barbie's head, Dale looked lovingly in Hanna's direction.

"Did something happen at home Honey?"

Hanna nodded slowly at Dale's understatement. She would try to share only the details she needed to. "I'm not sure if I can marry Jacob anymore." She'd already said more than she wanted to. It hurt to hear herself put it that way but it was the simple truth. Dale was quiet for a second, processing the surprising statement. He was expecting a less serious dilemma, like a disagreement between Hanna and Jacob or maybe a work issue that had overflowed onto the home front. He instantly wished Pam was still alive to help him and Hanna navigate the situation, whatever it was. He knew that something serious must have happened for Hanna to consider calling off her wedding to Jacob. Dale had taught his daughter to be honest with him. If he asked enough questions he would eventually have the answers."Did somebody make a bad mistake?"

Dale omitted their names hoping it would be easier for Hanna to answer him. She nodded again in answer to his second question. Jacob had definitely made a mistake. The more difficult question to answer was whether or not Hanna could find it within her to forgive him.

"Have you guys talked about what happened? Or is this a cool-down period?"

Unfortunately, they were past the cool-down phase and talking about what happened had only revealed more shocking details of Jacob's infidelity. Hanna had then complicated things by meeting someone else.

"We've talked. He's in England right now trying to win a contract with a new customer. I haven't talked to him in a couple of days."

Dale had been softly blowing his tea in an effort to cool it. When Hanna mentioned England, he stopped and lifted his head from his mug in surprise. Dale had always admired Jacob's ambition and desire to excel. This was disappointing.

"Must have been pretty important. Any phone calls or texts?" he prodded. Dale tried not to look troubled over the inopportune timing of Jacob's business travel. Hanna recalled the morning she thought he'd stopped in to plead for her forgiveness but was only heading to the airport. "We've spoken twice since he's been over there but the last call didn't go very well. I'm staying with Ava right now."

Dale's eyebrows pulled together, knowing that if Hanna had inherited his habit of grudge-holding, it would make things much more challenging for both her and Jacob.

"That's too bad sweetheart. I'm sure Jacob's feeling just as badly about things as you are. Does he want to work it out? What's his mindset right now?"

Jacob did feel badly about what happened and despite not being overly convincing, he said that he wanted things to work out.

"He said he was sorry and he asked me not to take my ring off. But he's also the one who suggested we postpone the wedding. He thought it was the better alternative to calling it off altogether."

Dale sipped his tea thinking things over. "Maybe he's just trying to give you some space. To let you clear your mind and cool off."

He was giving her some space alright. He'd given her so much space that she'd had enough time to have an affair with another man. Hanna knew that if Jacob had put more genuine effort into his atonement and shown her more remorse she might not have left for Ava's, and consequently been in a position to meet someone. "It's possible he sees it that way. But it doesn't seem to be helping his cause. You always told me that if you hurt someone you make sure they know how sorry you are. You show them. You tell them. I had no idea Jacob struggled so much with atonement until all of this happened."

Dale sighed deeply sharing in Hanna's frustration.

"It's hard for some people to show remorse, even when they know they should. It doesn't mean they aren't sorry for hurting you."

Hanna sipped her tea.

"What if I can't forgive him, Dad?"

Dale looked at Hanna adoringly. It was like she was eight years old again, learning a valuable lesson from her doting father.

"You'll know what to do Honey. It'll be ok."

Dale sipped his tea and grimaced slightly from the heat. "He hurt you deeply and it's a damn shame he made such a stupid mistake, but I will say that unless something's changed, that boy Jacob loves you deeply. I see it when you're together. This doesn't have to mean the end for you two Honey. You can still have a wonderful life together."

Knowing how tightly her father held grudges in the past, it wasn't exactly what Hanna expected him to say. After he attempted to reassure her about Jacob, she tried to take comfort in his surprising effort to offer hope. A life with Jacob had been all Hanna had ever wanted. Her father had just told her there was still a chance at a good life with Jacob. He believed it too. After all, Dale had been in love before. And to Hanna, it was the greatest love she had ever known. Her mother and father showed each other how much they loved each other daily. She could only hope she could have something as special as they did.

"You're right Dad. I just need to decide to forgive him and then live with the fact that three months before our wedding he decided to get drunk and…" Hanna trailed off as her voice broke. Barbie immediately jumped down off Dale's lap and sat at Hanna's feet, waiting for the signal to join her. Hanna lightly tapped her thigh, granting Barbie permission, prompting her to jump up. Barbie did her trademark circle check and then sat down in Hanna's lap. Hanna gently stroked Barbie's small head and soft back. There was something about petting Barbie's silky hair that always helped Hanna to relax. Hanna inhaled deeply and held it together. "What do you think Barbie?" Hanna spoke softly in a raised pitch. "Would you tell me what to do if you could talk to me?" The dog gave Hanna a couple of licks with her tiny tongue then rested her head on Hanna's thigh. Hanna thought that was probably the right note to leave off on for the night. They could talk and visit more tomorrow. She looked toward Dale and offered a small smile. "Should we call it a night Dad?"

Dale smiled, nodding at her suggestion. Those were the words he said to Hanna as a child each night after her bedtime story, and later to Pam when they were tired after watching nightly television. Hanna knew he would be thinking of Pam just as she was. The two of them got up out of their chairs and as Dale picked up the mugs, Hanna snuck a kiss onto his cheek.

"Night Dad. Thanks for the tea, and for listening."

"Night Honey."

CHAPTER THIRTY FOUR

That night Hanna struggled to fall asleep, thinking about her current dilemma. She wondered what Jacob was doing wherever he was, and at the same time, tried in vain to ignore the intruding thoughts and images of Isaac. She went over the events of her life from the past week and everything that had brought her here. It was Jacob who had caused the initial division between them. But it was Hanna's pride and unforgiving nature that prevented her from staying, committing herself to repairing their relationship and her self-esteem. Hanna remembered Lisa's words about forgiveness and how it was ultimately her choice. She didn't know if she'd be making a mistake by taking a chance at trusting Jacob again. If she could forgive him and their life resumed the way it was before the mishap, then maybe she would feel she made the right decision. Hanna knew she would have to tell Jacob about Isaac, no matter how difficult it was. Not because she would draw satisfaction from his pain, but because it wouldn't be a fresh start if they began with more lies. Hanna shook her head at the ironic possibility that Jacob might not even forgive the offence. It was unfitting, considering her time with Isaac to be an offence when it had brought them both so much pleasure. Hanna had tormented herself enough for one night and tried again to fall asleep.

Hanna dreamed of an alternate distorted reality. In her dream, Hanna had married Jacob. There hadn't been a ceremony but soon her tummy was big and round with her longed-for, first child. After several short days, Hanna had given birth to not only one baby but two beautiful boys. In this twisted nightmare world, Hanna was granted permission to take only one baby home with her. She had to choose which little boy would have a loving mother and which baby would be adopted by the state. Hanna cradled the babies in her arms waiting to see their beautiful, precious features. One baby opened his eyes revealing two perfect, deep blue eyes, just like Jacob's. Excluding Hanna from the decision, Jacob decided, this was the baby they would take home. The other baby was immediately swaddled by a nurse and taken away before Hanna had a chance to see him open his precious eyes. When it was time to leave the hospital, they walked past the nursery. Laying there alone in his bassinet was Hanna's other baby boy. He was wide awake but he wasn't crying. Hanna rushed to the glass to see the baby she'd been forced to leave behind. As if sensing her, he turned his tiny head to look at her through the thick partition. His eyes weren't deep blue like the other baby's but a beautiful mixture of grey and green. Hanna then bawled and screamed looking for a door to get to him. When it became obvious that there was no way to reach him, Hanna looked at the baby and told him she loved him. He stared at her and with only his grey eyes, he told her that he would always love her and knew that she didn't want to leave him. When Hanna woke up her cheeks were soaked with tears. Despite her relief that it had only been a bazaar and cruel nightmare, she was still reeling from the heartbreak she felt for the baby she couldn't reach. Looking at her phone Hanna realized it was later in the morning than she thought. Trying to abandon thoughts of the disturbing nightmare, she went to the kitchen for a glass of water. She then looked around for Dad and Barbie. They weren't anywhere within the house and she couldn't see them outside either. Hanna then heard the sound of car tires approaching on the gravel driveway. Looking out the front window she could see Barbie primly perched, high on the center console of Dale's car. Her curly tail wagged excitedly as she saw the house come into view and Hanna standing at the window. Dale had driven down the road to the bakery for coffee and morning tea biscuits. He was sure to have them at the house if Hanna and Jacob were visiting.

"Morning young lady." Dale handed a paper bag and one of the coffees to Hanna.

"Morning Dad. Thanks!" She peeked into the bag and smiled.

Dale headed to the covered patio out back while Hanna and Barbie followed. Dale spoke over his shoulder. "The Wilsons are having a big estate sale. The whole front lawn is covered. Probably lots of good ol' stuff if you're interested."

"Neat. Maybe I'll check it out after my coffee."

Hanna took a seat on the porch swing while Dale and Barbie took the large cushioned deck chair. Both Hanna and Dale enjoyed spending time gazing at Pam's flower gardens during the warm summer months. Pam had loved caring for the garden plants and being around them now helped both Dale and Hanna to feel close to her. The blooms returned yearly, reminding them she was still with them. "She'd be out there right now, wouldn't she?" Dale grinned, picturing Pam working away, out in her garden.

Hanna could almost see her beautiful mom crouched in the garden, wearing her old worn sun hat. "I think your right Dad," she agreed quietly.

They both sipped at their coffee, looking out at the lush gardens. Hanna ached for the chance to talk with her mom again. "What do you think mom would say about Jacob?" She wasn't sure if she expected Dale to answer or not.

Dale then sighed and looked as though he was pondering something.

"She'd tell you to go home and marry the boy."

When Dale had told Hanna that she could still have a wonderful life with Jacob she was caught off guard. Dale said he knew that

Jacob loved her and even defended him by claiming that some people weren't very good at showing remorse. She struggled to believe that her notorious grudge-holding father hadn't told her to '*give him the boot*' the way she expected him to. It was even harder to believe that he thought that her mother would think Hanna should rush home and forget all about what Jacob had done. Hanna shook her head in frustration. "Why are you so desperate to have me marry Jacob? I don't get it, Dad. Besides losing Mom, I've never been so hurt in my entire life. He cheated on me!"

Dale sipped on his coffee and Barbie watched him as if gauging his reaction to Hanna's defensive tone.

"I know what he did Honey. What's the saying? Those we love most, hurt us the deepest. It was one mistake. Sometimes we have to be strong, forgive and move on."

Hanna frowned. "I don't believe in that saying."

In her frustration, Hanna pushed her foot off the deck board, picking up the pace of her swing and glared out into the garden. "And, where is this even coming from? You're the one who always taught me to do the right thing, to be honest and loyal. If someone doesn't treat you the same...*to hell with em'*. Those are your very words."

Dale smiled pridefully, knowing she was right. Those were in fact his words. But exceptions could be made and he knew he needed to justify his stance. "It's coming from the fact that, if I had been less forgiving when I'd been in your situation, your mother and I would have been divorced and you wouldn't have been born."

Hanna's swing stopped swaying and she turned her head to look at Dale. He tilted his head downward and looked at Hanna over his glasses. "I'm only going to tell you this story Honey, because I think it might help your cause."

Hanna said nothing, anxiously awaiting the details of Dale's sudden and shocking revelation.

"It was a very long time ago and your mom and I had only been married less than a year. It was your mother's second year teaching at Glendale and I was still with the township roads department. We were invited to the annual teacher's end-of-year party at Brett Hastings, the school principal's house. We'd been there for half an hour when I'd been called in to work. They needed some emergency road repairs after a fiery accident on the Third Concession, down by the bridge."

Dale used his thumb to point backward in the direction of the bridge. "The repair took half the night and I never made it back to the party. At first, we assumed I'd be back, so your mom had stayed there socializing. She ended up getting a ride later and was home before me. When I got home she was sitting there at the table crying. Your mom told me she'd been drinking a bunch, which she never did, and made a horrible mistake at the party. When she said what she did, I wanted to leave her. But I didn't. We never had a single fight until that night. Your mom was sick with guilt and regret.

We both knew it only happened because she'd been drinking so much. She couldn't even remember all of the details. We talked and decided to give it time. Out of respect for me, she never drank again and even tried to quit her teaching job at the school. I told her she didn't have to do that but she thought she had to prove to me….," Dale swallowed the uncomfortable lump in his throat. "how much she loved me."

He sipped his coffee and continued. "Your mom became pregnant with you a couple months later, so when you were born she stayed home so she could be with you," Dale paused briefly, "and with me."

Hanna looked up at the sky as if that would keep her tears from falling. She was not only sad for her dad for having to endure the humiliating heartbreak her mom had caused him but also sad for her mom for having to live with the mistake her whole life. Hanna had only ever known her parents to be blissfully happy. Evidently, time and love had allowed them to put the painful ordeal behind them. "I'm sorry Dad. I had no idea."

Dale nodded slowly and half smiled. "That's good. You weren't supposed to know Honey."

Hanna was still in disbelief, thinking about her parent's near-perfect relationship. "But you two were so happy, like every day. How did you ever get passed it?"

"We loved each other. I had to accept that what happened had nothing to do with your mom not loving me. I didn't want to lose her love and I didn't want to stop loving her. In time I knew we could still be happy," Dale snorted lightly then added, "once it stopped pissing me off."

Hanna was absorbing Dale's words. "How long did that take?"

"Oh, a few years. I'm not gonna lie."

That sounded like an unrealistically long time. "Oh my god."

Dale could see Hanna was discouraged. "Honey, If I hadn't found the patience, I would have missed out on the best twenty-five years of my life. I got to spend all that time with my two favourite people, you and your mom. I know I made the right choice by not leaving here that night."

They shared a moment of silence before Dale then stood and kissed Hanna on the top of her head. "I don't mean to spoil the mood, but my coffee seems to have done its job. I have to go." Dale and Barbie made their way inside to use the washroom, leaving Hanna alone with her scattered thoughts. After a few minutes, Hanna got up from the swing and walked around the yard. She walked to the far edge of the garden where the tall pink garden phlox was blooming. The news about Pam had baffled her. She had always seen her mother as a perfect angel. The fact that her mom had possessed the capacity, whether sober or impaired, to hurt anyone at all, especially her dad, was a mind-boggling eye-opener. Dale had chosen not to take Pam's actions personally. Instead, he saw it as a careless mistake that burdened them both, possibly her sweet mom more so. Hanna didn't know how this new information couldn't alter how she viewed her own situation. From the raised garden beds to the small brick fire pit, everywhere she looked was validation of the happy life her parents had built together and cherished. There was no doubt the love they showed each other set the bar for Hanna's relationships. She felt she needed to carefully reassess what had happened between her and Jacob. Maybe she was taking the incident too personally. Standing there in the backyard, a strange new light was emitting from an invisible source, casting a soft new hue across Hanna's entire world. Her phone buzzed quietly from within her pocket. She glanced down at the screen to see the first text from Jacob she'd received in days.

Hi, Can we talk?

Hanna typed a short, courteous text to Jacob.

Sure of course

A few seconds later her phone rang. Hanna was instantly anxious and her fingertips dampened with sweat. She breathed deeply and then answered, trying to sound calm and neutral.

"Hi!"

"Hi, How are you?"

"I'm......ok, How about you?"

"Honestly? Not awesome."

Hanna heard Jacob swallow before he continued.

"I heard that you sent out a wedding postponement. My mom got the email and phoned, all in a panic. She was pretty upset about it so I told her it was because there was a problem with the venue. I didn't know what to tell her."

Hanna had temporarily forgotten that she'd scheduled the postponement email for this morning. "Oh my gosh! Poor Cathy. I should have called her." Hanna had always adored Jacob's mom. She was a sweet person and was excited that her only son was finally getting married. Cathy loved Hanna and would comically torment Jacob about grandkids in favour of Hanna's cause. Hanna suddenly felt like a spoiled brat. Both ends of the phone were silent until Jacob let out a sigh.

"I really miss you, Hanna."

She listened intently as Jacob continued.

"I don't want to be away from you anymore. I need to see you. I'm at the airport now and take off in an hour, will you please meet me at home?"

Sounding so sad and desperate, Jacob had reached through the phone and squeezed at Hanna's heart like a artist skillfully manipulating a ball of clay.

"Please say yes. I'm sorry for what I did Honey. I was so stupid. I know that. All I want is to be with you. Will you please let me show you how much I love you?"

If he'd been standing there in person, it might have been difficult not to embrace him. At the same time, something warned her to move slowly. She reminded herself she would have to tell Jacob how she'd spent the last couple of days. How would he feel after hearing about that? "I think you're right. We should talk." Hanna wondered if their talk should take place at home or somewhere more neutral.

"So you'll be home when I get there?" Jacob wanted to confirm.

Compelled by his desperation and the recent conversation with her dad, Hanna agreed.

"I'll be there."

"Ok! I gotta go. I have to check my bag and go through security now but I'll see you late tonight. Right?"

"Ok, you'll see me."

Hanna hung up the phone and stood there processing her feelings. She was thinking about all the *what-ifs* she'd tortured herself with, last night before falling asleep. And what about Isaac? She found herself thinking of the last, sweet kiss she'd shared with Isaac in the studio parking lot. It might have looked like an average kiss but what it revealed to Hanna was anything but ordinary. In that single kiss, he showed her how much she meant to him and wanted her. Without a word, he had confessed that his life would be incomplete without her. Kissing Isaac took Hanna far away and when they made love, she felt beautiful and cherished. *How would she ever be able to marry someone else when she felt all of that? After she'd had a life-changing affair with this man?*

The uncertainty of her life was enough to send her mind spinning. She needed a mental break. After eating one of the tea biscuits from the paper bag, Hanna dressed and brushed her teeth. For some much-needed change of scenery, she grabbed her purse and drove to the garage sale down the road at the Wilson's house. When she pulled into the driveway, Clare Wilson was carrying a stack of shoe boxes out from the garage and was heading toward a folding table set up on the grass. She was a short, chubby, energetic lady with a kind and jolly nature. Clare was Hanna's childhood babysitter when Pam and Dale had a date night or an event to attend. Hanna noted how much older Clare looked now with her grey hair. A testament to just how fast time, inevitably goes by.

"Hanna Richards? Is that you, my child? Oh my goodness!" Clare peered out from around the stack of boxes.

Hanna grabbed the top box from Clare and sat it on the table. "It's meee alright!"

Clare sat the rest of the boxes down on the table and pulled Hanna inward for an affectionate squeeze. "Look at you, Honey! You are more beautiful than ever! Oh! And I heard you were getting married!" Hanna smiled and nodded. Clare raised her stubby index finger and looked around eagerly. "Oh! You know what, I've got something for you! You left it here the last time you were here!" Hanna couldn't remember how many years ago that would have been. She guessed, at least fifteen. Clare reached into a cardboard box beneath one of the long tables and pulled out a pink plastic box with a white handle. Hanna's eyes were round with surprise. "Oh wow! Is that what I think it is?"

After carefully taking the case from Clare, Hanna placed it on the table. She flipped up the silver clasps and lifted the lid. Inside, stood her treasured, long-lost Wedding Wonders dolls, complete with an assortment of miniature wedding accessories. These were the small dolls that had helped influence her childhood dreams. Looking at the perfect, smiling dolls, Hanna felt like they were from another lifetime. She looked at the handsome groom wearing his tiny tuxedo then carefully shut the case. "Thanks, Clare. I wondered where they'd disappeared to. I thought I'd never see them again."

"I didn't even know I had them! When I found them this morning, I knew you'd probably want them back and set them aside." After about an hour of chatting with Clare and sifting through dusty boxes, Hanna headed home to Dale and Barbie. She'd ended up with a miniature wood sculpture, some vintage botanical postcards, a cool frame to arrange them in and of course her old doll case. When Hanna walked into the kitchen, Dale was at the counter making sandwiches for lunch. "There's some leafy lettuce out back in the west garden if you want some for your sandwich." Nothing tasted better on a sandwich than homegrown leafy lettuce. Hanna grabbed a bowl and headed out back. The vegetable garden was just beyond the big maple tree that housed Hanna's childhood tree fort. The first time she brought Jacob home to meet Dale, they had walked the property. Jacob had carved a small heart into the bark and in the middle, he scratched the letter *H*. Hanna stopped briefly to remember the sweet occasion. It was also where he'd asked her to marry him two years later. It was impossible not to feel like some higher power was trying to tell her something. She grabbed a few pieces of lettuce from the garden and headed back inside. After lunch, Hanna took time to arrange Ava's vintage postcards within the frame Clare had kindly given her. She used some old leftover wallpaper as the background and fastened the postcards on top of the paper. Hanna polished the glass until it sparkled then reattached the backing on the frame. She flipped it over to see her finished product. Ava would love it. "Not too shabby! Is it now Barbie?" Barbie tilted her head trying to grasp Hanna's satisfaction.

If she wanted to miss Friday night traffic, it was time to head back to the city. She carefully sat Ava's frame in her backseat, with her gym bag and long-lost treasures she'd gotten from Clare at the sale. She hugged her dad and thanked him for confiding in her and for being a good listener. She told him to wish her luck and that she'd be back again in a couple of weeks to visit, with or without Jacob. Dale didn't push but instead told her he loved her. "Drive safe sweetheart."

"Thanks, Dad! Talk soon!" She blew him a kiss through the car window and headed down the road. Hanna left feeling comforted but still unsure of almost everything. She was only a few miles down the road when she spotted the big sign in the air that read Ivan's of Ingleton. She couldn't help thinking of Isaac and his old pickup truck. Her mind then shifted to the classic image of him, leaning against the bar, wearing that tuxedo, giving her an incredibly sexy smile. She wondered what it would have been like if she'd met Isaac and not known about Jacob's infidelity. She would have been attracted to him but never would have gone home with him had Jacob not cheated. *Would she have?* Hanna shook her head at the thought of herself being so reckless. It didn't matter. She couldn't change anything now and she didn't want to. She would never regret going home with Isaac. The music on the stereo paused and Ava's ringtone came through the speakers. Hanna pressed the screen to answer. "Hello? Ava? that you?"

"What? Are you eighty all of a sudden?" Ava didn't even give Hanna time to defend herself. "Hey! Where are you? I stopped in at the studio and Ethan said you'd taken today off."

"Sorry. I'm in the car. It's hard to hear. I'm just on my way home. I was visiting my dad."

"I was hoping to meet up."

"Sure, you wanna meet me at my place? I'm actually going home now to talk to Jacob. He called me this morning. We're supposed to talk. I'm going to tell him about Isaac."

"Oh." Ava sounded annoyed. "As much as I'd like to see that, I was hoping to talk to you without him there."

"Ok. Well, he won't be home until midnight. Your paths shouldn't cross."

"Good, When are you home?"

"I just left. Maybe forty-five minutes. I need a quick shower first though. I'm grimy. I was digging through a bunch of dusty old boxes."

"Sounds good! How's an hour and a half?"

"Perfect! See you then!"

The rest of Hanna's car ride was spent thinking about her relationship with Jacob. Until the one isolated incident, their relationship had been almost perfect. After realizing that sometimes forgiveness can bring blessings, she convinced herself that their love was worth keeping. Hanna felt maybe she owed it to decency itself to give the relationship another chance, a fair chance. If she didn't find it in her heart to forgive Jacob, she would be, giving up on him, her home and her dream. He had hurt her deeply, but instead of giving herself time to heal she'd allowed her pride to steer her away from him and into the arms of another man. She felt guilty thinking about how he would feel once she told him. It would crush him. Jacob wanted to prove how sorry he was and make it up to her but instead of allowing him the opportunity, she walked away. If they needed to, they could go see Lisa Price as a couple. It would be a new beginning together. Eventually, they could talk about moving ahead with the wedding plans. They could still have, as her dad had put it, a wonderful life.

Chapter Thirty Five

Hanna turned onto Pinedale Ave and slowed, taking her time approaching the driveway. Now that it was daylight, she could see that her tall pink garden phlox had fully bloomed. Pam would be proud that the little divisions from her garden in Ingleton had done so well. Hanna pulled up to the house and parked the vehicle. As she was retrieving Ava's frame from the back seat something collided with her rear window, then fell to the ground. It was so loud that Hanna doubted that the window wasn't smashed. She stopped what she was doing and went around to find a small drone lying on the driveway. Hanna looked around to see its owner, a young man, running frantically in her direction from across the street. She bent to pick up the downed flyer and then glanced at her rear window. Sounding out of breath from running, the young fellow apologized for the incident.

"Oh shoot. Sorry. I didn't mean for that to happen."

After one last glance at the unharmed window, Hanna turned to respond. "That's ok. It looks like…." She broke off after looking at the young man. He was about thirteen. He stared at Hanna with the most arresting grey eyes that Hanna had only ever seen on one other person. For a moment Hanna was paralyzed looking into the child's eyes. Finally, she passed him back the drone.

"Thanks!" he said gladly, then headed back across the street.

Hanna carried her gym bag and Ava's art into the house. The brief interaction with the young man had caught her by surprise. His mosaic eyes had reminded her of someone who would likely no longer be a part of her life. The realization made her chest ache. Isaac had only been in Hanna's life for two days and yet he possessed the capacity to affect her beyond reason. Their time together felt more like a lifetime and at the same time a complete dream. Hanna now knew she would think of him every time she saw someone with those same grey eyes. *In time, would she learn to simply remember Isaac fondly or would she long for him and miss him from her life?* She felt deflated. Ava was on her way over shortly and she still wanted to freshen up. She hoped a shower would help wash away her darkened mood and maybe perk her up a bit. Hanna walked into the en-suite and turned the shower lever to hot, letting it heat up before stepping in. When they'd remodelled the Master bath, Jacob had requested they install not one shower head but two shower heads.

"We can shower at the same time," he whispered seductively into Hanna's ear.

Hanna thought it was a spectacular idea and didn't need any further convincing. The designer had made the custom shower extra wide and extra long. As requested, there was a shower head at each end with separate controls and a large central rain-head above. It was an impressive shower and a dream when shared with your lover. Jacob and Hanna had steamed up the large luxurious shower together on many occasions. Hanna draped a fresh towel over the nearby hook, slid the thick glass door closed behind her, and leaned her head back into the hot spray of the water. The heat of the shower immediately began to relax her tense neck and shoulders. Hanna closed her eyes allowing the water to work its magic on her body. It was truly amazing what a hot shower could do. Hanna washed and rinsed her hair then lathered herself with her vanilla-scented body wash. There was a chance she might still be in her robe when Ava arrived but there was no doubt she would be spotless and would smell good enough to eat. Hanna turned off the water and began the squeegee process. It was the one downside to a giant tile shower. The tile installer told them the shower would keep longer if they *squeegeed* the tiles as often as possible. Jacob didn't know Hanna was aware that he shirked his shower care duties, but she didn't mind doing it. If it avoided mouldy corners, it was well worth it. When Hanna finished swiping the rubber squeegee along the base of the shower, she looked at the glass portions, planning a quick and final swipe on them as well. A sudden wave of dizziness overcame her and she quickly knelt back down to avoid falling. Her vision was blurred, the heat and thick steam compounding it. This was the start of one of her rare aura migraines. A painless but blinding condition that could eventually lead to a stabbing migraine. Dreading the thought, Hanna took a few deep breaths and started to stand up. As she slowly raised herself to stand, she looked again at the glass and realized that her vision wasn't blurry after all. Instead, a clear substance had somehow gotten onto the inside of the thick glass wall. Hanna slowly traced her finger across the oily film. When she brought it to her nose she immediately knew what it was. She had smelled the scent before, dozens of times. Hanna slid the glass door open, stepped out of the shower and twisted a towel around her head. She threw on her robe, angrily tied the waist belt then went back to the shower and stood looking at its thick pane of glass. Now that she had stepped back from it, there was no mistaking exactly what it was that she was looking at. It was a subtle, oil imprint of a woman's naked upper body. A vanilla-scented oil imprint to be precise. Hanna and Jacob had sex in their shower before but never had Hanna pushed the entire front side of her upper body against the glass, with or without oil. The imprint wasn't hers, but she was confident she knew who it belonged to. She stared at the ghostly image, fighting the venomous heat building within her veins. Hanna felt stupid that she hadn't noticed it until now. She hadn't used the shower until this afternoon.

She'd had one bath after getting home from Halifax then left to stay with Ava. When she had taken her bath a week ago, she had to forego the drop of scented oil because she'd misplaced it. *Someone had misplaced it*. The shock of the discovery had jolted her wide awake and a series of questions about the imprint whirled crazily through her mind. While talking that night in their living room, Jacob said that Mandy had driven his car home for him because he was drunk. That in itself had shocked and enraged Hanna. The other half of the truth was that he'd not only invited the woman inside their home but lathered her in Hanna's oil and then taken her into their private shower. There was only one reason someone would do that. Hanna wondered about other things like how long she'd stayed in Hanna's bedroom and when she finally left. She thought about old Bill recalling the Taxi that left her house the morning he'd had his heart attack. *Had that been Mandy leaving in broad daylight? How many times had she been in their house? Did she peer at the photos of Hanna and Jacob placed around their home?* It would explain why Mandy was frazzled after Hanna and friends had visited The Pink Pearl. Hanna could hear her phone ring and a second later a doorbell camera notification. It was Ava, accompanied by a large suitcase. Looking crazed, Hanna opened the front door, allowing Ava inside. Ava could tell Hanna was already severely troubled by something but this couldn't wait. In unison, the two of them shouted the same words.

"I have to show you something!" Ava held up her phone while Hanna pointed down the hall. Hanna stormed off in the direction of the bedroom and Ava, feeling overruled, simply followed.

"Oh! Ok, you first then," Ava quipped.

Hanna showed Ava the imprint on the shower glass. "It isn't from me. The person who left it was slightly taller than me."

Ava listened, then looking repulsed, stepped into the shower and raised her arms, curling her fingers over the top of the pane. If Ava had been naked her silhouette likely would have matched with Mandy's. "Careful," Hanna warned her, "you'll get oil on you."

Ava lowered her arms and stepped out of the shower. "Wow, just when I thought the man couldn't be a bigger pig. He's got some brazen balls bringing her in here."

"He said the same thing about you," Hanna said dryly.

Ava's expression was one of challenge and delight. "Oh? Did he?" She then reached for the toothbrush on the counter beside Jacob's personal care products. She picked it up purposefully and then started with it toward the toilet.

"No. Ava don't!" Hanna pleaded.

"Why not? He'll never know and he damn well deserves it!"

Hanna was wearing a guilt-ridden expression. "I already used it to clean the sink."

Ava was pleasantly surprised but somewhat quelled by Hanna's admission. She glared at the toothbrush as if telling it how lucky it was she hadn't plunged it into the toilet. "Let's get out of here before

I get any more good ideas. It's my turn to show you something now." The two friends sat outside on Hanna's private balcony in the two outdoor chairs. Ava wasted no time pulling out her phone, exposing a series of private messages. "After we left The Pink Pearl I connected with Daisy, the girl who gave me the lap dance?"

Hanna rolled her eyes recalling the dancer. "Yes. I remember Daisy."

"When you were in the washroom that night, I tried to ask her things about Mandy and after she stared at us as we left, I knew there was more that Jacob wasn't telling you. Daisy, whose full name is Oopsie Daisy, because she was a surprise baby, told me that someone the girls at the club call Mr. Blue Eyes has come in several times seeking Mandy's services. Mandy has even left with him for over an hour before."

"But we know she left with him. That's when the photo was taken."

"Yes, but we didn't know that it happened over two weeks ago, or that he's been there a bunch of times!"

"But….two weeks? The Instagram post was only…"

Ava was quiet while Hanna pointlessly calculated dates in her head.

"There's no possible way I wouldn't have noticed that oil imprint if it had been in there for that long." As difficult as it was to believe, it was all sinking in. "That means the time he left with her was a separate time than when she gave him a ride home."

Then making sure she had all the facts, Hanna asked, "How does Daisy know this Mr. Blue Eyes is Jacob."

Ava scrolled down to the bottom of her text conversation with Daisy. "Because I sent her this."

It was a photo of Jacob that Hanna had posted to social media on his birthday. Hanna stared at the photo with a sober expression. Ava then threw the last few logs on the fire. "Daisy told me that no one gets to dance for Jacob, but Mandy, and that Mr. Blue Eyes likes to buy her shots of Jagermeister, her preferred drink. Not that it matters what she likes to drink."

To Hanna, it mattered. She took off walking through the bedroom and then into the closet. She reappeared a second later with the receipt from Jacob's jeans she had stowed in the drawer. "I found this in Jacob's pocket the day you took me to lunch. My instincts told me to keep it, but I didn't do anything with it. I was going to ask him when he'd started buying Jagermeister but didn't get the chance. It's dated for about two weeks ago, the same night I came home around midnight after working late."

Ava scanned the receipt and then typed the name of the convenience store into the map app on her phone. Ava used her finger to virtually scroll the area around the store where Jacob had bought the alcohol.

"Well, according to the map, it's right near a gas station, a sex shop, Pippa's Pizza aaand oh!" Ava was shaking her head, wearing a vengeful smirk. "Whattya know, it's right across from The Pink Pearl!"

Hanna felt ridiculous for letting Jacob talk her into meeting him at home that evening. In time, one foolish, drunken mistake might be forgiven but it was now clear that what Jacob had been guilty of, was something entirely different. She didn't know how many times he had met with Mandy and doubted she ever would know.

Feeling mentally depleted, Hanna took the towel off her head and hung it over the outdoor railing. Ava watched her, praying this was now enough evidence to prove that Jacob wasn't worthy of her. Hanna put her hands on the railing and stood taking in the view from her secret hiding place, one last time. She heard a man's loud chuckle coming from the neighbour's backyard. Through the small break in the trees, she could partially see Bill and Beatrice, sitting on their deck, enjoying their afternoon, probably after having puttered around in the yard all morning. She would miss them, Bill's tall tales and the scoldings Beatrice would grant him for his careless mishaps. Hanna was surprised by her sudden envy of them. She would miss her beautiful home and sadly she would miss Jacob too, or at least who she thought he was.

"You're not going to jump right?" Ava half-joked.

Hanna turned, giving Ava a small, sad smile.

"I think I'm ready to take you up on your offer now. Can you help me pack my clothes?"

Ava smiled proudly. "I thought you'd never ask."

Ava, having come prepared, jumped up and went to the front entrance and grabbed the large suitcase she'd shown up with. When they'd finished filling it with Hanna's clothes, she dragged it out to her car and lugged in another empty suitcase for Hanna to fill. Hanna laughed at Ava's dedication and had to hug her mid-step. Besides the clothes, there was only one other item Hanna wanted to leave with. It was a small box of photos, letters, trinkets and awards she'd won and accumulated throughout her life. When she kneeled beside the bed to look for it, she found the empty bottle of vanilla oil. She glanced at it briefly and imagined how it got there. She sat it on the bedside table and proceeded to pull out the box of memorabilia. After standing up with the box Hanna took one last look around her bedroom.

"I'm ready."

Ava took the box for insurance, in case Hanna tried to change her mind and then headed toward the door.

"Wait!"

Ava stopped when she heard Hanna call out. She slowly turned around to find Hanna holding out her hand.

"I need that receipt."

Ava feared Hanna was having sudden doubts about leaving. She hesitantly shifted the box into her one arm so she could get to the receipt in her pocket. Passing it to Hanna she asked,

"This is just for kindling right?"

"You'll see."

Hanna pulled a pen out from the drawer of the nightstand and scribbled on the back of the damning receipt. When she was done, she sat it beside the empty oil bottle. Ava curiously leaned in to read Hanna's impromptu exit note.

Jacob,
you can let Mandy know she
can find more oil online at mysilkyskin.com
Don't forget to use the squeegee in the
shower. I noted that the glass portions were
especially dirty and will need some extra cleaning.
Take care, Hanna

It would be pretty clear to Jacob why Hanna wasn't there to meet him at midnight when he got home.

CHAPTER THIRTY SIX

Hanna and Ava drove their vehicles to Ava's house, arriving early evening. Ava loved her framed postcard gift from Hanna and immediately following the removal of the suitcases from the cars, proudly hung the piece in her entryway. It was now close to dinner time and Ava thought it seemed like a good night for boxed mac n cheese paired with a bottle of wine, of course. The two friends spent the evening in front of the T.V. watching the latest romcom movie on Netflix. Hanna was understandably quiet but considering all she'd discovered about Jacob and left behind, she was doing well. Ava felt bad for Hanna but inwardly she celebrated the end of the Jacob era. Her instincts about him had been right all along, though she wished they hadn't. Hanna would find someone who would be true and faithful, someone she cherished and in return, cherish her. Hanna had narrowly dodged a bullet by finding out about Jacob so close to the wedding and not afterward.

Noticing her friend looked preoccupied, Ava wanted to check in. "We haven't talked much since you gave me the quick version of your night with Mr. Double O Seven Inches. Ethan and Shauni said you met up with him yesterday and spent the day together. When I stopped by today, Ethan said that if you didn't pursue him, he was going to."

Hanna smiled, imagining Ethan calling dibs on Isaac. "He introduced himself after he dropped me off at the studio. They liked him. Ethan even called him beautiful."

"He's certainly good-looking enough, how about the nice nickname Shauni's assigned him?"

Hanna smiled knowing what Ava was asking. It wasn't unlike the friends to converse about such personal details. "Are you asking me about Isaac's penis?"

"Of course I am. A man with that much confidence must have something to be proud of."

Hanna wasn't going to lie. She sipped her wine grinning as she recalled brief and pleasant images of Isaac's impressive naked body. "He's earned the nickname. I think you could say he's got a lot to be proud of."

Ava laughed at the innuendo. "Is it too soon for me to ask if you plan to see Isaac again? Do you like him?"

Hanna knew how she felt about Isaac but wasn't positive about Isaac's feelings toward her. When they'd parted ways after their boat ride, it sounded like he was giving her a cool brush-off. But then he embraced her and gave her a kiss so intimate, she could still feel the sweetness of it on her lips.

"If he wanted to see me, I would see him again."

Hanna remembered the moment she feared things may have been moving too fast. She sensed that Isaac felt it too. At the time, she hadn't yet known the extent of Jacob's deceit and was still contemplating their relationship. That was the silent communication that had been passed between them on the boat ride back. Isaac hadn't said a word, but it instantly altered his mood. Recalling his sullen expression when he dropped her off, made Hanna wish she could go back in time. Had she known about Jacob what she knew now, she would have gladly removed her ring when Isaac joked about taking it off. On second thought, she wouldn't have been wearing the ring at all.

"Why say *if?*" Ava asked. "Do you have a reason to believe he wouldn't want to meet up again?"

"I wouldn't be surprised if my heavy baggage scared him off. Besides, what type of person would I be if I jumped into a new relationship before my engagement has even ended? Jacob still thinks he's coming home to find me waiting there for him."

"Screw him! It ended when he cheated. Do you want me to text him and tell him you finally realized you're too good for him? After that, I can text Isaac and get him over here."

Grinning, Hanna shook her head at Ava.

"Let's just give it a beat Ave. Besides after our boat ride, Isaac told me that he'd be busy with work for a couple of days. I don't want to look desperate and embarrass myself. Not to mention, my self esteem couldn't handle the rejection."

"Ooooooo K, but a man that looks like that, probably doesn't need to be lonely for too long. It *is* Friday night. He's probably out right now."

Ava was only playfully teasing but she wasn't wrong. Isaac's striking, grey-eyed appearance was undebatable. Even the young waitress at the French cafe where they'd had their coffee, couldn't help staring at him. He could have the company of anyone he wanted with the tap of a finger. Picturing Isaac with another woman had instantly soured Hanna's mood. She finished her glass of wine and grabbed her phone. She opened her messaging app and stared at the text message Isaac had sent himself from her phone the morning in his bedroom. He told Hanna that he needed to see her again and she told him to forget it ever happened. Saying the words had felt wrong at the time but thinking about it now was even more painful. Hanna sighed deeply. She didn't want to forget it happened. She now hoped longingly that it could happen again and again. The text message he'd sent from her phone read *until next time*. It was made in an effort to keep in contact with her. Hanna smiled picturing him slyly typing his cell number into her phone and then sending the casual message to his own device. The next message was regarding the leak at the studio and why she'd left the renovation show. She thought she was texting Ethan, but instead, she'd unknowingly texted Isaac, who rushed over to help her. Hanna stared at Isaac's cell number wondering if he would reply if she sent him a text. *What if he was busy with work like he said or worse, busy with another woman?* Hanna immediately talked herself out of texting Isaac. She topped up her wine and for the rest of the evening, attempted to focus on the movie.

Chapter Thirty Seven

Over a candle-lit dinner, a bottle of wine and a delicious meal, Isaac was in the company of a beautiful brunette woman. However, the only task he was occupied with was trying to get the heckler, his younger sister Sadie, off his back. They were supposed to be enjoying dinner together at Bernard's. Instead, it had turned into an uncomfortable, one-sided questioning period that, to Isaac, felt more like a firm ball squeezing. When Sadie ran into Isaac and Hanna outside the elevator the other morning, she quickly picked up on the troubled, unfamiliar expression on Isaac's tired face. Now across the table from him, Sadie had already asked over twenty questions about the pretty mystery woman. After answering each question, Isaac's dismay over his yearning for Hanna became increasingly frustrating. Sadie on the other hand was beaming at the fact that her brother had finally found her. The one who had broken the spell, awoken his heart and was clearly ruffling his perfectly quaffed, unruffleable feathers. Sadie was the type that hoped every problem could be solved with a dramatic show of affection.

"Don't let the cheating fiance get in your way. You should go and find her right now and tell her how special you think she is."

Isaac sat there looking at Sadie like she'd just asked him to hula hoop naked. "I've already shown up once at her studio unannounced. Besides we spent an entire day together and at the end she looked like she was going to tell me she regretted it and couldn't see me again. I just did us both a favour and told her I'd be busy for a while."

Sadie sipped her wine thinking of the time she'd heard the lame line after the guy she dated had decided to step back from the relationship. If she knew her brother like she thought she did, he didn't want to step back from Hanna. He was being a coward and thought he was protecting himself from being rejected.

"Normally I wouldn't dare try to give my big brother dating advice but by giving Hanna your classic, *I'll be busy* brush off, you might be sending the wrong message."

"Ok." Isaac was irritated that for the first time in his life, he was obliged to ask his younger sister for advice about women, one particular woman. "Let's hear it. What would you recommend I do in this situation?" Isaac couldn't believe what he was saying, yet waited eagerly for her answer.

Sadie smiled happily at the opportunity to advise her brother about members of the opposite sex and matters of the heart.

"I'm no therapist and I won't pretend to be, promise. I'll just tell you what I would want you to do if I were in Hanna's shoes." Sadie continued. "You care for her and you should tell her. Ghosting her won't magically make your feelings for her go away. If she feels the same for you, she'll appreciate knowing how you feel. She might even find it impossible to turn your handsome face away."

Isaac smiled, rolled his eyes and listened as Sadie finished.

"If you go to her and she asks you to back off, at least you'll know it wasn't because you didn't go the distance. You have nothing to lose by telling her how you feel. The worst that can happen is, that you feel mildly rejected for a few days, then move on. Let's face it. You've got lots of other…" Sadie raised her hands and put air quotations around the word *people,* "to distract you from Hanna."

Isaac still couldn't believe he was considering taking advice from his little sister. As if they'd been discussing the sale of illicit drugs, he cautiously glanced around the restaurant to make sure nobody was listening to their conversation. "I'll think it over."

Sadie then shot him a joyous smile. "Let me know what happens. I'm hoping to meet this girl!"

CHAPTER THIRTY EIGHT

The next morning Hanna woke to find multiple texts on her phone from Jacob. He'd come home late last night, expecting to find her waiting for him. Instead, he found a half-empty closet and a note on the back of a receipt she'd left in the bedroom with the empty bottle of vanilla oil. None of his texts were heartfelt apologies or attempts at explaining the female body print in the shower. The texts simply read *'call me'* and *'we need to talk'*. Neither message had compelled Hanna to respond and she decided that she would prefer that he not reach out to her at all. She had already accepted that, by no fault of her own, the chapter of her life starring Jacob was soon to be over. Hanna would never know how many times he'd cheated or lied to her. No amount of time would compel Hanna to forgive him or want to marry him. She thought of the statement, *'You are the company you keep'* and then of Jacob's unscrupulous clients. Regarding Jacob, this statement seemed to be true. She wondered if Jacob had always secretly been this person or if that side of him had developed slowly over time. Maybe he simply enjoyed the thrill of keeping such a powerful secret from her. She would never be able to trust Jacob again, even if she wanted to, even if she tried to. There was no longer anything to decide or try to forgive, it was over.

Other than the finances regarding the house, they had nothing else to talk about. If she had to, she could even hire a lawyer to communicate with Jacob on her behalf. Aside from ignoring any further texts from Jacob, Hanna had a couple of tasks in mind for today. Shauni had texted Hanna to tell her that a mystery parcel had arrived for her at the office while she was at her dad's house. Work parcels typically arrived with Richards and Co. as the recipient, but this parcel bore Hanna's name. She would head over and grab whatever it was later this morning. She also needed to stop at the grocery store to pick up whatever she needed for the impromptu barbecue that Ava had planned for tonight. Hanna promised to prepare the appetizers, salads, and desserts. It was clear she'd be staying there for a while now and wanted to show Ava her appreciation, again. Ava had invited Jasper's bandmates as well as Ethan and Shauni. Hanna showered and dressed then told Ava her plans as she left for the studio. Ava was just getting out of the shower before dressing, planning to spend her Saturday out at the beach with Jasper. "You sure you don't want to come with us Han?"

"No thanks, especially if you plan to wear that white bikini. Poor Jasper won't know what to do with himself."

Ava imagined herself in the sleazy bikini and smiled brightly.

"Sounds good to me! I'm soooo wearing it."

Hanna gave a small laugh. "You're cruel!" She shook her head at the thought of Jasper desperately trying to maintain his manly dignity. "See you tonight Ave!"

When Hanna stepped out the front door she saw Jasper's truck had just pulled up to the curb. He opened his window. "Hi Hanna!" he called.

"Hey Jasper! Have fun at the beach! Don't forget sunscreen!" She thought of Ava's white bikini. "Oh and lots of ice water!"

Hanna jumped in her vehicle and waved out the window at Jasper as she drove down the boulevard and then across town to the studio. When she arrived at the studio she parked out front on the street knowing she wouldn't be there that long. Hanna unlocked the front door and went in to find a large beautiful metal sign reading the company name Richards and Co. hanging high on the wall above the presentation area. With its brushed metal finish, it was both modern and classy. Despite not having an audience, Hanna smiled pridefully, loving its presence. She didn't know how Shauni was able to keep it hidden from her while she crafted it. Hanna guessed she would have had some time while she was in Ingleton at her dad's. She would have to give her a big hug and thank-you, when she saw her later tonight. She then noticed the parcel that Shauni mentioned, sitting on her desk. When she opened the box she saw the sixty custom wedding favours she ordered six months ago. The supplier held them until Hanna's pre-selected ship date. Staring into the box, she figured that she now had enough potted lavender seeds to start up a lavender farm. She had chosen them in keeping with the French theme of her wedding. Each miniature pot had a small piece of French lace tied in a bow and the rims were sealed with clear plastic. They were filled with dry potting mix and buried lavender seeds that would begin to grow once watered. With each pot baring the couple's name, guests would have had a pleasant way to remember the special day. As she was deciding between donating the favours and maybe planting some at her dad's place, the door chime rang. Startled by the unexpected visitor, Hanna looked up to see Jacob's tall form standing there, wearing a blank expression. He looked exhausted as if he hadn't slept. After ignoring his texts this morning, she regretted not locking the door behind her. She had no idea when she was expecting to see Jacob next but it wasn't this morning. They stood there in silence for several stressful seconds, Hanna's anxiety level increasing as each second passed. She wasn't sure she knew him anymore and it felt like she was staring at a stranger. Finally, Jacob spoke in a solemn but calm voice. "I don't expect you to forgive me. I know that's too much to ask."

Hanna was silent, waiting for Jacob to finish speaking. "I'm just here to say one thing."

Nothing Jacob could say would surprise Hanna anymore, not even if he'd come to ask her for her ring back and perhaps that's what he was doing. He then took a step toward her and Hanna stiffened with alarm. Jacob raised his hands like he was trying to tame a wild animal.

"Hanna, I only want to say that I'm sorry. I know what I did is beyond forgiveness. That's why I never told you. If I could take it all back, I would. I was an idiot and will regret it for the rest of my life."

Hanna sighed when she realized he wasn't there to be hostile toward her. If anything, he was trying to own up to his mistakes. When she nodded her head as a sign of acceptance, Jacob continued. "I want you to know what happened with Mandy, it really is over. It was over before you even found out."

It was impossible to believe him.

"It probably doesn't matter now, I guess," Jacob added.

He was telling the truth about that at least. It no longer mattered to Hanna whether he would be continuing his affair with the stripper or not. She kept silent allowing him to finish.

"I want to be fair with the house. You put a lot into it and I'm not going to be difficult where that's concerned. We can probably both agree that I've already been enough of an asshole."

Jacob's eyes glistened as he listened to himself. Hanna almost felt sorry for him, knowing he realized that he alone was to credit for the circumstances between them. Hanna picked up one of the miniature pots from the cardboard box and held it outward. "Here," she offered quietly.

He smiled at its miniature size and held his hand toward the tiny bow-tied pot. He looked at Hanna, his expression weary.

"It's French Lavender," Hanna answered. "Remember? Our wedding favours?"

Jacob pulled his hand back as if the wedding favour had stung him. "If it needs any care other than air then don't give it to me, clearly I can't be trusted with it."

Hanna gave a half smile and put the pot back in the box. As difficult as it was, she had to give Jacob some credit for coming by today. It meant something to her that he told her in person how sorry he was that he'd crucified their relationship. Hanna hoped it was a sign that they could try to move forward on somewhat peaceful terms. Not all couples could say that after a split, especially if one person had cheated. Hanna hadn't planned on being at the studio very long and since Jacob had been decent it was probably best they leave on a positive note. She closed the cardboard flaps and began to pick up the box to carry them out to her car. Jacob stepped forward and took the box from her hands.

"Here, let me take that for you. Surely I can be trusted to simply carry a box to your car."

Hanna smiled as Jacob poked fun at himself. She remotely opened her trunk, followed him out of the studio, and then locked the door behind them. Jacob sat the box in the back of Hanna's vehicle and turned back to face her. He was wearing a wounded expression and paused before speaking. "When you left for Ava's, I promised you that wasn't going to be the last time I kissed you."

Hanna gave him a slightly ridiculing expression. "Yes, you did promise me some things."

Jacob ignored her gentle but sarcastic jab regarding his failed promises.

"Could I give you one last kiss? I won't ask for anything else."

Not wanting to ruin the softer-than-expected landing, Hanna decided to grant him a single kiss. It would be their last and final goodbye kiss. She looked into Jacob's dark eyes, soundlessly agreeing to the request. He pulled her close and gave her a gentle kiss on her lips. As he broke the kiss and pulled away he was frowning and slowly shaking his head. "God I'm such an idiot." Now grasping the full scope of his loss, regret jabbed sharply at his chest. Trying to distract him, Hanna reached into the box again and held out one of the lavender pots.

"Take it. All it needs is a little bit of water. It will give you a sense of accomplishment when it starts to grow. When it gets too big for the pot, stick it in the ground, out back in the garden."

Jacob took the tiny pot and held it with two fingers. He looked discouraged, peering down at it, but was comforted that Hanna took the chance at trusting him, even if it was only a non-existent plant.

"Thank you."

Jacob and Hanna agreed to talk again soon, regarding the next steps in dividing their shared assets. Hanna was relieved to hear that Jacob intended to be fair with her. He began the short walk to his car and then stopped. "Hanna?" His eyes were pleading. "Would it make you feel any different if I said it meant nothing?"

His words were meant to bring comfort, but instead, he had unintentionally summed up what he'd done, to being a complete waste. Hanna gave him a tiny smile, feeling badly for his ignorant blunder.

"No Jacob, it doesn't make me feel better knowing that we lost what we had for something that meant nothing."

Feeling the weight of her words, Jacob nodded his understanding and then finished the walk to his car. After watching his car drive away, Hanna sat in her vehicle for several minutes in the air conditioning, allowing the finality of their relationship to set in. She wasn't sure if it was right that she hadn't told Jacob about Isaac. In all fairness, it wasn't like he had come to her and confessed what he himself had done. Even when Hanna confronted him, he gave her only partial truths to ease his guilt. *How trapped would she have felt if the photo had been brought to her attention after they were married? Or years later, when they had children, permanently tethering them?* Her guilt evaporated immediately when she considered the possibility. If she was being honest with herself, the perfect life she thought she had with Jacob was over the moment she'd seen the photo. She no longer planned on marrying Jacob, she just hadn't admitted it yet. She had been holding on too tightly to her childhood dream, fogging her ability to see reason. She could have stayed and married him but would have been forced to accept their relationship was only a counterfeit of the deep love and honesty she had always hoped for. It would have required a ceaseless effort to be happy, knowing he'd been inside another woman, kissed another woman, and even brought her into their home. There were likely more details she still wasn't even aware of. Details that no longer mattered. Hanna sighed and reminded herself that she had a circle of great friends, a loving father and a career that gave her self-gratification. Dale would never have encouraged a rekindling with Jacob had he known the extent of his deceit. What happened between her mom and dad was very different than what Hanna had experienced.

Her thoughts drifted a distance and she found herself imagining Isaac introducing himself to her dad. He would like Isaac's genuine sense of humour. Dale would see how he made Hanna laugh and smile and that would be more than enough for him. Daydreaming of the imagined relationship between Dale and Isaac, she realized she was getting carried away. She promised herself to make an effort to push aside further thoughts of Isaac. She started the car and headed to the grocery store for the food items she needed for tonight's barbecue then made her way to Ava's.

When Hanna arrived, she saw Jasper's truck parked at the curb. They had arrived home from the beach earlier than expected but were nowhere in sight. Hanna wondered if Ava's white bikini proved too much for Jasper's self-restraint. It appeared they'd rushed home from the beach and went straight into Ava's bedroom. Hanna grinned and went to work preparing the appetizers and salads for tonight. Afterwards, she placed them on metal trays and bowls in the fridge. She then started on a dessert, oddly named *Sex in a Pan*. The dessert consisted of a crushed pecan crust, layers of pudding and cheesecake, then topped with sprinkles of shaved chocolate. It was easy to make and was Ava's all-time favourite. It was a delicious treat, but Hanna knew the naughty name had something to do with the appeal. The driving across town, the run-in with Jacob and the food prep had left Hanna beat. She decided to have a short nap before the guests arrived. As she laid her head on the pillow, there was a quiet knock at the door. "Come in!" Hanna called.

Wearing her short robe Ava stepped into the bedroom and closed the door behind her. "Hey, how's it going?"

"I'm good. Just a little sleepy."

"No wonder! You've whipped up enough food out there to feed a herd of hippos."

Hanna's eyes were closed and her arm was laid across her forehead. "Perfect. That's what I was going for. Did you see the dessert?" She smiled, knowing Ava would be moaning dramatically as she ate it.

"Han, That food out there looks awesome! You're going to put all my meats to shame. Oh hey! Speaking of meat, are you inviting Double O Seven Inches?"

Hanna smiled at Ava's dirty segue. "No. Been thinking about him all day though." Every effort Hanna made to avoid thoughts of Isaac had completely failed. She changed the subject. "You'll be happy to hear, it is officially over with Jacob now. He stopped by the studio to say he was going to be civil."

"Oh good. So he got the note."

"He did. He wanted to tell me he was sorry, in person."

Ava didn't care that Jacob was sorry.

"Good for him. Did he try to get the ring back?"

"No. But I wondered if he would. It's sitting in its original box now."

Hanna held up her bare hand, waving her fingers.

"Anyway, how was the beach today? You weren't there very long."

"We never actually made it."

Surprised, Hanna lifted her arm slightly from her head and peeked at Ava. She was smiling proudly, twirling her hair around her finger, prompting the corner of Hanna's mouth to curl up. "You showed him the white bikini, didn't you?"

"I sure did!" Ava laughed, patted Hanna's leg then left the room, allowing her to nap.

Hanna rested soundly while endless visions of a naked, dark-haired lover swam dreamily through her mind. They each took turns pleasing each other in every way imaginable. He pleasured and teased Hanna with his hands and mouth while his entrancing eyes spoke sweetly to the deepest parts of her soul. He brought Hanna to climax, first using his mouth, then again as he joined his body with hers. Hanna drew sounds of pleasure from him, conveying how thoroughly he savoured her. When they were both finally satisfied, he left her with a whisper of a kiss on her lips.

Hanna awoke feeling physically renewed, but a sense of restlessness poked at her nerves. Usually, after a nap, she felt calm, clear and refreshed. She showered, hoping to wash away whatever was causing her agitation. As she finished dressing, Hanna heard music and voices from the backyard, realizing the guests had arrived. She made her way out to the back deck, where an apron-laden Jasper was flipping burgers and chicken on the barbecue while Ava conversed with Ethan and Shauni. Noah and Felix, the band's keyboard player, drank beer and kept Jasper company at the barbeque. After Felix and Hanna introduced themselves, Hanna took a few minutes to thank Shauni for the amazing Richards and Co. sign. Shauni's cheeks were rosy from the slew of compliments that both Hanna and Ethan had paid her. Now that Hanna had seen it, Ethan could post pictures of it on their social media page. Soon, the food was ready, and everyone enjoyed the tasty summer meal on Ava's backyard deck. The weather was clear and comfortable, adding to the perfect outdoor atmosphere. As the night progressed, several bottles of wine had been shared, and a tray of chilled Irish whiskey shots were enjoyed by all.

Now that the sun had disappeared, strings of brightly coloured lights strung along the fence lit up the perimeter of the backyard. A mix of music rang out from the portable speaker, and everyone had gone out on the grass to show off their tipsy dance moves. In lieu of food or alcohol, Shauni brought along a box of flashing LED party favours that included jumbo-sized neon eyeglasses, bunny ear headbands, glowing bracelets and necklaces. Everyone excitedly threw on the glowing bling within seconds of opening the box. Ava's yard looked like a mini outdoor rave with neon shapes moving buoyantly in the dark. Hanna couldn't say she wasn't enjoying herself but the pestering distraction from earlier was still pulling at her nerves. Having consumed just enough wine, she could now admit to herself exactly what the source of her displeasure was. It was one man, or the uncomfortable absence of him that was bothering her. Ava had encouraged Hanna to invite Isaac, but something had prevented her. Isaac said he would be busy but also suggested they could meet up afterward like maybe he hoped to see her again. It was Saturday evening. Hanna asked herself what the chances were that Isaac would even be home.

CHAPTER THIRTY NINE

Ryan Vance arrived at Isaac's place later than expected. When no one answered, he used his key card to let himself and his two female guests inside the large apartment. Issac had already put a heavy dent in the pint-sized bottle of whiskey and wasn't his usual charming self. As Vance and the two attractive women entered the living room, Isaac glanced up lazily and scanned the brunette women in their short dresses. He then took a long sip from the bottle in his hand. Instead of getting up off the couch and introducing himself, he used the bottleneck to lazily point in the direction of the large sidebar where the alcohol was stored. "Drinks are that way, everybody!"

Vance took over the role of host, showed the ladies in and invited them to help themselves to some drinks. He walked over to Isaac on the couch, peered down at his irritated eyes, and spoke quietly. "Isaac, you're wrecked. You're drinking right out of the bottle."

Vance looked over at the women who were now pouring liquor into tall silver shot glasses then back to Isaac. "Should we maybe, put the bottle down? You want a glass with some ice?" Vance sounded like he was trying to convince Isaac to put down a loaded gun.

Isaac glanced down at the bottle and waved his free hand. "Don't bother. I'm just going to polish it off anyways."

Vance looked at the half-drained whiskey bottle thankful it was only a pint. "Did we lose a big fish you haven't told me about? What's going on here my friend?"

Isaac stared at Vance blankly as he lounged casually on the long leather sofa. He was thinking about the woman who'd beaten him at his own game and she hadn't even known she'd been playing, the woman who had managed to fill his body with groin-tightening lust and his heart with warm desire. She'd been a marvel to him since he first laid eyes on her that night at the charity gala. She was the woman who had compelled him to realize that he'd been looking for her his entire adult life.

"It's the Hanna girl, isn't it?" Vance looked annoyed. "Maaan, I told you that night, rivers of bullshit would rain down if you got involved with her. I knew it! Let's forget her! I've got two ladies here, and they're looking to party in your pants."

Isaac clumsily looked down at his jeans as if taking Vance literally, then stared distractedly again. He didn't want either woman in his pants. "You can have em' both, they don't do it for me. I probably can't get it up anyway."

Vance looked toward the two attractive women as if contemplating the idea then shook his head. "No. You're not fooling anyone, you can get it up. You've had a hard-on since you met her. Do you want me to get you a nice little blonde over here? Just give me twenty minutes."

Isaac shot him an offended glance then took a sip from the whiskey bottle.

"Is that a yes then?" Ryan teased and then pulled out his phone.

Isaac got up from the couch, went to the stereo, and contrary to his mood, cranked up the dance music. The two brunettes cheered joyously and carried him over one of the silver shot glasses. At least they were making themselves useful. Isaac threw back the shot, telling himself that each ounce would bring him closer to forgetting about Hanna.

CHAPTER FORTY

Hanna wondered how rude she would be if she left the barbecue to take a chance that Isaac was home and wanted to see her. She decided it didn't matter if he didn't want to see her. At least she would know how he felt about her, and she could make the Herculean effort to forget him. Hanna went into her room, reapplied a little makeup, then removed the elastic from her bun, letting her hair fall in big honey waves. She then checked her outfit in the mirror. Loving its flattering short length and crisscross back, it was Hanna's most loved sundress. Looking it over for wine spills, she was happy there were none. She grabbed her cardigan and purse, stuffed several items inside, and then went to tell Ava her plan. Through pink, glowing glasses, Ava opened her eyes wide and smiled drunkenly at Hanna. "Go get 'em, girl! Woohoo!"

Ava spun around, put her arms up in the air and waved them loosely back and forth to the music. After asking Jasper to take care of Ava in her altered state, Hanna hugged Ethan and Shauni goodbye, then ran out front to jump in the Uber that had pulled up to the curb. After a twenty-minute ride, she arrived at Isaac's building. Hanna never expected to find herself back at Isaac's apartment, and now, here she was, just hoping he was home. Hanna stared out the car window at the large modern glass doors. When the driver finally turned backward, hinting for her to get out, Hanna grabbed her purse and hesitantly exited the Uber. "Thanks!"

Hopeful her nervous knees wouldn't buckle, Hanna walked to the entrance and stared at the series of shiny silver buttons. She knew from her previous visit that Isaac lived on the fourth floor. She took a deep breath in preparation and then pushed the button. She waited a couple of minutes and when there was no response, pressed it again. As she focussed on the intercom, wondering if she should leave, a friendly voice sang out from behind her. "Hey there! It's Hanna, isn't it?"

Startled, Hanna jumped like a baby kangaroo and pivoted to find the small dark-haired woman from the other morning in the elevator. It was Sadie, Isaac's sister. She was just getting home.

"Oh hi! Sadie? Am I right? Nice to meet you."

"Very nice to meet you Hanna, You here to see Isaac?"

Hanna felt silly now for showing up unannounced.

"I wasn't actually invited," she admitted sheepishly. She felt even less certain now than she had only minutes before when she cowered to the door.

Sadie pulled a plastic card from her pocket and tapped it against the sensor on the door.

"I'm inviting you. Go on up!"

Sadie and Hanna entered the building and rode the elevator together briefly until Sadie got out on the second floor. "This is my stop here, Hanna. Just press number four and ring the doorbell. He'll be happy to see you!"

Hanna gave Sadie a small wave as she walked away.

"Thanks, Sadie."

Sadie smiled at Hanna brightly as the door slid closed again. It was a relief that Sadie was as friendly as she was on the morning she made fun of her brother's outfit. Hanna figured she might like her, given the chance to know her. The elevator dinged quietly as it stopped on the fourth floor and slowly opened. Hanna recognized the luxurious furniture down the hall and, of course, Isaac's apartment door. Hanna nervously stepped out of the elevator and walked over to the door. She could hear loud music coming from within the apartment and hoped that explained why she was never buzzed in. She took a deep breath and remembered Sadie's comment about Isaac being happy to see her. Hanna reached out to press the doorbell and grasped her purse strap tightly at her shoulder as she anxiously waited. A moment later, the door opened slightly, and Hanna peeked around it to see someone walking away, back toward the living room. It was Isaac. He then called out loudly in the opposite direction of the door.

"Vance! Your friend is here!"

Isaac walked purposefully toward the sidebar with the now empty bottle of whiskey. Hanna had stepped just inside the door and closed it gently behind her.

"Actually, I came to see you," she announced timidly.

Isaac froze as the sweet familiar voice registered in his ears. He wondered if he was so inebriated that he was now hearing things or if the loud music had made him half-deaf. He then turned slowly to face the owner of the voice. Hanna stood there looking pretty and perfect in her floral summer dress and her long, brown sugar waves of hair. Looking bewildered, Isaac walked toward her and stopped several feet away as if he'd just remembered something unpleasant. He swayed slightly and Hanna looked at the empty bottle in his hand.

"Hi!" Happy to see him, she smiled at the unexpected display. "I didn't mean to interrupt your evening, I just came..."

"You interrupted nothing." His unfriendly tone caught Hanna off guard.

There was a heavy energy in the air, making it difficult for Hanna to breathe or relax. She hoped Isaac would invite her in or say something to lighten the mood but he just stood there with a half drunken stare. Hanna then reached into her purse and pulled out a small wrapped gift. It was about the size of a watch box. Smiling shyly, she held it out toward him. As she waited for him to register that it was for him, she explained how she came to find it.

"It's kinda silly. I found it at a yard sale in Ingleton and it was impossible not to think of you after I saw it sitting there. So I grabbed it. It's to remember our…" Hanna trailed off not sure of the best way to say what she meant. "Anyway, I thought you should have it."

If their time together had meant as much to Isaac as it did to Hanna, he was sure to treasure the gift. Isaac stared downward at the small box in her hand. Wearing an offended expression, he spoke quietly and coldly.

"I don't want your goodbye gift. And I won't need a reminder."

Hanna was stung by his reaction and unprepared for Isaac's use of the word goodbye. If she wasn't sure where they stood before arriving, she certainly was now. She quickly tucked the small gift back into her purse and mentally readied for her awkward exit. Coming to see Isaac had been a terrible mistake and she felt like an intruding bimbo. Just then a woman's voice called down over the upper balcony. "Isaac! We need more ice! It's hot up here!"

Another woman's voice then called out. "Bring up the shot glasses when you come!"

Hanna stared upward in the direction that the voices had originated then looked back at Isaac. Unless Isaac had more sisters, he had multiple women upstairs, with whom he'd been drinking. Hanna felt incredibly stupid and a deep stab of jealousy, worse than any migraine, slashed her fragile composure.

"I'll let myself out. Sorry I bothered you. Enjoy your night." Hanna turned, walked as fast as she could to the elevator and jammed desperately on the downward button. As the elevator door opened, Isaac appeared beside her. Hanna ignored him as he stepped with her into the elevator. He was standing behind her and Hanna turned around to face him. Towering over her, his arms were crossed over his chest like he was angry. "Why are you here?" He asked sternly, staring intently.

She was embarrassed she'd interrupted his evening and it should have been obvious that she was trying to leave as quickly as possible. "I made a mistake, I'm so sorry. I'm leaving."

"I don't think so, Miss Richards." He wasn't smiling and instead, slowly shaking his head. "You're not leaving here until you tell me that you didn't love being with me just as much as I loved being with you."

Hanna couldn't believe he'd chased her into the elevator so he could hear one last time how wonderful of a lover she thought he was, all while having two different women calling out for him back in his apartment. She looked at him like he was absurd then looked away. "Does it matter that much to you? Do you really need to hear from every woman how thoroughly they enjoy your body?"

Hanna glanced upwards thinking of his current female guests. "Can't you get your friends upstairs to stroke your ego for you?"

Issac couldn't help smiling at her choice of words. The realization that the women upstairs had made Hanna jealous had shamefully helped to extinguish Isaac's ire. He answered her, this time speaking less indignantly. "No. I don't need to hear it from everybody. Just you."

Hanna shook her head, unable to believe this was the same man she feared she could easily fall in love with. She searched his face as if to confirm that it was Isaac. The wine she'd drank at Ava's was still pumping through her veins and had unwittingly loosened her restraint toward the qualities that had made him so irresistible to her. She noticed that his striking eyes looked a deeper-than-usual shade of grey. Isaac's dark hair was tousled, and Hanna tormented herself by wondering if someone had found it too tempting to keep their fingers from it while they had kissed him. She shifted her eyes downward to his mouth and lips. When she glanced back to his eyes to see him watching her, she inwardly berated herself. Aside from the bravery she'd acquired from the two glasses of wine and the single shot, this was her own fault. She'd come here on her own. She would tell him exactly what he had done to and for her, and then she was leaving. Eventually, she would have to forget the lips that kissed her so gently and those grey eyes that had never ceased to pull her in. Despite being honest, she would deny him the satisfaction of sounding sincere.

"Kudos. You are the new gold standard. Sex for me will probably never be the same. I won't be able to look at another man's body without comparing it to yours." Isaac frowned at her sarcastic tone not knowing if her words held any truth.

The words Hanna spoke were honest and true. Now hearing herself say them out loud had partially sobered her and she replaced her sarcasm with her soft natural voice. "No one else's hands will leave behind a trail of heat on my skin the way that yours do. And," Hanna gazed at his eyes wishing she didn't think they were so beautiful. "I will never be able to look at anyone with the same grey eyes without thinking of you every time."

He could do what he wanted with her confession. She had nothing and no one left to lose now. Isaac had made it clear how he felt when he'd domineeringly chased her out of his apartment. The elevator opened slowly as it reached the ground floor. Instead of stepping out of the way and allowing Hanna to exit, Isaac uncrossed his arms and reached out to push one of the elevator buttons, still holding eye contact with her. The elevator door closed and began moving them upward again.

"Racing back to your apartment to rejoin your harem?" Hanna asked in an irritated tone.

Isaac was torn between childishly enjoying her jealousy for the second time and saying something funny in hopes of getting her to smile so he could enjoy the magical effect. He knew that confining someone to an elevator was likely against the law not to mention beyond desperate. He'd never confined anyone to anything against their will before Hanna had appeared tonight at his door. It was abundantly clear this woman brought out the best and regrettably the worst in him. If Isaac hoped to uphold his dignity he would eventually have to step aside, allowing her to walk out of the elevator and out of his life. He didn't know how he would bring himself to let her go. If he could have one last kiss, it might give him the strength to walk away from her. He stared at her looking overthrown, prompting Hanna to speak.

"Happy? You've heard it all now, so if you plan to ride the elevator up and down all night, you can let me out here and I'll use the stairs."

Isaac grinned at her saucy remark, and Hanna found it impossible to ignore his arresting smile. It was the most powerful, provoking smile Hanna had ever seen. She knew it when she'd met him at the gala and she knew it now as she gazed at him. Hanna needed to leave before she was emotionally overwhelmed. She'd come here tonight hoping to spend time with this remarkable man. She had hoped that he might be happy to hear that there were no longer any obstacles or decisions to be made regarding her future. Hanna allowed her childhood dreams to impede her ability to accept the sad fate of her engagement. She faltered, and now she was paying the ultimate price. That night on the boat, Hanna thought she needed to take a step back from the affair with Isaac. The time she'd spent with him had been so wonderful that she thought it was impossible to be true. She wanted to tell him tonight, that her life had changed the moment she'd met him. She may have been wearing another man's ring but every minute Hanna spent with Isaac, she belonged to him. She wanted to tell him that too, if she'd had the chance.

They'd reached the fourth floor. Looking entirely unreachable, Isaac stood there intentionally blocking the elevator door. Hanna watched him and waited for him to move so she could finally leave. He had been crossing his arms at his chest the entire time to prevent himself from reaching out and pulling her against him. Isaac uncrossed his arms, took one slow step toward her and cradled her head in his hands. He leaned down, leaving a long gentle, kiss on her forehead. It was the same sweet gesture he'd shown her the morning after the gala as she waited for her ride. He didn't want her to leave then either. "Goodbye, Hanna," he said softly, then stepped out of the elevator.

Hanna quietly gasped, trying to recover from what felt like a punch to her abdomen. Isaac's two words hurt her deeply. She stood in the elevator and watched as he turned around to face her for the last time. Looking just as tortured as Hanna, Isaac said as genuinely as possible, "I wholeheartedly hope he makes you happy."

The doors then closed and Hanna was left in the elevator alone. As it began moving downward, her mind flashed to Isaac's anguished expression and she mentally repeated his last words over and over. *Who exactly was the 'he' that Isaac was referring to? Did Isaac believe Hanna had chosen to continue her engagement with Jacob? Was that what had caused the confident, attentive man who'd flirted with her and made such sensual love to her, to become so resentful toward her?*

Hanna began frantically tapping on the upward button as fast as her finger would allow, switching between pressing and holding the button and tapping it incessantly. When the elevator stopped, Hanna hurriedly squeezed out between the partially opened doors. She rushed toward the apartment and was about to ring the doorbell when out of the corner of her eye, she noticed a slow subtle movement. It was Isaac. He was sitting there alone in one of the large lounge chairs at the end of the hall. His eyes were closed while his fingers were clasped together behind his head. The loud music was still pumping loudly from within the apartment and could be heard in the hall. That, and the whiskey he'd consumed had caused him not to notice the subtle opening and closing of the elevator. Hanna carefully walked over to where he sat. Looking at him, Hanna thought Isaac was not only the most handsome male she had ever seen, he was the most passionate and arousing lover Hanna had ever known. He made her laugh and smile. She wanted to explore every corner of his fascinating character. He looked defeated and vulnerable sitting there alone, unaware of her presence. She wanted to grab him and kiss him so badly but couldn't allow him to think for one second longer that she'd foolishly chosen someone who took her for granted, over what she had with him.

"Isaac," Hanna called his name in a half-whisper.

Isaac slowly opened his eyes, glanced back and forth, then up at Hanna as if he had briefly forgotten where he was. He looked into Hanna's eyes, waiting to hear the reason for her return.

"Isaac, did you come by the studio this morning?" she asked softly, holding back her tears. In answer, Isaac frowned and looked away, not just from the embarrassment but the unpleasant memory. He'd made himself vulnerable to a woman, for the first time in his life and now Karma was laughing at him. He'd fallen for a small-town girl who was smart, beautiful and cared about her elderly neighbours. He loved that she thought keeping her word was the highest honour in the world. After Isaac had spoken to Sadie over dinner, he swallowed his pride and decided he would find Hanna wherever she was and tell her that he cared about her, wanted her and needed her. He wanted to tell her that when he touched her, he never wanted to stop and when he was with her, he never wanted her to leave. He didn't want to live without the feeling he had after seeing that precious smile on her face and knowing he was the one to credit for putting it there. He wanted to ask her if he could take her to France so she could visit the castle she named and maybe they'd have coffee at one of the sidewalk cafes she talked about. Isaac had gone to her studio this morning to find her so he could tell her how he felt and when he'd pulled up to the curb he saw her standing on the sidewalk kissing her cheating fiancé. Isaac vowed never to leave himself that vulnerable again then drove away with his battered dignity.

"Isaac, there is no '*he*' other than you. And, '*you*'," Hanna emphasized, "are the only '*he*' I want. If you still want me that is."

Isaac was listening attentively but also had alot to drink and wanted to be sure he was fully comprehending.

"Hanna, are you telling me it's over between you and Jacob?"

Hanna hoped his question confirmed that he did still want her.

"What Jacob and I had, is over." She held out her ringless finger.

Isaac closed his eyes and breathed deeply, savouring the instant infusion of relief. Hanna continued. "I saw Jacob briefly this morning at the studio. I didn't know he was coming. He wanted to say one final goodbye in person."

Isaac gave a slow subtle nod. "Yes. I think I watched him doing that, in front of your studio."

Hanna let out a pained whimper, unable to handle the guilt of the hurt she'd caused him. She had allowed the kiss, only to keep the peace between her and Jacob and in turn caused a near-catastrophic misunderstanding between Isaac and herself. The thought of Isaac sweetly coming to see her and then having to watch her be kissed was humiliating.

"I'm sorry that happened. Jacob asked me if he could, and I wanted to end things on good terms."

Hanna shook her head, now regretting the kiss. "After he left, I had to keep busy to prevent myself from driving straight here to your apartment. You said you'd be busy for a few days so I decided I should wait until Monday. I couldn't wait, I came tonight instead."

Enjoying the loveable, warm flattery of her comment, Isaac gave Hanna a small, affectionate smile. He leaned forward in the chair, put his hands on Hanna's hips and gently pulled her downward into his lap. They both felt like they had suffered the profound loss of each other and, after a brief but heartbreaking ordeal, had gotten each other back. When Hanna and Isaac were finished sharing a sweet and thorough kiss, Hanna reached into her purse and, for the second time, pulled out the small wrapped box. "This was never meant to be a goodbye gift," she assured him.

Isaac looked regretful, remembering the way he'd coldly rejected Hanna's gift. He took the box from her hand and tossed the wrapping onto the floor. When Isaac lifted the lid, he found a small wooden, hand-carved castle. It had a miniature hinged door with a tiny wreath, which Hanna added to replicate the one on the Blythe castle. Isaac smiled at the precious little gift and its secret significance. Using a single finger, he pushed the tiny door inward revealing the words *until next time* written in metallic gold pen. Isaac recognized the words because he'd written them in the text he sent himself from Hanna's phone the morning he realized he desperately wanted her. He placed a kiss on Hanna's cheek and thanked her for the gift. They sat in the chair enjoying the togetherness, Isaac protectively cradling

Hanna in his lap. After a few moments, Isaac sighed deeply at the folly and wondered how many years had been shaved off his life expectancy after the extraordinary stress of thinking Hanna wouldn't be a part of his life. He then smiled mischievously thinking of something they could do that might help add the stolen years right back on.

When Isaac returned to his apartment with Hanna at his side, Ryan Vance smiled knowingly, said *hello* to Hanna and then left promptly, taking the two brunettes with him. For the rest of the night, Isaac enjoyed spending his time with his first-ever *invited* sleepover guest. They spent hours talking, laughing and lovemaking under the covers, doing their best to add those lost years back to their lives. Isaac got the chance to tell Hanna he wanted to take her to France, and she ecstatically accepted.

Right before Hanna fell asleep in Isaac's arms she relayed a brief message she'd received earlier from Sadie as they rode up together in the elevator. "Oh! I almost forgot. Your sister told me to tell you that she's got your sling all ready for you."

Isaac's joyful laughter rang throughout the apartment. He recalled Sadie's comment about having his heart stolen and never getting it back. He happily admitted to himself that Sadie was right, Hanna had stolen his heart. Isaac then decided that if this was what having your heart stolen was like, then he was more than ok with that.

About the Author

Sierra Chandler lives in Ontario Canada with her husband and four children. When she isn't writing, she likes to take nature walks on her small farm near Burlington.